A Dark and Alien Rose

A Dark and Alien Rose

Josephine Edgar

St. Martin's Press
New York

Library of Congress Cataloging-in-Publication Data

Edgar, Josephine.
    A dark and alien rose / Josephine Edgar.
      p.   cm.
    ISBN 0-312-05843-8
    1. World War, 1914–1918—England—Fiction.
I. Title.
    PR6015.0857D37   1991
    823'.912—dc20   90-28550
                                                  CIP

First published in Great Britain by Judy Piatkus
(Publishers) Limited.

First U.S. Edition: July 1991
10 9 8 7 6 5 4 3 2 1

A Dark and Alien
Rose

Chapter One

The Riviera town of Nice was enjoying its usual pleasant autumn warmth, which brought so many visitors to enjoy the magnificent coast line and, presumably, the exceedingly uncomfortable and pebbly beach. The sixth-form classrooms of the Convent of the Holy St Teresa of Lisieux smelled of damp serge-clad armpits and hot girls – for winter uniform was worn from the start of the term whatever the weather – all the girls except Shareen Abderhazy who always seemed to stay maddeningly cool and pretty. She was commonly called Rose, said to be the meaning of her Persian name, as the sisters considered it less foreign.

The nuns took the girls for walks in crocodiles along the *Promenade des Anglais*. The palms were green and the sea stretched in pale blue and silver to the horizon, sparkling like diamonds.

Diamonds always made Rose think of her mother, the Baroness Abderhazy. Her earliest memories were of long afternoons on her mother's big satin-quilted bed, where the Baroness lay propped upon her pillows of fine lawn lined with pink silk and trimmed with lace. She always wore négligées of lace, frilled chiffon, and rosy crêpe-de-chine. Very thin and pale, her beautiful tumultuous hair spread over the pillows in coppery curls and ringlets, and her eyes were sapphire blue, sometimes glinting green like her emeralds.

Rose did not live with her mother, but once or twice a week Madame Respigny, who had always cared for her, took her round to the huge gilded apartment overlooking the *Promenade des Anglais*. The two vast reception rooms, which in the

1

past had seen such famous parties, were shuttered and the furniture draped in ghost-like dust-covers. Her mother lived in her bedroom and her boudoir. She could not remember her mother ever being really well.

When Rose was a baby the Baroness liked to have her on the bed beside her. She would tell the maid to bring her jewel boxes, and then she and Rose would play with the glittering contents, decking themselves out in the earrings and necklaces until the child, with her dark creamy skin and great black eyes, looked like a little Eastern idol, and Charmian Abderhazy would run her beautiful hands through Rose's waist-length hair and call her '*Ma belle petite Arabe*,' 'My little doll baby,' adding, 'You are not a Normanby, but you are still very beautiful.'

'Is it nice to be beautiful?'

'It is very nice – but it gets you into scrapes.'

'What are scrapes?'

And her mother would laugh, or lose patience, and if Rose persisted would ring for the maid to take her into the kitchen until Madame Respigny called for her. While she was a baby Charmian treated her like a pet; when she grew into a thin leggy child, Charmian lost interest in her.

Madame Respigny lived in the old town above Monsieur Respigny's bakery. In the morning Rose would run downstairs to the shop for warm croissants for breakfast. He had been at work since four and the small apartment above always smelled of fresh baking and the sugary smell of vanilla.

Then she would go to the kiosk on the corner to buy Madame Respigny's newspapers, for she was an educated Englishwoman and read all the news. Rose always spoke to Respy in English, and to her mother in both languages, and to everyone else she knew in French.

Monsieur Respigny was a kind man, a good deal older than his wife. He would give Rose delicious little cakes flavoured with lemon or orange, but he was no father figure. To him she was a little lodger who contributed to their income. When she grew older Rose often wondered what on earth had brought the Respignys together but she did not dare to ask, for she knew Respy would say reprovingly that it was extremely offensive to ask personal questions.

2

There were never any visitors to her mother's apartment when she was there, except old Monsieur Ferdinand Léon who occasionally called for tea or a small glass of crème-de-menthe. They would gossip together, and he would hold his cup delicately, always watching Rose with his bright old eyes. He was very critical of her manners, and her English accent and, now she was growing up, her deportment. But sometimes he took her out to tea at one of the big hotels where all the rich and famous people stayed. She loved that. He talked mischievously about them all as though she was grown up, but he never told her anything about her mother or her father, the Baron, whom her mother never mentioned. She became aware when she was very young that there was a conspiracy of silence surrounding her. That she was a mystery.

Sometimes when Charmian had drunk too much champagne, her mother would talk of someone called Maggy, a disapproving person whom Charmian delighted in annoying. When Respy ventured to suggest that the headache would be better without champagne, she would cry, 'God! You sound just like Maggy, my sister Maggy. No one would ever have any fun, if they took any notice of Maggy. A real old killjoy, my sister Maggy – Maggy the dressmaker.'

This made Rose think of someone kneeling at her mother's feet with a mouthful of pins, adjusting her skirt hem for alteration, one of those insignificant women whom she employed when cash was short, and who dunned her, pathetically, for the payment of their small bills.

Rose did not want a relation like that. She preferred to dream of a rich and powerful father, perhaps an eastern king, arriving in great magnificence to claim her – the Princess.

But if gentlemen came to call – her mother's visitors were all gentlemen – she was immediately led off to the kitchen. She listened to masculine voices and laughter, and the pop of champagne corks, and caught the heavy fragrance of cigars through the closed doors.

Sometimes she saw her mother driving along the *Promenade des Anglais* in a carriage or in one of the splendid new motor cars, always ravishingly dressed, always with a wealthy-looking gentleman. Sometimes she saw her sitting in the sunshine at the most fashionable cafés, with a champagne

3

bucket beside her and a gentleman sitting at the table, while she smiled at him with her brilliant eyes. And more gentlemen would stop and kiss her hand and join them at the table, and order more champagne, until she was surrounded by white Panama hats and only the top of her own elegant hat could be seen.

Her mother would never give even a flicker of recognition if she saw Rose, and Respy would hurry her away. She was never allowed to greet Charmian in public, and she never questioned it. That was how it had always been.

At the Convent school the girls said that her mother was the most notorious woman in Nice. They had heard their mothers and sisters say so. But they did not bait Rose herself about this, because she could beat them all at that cruel game and had once hit a senior girl and was very nearly expelled. But by the time she reached ten she knew her mother was a whore.

The Baroness became increasingly pale and listless in the afternoons. She would lie back on her pillows and cry, and not so many gentlemen called. She would sip champagne alone, or she would take her little white pills, and sometimes a yellow-skinned doctor called and gave her injections after which she would drop into a heavy sleep or begin to sparkle and talk vivaciously. And then one morning when Respy called Rose, she told her that her mother was dead. She had died in her sleep.

'Who will pay for me to live here with you?'

'Monsieur Léon will tell me.'

'Shall I have all the jewels?'

'What a strange child! She was your mother. Are you not sad?'

Rose considered this.

'I don't *feel* sad. She was very pretty but she was very silly.' Then, quite unexpectedly, she began to cry – but it was more from fear than love.

Monsieur Léon took her to the funeral, and they stood with Respy behind the more distinguished guests. There were many of the elegant gentlemen, and many exquisitely dressed and over-painted ladies. They glanced at the child's small black-clad figure and whispered behind their hands. A few of the ladies kissed her and said, '*Pauvre petite*, what will

4

become of you?' And a stout foreign-looking lady said, 'Has Charmy done *anything* for this *pobrecita*?' Monsieur Léon assured them Rose would be cared for, and they fluttered off chattering like a crowd of brilliant peacocks. Respy took her back to the apartment over the pâtisserie and she never went to the apartment in the *Promenade des Anglais* again.

She was told that Monsieur Léon was now her guardian but apparently all that meant was that he paid her expenses and occasionally took her out to tea.

For what seemed a long while life went on as it always had. Daily attendance at the Convent, the routine of her life with the Respignys. Then, as the summer advanced, Respy would take her swimming.

The sea was the only freedom she had ever known. Respy, who had been a spartan trainer of British children, had taught her well, although she no longer swam herself.

It was a fine morning in the late summer, but too early for the sun to have found its full strength. They hired a wooden changing hut and Rose got into her red flannel bathing suit, with its sailor collar, knee-length tunic and tight boyish knickers. Her long hair was tied up with a scarf, and a clumsy life belt of cork biscuits was fastened round her waist.

'Don't swim out too far, or out of sight, or speak to anyone you don't know,' Respy admonished, then settled down in her deck chair and shook out her morning paper. She knew it was hopeless. Rose was in her element in the sea. She would go out as far as she wished, and there was no use calling frantically from the shore. It was better not to watch.

But what Respy did not know was that Rose would swim along through the chill morning sea in the shelter of the great stone bastion which guarded the harbour, and once out of sight of the beach would unhook the life belt, slide out of the hideous suit which sogged and dragged at her limbs and fasten ⁺hem to an iron hook driven into the stone. And then, naked and free, she would dive down until she could touch the bottom of the wall.

The rising sun was warm on the water and shoals of small transparent silvery fish slid past her. A jelly fish like a beautiful purple flower pulsed nearby and she shot away to the surface, knowing how it could sting.

She struck out seawards into the really deep water, blue now under the deepening blue of the sky, playing in the water like a dolphin, diving over backwards and rising with her body arched until her small breasts stood firm like pink-tipped apples, then raising her legs until her toes pointed upwards like a dancer before plunging down into the water again. Her scarf loosened and her long black hair spread and floated about her like seaweed as she broke surface again, laughing into the sunshine.

Up on the bastion above her a tall, fair young man was looking down at her with interest and amusement, thinking he had never seen anything so full of joy. He watched her thin dark body twisting and turning with the long hair spiralling around it as though she were a mermaid. She looked up and their eyes met and he began to laugh. Rose struck out for the shelter of the bastion, the colour flaming in her cheeks. She scrabbled along the slippery wall, grabbing her red bathing suit bobbing on the cork belt, and went round the high stone wall, hopefully out of sight.

She heard the splash of his dive as she struggled back into the hated wet red flannel, dragging the cork belt round her waist before she cautiously swam back to where she could see him, fair head catching the sunlight as he rose on the stroke, far out to sea. Well, he might have laughed, but at least he was a gentleman. He was giving her the chance to get dressed and away.

She thrust off the wall with her feet and swam slowly back to the beach. Respy came stumping over the pebbles to wrap her in a big towel.

'You were very quick this morning.'

'It's cold.'

'No more than usual at this season. Where's your scarf?'

'It came off and I lost it.'

'Why, there's another swimmer out there – so early,' said Respy. 'A man.'

'Yes.'

'Did he speak to you?'

'No.' She stood in the wooden chalet while Respy rubbed her down and dried her hair. Her heartbeat was quietening. She had a vivid memory of a pair of intensely blue eyes, the

6

colour of her mother's, staring down at her from a smiling brown face crowned with a thatch of wheat-blond hair. She thought it would have been wonderful to swim out so far with him, and sighed.

'Hurry up, quickly now, and get into your clothes.'

They climbed slowly up the steep beach towards the promenade.

'Monsieur Léon is coming for you today, to take some flowers to your mama's grave.'

'And take me out to tea?'

'No doubt. If you behave.'

'I always behave,' said Rose, and tossed her head.

Monsieur Léon called for her that afternoon with a carriage and told the driver to take them to the cemetery.

Up the hill at the back of the town it seemed cooler, but Monsieur Léon leaned back in his seat, his breath a little short, and a damp trail of sweat ran wormlike down his raddled cheek. 'Are you unwell, M'sieur?' she asked anxiously.

He glanced at his reflection in a small pocket mirror and exclaimed in horror, taking out a large white handkerchief and dabbing carefully round his eyes. 'It is the heat,' he complained. 'Tell the driver to pull up in the shade of the trees and to put up the sunshades. I will wait for you here. Take the flowers. And don't be long.'

'You will be all right, M'sieur?'

'Of course,' he said tetchily, sniffing at a cut glass bottle of salts. 'Off you go.'

Rose picked up her own small posy, and his beautiful sheaf of white orchids and small pink roses, and set off down the wide gravelled walk towards her mother's grave. Yews were planted down the paths between the elaborate French tombstones, some with weeping angels and cherubs, and ugly immortelles propped against the headstones.

Fancy putting iron flowers on a grave, Rose thought. *Mon Dieu*, it is disgusting! Who would want to be remembered by iron flowers adorned with horrid little glass beads?

As she turned the corner of the cypress hedge she stopped abruptly. A tall, very handsome young man in a white suit and a Panama hat worn at an angle of his fair head, stood looking

7

thoughtfully at the bronze plaque mounted on her mother's simple granite stone. To Rose he seemed very old. Actually he was just twenty.

Her black eyes widened with curiosity. Surely this was the young man she had seen in the sea that morning. Who had laughed at her nakedness and then gone tactfully away. He had just laid flowers on the grave. And such flowers too. A large sheath of pale pink roses. Her mother's favourite flowers. How did he know that? He was surely too young for the Baroness, although she had heard once that her mother had been attracted by young and unsuitable men. But this one did not seem at all unsuitable, and was handsome enough to attract any woman.

Tom Grimshaw heard her footsteps and glanced up. He saw a French schoolgirl in a grey gingham uniform dress, black cotton stockings and button shoes. Her hair was scraped back from her face into two waist-length plaits and she wore a round hat of black straw with a school band. She was gazing at him with catlike curiosity.

He had been reading the inscription on the bronze plaque mounted on the plain headstone of coral-coloured travertine marble, paid for by Monsieur Léon. It read very simply: "The Baroness Charmian Aberderhazy, wife of the Baron Philippe Aberhazy. Greatly loved by all who knew her." He noted that no age was given and thought his mother would smile at that. They were twins.

The French schoolgirl took a small rake out of a bag over her arm, and a stiff little hand brush, turned back the skirt of her uniform very precisely, knelt down without a word and began sweeping up a few fallen leaves from the grave before laying her large sheaf of white orchids and small pink roses and another posy of Parma violets on the grave beside his flowers. Then, for the first time, she looked up at him and he was startled by the extraordinary beauty of her eyes. They were almond-shaped, slanted upwards, of a brown so dark they seemed black when the sunlight did not catch them. They were shadowed by long, sweeping lashes like those of the women in Rajput paintings. And her skin was that colour called olive because its creaminess held a strange, almost greeny light, and the lashes were so long that they cast small

8

pointed shadows on her high cheekbones. Her red-lipped mouth looked very controlled and severe. There was something familiar about her that he could not place. A look, somehow, of his mother, whose blue eyes also held a catlike mischief when she did not want to give her thoughts away.

'Please,' Rose burst out uncontrollably, 'who are you?'

She spoke in French so he replied in French.

'I am called Tom Grimshaw. And who are you, Mademoiselle?'

The name meant nothing to her. His accent was obvious so she replied in her precise English: 'Oh, I'm nobody in particular.'

'But everybody must be somebody,' he teased gravely.

Her chin came up and she flushed under her beautiful skin like a dark rose. A dark and alien rose. She said, 'Well, I live with Madame Respigny.'

He suddenly remembered the archetypal British governess in her gray woollen cardigan, waiting by the changing hut that morning. He could scarcely believe it. This was his naked mermaid and she was obviously hoping he would not recognise her.

'I see,' he said, meaning he did not see at all.

'Well,' she said diffidently, 'I just live with her. That's all.'

She hurriedly finished tidying the grave and arranged her bouquets carefully by the headstone.

'What beautiful flowers,' he said.

'Yes. The roses and orchids are from my guardian. The violets are from Respy and me. They cost us nothing. Old Monsieur Celeston in the market always gives them to us. He always did give the Baroness flowers. She never paid him, of course. He admired her very much.'

'Was she very beautiful?'

'Yes, very.'

'You knew her well?'

'I knew her,' Rose said guardedly, and then with sudden passion, 'Yes. She was very beautiful. One saw her driving along the *Promenade*. Her clothes and jewels were magnificent. All the gentlemen admired her. She had blue eyes. Very blue.' She looked directly into his eyes for the first time and saw they were the same azure blue as her mother's had been.

9

She rose to her feet, sighing. 'All the jewels, everything will be sold this week!'

'So I hear – will you go?'

'Me? No. Why should I go? I have no money for jewels. Will you go, M'sieur?'

'I think I will.' He felt he owed her some explanation. 'She was my mother's sister. They were twins. She was my aunt. I am in Nice for a holiday with my brother, and so my mother asked me to put some flowers on her grave.'

She brushed down her skirt and gave a little curtsey. 'Goodbye, M'sieur.'

'May I walk with you, Mademoiselle?'

'Certainly not. My guardian is waiting for me.'

She walked away towards the entrance, straight-backed, trying to be very dignified, like a little wooden doll. Then, as children and young animals do, bored with thinking about her deportment, she broke into a run, skirts and plaits flying, her lamblike skips and jumps showing her long slim legs.

Tom smiled to himself. A funny little ha'porth. About thirteen or fourteen? A convent-bred bunch of adolescent mischief. But he hurried after her, screened by the long yew hedges, and reached the gate just in time to see her get into a carriage waiting beneath the trees, where a very old gentleman in superb English clothes of a style at least a generation past sat waiting for her. He had an elaborate maquillage and his scanty hair and pointed beard were dyed an unlikely pale brown. The driver whipped up his horses and they trotted off down the hill towards the town.

Tom signalled to a passing taxi and drove back to his hotel.

Monsieur Léon took Rose for a ride through the villages along the lower *Corniche*, through the carnation fields with their windbreaks of bamboo and tamarisk, and then announced, 'We will go to the Grand Hotel for tea. You will like that, *chérie*?'

Her eyes lit with delight. '*Bien sûr*, Papa Léon.'

He liked giving her treats and he was such a change from Respy. He talked to her as though she was much older. And sometimes some of the exquisite ladies who lived in Nice through the winter, and people from the theatre and the opera house, paused at their table to tell him all the gossip from Paris, and all about the fashion trade and fashionable people, while Rose sat demurely with her hands folded and drank in these tales from a rich but distant world.

There was a *thé dansant* every afternoon at the Grand Hotel. Rose knew they would not sit near the dance floor but from their secluded table, discreetly screened by palm trees, as though a rendezvous for secret lovers, she could see the circle of polished floor.

The small orchestra tuned up in its nest of palms and azealeas, and people began to arrive for the dancing. They were mostly in couples. Devoted partners gliding across the floor, middle-aged men with pretty young girls, middle-aged women with smooth, good-looking young men, and parties of people enjoying the new craze for dancing at all hours and every opportunity.

Papa Léon ordered tea, pekoe with lemon, allowing Rose a lump of sugar with hers although really he disapproved. The waiter brought them tiny sandwiches of paté and cucumber and a salver of pastries. Papa Léon had a small cognac with his tea but ate nothing. Rose ate nearly all the sandwiches, knowing he would only allow her one pastry, and anyway she could get any sort of pastry she fancied from Monsieur Respigny.

'Selection,' Papa Léon told her, 'is the basis of all good taste. Greed is vulgar and undisciplined.'

She chose a small biscuit, and asked: 'Was Mama undisciplined?'

The bright eyes in the tired old face assessed her critically, her straight shoulders and delicately poised head. The dark hair was drawn back tightly into plaits, showing small, flat ears. He looked at the dark oriental eyes and exquisite hands. Her mother's hands.

'Sit up straight,' he said peremptorily. 'You will never wear clothes well if you slump. Yes, your mother was completely undisciplined. Otherwise she would have accumulated a fortune. I brought you here today to take you away from the Respigny woman whom I shall continue to pay so long as you are in her care. But there will be no money, you know. Everything will have to be sold to pay her debts.'

She put down her pastry fork abruptly.

'What's to become of me?' she asked anxiously.

'Oh, nothing will happen to you,' he said testily, then realised he was talking to a very frightened child. 'I am not without money.'

'What will happen to all the jewels?'

'As I said, they are to be sold. Her debts were enormous.'

'She gambled,' Rose said, 'I know. She never paid anyone.'

He was startled. 'You knew?'

'But everyone knew! She would lose ten thousand francs at a sitting. When Respy took me round one day she was too drunk to see me. I think a gentleman lent her some money that time. He must have been rich. But all her gentlemen were rich. The whole school talked about it. I blacked Martine Lebrun's eyes for calling her a tart and they nearly expelled me. But they did not call her names again.'

'I know, *chérie*. I had to go and soothe the Mother Superior. A most pernicious school. But your mother had some idea that a convent education would shield you from the world. I see I have been neglecting you. We must change all that. A crowd of gossiping *bourgeoises* – the narrowest class in France – how could they appreciate a bird of paradise like your mother?' Rose glowed with understanding. 'But it did not cost her a great deal, as your fostering with the Respignys was exceedingly cheap. I could never get her to spend money on you. She thought any money not spent on herself wasted. It was the money-lenders that had it in the end. I doubt whether the tradesmen were ever paid.'

'But did you *like* her?' asked Rose, puzzled.

'No – I loved her,' he said. 'I loved her beauty. It is my weakness. I spent my life creating beautiful clothes for beautiful women to wear, and no would could ever wear clothes like Charmian. She was silly, vain, idle and really very mean – but she was beautiful, and she could be charming.' He paused and shook his head, as though the memory of the Baroness tormented him like a summer fly, 'You too will be beautiful, Rose, but you have a good, sharp head on your shoulders as well. Value that. Use it. Don't waste your gift of beauty like your mother did. Do not give it away to any fool you happen to take a fancy to, or for a diamond bracelet that any rich libertine can pay for. *And*,' he added unexpectedly, 'keep

12

yourself pure. Until you are married. A beautiful married woman is like a queen. All men desire her. A mistress, unless she is very clever, is always dependent on a man's whims . . . it is the way of the world today.'

'Yes, M'sieur.' She nodded gravely. He was the only grown-up she knew who gave her really sensible advice. Respy was full of warnings and admonishments, and the nuns *expected* her to go to the bad. They sometimes prayed for her. They said, "Keep your feet together, never cross your ankles, never shout or run in the street, put on your gloves leaving the house, never speak to strangers . . ." Why was it virtuous and ladylike to behave like this? Great ladies did not bother. Monsieur was *very* sensible.

She knew perfectly well that she was beautiful – men's eyes and other girls' jealousy had told her so. Her mama had told her so, draping her in diamonds and calling her "My beautiful little Eastern idol." Monsieur was saying, "Put a value on yourself." And it was good advice. To regard one's looks as an asset like good family breeding, brains or wealth had never occurred to Rose before. Papa Léon was very sensible and wise.

'I have just one piece of jewellery in my care for you. It was given to your mother by her grandmother, Lady Margaret Normanby, many years ago. It is a string of pearls. Your great-grandmother had a long strand, perfectly matched, and she had it split between your mother and her twin sister. Your mother gave hers to me to keep for you. I shall give it to you when you are old enough to wear it,'

'My mother left it to me?' she said incredulously.

'It was one of the few sensible things she ever did,' he said in amusement. 'The other was to make me your guardian. But perhaps you would have preferred some of the diamonds?'

'No, I love pearls. But I would have liked the golden bangles with the engraved patterns and tiny stones. They are so thin and fine. Mama said her husband gave them to her and that they had belonged to a Ranee in India. I suppose my grandmother is dead?'

'Yes.'

'Are any of my mother's people alive? Apart from the dressmaker? I mean the sister she always quarrelled with?'

13

'There is a cousin, I believe.'

'Called Tom Grimshaw?'

'How do you know?' He was startled.

She told him about the young man who had brought flowers to their mother's grave that afternoon. 'There was a card which said – "To Charmy, with my love and so many regrets that I did not keep on trying. From your sister, Maggy."'

'Ah, *mon dieu!*' To her astonishment Papa Léon took out his fine lawn handkerchief, smelling of chypre, and carefully dabbed at his eyes. She was surprised to see that they were full of tears.

'Charmian was always hopeless,' he said, shaking his head. 'Dear Maggy! How hard she tried with her, but it was hopeless. Everyone loved Charmian and spoiled her, and she was so quickly bored. Darling Maggy . . . Did you tell this young man who you are?'

'No. I'm never allowed to talk about me. Mama did not like it!'

'You were discreet. But don't worry, my child, you are quite safe, I promise you.'

Rose sat up, bright-eyed. 'They are going to dance. Oh, may we stay and watch? Just for a little while, please, Papa Léon?'

He seemed about to agree when a party of four young English people came in. One of them was the young man she had seen at the cemetery. The two girls were very pretty but Rose did not think them smart in their flowery summer dresses and flower-trimmed hats. The other young man was like a shadow of Tom Grimshaw. The same ruddy golden skin, the same thick fair hair, but he was shorter, slimmer, a little more dandified and delicate, and when he took one of the girls out on to the dance floor she could see that the sole and heel of his left shoe were built up and he walked with a slight limp, although he danced beautifully. They were a gay and self-confident party of rich young English people, dancing, laughing and flirting together, so different to the chaperoned French and Italian girls.

'Papa Léon,' she began excitedly, but the old gentleman was already on his feet, his hand beneath her elbow.

14

'*Allons vite!*' he said abruptly. They left by a side door going on to a narrow back street and had to walk round to the front to get a carriage, which made Papa Léon extremely short of breath.

'But, M'sieur,' she said, 'that was Tom Grimshaw! The tall one.'

'Yes. And that was his young half-brother Stephen,' he said shortly. He looked so preoccupied she did not dare speak while the commissionaire called a *fiacre* to drive her back to the apartment in the *Rue des Boulangeries*.

She got down, made her curtsey to him, and thanked him politely for her tea. He had been silent on the way home but now he retained her hand, looking down at her in a puzzled, doubtful way.

'Monsieur?' she asked, equally puzzled. One never expected anything but exquisite self-possession from the old gentleman.

'I have neglected my duty to you,' he said, 'but I made a foolish promise to a dying woman and I will keep it as long as I am able.'

To my mother, she thought, then smiled and shrugged. 'I do not know what you mean, Papa Léon. But if your promise was to poor Mama, I do not think she will care now one way or another. But for me, it is most important that whatever you decide will ensure me some kind of future.'

He gave an affectionate cackle of laughter.

'So speaks my little cynic! No sentiment, and perfectly right too. You are going to be *formidable* as well as beautiful, my Persian rose.'

'I shall wait for your news. *Tout à l'heure*, Papa Léon, and many thanks.'

He told the driver to take him home. He looked tired. He had found it an exhausting day.

Back in his cool apartment, taking his apéritif before dinner, he thought of that promise he had given which, of course, he had known could not be kept. But Charmian had been very high that day. She had had a lucky afternoon at the casino and when he called had been sitting at her triple mirror, with champagne in an ice bucket on hand, having her

15

hair dressed before going out to dine. He had tried to talk about the provisions he was making for the child, Rose.

'Oh, nonsense, Ferdi! I'm not old enough to talk about such things. There's plenty of time.'

The doctors had told him differently.

'Charmian, your allowance from the Baron your husband is only for your lifetime, and makes no provision whatsoever for this child.'

'Now you're trying to frighten me.' She dismissed the hairdresser, and when he presented a bill, handed it to Léon, saying, 'See to this for me, will you, Ferdi?' Her maid brought a hat of swathed paradise plumes, and Charmian pinned it carefully in place and made secure her topaz and yellow diamond earrings. She was in golden tawny colours tonight, glittering and brilliant. 'I don't know why you worry. Respy will always look after her. She adores the child. Rose thinks more of her than she does of me.'

'Respy cannot afford to do that indefinitely. The child must have some money behind her. Charmian, I shall have to get in touch with Maggy unless you help me.'

A look of fear and fury, of childish stubbornness and spite, came into her face. 'I will not have Maggy know anything about me! She will pester me with letters and lawyers! I tell you I will *not* have it. Promise me you will not tell Maggy anything!'

'Until when? Rose needs a family behind her. She needs education. Look, if you let me be her legal guardian, then I will promise. You can give me a limit to that promise.'

'How about until I am dead?' The bright smile was suddenly tremulous with terror. 'No, until she is grown up. Yes, until she is grown up.'

So he had persuaded her to make the guardianship legal in a slightly drunken impulse, to give him the pearls into his keeping. Until the child was twenty-one. He had it legalised as soon as he could extract her signature, for she had forgotten the verbal promise immediately. He knew a time might come when he might have to break his promise. But he had loved Charmian and would keep it as long as he could.

So he had persuaded her to make the guardianship legal and, on impulse, to give him the pearls. And in return he

16

promised he would never tell her sister that the child Rose existed.

He loved her. He always had. Not as a man loves a woman, for he had not been the kind of man who had loved women, but as a goddess of beauty. He had loved his wife, Maggy, whom he had never touched in sexual love. He had never been jealous of her lover Henry Grimshaw, the father of her handsome boy. Léon had not seen Maggy now for some years. Not since he left Paris to live in the warmth of the Riviera sunshine. But Charmian had now been dead for six months, and the boy had turned up with flowers from his mother and he would ask questions, and then Maggy would know. She was the child's only relative – she and her bonny Grimshaw son. But it was summer and hot, and he felt quite well. He would keep his promise to Charmian as long as he could, but he would change things for the child now.

The first thing was a new school. He found her a place in an exclusive academy for girls, run on English lines by two English women. It was for the children of expats. The English, who by the nature of their work lived in the district, or those who chose to do so because they were rich.

Rose was to be a weekly border, still going back to the Respignys at weekends and holidays. That connection must not be broken abruptly. She needed affection and he could not have a girl child living with him.

Rose found the change stimulating. The new and quite different clothes, summer uniforms of striped white and green cotton. A smart green blazer and a panama hat with a striped ribbon and a school badge. Gym clothes, and a party dress for the weekly dancing class where one middle-aged French lady thumped the piano and the other called the time with high-pitched authority. Once a month the school shared a dance with a similar school for boys, shy youngsters sweating in the Riviera heat in their formal Eton suits. Rose did not find the boys attractive and thought them all terrible dancers. She remembered Tom Grimshaw in his well-cut linen suit, fox-trotting skilfully across the dance floor at the Grand Hotel . . .

She found the lessons interesting and worked hard, her fluent French a great advantage over the English pupils. She

17

found the beach cricket sheer misery, and the swimming competitive and therefore not enjoyable. No one wanted to dive into the depths and play at being a naked mermaid. Instead of hourly prayers and innumerable Hail Marys, there were just two morning prayers: one the Lord's Prayer, the other calling for a blessing on King George V and his family. All very fervent because the senior girls were crazy about the snub-nosed, blond Prince of Wales, and pasted photos of him in the lids of their lockers.

Monsieur Léon found he was beginning to value Rose's bright, childish presence more highly, and to enjoy spoiling her. He took her to Monte Carlo to see the Ballet Russe, and afterwards, on the great terrace, she met his friends from the company: the great dancers, and even on one occasion the famous impresario himself with his white-winged hair and his attendant retinue of brilliant composers, writers and artists, and exotically beautiful young men. She sat silently beside Papa Léon while he chatted, and made them laugh, always introducing her as, 'My step-niece – if there is such a relation. She is the daughter of the late Baroness Abderhazy.'

This always caused a flutter of interest because of course they all knew of Charmian, many of them intimately. They spoke of her beauty, and her clothes, and her jewels, and her admirers at an earlier time, before Rose was born, before the lines had deepened round the azure eyes and the pretty mouth.

He took her to lunch at the Café de Paris, and to the opera, and sometimes they drove up into the mountains to the beautiful inland towns and to small but famous restaurants where he was well known. The cuisine was excellent, and he always let her order so that her small, sedate presence became quite a feature of these excursions.

But there came a day towards the end of the summer when instead of calling he sent a carriage for her. She had never visited him at home before. She felt curious, because she had always wanted to see his apartment, yet apprehensive too. There was something in Respy's expression as she waved Rose goodbye which she could not understand. She felt a sense of being abandoned again.

Papa Léon lived in an apartment on the eastern side of the town on the first floor of an ancient mansion. The concierge spoke through a tube on the wall and within moments an Italian manservant appeared and escorted Rose into an elaborate gilded cage of a lift. She was ushered through a spacious foyer into the large drawing room, the walls of which were hung with yellow silk and the high ceiling elaborate with gilded plaster work. It was lined with shelves of books on costume and design, and there were signed photographs of lovely ladies and distinguished people in the world of fashion. Rose could have spent hours looking at them. The clothes were all of two decades past; the people stars of yesterday.

The manservant announced her: 'Mademoiselle Shareen Aberderhazy, Monsieur,' which gave her a pleasant feeling of self-importance.

'Thank you, Luigi. You may bring tea now. Come and sit by me, my dear Rose, out of the glare of the sun.'

He lay on a sofa near the window over-looking the bustle of the harbour. Newspapers and magazines lay about, and there was a pair of binoculars on a small table with which he had been watching the shipping in the harbour. The big yachts were coming in for the autumn and a British battleship, long and grey, like a dangerous sea animal, lay at anchor outside.

He put down his binoculars and said, 'There will be dancing down at the port tonight when the sailors come ashore.'

'Yes, I would love to go and watch. But Respy said it was not *comme il faut*.'

'She is perfectly right. Not for a young lady.'

Luigi brought the tea and Monsieur dismissed him, preferring to serve himself.

She realised how very old he was and how fragile. He had not done his face and his scanty hair and beard were showing rims of white. There was a shawl over his shoulders and a rug across his knees, although the weather was warm and sunny.

When she had made her curtsey and kissed him, his shrivelled skin smelled of dead perfume like a bowl of stale rose petals. She sat down and folded her hands. She was dressed like an English schoolgirl now, not a French orphan. But she did not look like either. She was growing, and her womanhood burgeoning like an opening flowerbud. A dark flower, he thought. When she took off her blazer he noticed the firm curve of her young breasts and the poise of her head on its slender neck. Her back was straight as a ballet dancer's. He smiled appreciatively. For him no woman was worth creating beautiful clothes for unless her breasts were in the right place. Proportion was everything, and to waste time creating beautiful clothes for women who did not possess it had always been a bore. But to create clothes for Charmian Abderhazy had been an inspiration. And one day this strange, dark child would be equally rewarding.

'I am going to Paris to see my doctor, Rose.'

'You are not ill, M'sieur?'

'No.' He saw her instant alarm. 'I am just very old.' He paused and said sheepishly, 'I shall be eighty this year, Rose.'

'Papa Léon, I cannot believe it!'

'How charming of you to say so . . . But unfortunately it is true.'

'When will you be back?'

'That is uncertain.'

There was a sudden silence between them. Then he shrugged and said, 'I do not complain. Taking it all in all, it has been a wonderful life.'

But Rose was terrified. Her black eyes widened like a captive hare's. 'But without you, Papa Léon, I shall be quite alone.'

'No, I do not think so. In Paris I shall make some new arrangements.'

'But you will not desert me?'

He kissed her hand comfortingly.

'I may not have any choice about that. But I cannot tell you because I do not know. In Paris I shall see my solicitors and arrange about my will. You will not be without money, but that is not all . . . Wait a little, eat one of these.' He offered her some small lemon cakes. 'There is a matter I have to speak to you about.' Out of a drawer in the side table he took a square leather jewel case which she recognised.

'That contained Mama's Indian bangles.'

He opened the lid and revealed the ten thin golden bangles, each engraved with delicate scrolls of leaves and flowers and studded with small white diamonds.

20

'Did you buy them at the sale, M'sieur?' The colour was warm in her cheeks but her eyes were puzzled and innocent. 'There are ten, five for each arm. How did they come here?'

'You have no idea?'

'Of course not.'

'The sale went well. But when all the debts were paid, there was nothing. Well, I will tell you about the bangles. Before he left Nice, your Mr Thomas Grimshaw called to see me. His mother had asked him to call on me after he had laid flowers on your mother's grave. He told me he had lodged a bid with the auctioneer for these, and if it was successful had arranged for them to be sent to me. This little card he left with me.'

He passed her a card which read: "Thomas W. Grimshaw, Cliffs Edge, High Thornsby, Yorkshire." She turned it over and read the message.

"For my little Miss Nobody, in the knowledge that one day she will be Somebody very beautiful indeed, and will wear them and enjoy them. Tom Grimshaw."

'Oh!' Rose's cheeks flushed, her eyes shining. 'How could he know about me?'

'Apparently he saw you leaving the cemetery with me. When I lived in Paris Margaret always came to see me, and once she brought him with her. He was about eighteen. You see, Rose, if your Aunt Margaret had known about you she would have tried to make your mother do more for you. To give you a different life and send you to a very good school. Charmian could not bear that Maggy should know about you. It was always the way between them. Maggy trying to make Charmian think and plan her future, and Charmian never following anything but her own feckless impulses, or the next man who caught her fancy, trusting to luck and beauty and charm to get her out of trouble, which it did – until she began to get old.'

'Did she know who my father was?'

'Who knows? It was not her first husband, a young army officer. He was in Bombay for three years before you were born. He made your mother a very adequate allowance – but nothing for you. He appears to have no knowledge of you. But she was always surrounded by men from the Middle East because of his business connections. There was one, a

21

nephew of Abderhazy's, a Prince Mahmoud, with whom she had a momentous affair. I think it must have been him. He was extremely handsome, and fifteen years younger than her. It was rumoured that he spent a fortune on her before the family ordered him home, but no one really knows. I'm sorry – I can't help you there.'

'Miss Nobody is a very good name for me,' she said bitterly.

'Do not let it worry you. I, too, never knew who my father was. Be proud of yourself.'

She picked up the gold bangles and slipped them on to her bare brown arm, thin and glittering above her long fine hand.

She sighed. 'They are so beautiful – is it correct for me to accept them?'

He was delighted at that. 'I think not. It would be correct if I accepted them for you until you came of age.'

'Very well. I can scarcely wear them at school.' Reluctantly, she put the jewels back in their case.

'It was kind and clever of Tom to choose the only pieces I really loved. Do you know where to write to him?'

'Oh, yes. I write often to his mother – your mother's sister.'

'Oh! The dressmaker?' she said disconsolately.

'You would have preferred a countess?'

'I would prefer a real family.'

'There is nothing wrong with being a dressmaker. I was a dressmaker. Margaret Normanby – Maggy – was my partner. We had the greatest couturiere salon in London.' He looked at her gravely and came to a decision. 'She was my partner and my wife!'

'You were *married*, Papa Léon?' she cried in astonishment. She could not imagine it. 'And this young man Tom – who exactly is he?'

'He is her son, as I said, but not mine. He was adopted by Henry Grimshaw, a wealthy Yorkshire wool manufacturer. A handsome, powerful man, his father . . . Tom is your first cousin. I am your uncle by marriage and now your legal guardian. It was the only sensible thing your mother ever did. I kept my promise to her while she lived, but now I must break it to do my best for you. You must wait until I return from Paris. Then I shall know what to do with you.'

22

The next morning he departed for Paris with Luigi in anxious attendance, carrying a medicine case, extra pillows and a rug. Rose and Madame Respigny went to see him off. He was wheeled along the platform to his first class *wagon-lit* and the manservant and a porter half-carried him into his reserved car. He looked incredibly frail, kissing his hand to them as the train moved off.

'I wonder if we shall ever see him again?' Respy said, and Rose wished she had not spoken. This frail old man seemed the last person between her and a sort of nothingness. She did not belong to Respy. She did not belong anywhere.

Two weeks later a letter came from Paris from Monsieur Léon's solicitors, Edouard Raymond et Fils. They regretted having to break such distressing news: their client Monsieur Ferdinand Léon had died suddenly of heart failure while awaiting an operation. They would communicate with Mademoiselle Abderhazy later, for Monsieur had set all his affairs in order and had appointed Madame Margaret Léon, of the firm of Margaret Normanby of Hanover Street and Riverside Mansions, Chelsea, London, as her new guardian.

Raymond et Fils had written to Madame Léon and were awaiting her reply. Monsieur Léon would be buried in Père Lachaise cemetery this week. The lawyers enclosed a cheque for current expenses and added that Monsieur Léon had left his ward adequately provided for.

Both Rose and Respy would have liked to go to the funeral but there was nothing they could do but wait and do everything as usual. Go to school, swim in the warm sea, return to Respy's at the weekend. Wait, wait, wait – like a parcel in the lost property office waiting to be collected.

The Parisian and Riviera newspapers gave a column and front page photographs to the funeral. Along the Rue de la Paix the great couturiers had lowered their blinds and closed their premises as the cortège passed, and the saleswomen, the seamstresses and the embroidery hands stood with the great designers themselves, bareheaded in the street. Madame Léon, although husband and wife had long been separated, had come from London, and her famous business Margaret Normanby had also been closed for the day.

Many ladies of title and high fashion had attended, many ladies of the theatre, and several members of the great Parisian demi-monde had wept and heaped flowers on the grave. There had been writers, actors, singers, dancers – everyone from the heights of fashion to the heights of Bohemia had valued Ferdinand Léon. Paris did not care about the old scandals which surrounded him, his flight from England, his dyed hair and eccentricities. He had been a gifted man and was therefore to be honoured.

Rose was astounded. She had loved the old gentleman and laughed at him more than a little but she had no idea of his fame.

She would have liked to be there. She looked at the photographs in the *Paris-Soir*, and there was one which caught her special attention: an elegant woman standing among the mourners leaning on the arm of Tom Grimshaw. It was raining and he held an umbrella above her head. The caption read: "Madame Léon, better known as the head of the firm of Margaret Normanby, receiving condolences from admirers and friends. She was accompanied by her son."

Her mother's twin sister, "the dressmaker".

But this was a woman with more than chic. She was a woman of distinction rather than a woman of great beauty, like Charmian. She seemed to have character and confidence, and in spite of the painful sadness in her eyes, humour. She looked like a woman who could laugh as well as weep.

'Respy, this is my Aunt Margaret, whom Mother called "the dressmaker". I didn't know she was a *great* dressmaker. I didn't know that Papa Léon also had been a great designer, and that she was his wife and partner.'

At the end of that week they heard from Monsieur Raymond again. Apart from minor bequests, Monsieur Léon left his entire capital between Rose and his manservant, Luigi. It would bring her in about £400 a year.

Respy was delighted. 'You are now a young woman of means,' she said happily, 'and it appears you have a new guardian . . . you have a family.'

The solicitor wrote again. He had heard from Madame Léon who would like Rose to travel to London at once, if she wished. She had asked if Madame Respigny would be so kind as to accompany her.

'As though,' Respy said indignantly, 'I would dream of letting you go alone.'

If Rose agreed to this rooms would be booked for them at the Hotel Ventura Royale where Madame Léon always stayed when she was in Paris and the following day they would travel on to London. Edouard Raymond would be glad if she could let them know immediately so that reservations could be made. All Madame Respigny's expenses would be paid. He advised Rose strongly to accept this offer, but she must realise that until recently Madame Léon had been totally unaware of her existence.

Rose and Respy read this together in Respy's small, neat living room. The smell of the midday bake was drifting up from the bakehouse below. Children on their way from school were buying the fresh loaves. It was the only home she had ever known.

'I must go, mustn't I?' she said.

She felt strange, almost without identity, wrenched out of her two contrasting worlds: this neat bourgeois room, and the big satin bed with the jewels spread out in sparkling cascades in the afternoon sunlight. No known father. A mother who had never publicly admitted her existence.

'Of course you must go,' said Respy. 'You cannot spend your whole life here with me. I'm getting on now and I cannot take on such responsibility. Monsieur has left me a little money also, which will give me some independence. I shall take private pupils again. Of course you must go to your aunt. She is behaving very well, and she is your only relative.'

Not quite. Not *quite*. There was Tom Grimshaw. The thought of him and his impulsive gift of the sparkling jewels warmed Rose's heart.

'I wonder why Aunt Margaret gave me the choice?'

'Perhaps,' Respy's voice was unexpectedly husky, 'she thought we might have a great affection for each other – it sometimes happens with foster children.'

'Oh, Respy!' Rose threw her arms round here. 'There is – there is!'

25

Respy dabbed her eyes, blew her nose and adjusted her pince-nez. Then she patted Rose's hand.

'Now,' she said, 'don't cry. It has been a great joy for me having you. I remember going to the Baroness's apartment to fetch you when you were tiny – two months old. Madame had a nurse until then who, thank goodness, stayed with me for another month. I had taught many children but none under five. So I was your foster mother.'

Rose realised for the first time what an odd burden she must have been to this essentially unmotherly woman. Respy had never gone in for any shows of affection. Indeed, Rose had come to regard her as a sort of permanent governess. But she had always been there. Steadfast, firm, irreproachably fair and kind, keeping Charmian's secret, doing her very best.

'I really do love you, Respy.'

'Yes, yes. I'm sure you do. But you must go to London. And I really think you want to.'

'Oh, yes. Yes, I *really* want to go.'

'Well, we will write to this Monsieur Raymond and tell him we will meet him in Paris, and then I think we should start to pack.'

The solicitor wrote by return, sending money for their journey and first-class reservations on the Paris Express, and saying that rooms had been reserved for them at the hotel.

The school had been notified of Rose's departure, the packing was done, her goodbyes said to Monsieur Respigny who kissed her on both cheeks and gave her a box of freshly cooked biscuits, and then they were off. Rose was fascinated by the train: the comfortable beds that folded up into seats during the day, the washbasin that was mysteriously hidden within a mahogany panel. There was a dining saloon with shaded lights and uniformed stewards. At dinner Respy ordered half a bottle of champagne. Together they toasted the future, Madame Respigny beaming through her pince-nez. Rose wondered what she really felt. Perhaps she was relieved to be done with her responsibility?

In the top bunk Rose pretended to sleep while Respy undressed, peeling off layers of petticoats under the discreet tent of a voluminous white nightdress, long-sleeved and high-necked. Her thin greying hair was brushed and plaited. Her teeth were cleaned, a glass of water and an English Bible laid on the small night table. Then Respy took off her spectacles, knelt in the bunk and said her prayers, drew the covers up to her chin and in a very few moments was gently snoring. Rose lay awake a long time as the train swayed and rattled, every now and then giving a plaintive toot as it raced through the night.

It was after midday when they arrived in Paris, and took a taxi to the Hotel Ventura Royale, which was very grand and seemed to unnerve Respy who had, hitherto, been very competently in charge, although Rose noticed that both the railway porter and the taxi driver had looked rather reproachfully at their tips.

But Rose, schooled by Monsieur Léon, felt very much at home in the resplendent cream and gilt foyer.

'I had not expected anything like this,' Respy whispered as they followed the porter into the lift, which was a cage, festooned with gilt roses. 'It really is overwhelming.'

'It is very splendid but a bit old-fashioned,' said Rose, and whispered as the porter unlocked the door and stood back for them to enter their room, 'Tip him three times what you planned – he will expect it.'

This time Respy got a smile and a bow, and a small mine of information as to how to ring for the *femme-de-chambre* if they wished her to unpack, and how to use the telephone to gratify their slightest wish. He presented Madame Respigny with the keys and wished them both a pleasant visit to Paris.

'Will you please draw back the curtains?' said Rose, and when he did so raced across to look out at the city. The window opened on to a small iron balcony and the man, smiling at her excitement, unbolted and opened it for her. The streets were crowded with traffic. There was an oblique view of the Arc de Triomphe. It seemed a bold, big, brilliant-looking city.

Their room was cream and gold. There were two large single beds dressed in cream satin covers, and built of carved cream-painted wood with panels of gilded wicker work. There were mirrors everywhere, and a big bathroom tiled in a pattern of birds and blossom, with two immense washbowls set in slabs of marble. Rose raced about, squeaking with

27

delight at each new luxury: the huge, warmed bath towels on a heated rail, the wrapped soap tablets, smelling of lily-of-the-valley.

'It is really too much,' said Respy, 'a simple pension would have done quite well.'

'But not so much fun!' cried Rose, '– my aunt must be rich if she always stays here. I think it is lovely!'

Respy looked at her severely, catching a glimpse of Charmian. She wondered just how much she was her mother's daughter, so that Rose, who guessed exactly what she was thinking, rushed across and hugged her, bubbling with laughter.

They dined at the hotel, Respy wearing a semi-evening dress of dark blue, long-sleeved with a discreet neckline; Rose one of her new school party dresses. She combed her hair up high and fastened it with a large diamante clip she had bought from a market stall in Nice, so that the pure lines of her face were revealed and the straight, black hair hung below her waist. She was quite aware that even in their secluded corner she attracted masculine attention and of Respy's slightly disapproving glances.

She could not persuade Respy to venture out into Paris on foot, but after dinner they did take a cab and drive down the Champs Elysée and round by the Place de l'Opéra and back. Rose thought the city very beautiful at night – so many lights and so many people. And soon she would be in yet another city – London!

At ten o'clock the following morning Monsieur Paul Raymond, from Monsieur Léon's lawyers, arrived. He brought their *wagon-lit* reservations and more cash for their journey to London. He assured them they would not have to worry about the hotel bill, and they would be met at Victoria Station in London. Madame Léon would have come to Paris to meet them but she had been slightly unwell.

He was a busy young man and had allotted just sufficient time for this interview, but he found something irresistible about the little girl – for she was, he told himself, only a little girl, in spite of her precocious charm which was sometimes naive, sometimes innocently bold.

He loved the way she was fascinated by the luxury of the hotel. She told him she had been in all the fine hotels in Nice with Monsieur Léon, but only to tea. She had never stayed in one before, so Monsieur Paul cancelled his appointments and took them out to lunch and on to a tour of Paris first – the educational tour which Respy had hoped for.

After he had dutifully showed them Notre Dame, the Senate House and the Eiffel Tower, he persuaded Respy *not* to go round the Pantheon, Rose protesting that she was not interested in stone coffins full of dead people, however famous, and whisked them off to the Rue de La Paix where he was delighted by her pleasure as she strolled from window to window, exclaiming, comparing, criticising and admiring. She was not very attracted by the jewellery – it was the clothes that fascinated her.

'One can wear artificial jewellery with an air,' she said, 'but clothes you cannot fake.'

'I am quite sure,' he said, 'you are going to like your Aunt Margaret.'

The following morning he drove them personally to the Gâre du Nord, saw to their luggage, bought chocolates and magazines, and finally offered Rose a long, flat box, wrapped in pale lilac tissue and sealed with the gold seal of a famous glove shop.

'A souvenir of Paris, from the Rue de la Paix.'

'*Monsieur*! How kind. May I open it?'

'But certainly.'

It was a pair of long-wristed, hand stitched gloves of cream-coloured kid, smelling of muguet.

Her eyes opened wide as she thanked him again, ignoring Respy's somewhat alarmed frown.

'The only correct gift a gentleman can give to a young lady,' he teased. 'To wish you well in your new life. My compliments to Madame Léon, and my father's compliments and good wishes for her health.' He stood back and removed his hat as the train began to pull away.

Rose jumped up and leaned out of the window, calling, 'Many thanks, M'sieur, you are very kind. I shall tell my aunt how well you looked after us!'

She sat down to try on the beautiful hand-made gloves as the train moved northwards and Respy, watching her smoothing them meticulously round her wrists, wondered, as she so often did, how much she was her mother's child.

Chapter Two

Riverside Mansions was a large redbrick building over-looking the Chelsea Embankment. Madame Léon's apartment on the first floor looked down upon a railed London garden planted with plane trees and shrubberies and the embankment and, beyond, the green of Battersea Park.

The apartment was large and airy, decorated in pale colours, the furniture had been chosen with care. There were many pictures and rare objects of interest and good taste, but it held no hint of the opulent Victorian fashions of Margaret's youth.

There was a large octagonal bay on the corner of the living room where stood a long lounge chair in which she would sit with her feet up, a small adjustable table by her side, the telephone and her papers within reach. She had taken to working at home two days a week. She disliked this inactivity, but had felt unusually tired recently. Besides she could trust her manager Roy Brinkley to run everything efficiently and to keep her well informed.

She was a small, spare, very elegant woman. Even when resting, with no one there to see her, she wore a jade green Japanese kimono embroidered with purple irises, and her small feet were clad in curl-toed Eastern slippers also embroidered with gold. She loved beautiful things made with craftsmanship and care.

She still looked a young woman, although her hair was a rusty grey, shining with the gleam of the red it had been in her youth. She had recently had it cut short, and it curled charmingly about her head. A new fashion from America, still very startling in London, especially in a woman of her years.

She heard the turn of a key in the lock and sat up sharply, her eyes lighting with pleasure. The sun-light picked out the laughter lines at the corners of her eyes and mouth and made shadows under the beautiful cheekbones in her small face.

It was a middle-aged face which would never lose its intrinsic charm.

That's my Tom, she thought happily. He was down from Yorkshire for a week and had come to lunch with her. The apartment was his second home. He always stayed with her when he was in Town.

She put the letter from Monsieur Edouard Raymond, Léon's solicitors in Paris, away in her handbag. Today she would have to tell Tom about the little French girl.

She rose quickly, irritated by a small pain which shot up the left side of her chest and vanished instantly. Her health had always been perfect, her energy inexhaustible, but the doctor said she had lived at a pitch of energy beyond her strength and it was time to slow down. After all, there was no need for her to work at all. Had she never considered semi-retirement?

She certainly had not!

Would she not like to see more of Europe – travel – see her friends?

She had plenty of friends, and she had always travelled, and worked as well.

'Great heavens, man,' she said crossly, 'there are many women still running businesses successfully well into their sixties.'

But she could not deny she felt tired. And every so often a sudden movement or a swift mounting of the stairs from the salon to her office would bring about the lightning stab of pain.

Ferdi's funeral had been an exhausting ordeal – emotionally as well as physically. The graveside tributes from the smart, the fashionable and the brilliant had seemed interminable. She had been grateful for Tom's strong arm and steadfast support. And it had rained. How it had rained! She had taken a chill, and was not quite back to full energy and strength.

Tom came bounding into the room, filling it with his vitality. Big, fair, handsome, with the deep blue eyes of the Normanbys, he was the delight of her heart.

'What's all this?' he demanded, bending to kiss her. 'I rang the salon thinking you would be there and I could pick you up, and they said you were taking a day off. I couldn't believe it! You're not ill, are you, Mama?'

'No, I'm not,' she said impatiently. 'Sit down. It's just that I can't shake off that chill I caught at poor Ferdi's funeral, and feel a bit overtired. I've been to the doctor. He just said I'd been overdoing things.'

'I've told you *that* often enough,' he said a trifle smugly. He liked to take care of her. 'You've got an excellent staff, and Brinkley could take over completely.'

'What would you like to drink?' She changed the subject abruptly. 'A sherry? A hock and seltzer?'

'That sounds very Edwardian,' he teased. 'Nothing for me, Mama. I have business appointments this afternoon. Stevie should be doing this trip but My Lord is too busy with his social round! And as I wanted to see you, I offered to do it.'

The dining room, equally spacious and charming, also overlooked the river. They were served by a middle-aged woman, not in uniform but wearing a large white apron over her skirt and blouse. She smiled affectionately at Tom.

'Nice to see you, Mr Tom.'

'Hello, Sarah. Nice to see you.'

'All well in Thornsby?' she asked as she set the dishes before them. 'Is your father well, and Mr Stephen?'

'Yes, Dad's fine. Stevie is his usual charming self.'

'Aye, he's a right charmer, that one,' she said, shaking her head. 'You were a right pair, you two lads!' She had worked at his father's house in Thornsby when they were boys.

'I don't know whether she's being complimentary or not,' Tom grinned when she had left the room. He noticed Margaret was sitting with her chin propped in her hand, not attempting to eat. 'What *is* the matter? Are you sure you're quite well?'

'Quite sure.' She paused, sighed, lifted her fork, put it down again. 'I've got something to tell you.'

'Well, can't we eat while you tell me this terrible secret?' He started on the smoked salmon bought, he knew, expressly for him.

Margaret's eyes suddenly sparkled with amusement. 'This may come as a shock to you, but I've suddenly inherited a niece.'

'A *niece*?' He stopped eating, astonished.

'Yes. It was a shock for me too. Shareen Abderhazy, my sister Charmian's daughter. Ferdi wrote a letter to me just before he died – it was to be delivered if he did not survive the operation. He had left her half his money, a nice little fortune, and he has named us as guardians and executors.'

'Me?'

'Yes.'

'You're joking, Mama!'

'No, I'm not. Here.' She handed him the French lawyer's letter. He read it through gravely and handed it back to her.

'I'm, to be the guardian of a kid of fourteen! He couldn't just do this – without asking us!'

'No, but he expected us to help her. You can refuse, of course, but I can't. Tom – she has no one else.'

'So – what are you going to do?'

'What he has asked. Bring her here. Make a home for her. We're her only relatives. I telephoned Ferdi's solicitors at once, gave my consent, and then confirmed it in writing. I'm hoping you will too. She has nothing from her mother. Charmian left only debts!'

'But why didn't he tell you before?'

Margaret looked both sad and amused. 'Ferdi adored Charmy.' She glanced at her son. 'Ferdi was not a man who loved women, you know.'

'I think he loved you.'

'Oh, yes. As partners and friends we loved each other. But Charmian was more than a woman to him. When she came back from India after her first husband died, she stayed with us for a while. To Ferdi she was the perfect model. The dream woman on whom he could create clothes. He did – marvellous clothes. And sophisticated old sinner that he was, thought nothing of her lying and her frivolous disloyalties. But I was her sister, her twin. I wanted her to live a good life.

34

He was always loyal to her, and so made this absurd romantic promise – he would not tell me about this child, Shareen, during Charmian's lifetime *if* she would make him the girl's legal guardian. Ferdi kept his promise. Shareen never lived with her mother – she was fostered by a woman called Madame Respigny.'

Tom suddenly sat up, alert.

'You knew her?'

'I've seen her. And I think I've met your niece.'

'*Met her*? Why didn't you tell me? How?'

'When I was in Nice late last summer with Stevie, I took flowers to Baroness Abderhazy's grave, as you asked me to. And this funny little kid was there, doing the same thing. She drove off with an old fellow, a real old queen, but – distinguished. I also, at your request, called on Monsieur Léon and behold, it was the same old fellow I had seen at the cemetery. I told you about that visit!'

'But you did not tell me about the child! And don't speak of my husband like that.' Her eyes glinted warningly. 'Ferdi was a brilliant designer and a good friend. Besides – it was vulgar.'

'Sorry. But I spoke to her at the cemetery and she did not say she was Charmian's daughter. I did ask her who she was, and she said merely that she lived with a Madame Respigny. I did ask Monsieur Léon directly, but he just said she was a young girl he knew, who was his ward, although she did not live with him. He talked a lot about your sister and the celebrities for whom you designed clothes in the good old days.'

'Well, will you accept the guardianship?'

'If you wish it – and if she consents. But I think you're crazy. A young girl of fourteen! I thought you had decided to take things easy.'

'Oh, Tom, she won't be here all the time. I will find a good school for her. Apparently Charmian told Ferdi that if I had known about the child I would have worried about how she was being brought up, and nagged her all the time – and insisted that Shareen should be well provided for.'

'Which, of course, you would have done,' he laughed, and she laughed too, and took his hand where it lay on the table.

'Yes, of course. Our Charmian in charge of a child? She couldn't take care of a lapdog! Or herself.' She regarded him with gentle mockery. 'This child – you seem to have taken quite a fancy to her. I gather you bought a present for her at the auction sale?'

He coloured a little under his sunburn. 'Oh, I put in a bid for one lot and it was knocked down to me. I told them to deliver it to Monsieur Léon. Odd to think he was still your husband. I never thought of you as anyone's wife – except Dad's.'

'I know. That was nice of you. Don't evade me – this present?'

'Oh, well,' he said a trifle sheepishly, 'I went to the sale of Charmian's things, clothes, furniture, jewellery – the lot. And I saw these bangles. They made me think of the little girl somehow. I don't know why. They were so oriental, and so is she under the prim French schoolgirl look. So I bought them for her.'

He kept the memory of the naked sea-nymph with the black hair floating in the blue Mediterranean water to himself. 'I was sorry for her. The way she said, "Oh, I'm nobody. I just live with Madame Respigny."' He rose and went to the window, lighting a cigarette. 'I saw the child next day in the town with this governessy person, but I did not speak to her. She had said that Monsieur Léon was her guardian, so I gave the bracelets to him and asked him to give them to her sometime. On her birthday, perhaps. He agreed, put them away, and did not speak of her again. Only of you and Hanover Street. And how happy you were.'

'Those were our great days together. But tell me what she's like – this child of Charmian's?'

'Not like you. Or . . . I don't *know*. Yes, there is *something* about the way she holds her head. That cocky little tilt you have when you want your own way. Something about the upward slant of her eyes. But otherwise she is dark, olive-skinned, black-haired, an Eastern child. Was Abderhazy from the Middle East?'

'A Persian, I believe. I never met him. He was her second husband.'

'Well, this little cousin of mine is straight out of the Arabian Nights.' He smiled mischievously. 'She might even be a great beauty one day, like her mama.'

'God forbid,' said Margaret fervently. 'I couldn't live through another Charmian.'

'What's all this then, in this letter? That there is some doubt about that child's parentage?'

'I don't know. Ferdi was always a great gossip. My only concern is that, whoever the father may be, she is my sister's daughter. She is only fourteen, and has no one to turn to but me.'

'Another little bastard in the family?' he said, grinning, 'That makes two of us. And splendid parents you have been to me. So, you want me to tell Dad?'

'Please. I don't want him bothered – it is not really his responsibility, but he must know. Now that's settled,' she began to eat at last, 'tell me about everything at Cliffs Edge. Is everything all right up there?'

'Between Angela and me? As right as it ever will be. I live at my cottage, and make a duty call once a week for Dad's sake. Usually for dinner – there's the usual touch of frost, especially if Stevie's out. Business is booming, though. A lot of uniform work.'

'And – my Henry?'

'Grand. You'd think him ten years younger than his age. He seems indestructible to me. He sent his love and says he will get away to see you in the New Year. He does twice as much work as any man in the business. Doesn't really like to delegate.'

She smiled to herself – neither did she.

'I know, I'm the same,' echoed Tom. 'I like to bear my own responsibilities. But it suits Stevie who'll never settle down while Dad spoils him so.'

She stayed silent. She knew why Henry Grimshaw spoiled Angela's boy. It was because he loved Tom, his love child, the best.

'Well, I've work this afternoon but I have a free evening. What shall we do with it? See a show? Dine out?'

'But my new niece arrives from France today. I must meet her, and make her welcome.'

37

'Let me go,' he said quickly, 'if you're tired. She may remember my face . . . we did exchange a few words. It would be better than arriving in a strange country and being greeted by someone she has never seen – however charming.'

'Tom, I was hoping you would. You seem very taken with this new cousin. Take warning – age is no barrier. Look at your father and me.'

He laughed and kissed her. 'Well, that worked very well. As well as anything works out in this uncertain world. But she is only a child – about fourteen, I should guess.'

'And, when you get back to Thornsby, you'll explain all this to Henry?'

'He'll think you're crazy too. And so you are, but I love you for it. And that little Miss Nobody deserves a better deal. What time is the train?'

'Four-thirty at Victoria.'

'I'll be there.'

Rose and Madame Respigny crossed the Channel by the early packet. It was a calm sea and they decided to risk lunch on board. They both realised with a slight shock that they were already in England. The waiters were all speaking in English and the menu was surprising.

'Roast beef with Yorkshire pudding? What is that?' Rose asked. 'This pudding is served *with* the meat? And roast lamb with mint sauce?' She was appalled. 'They eat *mint* with lamb?'

'It is chopped mint mixed with sugar and vinegar.'

'Ugh!'

'It is a traditional dish.'

So they had it, and even Madame Respigny herself pulled a sour face over the mint sauce, though the lamb was excellent, if overdone. They began to realise how very French they were. Madame Respigny found that she now spoke with a faint French accent, and Rose was surprised to find that though her English accent was excellent, there were still many words she did not understand.

At Dover they regarded the white cliffs and the castle and the neat row of villas overlooking the harbour, and tried to get used to the feeling of not being in France. Even the sky seemed smaller.

The train took them through hop fields and cherry orchards, the fruit long picked and the trees bare except for a few lingering yellow leaves. Past neat villages, everything looking very spick and span, with little gardens where autumn flowers still bloomed, and no smoking, smelling, manure heaps stood in the road outside the farms. They approached London through clean outer suburbs, with many green spaces and neat well-kept houses, then grey streets squashed between railway sidings, huge gasometers on one side of the track and a pretty park on the other. Then they crossed the wide grey Thames and the train curled slowly into the station.

Rose jumped out on to the platform. Respy was fussing, trying to find a porter, but Rose just stood there, gazing around. Respy had allowed her to abandon mourning since Monsieur Léon had expressly forbidden anyone to wear it for him. But even in the dark grey school coat she wore, and the round felt hat, her waist-length hair plaited into two long pigtails tied with neat black ribbons, nothing could make her look like an English schoolgirl. She felt a rising panic. They had been told someone would meet them. Who? The unknown aunt – the dressmaker? Another solicitor? A servant? Would they recognise her? If only someone she *knew* was there.

And then she saw Tom Grimshaw.

He looked curiously different in his well-tailored grey suit, a grey Homburg on his bright fair hair. She remembered the tall, graceful, handsome young man in his white linen suit and Panama hat. She recognised him instantly and as she did he saw her, a big smile instantly lighting up his sun-burned face. He raised his Homburg, waving it like a boy, and began to run towards her.

She felt an explosion of joy so intense that for a second she could not move, and then she too began to run, flying towards him, plaits flying, skirts flapping, arms outstretched, and both abruptly halted, and he stood gazing down into her wondering eyes, his face full of laughter.

'Miss Shareen Abderhazy, I presume?' he said.

'Oh, yes,' she gasped.

39

'And I am your new cousin, Tom Grimshaw. My mother, your Aunt Margaret, has sent me to meet you. Welcome to England.'

She held out a shaking hand, but he put his arms round her and gave her a kiss on each cheek, saying again, 'Welcome to England, my little cousin.'

'Oh, *thank* you, M'sieur!'

'So – little Miss Nobody has turned out to be my own cousin. Shareen, why didn't you tell me who you were, that day in Nice?'

'Oh, Mama never let me tell anyone. I do not know the reason. She seemed to like me when I was a baby. Perhaps because she was embarrassed to have a great schoolgirl daughter.'. Her creamy dark cheeks flushed enchantingly. 'Shareen means rose in Persian, I am told, so everyone calls me Rose. I am so glad you came to meet me – someone I know. I don't feel so much of a nobody now.' She stopped talking for lack of breath, while Respy stood listening in astounded silence.

Tom held Rose away from him. Suddenly she put her head down and rubbed one of her cheeks against his hand, like a kitten.

'Let's have a look at you. Yes, older and taller – and I'd say prettier, or shouldn't I say that?'

'Please *do* say it – I like to hear it very much.'

'I'm not going to – you'll get very vain. I think you are really quite vain as it is.'

'I am not! I am not!'

'Oh, yes you are, Miss Abderhazy. Wait until you meet my stern mama, your aunt. She's a gorgon.'

'With snakes for hair?'

'No, actually it's bobbed.' He saw the coquetry die in her eyes, and the touch of panic rise again, and said quickly, 'I'm teasing. She's a lovely person. I shall have to be stern myself or she will spoil you silly.'

'What does that mean?'

'It means she is looking forward to having you.' The white lie slipped carelessly off his tongue to reassure her. 'There are no girls in our mixed up family.' He became aware of Respy, and held out his hand apologetically. 'Madame Respigny, I am so sorry. Let me help.' In a few seconds he had called a porter and their luggage was collected and wheeled away along the platform. 'Mama asked me to come as I was in town. I keep my old room at her flat and stay there with her when I am down from Yorkshire. We'll get a taxi – it is not far to the apartment where we live.'

'Thank you, it is very kind of you.' Respy was stiffly formal. 'I trust your mother is well?'

He gave a little worried frown. 'Yes, but not as well as I would like her to be. She caught a bad chill at that great long funeral of Monsieur Léon's in Paris – it poured, and it was cold, and the speeches went on forever. She has seemed a little tired lately.' Respy was touched by the boyish anxiety in the handsome young face. 'I suppose,' he said, 'you do get more easily tired – when you are older?'

'I am afraid that this is so,' Respy said gently. 'It is to be expected.'

'But she's only in her fifties – and she's always been so full of fun! She's given up driving the car – says there are too many cars in London. But she still goes to the salon in Hanover Street twice a week. I suppose she was very upset over Monsieur Léon's death – did you know that although they had not met for some time, he did an occasional design for her right to the end of his life?'

The taxi had turned into a wide carriage way running along beside the river, with bronze lampposts with two large globes which a man with a long pole was methodically lighting. There were tall plane trees like a Parisian boulevard.

'Why are there no bookstalls along the river walls?'

'I've often wondered – perhaps it's a bit colder and a bit wetter than Paris. I suppose that's why we don't have cafés where you can sit outside. That's Battersea Park across the river. And the garden on this side is the Herbalists' Garden. We live a bit further along – past that little white pub.'

'An inn? Will you take me there?' asked Rose.

'You're not old enough.'

'Why not?'

'It is the law.'

'Against girls?'

'Against boys and girls under eighteen.'

41

'But if you were with me?'

'It would make no difference, you are too young still. Besides, well brought up young ladies do not go into pubs.'

'But why is this so? Papa Léon often took me into cafés when I was quite small.'

He could see the small dark child perched up on a café seat in the Nice sunshine while Léon chatted with his cronies. 'They don't believe in encouraging alcoholic drink among the very young. Look,' he pointed with relief to the large five-storey building on the next corner, 'that is where my mother lives – on the first floor on the right. Come along.'

Rose stepped out. The wintry wind along the grey river was cold, whipping little angry waves. She shivered. Her coat, bought for a Riviera winter, seemed thin.

'*Mon Dieu, c'est froid!*'

'Yes. Let's get you in where it's warm – it's colder still where I come from in Yorkshire. We already have snow on the moors. But here the gardens are very pretty in the spring. In the one beneath my mother's windows there are lilacs and almond trees in blossom in April.'

Respy sniffed. Her nose was quite red. The climate was another thing she had discovered about England.

A uniformed porter came out of the building and with the help of the taxi-driver, carried their luggage inside.

'Good afternoon, Mr Grimshaw.'

'Good afternoon, Williams. This young lady is my cousin from France who is going to live with Madame Léon.'

'Pleased to meet you, miss. You go on up, sir, and I'll see to this lot.'

It was warm in the entrance hall. It had a red carpet and was panelled in mahogany, and there was a porter's desk, with hooks for keys like an hotel, and a telephone. Tom took them up to the first floor in the lift. Rose felt her chest tightening with apprehension. She was going to meet her aunt, the fabled Margaret Normanby, whom her mother had dismissed with pettish spite as "the dressmaker". The corridor was wide, with polished parquet floors and runners of thick carpet. All the doors opening on to it were mahogany with elaborate brass fittings. Number 4 was at the end of the corridor. Tom opened it with his key and showed them into a white-walled hall, large and charming, with a Persian carpet and a light oak table on which stood a telephone and an arrangement of copper-coloured leaves and chrysanthemums. On the walls were sketches and photographs of model gowns, covering the fashions of the past twenty years.

Rose stopped at one sketch, recognising the provocative tilt of the pretty head on its long delicate neck. The hair was a beautiful reddish-gold. It was her mother wearing a dress of Nile green satin, cut very low. The skirt swirling from a tiny waist was embroidered in a design of variegated pearls. Written in the corner, in Monsieur Léon's handwriting, was "Charmy in the Langtry ball gown. 1895".

'That's Mama,' she said, 'I didn't know she was a mannequin?'

'I think so,' said Tom, 'when she was very young. Mama told me it was when she came home from India and her first husband died.'

'Her hair was not like that – much redder, and harsh. She dyed it.'

At least she would learn all about her mother now. About her first marriage, and before that when she was a girl. You knew all about your mother when you really had a family.

Tom led them into a large airy drawing room overlooking the river. In the corner was an octagonal bay with eight small windows, and a chaise longue where a woman was sitting with a light rug over her knees. The grey skies and early twilights of autumn made it shadowy, except for the firelight flickering on white walls. Tom pressed down the light switch and revealed a lovely room with light walls and flowers, paintings, and many shelves full of books.

The woman looked up over a large pair of spectacles then took them off and rose to her feet, a half-smile on her face.

She was not tall, and very slight; the first thing Rose noticed was that her hair was cut short, ear-length, and that it curled charmingly about her pretty head, and that there were still glints of red in the grey curls. She heard Respy draw in a sharp breath of astonishment – they had seen sleek-haired young beauties occasionally in Nice, usually Americans with their hair cut like the child star, Jacky Coogan, but never a woman of Respy's own age. Margaret was small but gave the impression of height and authority because of her straight back and beautifully poised small head. She was wearing a Japanese kimono of pale silk embroidered with irises, and there were gold-embroidered slippers on her small feet.

'Here is Rose, Mama,' said Tom. He seemed very tall and wide-shouldered, a masculine presence among the three women, 'and her companion Madame Respigny. Rose, this is my mother, Madame Léon.'

Margaret looked at her gravely, the close, shrewd look of a woman who has engaged and controlled staff, who has dealt with many types of people, who would be hard to deceive. Rose had no wish to deceive her. She wanted to be accepted. She made a small bobbing curtsey in the French manner, her dark eyes meeting the searching blue scrutiny of her aunt's with a touch of defiance. Then suddenly Margaret took her hand and smiled brilliantly, and for the first time Rose caught a glimpse of her own mother. But this was a straightforward approach with none of Charmian's wheedling, petulant, devious wish to please at any cost which could change to impatience, and from impatience to dismissal and denial, within seconds.

'I am your mother's twin sister,' said Margaret. 'I have only just learned about you. I am very glad Monsieur Léon sent you to me.'

Rose found herself smiling in sheer relief. Margaret put a hand on each of her shoulders and kissed her. 'You are as tall as me,' she said, 'and so very pretty. But not like your mother at all.'

They stood for a long moment in silence, weighing each other up. They were alike but unalike, dark and fair, East and West, but each of them was reassured by what they saw in the other's eyes.

Chapter Three

Margaret sat propped up with pillows in her comfortable wide bed. It was late evening. The room was a bedroom and office combined for in spite of the feminine elegance and comfort there was a large mahogany desk and filing cabinet. At the moment the desk was strewn with letters and prospectuses from girls' schools.

She leaned back on the pillows with the unpleasant sensation of a sudden draining of energy. It had happened frequently of late; she would begin the day with her old drive, and then quite unexpectedly the unpleasant lethargy would take possession of her.

I must be getting old, she thought. And then rebelliously, Rubbish! I'm only in my fifties. Women of my age have many good working years ahead, and so have I.

It would be several days before she would receive answers to her letters and then she would take Rose with her to visit the schools and make their final choice. The schools were half-way through their autumn terms and she would like Rose to start immediately after half-term so she would get the feel of it before Christmas.

At the Salon in Hanover Street they were in the middle of the pre-Christmas rush of orders and she should be there every day. What on earth could she do with a fourteen-year old? After Christmas she would have more time, and had considered taking Rose on holiday before the start of spring term.

She rang the bell and Sarah came in with her nightly drink

of warm milk with a dash of brandy and set it on the beside table, shaking her head warningly.

'You look tired, ma'am. I hope this young miss won't be too much for you.'

'I hope so too,' Margaret smiled, 'or she'll be the first young miss who ever has! Is she in bed?'

'Yes, ma'am. And that French-English lady, Madame – what's her name?'

'Madame Respigny.'

'Yes.'

'And Mr Tom?'

'Oh, he's not in yet. It's early for him yet, ma'am.'

'Yes, of course.' She leaned back on the pillows. 'Will you brush my hair, Sarah, just for a few moments? Like my old nurse used to? It's silly, I know, but it's soothing. I find it tiring to lift my arms for any length of time at the end of the day. Just five minutes, and then you can go to bed.'

'Of course I will, ma'am.'

She took the two brushes, one stiff, the other soft as silk, and began to brush the short grey hair. It curled from the brush, the latent red glittering as it sprang back. Across Margaret's forehead was a wing of pure white. She put a small tablet beneath her tongue. She closed her eyes like a cat and the feeling of tightness across her chest slowly faded and her breath came with blessed ease. Tomorrow morning, she thought, I'll take the child to the salon with me. In the afternoon, perhaps Madame Respigny will take her out, or Tom will amuse her, and I'll go to see Dr Nathan and get him to give me a tonic.

Rose found the Salon quite enchanting. Margaret told her she could go where she liked, and sent a young assistant with her to introduce her to the heads of each department. She told the girl to ask any questions she wished and was amused by the complete confidence with which she did so. Lunch was sent in from a local restaurant at midday, and they served themselves at a small table set for them in the office.

Margaret regarded her composed young niece with amusement. 'How would you like to work in the fashion trade?'

'You mean – when I'm grown up?'

'Of course. Although I wasn't much older when I started my apprenticeship.'

'It is not what I had thought of for myself, or what Papa Léon had thought of for me. Mama never discussed my future. I love the beautiful dresses, the fine workmanship and the gorgeous materials. I would like to wear them. But I did not realise what a difficult business it is to learn. Buying, choosing, cutting, fitting, sewing. I would not mind working in the salon, but not forever, I wish very much to wear nice things, not to make or sell them.'

'Well, that's positive enough – though it makes me think of your mother,' Margaret said drily. 'She did not like work at all.'

'What is wrong with that?' Rose blazed unexpectedly, her black eyes sparkling. 'She was most beautiful and elegant, and greatly admired. I have often thought it might be quite a good life.'

'What was she then?' Margaret asked gravely.

To her astonishment, Rose said, 'She was an expensive whore. You are shocked? But you *knew*.'

'Yes, indeed,' Margaret said bitterly.

'But she was a fool. There are several such ladies in Nice who were Mama's age but still had their mansions, their money and investments, and also their faithful protectors. One or two married rich men with titles, and people came to respect them. But Mama drank, and took those little white pills, and gambled all night at the casino, and she could not be faithful to anyone. Not even to me. She would break faith for . . . for . . .' She sought for words, and Margaret found them for her.

'For the sake of half an hour's pleasure?'

'Yes. But I am not like my mother. If I was a lady of pleasure, as Papa Léon called them, I would never drink or gamble or waste my time with worthless lovers. I would look to my future.'

Margaret recalled the time when she had tried to protect the beautiful young Charmian, and how from the start it had always been hopeless – that luscious beauty with its bird

47

brain. Her daughter was certainly made of sterner stuff. She pretended to take her seriously.

'So you are thinking of a life as a lady of pleasure?'

'You are laughing at me, Tante Margaret,' Rose accused, but she burst out laughing herself. 'Of course not. Papa Léon said things of great sense to me. He said a great beauty was like a great talent – a gift of God – and should not be wasted. He said a mistress had no real security unless she was very wise, and if she was wise then she would not be a mistress! Marriage was the thing. He said a beautiful woman who was married and rich was like a crowned queen.'

'It was just what he *would* say – I can hear him as you talk. Preaching cynicism and ruthlessness, and he with a heart as soft as putty.'

She was a mixture, this fourteen year old. A mixture and a mystery. The charm of France, the subtlety of the East, and something else – pragmatic, not self-deceiving. A bit of Margaret herself, perhaps? A bit of Yorkshire.

'So your ambition is to marry a rich man and be his beautiful wife? You think you are beautiful?'

'*Bien sûr*. It would be foolish to pretend I do not. Of course I see myself in the mirror, and I notice the way people look at me.'

'Men?'

'Yes, of course. Are you shocked again, *ma tante*?'

'I'm not easily shocked. But I do believe that the only reason for a marriage or a love affair is love. On both sides.'

'Oh, yes, of course.' Rose sounded very French and practical. 'But one cannot always have everything. One finds the man one loves, but perhaps he is poor, or not free, anything. And position and money count a great deal – particularly for someone like me.'

'What do you mean?'

Rose laid her beautiful hand against Margaret's. 'I am a hybrid,' she said simply. 'People do not always accept that, even if my mother was a Baroness. I must charm twice as successfully, be better than any, climb above that prejudice. I *know* – I learned that at school. At the convent a girl once called me a nigger. Here in England too people look down on people like me, but I am *not* going to be humble about it.'

'What did you do about the girl – the one who insulted you?'

'I blacked both her eyes. Papa Léon had to soothe everyone – but he always paid my fees in advance, so that was all right.'

Margaret burst out laughing, and then put her arms round Rose and kissed her.

'You're all right,' she said, 'Ferdi taught you the only way he could. Cynically but well. But don't forget you have a heart too – it may catch you out one day. Now, tell me what you hoped to find here in England?'

Again the expressive little shrug. '*Everything*. A family of my own who is not ashamed of me. A good education. A chance. But what else could I do? Respy could not have me for ever. Papa Léon was fond of me but he could not take a *jeune fille* into his *ménage*.' The dark eyes were knowledge-able and a little amused. 'You say you believe in love, Tante Margaret, and yet you married dear Papa Léon who, for all his brilliance was – well – what he was. I cannot believe you did not know. But if so, why did you marry him?'

Margaret flinched, but she had to be honest.

'I was in love with Tom's father. Ferdi and I were intro-duced by a dear mutual friend. Ferdi was looking for a manager. He had capital and talent, I had management experience. He wanted to open a first-class salon in London. In a way it was a bit like falling in love. We were wonderful together, Ferdi and I. He was free to design, while I saw to all the rest. The salon workrooms, cleaning staff, the accounts. Everything. As time went on, we became very successful. We were close friends. I liked him and I liked his friends – all interesting people in the arts and the theatre and music worlds. Ferdi introduced me to a wider, more sophisticated life, and then he asked me to marry him. It seemed a good idea. Although I was twenty-five and was perfectly aware of homosexuality, I never thought about it with regard to him. So I married him, and then I found out. Still, I loved him. We were comrades and partners. We managed very well, until in Paris one day we met Henry Grimshaw. He too had an empty marriage. We had been in love since I was a little older than you are now. I was twenty-five when we met again and he was

49

twenty years older. A wonderful man. We went up like flames through straw.'

'But why did you not go and live with Mr Grimshaw?'

'Ah – because I was me, not Charmian. No one was going to take my business from me, and Henry was tied to his great business in the North. I was not going to live tucked away in Harrogate or Scarborough. But I was pregnant with Tom. And then his wife, when they had given up all hope, became pregnant too. He could not leave her. It was an impasse. Then poor Ferdi got himself into a scandal and had to leave England, and Henry loved our boy and wanted him – and I found I could not keep Tom *and* my independence . . . So Henry and Angela adopted him. Maybe we were all wrong, but that was how it was. But I don't know that I would have married Ferdi had I realised how it was with him.'

'*Mon Dieu*! It cannot be possible that you did not know? Mama knew all about these things and told me.' Rose laughed suddenly, remembering all the things Charmian had said which she had never repeated to Respy. 'Mama knew many such men, and Papa Léon knew everybody. I would see him driving with his pretty young men. But he was always kind to me, and he also loved you. "Maggy," he said, "is true gold."'

'Oh!' Margaret's hand went up to stop the sudden trembling of her lips. 'I'm glad I married him. As I said – we were comrades. I miss him every day. When the telephone rings and it is from France, even now I still think for a second it is Ferdi calling me with all the news, the fashions and the scandal.'

For a moment neither of them spoke. 'Now I'll tell you what I propose to do,' Margaret said at last. 'I am looking for a school for you – the best we can find, for you cannot stay here all the time. You would get bored, and I am too busy. For holidays you will be here, and we will also go away – to France or Italy, or to visit your Respy in Nice. At least I can give you a good home, a good education, and I hope we shall like each other.'

'And one day, like everyone else, I must find my own way?'

'As you say, it happens to everyone. Perhaps you will become that rich and beautiful woman, like a crowned queen, that Papa Léon described. At least you have arrived safely

50

here with me, and I will do my very best for you. That I promise you, Rose.'

For almost the first time in her life Rose's mask of pert assurance fell away. She kissed her aunt. 'And I too, Tante Margaret. I am very happy that I have come here. And am happy to have an aunt and a cousin, for I shall see Tom too sometimes.'

'Oh, often,' said Margaret turning back to her writing. 'He is here whenever he is in London, and when he is here you are bound to see him.'

For the first time in her life, Rose felt a glow of pleasure and of hope. At last she knew where she belonged, and paramount in her mind were Tom Grimshaw's smiling blue eyes.

Yet when Madame Respigny's departure came it was like the cutting of an umbilical cord. They had been together for so long. It was a grey day. Respy was restrained but red-nosed from sniffing, and Rose pale in the dingy London light.

Tom, in London for a few days, drove them to the station, and with his usual understanding warmth made a great fuss of Respy, escorting her to her seat, booking her first class through to Nice, bringing gifts of flowers and magazines, tipping the steward to look after her.

'You will write, *chérie?*' Respy asked.

'Yes. And you will write to me, *ma chère institutrice*, and tell me all the gossip of Nice, and put in a little mimosa flower to remind me of the blue skies. And give my love to the dear flower market and to the deep blue sea.'

'Ah, Rose!'

As the train drew out Rose felt the tears sliding down her cheeks, and hurriedly dabbed at her eyes. Tom put a comforting arm about her shoulders.

'You're sad to see her go?'

'I did not think it would be like this! But she has always been with me. I have lived with her in her little apartment over the *boulangerie* as long as I can remember anything. And she is going to the south and the blue sea . . .'

'Where you used to swim like a mermaid,' he said.

Rose went scarlet. 'You *did* see me that day? It *was* you?'

He grinned. 'Yes, you know I did, and I'm glad. You looked like a mermaid and swam like a little fish. We must

51

find somewhere for you to swim in London – and you will be able to swim at the new school again. Don't be sad, *chérie*, Mama would have asked Respy to stay if you had said so.'

'No, I did not want that!' With a wise little smile, 'And neither did she – I was always a great responsibility and worry for her, and I think she is relieved.'

'And now the poor little orphan child is alone among cruel strangers.' She knew he was laughing at her, and thumped his shoulder. He caught her hand and drew it through his arm, leading her back to the barrier. 'Cheer up! I'll take you out to lunch.'

'Will Aunt Margaret permit that? Alone – without Respy?'

'Of course. You are in England now. English men, as no doubt you know, are phlegmatic and not given to leaping on undefended schoolgirls.'

'I think,' she said, dark eyes glinting mischievously, 'men are much the same everywhere, depending upon the circumstances.'

And so the happy time began, those few weeks before a school could be found which could take her at the half term before Christmas.

Tom seemed to find time to travel down to London quite often, and time to amuse and entertain this enchanting young cousin, and Rose, too young to realise what was happening to her, waited eagerly each day for the telephone to ring or his key to rattle in the door. To her a man of twenty-four was excitingly old, but not *too* old. She had never found boys of her own age interesting, and was trained to admire sophistication. But to Tom she was just an enchanting and funny child.

He took her out to lunch at expensive restaurants, amused at the way she loved it all, reading the menu with all Monsieur Léon's assurance. They went to the cinema and to matinées, to all the London riches of museums and historic buildings, arriving back at the flat in the early evening to take an apéritif with Margaret who would just have returned from Hanover Street. Sometimes Tom would stay to dinner, but he had many friends in London so usually Rose and Margaret dined alone.

Before she went to bed Rose would sit on the edge of Margaret's *chaise longue*, pouring out the excitements of her day, asking questions about Tom, and his father, and Stephen and the mysterious Yorkshire where he lived.

'If Tom is going to run you around London before you start at school,' said Margaret, 'you had better come with me to the Salon and we'll make you some clothes. You need them badly.' And in two or three magical days the clothes were made and finished, clothes suitable for a very young girl yet exquisitely different from any Rose had ever possessed: two day dresses, two evening dresses, and a chic warm winter crimson overcoat with a little collar of white mink and a cossack cap of the same soft fur.

'It is no use trying to make you look like an English rose,' Margaret said, 'you must wear things which flatter your difference. You are growing so fast, it is absurd to dress you like a little girl. I shall enjoy making clothes for you. I like my customers to be advertisements for me.'

When Tom was not in town Rose went to the Salon with Margaret, and slipped easily into the role of general assistant. She fetched and carried for the showroom, helping to display the rolls of beautiful materials, watching with eager eyes the society women and beautiful actresses who bought their clothes at Margaret Normanby. None of them was quite as beautiful as she remembered her mother to have been. She studied the superb assurance of women born to privilege, or women who had used their talents to fight for privilege and position, as closely as she ever studied at school.

But best of all, Rose liked the restaurants where Tom took her to lunch. She liked to watch the clothes of the women, wondering who they were, and where they had their clothes made, criticising them and asking his opinion, and could not understand his indifference. She knew that he preferred to watch the changing expressions on her face, even though he laughed at her.

She spoke to the waiters in French or her fluent but not quite so perfect Italian, seriously studying the menu like an old gourmet, preening when at one of the restaurants in Soho, the proprietor presented her with a rose, for the *bella ragazza*, and she pertly corrected him, 'You mean, *la bellissima signorina*.'

Tom laughed at his profuse apologies. 'D'you speak Italian?'

'Fairly well. There were many rich Italians at the convent. *Contessas* and *principessas*, some of them. But I do not speak it too well. Respy always spoke to me in English and her husband in the local patois. He was a Niçois.'

'And your mother?'

'Always in English – her French was not good. And Papa Léon spoke to me in English, although he was French. He would always correct my accent and grammar if I spoke French. He liked very much to take me out, and I liked to be with him for he knew some very famous people, but it becomes boring, sitting listening with one's hands folded, always the *petite fille*.'

'The grand-daughter?'

'So. But – it is useful to speak many languages.'

'What language did your father speak?'

She flushed, resentment in her beautiful eyes, and he marvelled at the way the warm ivory skin suffused with rose, like her namesake. Rose. A dark and alien rose.

'I don't know. I never saw him. Many languages. He was Persian by birth – but he had great houses everywhere, and horses and yachts, and entertained a great deal.'

'But he never asked to see you in Nice?'

'No,' she said coldly, 'he knew I was not his child. When he came to France he stayed in Paris and Mama used to travel up to see him, but she never took me. She always came back with a lot of money, and new jewels and clothes, and a list of new friends – men he wished her to cultivate for him to do business with. Sometimes his yacht would come into the harbour, and Mama was always there, but he never came ashore, and I was never taken there. I don't think she liked him – I think she was very much afraid of him. Someone told me he had ordered her to get rid of me, but she had not the courage to have the operation. Don't look so sad – I *am* here, after all.'

'Yes, here you are, and very sweet you are, and now you are our girl.' He grinned. 'I shouldn't worry about it.'

54

'Of what use is it to worry? Papa Léon left me some money so I am not poor. And I know you and Aunt Margaret are real relations. I belong to a family now. Has Aunt Margaret told you we have found a school?'

'I'm glad.'

'It is very upper-crust.' She flicked a finger under her nose with an expressive gesture. '*Très snob*. But very good. It is by the sea, with many girls. About three hundred. I will arrive for what they call the Christmas half. And in the holidays I will live with Aunt Margaret. In two weeks' time I go.'

'Only two!' he cried. 'I must get down to London as often as I can.'

'I think Aunt Margaret thinks you should go home more often because your father telephones and is cross.'

He laughed. 'He's not really cross. He knows I'd never let him down. But he's right. Every time I telephone the office, he or someone else tells me so. But it's not often a chap discovers a pretty new cousin out of the blue, and if Stevie were here he'd be trying to cut me out. He's a lazy young dog. He can do some of the hard work for a change.'

But he ought to get back to Thornsby and he knew it. He had wasted nearly a month since Rose had arrived. He had done a great deal of work, seeing customers in and about London, but that was not really his province. The sales side was Stephen's responsibility, and Tom had discovered he had been neglecting it. His charming, gentlemanly younger brother did not care for business at all. But he, Tom, was considered the back bone of the firm and ought not to waste his time on this young cousin whom it had given him such unexpected pleasure to amuse and entertain.

The school they had decided upon was in Sussex in the beach country near Arundel. Margaret had gone through all the correspondence and curriculae with Rose, giving her freedom of choice, something which had never happened to her before.

They had brought the choice down to two.

'This school, St Barbara's, attracts me,' said Margaret. 'They are very interested in creative work and the arts. But

55

Lady Pendrill's is more exclusive. From what you have told me of your ambitions, Rose, Lady Pendrill's is the one I think *you* will choose?'

'You mean, they will teach me to be a great lady?'

'Well, they will try!'

'You are laughing at me, Aunt Margaret.'

'Just a little. But at Lady Pendrill's you will certainly meet some very well-bred and rich young ladies, many of whose mothers are my customers, and whose fathers are very well-known men.'

'*Lady* Pendrill's? Is this school, then, run by a lady of rank?'

'No. It was founded by a lady of rank three hundred years ago. She thought the daughters of gentlemen were only taught to entertain men, that most of them were frivolous and foolish, so she started a school to educate ladies. Now what do you think?'

'But, Aunt Margaret – it is for you to decide. You who are so generously paying for this school.'

'Not really. *You* must try to know what you want from life. I wanted to earn sufficient money to keep the family. Charmian wanted romantic dreams. I mustn't make any mistakes with you. Suppose we visit both these schools? Of course we shall have to find out whether they will have you.'

Rose was surprised. 'You mean they will not always take pupils, even if they can pay?'

'Yes. Particularly Lady Pendrill's.'

'That one, then, is the one we should choose,' Rose said decisively. 'It seems the most prestigious.'

Margaret smiled, and shook her head. She was beginning to see small reflections of herself in this strange dark child. The definite choice was not from snobbishness but from opportunism. To be a great lady one must associate with ladies . . . it was simple. Just as she had thought that to be a great dressmaker one must associate with the best creator of clothes. That was why she had married Ferdinand Léon all those years ago.

The schools were a surprise to Rose. Both the establishments she had been to in Nice were housed in large suburban mansions, but these English ones were out in the country with

56

wide playing fields, buildings for gymnasiums and both near the sea. Lady Pendrill's had stables, with horses for the girls who wished to ride, and a large library for quiet study.

During her interviews with the two head mistresses Rose sat with her hands folded, a model of decorum, answering questions in her charming, faintly accented English. Her knowledge of French and Italian was impressive. She had decided unhesitatingly on Lady Pendrill's and Margaret was relieved when she was accepted. She knew her family names, Normanby and Abderhazy, overrode the child's colour, and when they were taken on a tour of the school and met other members of the staff, Margaret saw for the first time how skilfully she could use her charm. The beautiful smile, and the sudden lapses into childishness which Tom at that first brief meeting in Nice had found so endearing. When they came to a high point in the garden and through a gap in the downs could see the Channel shimmering in the sunlight, she threw up her arms and raced to the highest point, shouting, 'The sea – the sea! Shall I be able to swim?' Then the grave headmistress burst out laughing. 'Tante Margaret,' she cried, 'Shall I be able to swim?'

Christmas came, and went with dinner at the Savoy with Margaret and Sarah, in her best new hat, and presents in the morning after breakfast. New Year passed – and it was the day before Rose was to travel down to Sussex to the new school.

Margaret and Sarah had helped her to mark everything and pack her school trunk – there seemed so many garments for so many activities – and all day her heart had beaten a little faster, and her eyes shone with eager anticipation, because Tom was coming on this last evening to take her to dinner and the theatre – not to a matinée and tea at Rumpelmayer's but an evening performance and out to dinner, as though she was really grown up.

Margaret had said she would stay at home. Business was hectic at this time of the year and she was tired. Tom came into the drawing room to wait for Rose, and when he did so his mother had the feeling, as she had always done with Henry, that the room was not big enough for him. It was not that he was excessively tall but that there was a superb, masculine vitality about him that needed large rooms, wide fields and generously-minded people. She remembered the big, handsome boy baby who had been such a treasure and such a problem to her, and could not believe he was this quick, strong, graceful young man, so good at everything he touched, whose charm was irresistible because it was simple and kind without a touch of self-consciousness. The self-willed Grimshaw set of the mouth and chin belied the beautiful, teasing Normanby eyes.

He dropped into a chair beside her, took her hand and kissed her.

'I'm sorry you're not coming, Mama. It's a long while since we had a jaunt together.'

'Well, you know what it's like at this time of the year. Later, when Rose is at school, we'll have a night out. Just one thing, darling.' She paused a moment. 'I hope you haven't told your father I've been feeling tired lately.'

'No. Why should I?' His faced showed instant alarm. 'You're all right, aren't you? I mean, I just thought it was the seasonal pressure of work.'

'And so it is. And of course I'm not as young as I was.'

'Have you seen the doctor?'

'Yes, he says I'm just over-tired. Which, as you say, I always am at this time of the year with the pre-Christmas sales rush, and preparing the spring collection. But I don't want your father rushing down here when I'm so busy. He's coming down after Christmas and we had planned a short holiday together, after Rose is back at school.'

'A good idea – and don't worry, I won't tell him. But take care of yourself, darling.'

'I always do.'

'You're sure Rose isn't too much responsibility?'

'Responsibility? I'm used to that. In a way she's a blessing. She's so funny – up and down, in and out of childhood in seconds. I shall miss her when she goes to school.'

Rose came in, making an entrance in her new gown, her eyes opening wide with pleasure at the sight of Tom in evening dress.

'*Mon Dieu, tu est très chic dans ton habit de soirée!*'

58

She was wearing the new evening dress that had been made for her at Hanover Street. Her eyes were shining as she came into the centre of the room and turned slowly as she had seen the models do in the Salon, smiling back over her shoulder into his admiring eyes.

It was a young girl's dress but designed and made by master hands – a glowing rose-pink taffeta masked with gauze of silver grey, the neckline a discreet bow, the sleeves puffed well above her elbows, the bodice fitted to her long slender waist, the full flared skirt looped once with a silver rose. She wore her hair loose, brushed straight and shiningly black, held behind her ears with two of the same silvery-pale grey flowers. She glowed as she paraded before them, knowing she was beautiful, revelling in their admiration, then coming with a rush to kneel by Margaret's chair.

'Aunt Margaret, thank you, thank you! It is a most beautiful dress. Never have I worn anything so beautiful. No other girls in the school will have a dress like this!'

'Not like it,' Margaret agreed, 'but maybe as good. I have made several of the senior girls their first ball dresses this term. But their mothers usually favour white. You look lovely my dark Rose, and will certainly bring in many orders in the spring.'

Rose swung round on Tom. 'You too think I am beautiful?'

'Not bad for a skinny one,' he said, then seeing the hurt in her eyes, 'Of course you look lovely, Rose, and you seem to grow taller every minute.'

'I do not wish to be a giraffe sort of girl. Proportion – that was what Papa Léon always said. He said that to make clothes for my mama was wonderful because not only her face but all her proportions were beautiful.'

'Yes, they were,' Margaret said wryly. She saw the expression in Tom's eyes as he looked at this new young cousin, and said, 'Now forget yourself or you'll spoil the whole effect. But come here a minute, Rose.' She took the long string of pearls from her own neck and slipped them over Rose's head. Tom involuntarily stepped forward and lifted the waterfall of shining black hair so she could settle the pearls about her neck. Rose was speechless with delight. She dropped down again by Margaret in a billow of silk and gauze, and kissed her on both cheeks.

'You have some of your own, which belonged to your mother. I believe Papa Léon secured them for you. It was one long rope belonging to our grandmother, Lady Margaret Normanby, and she had it split into two for your mother and me when we were twenty-one. But tonight you can borrow mine. Pearls are for you – diamonds are for lesser women.' Rose frowned, puzzled. Tom met his mother's eyes, bent and kissed her.

After they had gone Margaret had a warm bath (not too hot, the specialist had warned her), changed into one of her silk wraps and put her feet up on the chaise-longue, where Sarah brought her dinner on a tray. All this sitting about when there was so much she wanted to do! High blood pressure and a slightly irregular pulse, the specialist had said. 'Take it easy. Have a break. Come and see me again after Christmas.' She hated this slow erosion of her vitality. She had not minded her greying hair, nor the few wrinkles round her eyes, but she hated this. But if she was to go away for a brief holiday with Henry after Christmas, she had better do as she was told. They saw each other so rarely now, and time was passing. He was seventy-four, but still strong and a fine figure of a man. An oak tree, she had always said, rooted in his north country soil. They spoke to each other over the telephone, and still longed for their meetings like young lovers.

Tom had planned a gala night for Rose. Dinner at the Cecil, then the pantomime at the Lyceum, for she had never heard of, much less seen, a pantomime. It was both funny and magnificent, especially the transformation scenes in the underwater world with mermaids swimming about in midair, when Sinbad, a handsome lady in tights, was shipwrecked by a sunken treasure chest from which the glittering fairy queen issued to produce a magic fortune. Rose was enchanted. Tom explained to her the strange tradition of girls playing the boys, and a man playing the comic old lady, which made her laugh.

'It is all so complicated and absurd,' she said. 'I always thought pantomime was silent. But this is like the Folies Bergères – without the naked ladies.'

'You have seen the Folies?'

'Oh, *no*, but I think that Papa Léon would have taken me one day. But you have been?'

'It is the first call of the Englishman abroad. The first time I went with Mama. I was eighteen. She said it would widen my horizons.'

'Oh, she is funny, lovely, and so very clever. I shall miss her so much when I am away at school.'

The theatre was over, and they came out into the cold Strand, among the departing audience. There were many children – small girls in velvet cloaks and hoods, and small boys in Eton suits – shepherded by smiling parents. There were bigger boys self-conscious in their first dinner-jackets, and many girls of her own age, but none of them had a dress and cloak like hers, and none of them had an escort like Tom. She felt very proud when he drew her hand through his arm.

'We will go and have a little supper,' he said. 'I will take you to Romano's. It is not at all suitable for your age, but I will look after you, and we will both feel extremely wicked and sophisticated, and you can impress all the girls at your new school by telling them about it.'

'I cannot eat anything else.'

'We'll have a glass of champagne, a sandwich and a dance,' he said, 'and you will see all the theatre people who come after the show.'

'Shall I see you in the holidays?'

'I don't know.'

'Aunt Margaret says she often sees you in the New Year?'

'We shall see.'

She should have enjoyed Romano's. Tom duly pointed out the theatrical celebrities. They danced, and that was lovely; moving in his arms gave her a feeling of sheer delight. And yet she had the same hollow feeling of being deserted that she had felt when Papa Léon had died. The thought that she might not see him for a long while left a desolate, hollow feeling inside her. The wine should have made her happy, but it did not, and he sensed her mood immediately.

'Time I took you home, *chérie*,' he said, ' and don't look so sad! You'll make many friends at school. There will be parties and dances and plenty of nice boys who will fall in love with you.'

'But I shall see you during the holidays?'

'Oh, I expect so. Possibly not. I always spend my Christmas at Cliffs Edge or it's a case of "Off with his head" from my stepmother. She takes the great family feast very seriously.'

Rose persisted. 'Aunt Margaret says you often come during the New Year.'

'Well, we shall see. My father usually manages to get down to see her, but Stephen and I will go skiing or climbing. We have not yet decided where.'

He was being evasive and she knew it. She was suddenly adrift, outside her experience. She wanted passionately to capture him, to charm him, and she who had found this so easy before did not know how.

In the taxi she burst out, 'Nice boys! I have met some of your nice boys at the English school at Nice. I do not wish to meet nice boys who stammer and have pimples and tread on my toes. I want to meet men.'

'Well,' he said teasingly, 'I expect you will in time. And you may find some nasty boys among the nice ones for you to dismiss with withering scorn.'

To his surprise she put her head down on her knees and began to cry in a tearless, savage way, hitting the leather seat with clenched fists.

Tom put his arm about her. 'If you throw tantrums, I certainly shan't come to see you.'

'Do not mock me, Tom. I am getting so tired of not being grown-up! All these years I shall still be at school! It is terrible. I want to start my life – and it will be years and years yet. It will be like a prison.'

He burst out laughing. 'You're like an angry kitten! Here, let's wipe those eyes or Mama will think I have been beating you.' He took out his handkerchief and gently wiped away the angry tears from the long dark eyelashes. His hand was on her shoulder. Her cloak had fallen back and through the thin silk he could feel her warmth and smell her perfume, and said, 'Why, you smell like a rose . . .' And instantly her tear-wet lips came up, soft and avid against his own, and her arms were round his neck and her young breasts against his chest. He was caught unawares. He knew she was perfectly aware of the desire she aroused in him. She was a kid acting blindly on her precocious sexuality, a kid still at school.

He loosened her arms from about his neck, pressed her gently away from him, flicked the melting, tempting face teasingly. 'Come on now, baby, don't try too hard to be grown up. You'll learn all about it in time. And don't try those tricks with any other bloke – he might not be as considerate as me.'

She drew back, her hands knotted together, her face and body rigid, and he was full of remorse, remembering some of the gaffes of his own adolescence.

'Rose.' He took her hands, but they were tightly locked with anger or shame, he did not know which. 'Rose,' he tried again, 'growing up is difficult. Especially for very attractive people. Remember Papa Léon told you beauty was a power? Well, it is easy to learn to play power games too soon.' Still she neither moved nor spoke and he said impatiently, to the child she really was, 'Rose, you must not provoke men. You musn't play the baby Venus. It's a dangerous game.'

She exploded suddenly into a torrent of tears, shuddering with temper and humiliation. '*Now* you despise me. You sound like a school ma'am, trying to make me ashamed. Do you think I would have wanted any other man but you to kiss me? You say I am not grown up, and that is so, but I am also not a fool. I know what I want. And always girls talk about this wonderful first kiss, and so I wanted to know. Why not?'

Tom sat with his arms folded not quite knowing whether to laugh, to lie, or to run away. Then he turned to her briskly and lifted her bodily on to his knees.

'So – you want to know what it is like to be kissed? You were experimenting. Well, then, we will experiment.' She stiffened like a wary kitten. 'Let's get it over.' Very firm and matter-of-fact, he kissed her – and both of them were quite unprepared for what followed. The ripple not just of delight and pleasure as their lips touched, but the almost overwhelming rush of feeling, of giving, taking and loving. She was still breathless and entranced when abruptly he released her, lifted her off his knee and set her down on the taxi seat. '*There*! Now you know and can tell the girls at school how extremely experienced you are.'

'Yes,' she said shakily. 'Yes, I now know something. Not everything, but something. It is always so?'

He laughed shortly. 'You manipulative little brat! No, sometimes it is extremely boring. It depends entirely upon who it is you kiss.'

'And you – you have kissed many ladies?'

'Ah, one thing a gentleman learns is never to kiss and tell. But you have to learn to be a lady. Have you done with experimenting?'

'Oh, yes.' She tucked her hand in his arm, confidingly, apparently quite recovered from her tantrum. 'For the present anyway. I do see now why people have warned me about what I permit a gentleman. It could be very dangerous because, don't you think, it would be very easy to *imagine* oneself in love?'

He heard the mischievous challenge and ignored it. He had never, or not for many years, felt uncertain of himself with a girl. He said, quite seriously, 'It would be both unkind and dangerous to arouse such feelings in the wrong sort of person. They might never forgive you.'

To his relief the taxi drew up outside Riverside Mansions. She walked ahead of him, her head as high as ever, her beautiful dark eyes smiling at some unspoken thought.

The apartment was silent, the drawing room empty, Margaret's light rug folded neatly on her chair.

'Mama must have gone to bed,' said Tom. 'And I go back to Thornsby early in the morning. I shall be off before you are up.'

'You will write to me?'

He gave a small dismissive shrug. 'I don't write many letters – I usually telephone. So goodbye, *chérie*, for the present. Enjoy school. Make real friends, learn what they can offer, and make the most of it.'

'I intend to.' She stepped up to him, put her hands on his shoulders and kissed him lightly on each cheek. '*Au 'voir*, my dear cousin. I do really love you, Tom, and Aunt Margaret. You have both been so very good to me.'

It was so completely sincere and innocent that he was startled, relieved, and perhaps, in some hidden corner of his heart, disappointed.

Rose sailed into her first half-term at Lady Pendrill's College with some confidence. She was armed with a family, money, the right clothes, and a new awareness of the power of her looks and charm. She cultivated girls whose friendship she felt might be useful to her, made a few who were really friends, and enjoyed receiving an education which was modelled on the lines of a boys' public school.

The staff were impressed by the new pupil. The end of term report which accompanied her to Riverside Mansions at Christmas was enthusiastic. "Rose is agreeably determined and tenacious about mastering any subject, and is extremely good at languages. She has an instinct for all the arts subjects. Her only failure appears to be games although she is good at dancing and gymnastics, and splendid at swimming. We would like to see a little more team spirit, and competitive effort."

Margaret's brows went up over that word "tenacious." It had so often been applied to herself.

Christmas drew near, and as Tom had prophesied Rose received many invitations for the holidays. She had made particular friends with two other pupils. Marian Palmer was the same age as herself. Marian lived in Bayswater, her people were rich and her father a rising politician. She was the only girl between two older and two younger brothers. She was plumply pretty and spoiled; she fell in love with Rose at first sight, and wrote her some highly coloured letters of adoration which Rose returned with a tactfully kind note, without any mockery, saying she hoped they would be good friends. Marian came from an important family, and her brothers would be useful partners at the holiday parties. And then she found she really quite liked the shy, awkward, affectionate girl who made a devoted friend.

Her second friend was one of the school elite, Jane Shawcross. She also had brothers, was a prefect and her interest was useful in school. She came from a wealthy provincial family, but her great attraction was that she lived at Thornsby and knew Tom Grimshaw and his brother.

Jane had introduced herself. 'I hear you're related to Tom Grimshaw?' she said eagerly. 'We live at Thornsby too. He and his brother are ripping sports.'

65

'Yes, Tom's a cousin of mine. My mother was called Normanby – she and Tom's mother were sisters.'

'Oh, yes,' Jane went on rather hurriedly. Like everyone in Thornsby she knew about Tom's parentage, but he was far too popular and eligible for that half-forgotten scandal to be a drawback. 'He was adopted, wasn't he?' she said vaguely. 'Anyway, my sisters know him very well. They're out, of course. He and Stephen are going to Glockenschule for the winter sports and so are we. They're both splendid skiiers and skaters. You'd never guess Stephen was a little bit lame. Do you ski?'

'Not yet,' Rose said cautiously.

'You must get your people to take you – you're awfully good at gym and dancing, so you ought to pick it up easily.'

That week brought a letter from Margaret saying that now Christmas was nearly upon them, she had more time to rest, and she had been thinking it would be pleasant to go away early in the New Year. Where would Rose like to go? Would she like to visit Madame Respigny in Nice? Rose wrote back at once, saying that many of her school friends were going skiing, and it was a sport she would like to try because it was becoming very chic. One of the girls had recommended a place called Glockenschule where she was going with her family. It would be nice to go somewhere where she knew some young people.

Margaret was happy to agree. She would have preferred a warm, sunny climate and had never been to Switzerland in the winter. But she knew the hotels were good, and the food excellent, and she could look at the mountains and have a real rest.

Margaret was astonished by the amount of invitations to parties and junior dances which began to arrive when Rose came home. The rich Marian Palmer besieged her; her mother called on Margaret, saying how pleased she was her shy little girl had made such a nice friend. Invitations from the Palmers mushroomed. The Harrow-educated elder brothers were obviously captivated and, as Rose had foreseen, useful assets.

Margaret found herself having to return society hospitality, something she had never bothered with before in her busy

66

professional life. As she did not own a large house, she invited Rose's friends to a matinée and a junior tea dance at the Savoy.

'You've made a lot of friends in a short while,' she said as they sat filling in the invitation cards.

'Yes, I've worked at it,' said Rose, and catching Margaret's eyes, began to giggle.

She had sent Tom Christmas greetings, and he had sent her a card with a brief message of good wishes. She threw it away angrily, then frantically searched through the waste paper basket for it, and put it away carefully in the Book of English Prayer Respy had given her years ago.

On New Year's Eve he telephoned his mother to wish her a Happy 1914. He said he was going to Germany immediately after Christmas. There had been an unusual drying up of business there though the home market was booming – they were working full-time on uniform material – and afterwards he and Stephen were going skiing for a couple of weeks.

'To Glockenschule?'

'Yes. How did you know?'

'I'm taking Rose there – it was her suggestion. She says she wants to learn winter sports.'

'The devil she does,' said Tom, and started to laugh. Then he said, alarmed, 'But you *hate* the cold.'

'Well, I have bbeen assured that I shall be safe in an extremely comfortable hotel with magnificent views. That I can go on sleigh and carriage rides to excellent restaurants, or take short walks when the sun is shining. Rose has gone into it thoroughly.'

'Is she in?'

'No – she is at a party with some people called Palmer. The daughter is a school friend.'

'She has made friends, then?'

'I should say, rather, she has cultivated people,' Margaret said dryly. 'I am getting very fond of her, Tom. She makes me wish I had a daughter. My sister, when we were young, was always such an anxiety to me. But although Rose can be a scheming little Frenchwoman, she is also extremely sensible and great fun. She has a trick of standing back from herself and laughing – it's then I really love her.'

'Well, don't spoil her silly.'

'I doubt anyone could do that.'

There was a brief pause. 'Wish her a Happy New Year from me. I shall be seeing you in Switzerland in the New Year. And look after yourself, my darling Mama. Spoil your new little girl by all means, but don't let her wheedle you into doing tiring things. Goodbye.'

'Goodbye.' Margaret put down the telephone. She would not this year, have a lonely Christmas like so many of hers had been, while Tom dutifully attended the seasonal feasting with his father who worshipped him, and his stepmother who resented him. A family feast for a family with no heart, a concession to Angela Grimshaw's unhealed wounds of jealousy. Margaret could not blame her, but she would so much rather Angela had loved the boy Henry had made her adopt.

The car brought Rose home at eleven-thirty. Margaret only chaperoned her when there was no way of getting out of it. Listening to society mamas talk about their offspring appalled her. She had enough of them all day at work. She pleaded fatigue, and slight ill health, and evening business appointments – some of which was true. She was happy to let Mrs Palmer take over this duty.

Rose came in regally, wearing a gold paper crown, her long black hair falling over her shoulders. She had a pretty Japanese fan in jade and gold, another party favour, and was wearing her pink and silver dress. Margaret marvelled at her exotic beauty. She was growing and developing fast. She would be fifteen after Christmas but could pass for nineteen or twenty. She made a low curtsey, then pushed back the crown with her thumb nail, and flopped down on a low stool by Margaret's lounge chair. Every night while she was at home, they sat and talked for a while before going to bed. They both enjoyed it. The party, she said, had been a bore. Children's games – one called postman's knock. She had been kissed by an Etonian with buck-teeth. There had in fact been so many "knocks" for her, that she had hidden upstairs until the daft game was over. "Daft" was a word acquired from Tom.

'Kissing is not a children's game,' she said firmly.

'Tom telephoned,' said Margaret, 'he sent good wishes for the New Year. He was surprised to hear we should be at Glockenschule.'

Rose's black eyes glanced up, sideways like a blackbird's.

'I thought he might be. I really fixed it, didn't I?'

'I had realised I was being manipulated.' Margaret tried to look disapproving but Rose saw the corners of her mouth twitch.

'But what fun we shall have, Tante Margaret! I want very much to meet the irresistible Stephen – Tom's half-brother, isn't he?'

'Yes.'

'According to Jane Shawcross, all the girls round Thornsby are nuts about the Grimshaw boys.' She spread the gold and jade fan over her wrist, the dark eyes with their incredible lashes smiling mischievously over the top. 'I find that girls of my age spend most of their time imagining they are in love. If they don't they either are in love with the horses they ride, or with actors like Owen Nares. Oh, *and* there is another boy coming to Glockenschule. He comes from Yorkshire too, from the big manor house near Thornsby.'

'Danesfell Hall? The Stoneberrys live there now. Sir Miles and Lady Stoneberry. They are tenants. The manor house and land belongs to Tom and Stephen. It was left to them by their aunt, a dear friend and customer of mine. This young man must be the Stoneberry's nephew.'

'Yes, he is called Alban, and Jane says he will be Sir Alban one day because his uncle has no children. Jane says that's about all he's got to recommend him, and her brothers say he is a pip. She says the Stoneberrys are awful stuffed shirts and can't really afford to live at Danesfell. But she said Alban is good-looking, if you like that sort of thing.' Her nose wrinkled thoughtfully. 'I wonder what she means by that?'

'I know Lady Stoneberry,' said Margaret. 'She was once a customer of mine. A sour woman. She always took a long time paying. She sometimes brought the little boy with her to the salon and a very tiresome child he was. There was some trouble about a bill – I do not wait forever for my money. I will not tolerate the "Who do you think you are?" attitude from anyone. I say, "I am Margaret Normanby, I have the best couture business in London, I employ wonderful crafts-women whom I pay well, and I do not work for nothing." She was not a customer I regretted losing.'

Rose had listened wide-eyed, and when Margaret had finished, clapped her hands. 'You are wonderful, Tante Margaret.'

'Is this future baronet one of your reasons for going to Glockenschule? Part of your upward climb to becoming a great lady?'

Rose laughed – her early ambition to personify Papa Léon's idea of a great lady had become a joke between them.

'Well, perhaps,' she said. 'I want to see this boy who will one day be a baronet, even if he is a pip. But really I want to see Tom again, because he has been neglecting me, and also to meet his so attractive brother.'

'You're a scheming little monkey,' said Margaret and her heart lifted at Rose's flashing smile.

'And as I said, it is extremely chic for English girls to ski. And I am now typically English, is this not so?'

'Not typically,' Margaret said, so dryly that in a moment they were both laughing.

Suddenly her smile vanished, she felt chilled and drew her fine, gauzy shawl round her shoulders with an involuntary shiver as the small stabbing pain came and went like lightning beneath her left rib. 'Ugh, someone is walking on my grave.' Then she explained to Rose's blank look, 'It is an old superstition – when one shivers without reason.'

'You shiver because you feel cold,' Rose said practically, and tucked the shawl tighter round her aunt's shoulders before stirring up the dying fire.

Sarah came in to say she had taken the hot milk to Rose's bedroom, and the girl kissed her aunt affectionately. Margaret held her for a moment, smiling up into the dark eyes. 'Don't be in too much of a hurry to grow up, Rose of Sharon. You have plenty of time.'

'How strange – Tom said exactly the same thing to me. But I am growing up so quickly, except in years, and I wish to catch up with my body. At school they all say I could be taken for nineteen. I wish I *was* nineteen. It seems a long way away. Goodnight, Aunt Margaret.'

70

Margaret watched her go out of the room, an exotic gold-crowned figure, like a princess out of the Arabian Nights. So sophisticated, so naive, and with all her mother's dangerous attraction.

Margaret sighed. It had been her sense of duty that had made her offer Charmian's girl a home. She had not expected to give her heart away to this beautiful alien child.

Chapter Four

Seen in profile as he stood on the Terrace Palace Hotel at Glockenschule, Alban John Stoneberry appeared to be a very good-looking young man. It was only when he turned full face that his long-lashed grey eyes were seen to be a trifle too close set, and there was a blurred look about his nose and upper lip, a hint of malformation just avoided, or corrected by surgery, now concealed by a newly grown fair moustache.

He had been born in India. His father had been a regular officer, attaining the rank of Major, and was the heir to the Baron of Stoneberry as his elder brother, Sir Miles, had no children. Both Major Stoneberry and his wife had died in a cholera epidemic. The boy had been five when he was sent home to his aunt and uncle at Danesfell Abbey where Sir Miles had legally adopted him, although Alban was now the heir by birthright. Neither his father nor his aunt and uncle had ever let him forget that one day he would be Sir Alban and inherit the comfortable, but not vast, inheritance. Certainly not vast compared to the manufacturers of the north of England like Grimshaw with his two handsome boys.

Shading his eyes against the sunglare from the snow, searching among the skaters below for his friends, Tom and Stephen Grimshaw, with whom he had been at prep school, Alban was feeling extremely irritated. They were not staying at the Palace Hotel, but at a small place up the mountain popular with experienced skiiers. It was Alban's first visit to the winter sports, and he hated submitting to the comical clumsiness of learning. He was clumsy, uncoordinated, and found any rhythmic accomplishment difficult to acquire.

The terrace looked down on the Kleinersee, a miniature lake immediately below the terrace, now a hard white floor of ice where the morning skaters were stumbling or swirling according to their prowess. Beyond the lake was the fabulous panorama of the high snows. To the right, nestling below a mild hillside, were the nursery slopes, and the small fairy tale village of Glockenschule.

He was quite unreasonably annoyed because the Grimshaws were not on the terrace waiting for him. Not that they ever waited for anyone. They were the undoubted leaders of the social group in the district round Danesfell and Upper Thornsby, as they had been leaders at school – good-looking, graceful, accomplished and unaffected youngsters, deservedly popular. They had been at the Wool Manufacturers College, he at Eton.

Then, on the ice below, he saw Tom Grimshaw, his fair hair bright in the brilliant sunshine, teaching a girl to waltz. The hissing of the skates rose in the clear, still air. The girl with Tom was dark – dark-skinned, dark-haired. She wore a white fur cap and a padded red jacket cuffed and collared with white fur, and a knee-length, swinging white skirt. Her hair was woven into a waist-length pigtail which flew behind her as the skirt twirled and swung with the easy movements of her slender hips.

Alban envied Tom, as he had always envied him. He watched Tom's warmly gloved hands holding and guiding his young partner precisely, so that she gained confidence, and as they passed close below the terrace he saw her radiant smile as she achieved a simple turn, then heard her squeal of alarmed laughter as she nearly fell. Tom caught and righted her, scarcely missing a note of the waltz music.

Alban envied almost everything about the Grimshaw boys: their looks, their charm, their uncomplicated ease of manner. They even owned the great house of Danesfell Abbey which Alban's uncle rented from them. He envied them their money. The only thing he did not envy them was their connection with trade. They were a manufacturing family while he was landed gentry, though unfortunately without land. They both worked in their father's great business. Stephen was lame. Yet they possessed all the assurance and

73

ease of manner which he did not possess but thought should be his by birthright. They were the examples his uncle continually held up to him. It was unfair that these jumped-up tradesfolk should be so easily accepted by local society, and able to refer to the great house of Danesfell as "Dad's white elephant."

In coming to Switzerland with them he had hoped to escape from the gloomy dignity of Danesfell, and had at least succeeded in that. The hotel was filled with lively young people, a large group from Thornsby. But, as always, he was an outsider. He felt cheated. He knew they had only suggested that he should go because Stephen's mother was friendly with his aunt. It was as though the two boys had stolen something from him, just as they had inherited Danesfell Abbey by chance from an actress who had married a millionaire.

Alban went back to his table and ordered a brandy with his coffee. He was damned if he was going to run after the Grimshaws.

It seemed an interminable time before the band ceased the morning session, and two horse-drawn sleighs came jingling up from the ice-rink, disgorging the skating party on to the terrace with a great deal of chatter and laughter.

The two Grimshaw boys, the two tall, sandy Shawcross girls with their copper-haired sixth-form brothers, two small and two tall adolescents, and the girl Tom had been dancing with, made for two tables drawn together where three ladies, wrapped in furs and rugs, were seated.

Alban saw immediately that the dark girl whom he had never seen before this morning, the girl who had been skating with Tom, was the queen of this small group, the focus of all eyes with her brilliant smile and glowing dark skin. She shone among them like a dark star. He rose as though magnetised and began to walk towards them.

He knew Mrs Shawcross but not the other two ladies. Tom greeted him blithely, as though he had not kept him waiting over an hour, and began the introductions.

'Mrs Palmer from London, wife of the MP Roland Palmer.' And then, 'This is my mama, Madame Léon.' Tom had no embarrassment about the irregularity of his birth, which was known all over Thornsby, although his mother never came north.

'Well, of course, she wouldn't!' Alban's aunt had once said. 'The less she puts in an appearance, the easier it is for poor Mrs Grimshaw.'

Mrs Léon did not give Alban her hand. Two brilliant blue eyes raked over him. She was a small, distinguished lady, with great elegance and assurance, muffled up to her chin in magnificent furs. She lifted a pair of gold rimmed pince-nez and smiled up at him.

'How do you do?' she said. 'Your mother used to be a customer of mine – way back. She brought you to the salon once or twice, and you were the naughtiest child I ever met – apart from Tom who almost wrecked the business before he was sent to join his father in Yorkshire.'

Alban stammered, and everyone laughed. The dark girl took the chair beside Madame Léon as Tom continued: 'You know everyone else. Oh, no – my cousin, Rose Abderhazy.' Tom put a friendly arm about Alban's shoulder. He did not care for young Stoneberry, but always felt sorry for him. He was sorry for anyone who had to live with Sir Miles and Lady Stoneberry at Danesfell. It was a great house, meant for splendid and lavish entertaining which the Stoneberrys obviously could not afford. And he was sorry for Alban because he did not seem to fit in anywhere.

'When did you arrive?' he asked, unwinding his long woollen scarf, his thick fair hair blowing in the frosty wind. 'We looked for you this morning. Steve and I were out skiing early, before breakfast, and afterwards skiied down to the village here. You must talk to Rose – she's a real little whizzer. She caught on to skating right away. Natural balance.' The dark girl had risen to speak to some friends, and he called, 'Rose!' and caught her sleeve as she passed. 'Rose, this is Alban Stoneberry who lives at Danesfell, which once belonged to Dad's sister, my Aunt Mildred.'

She turned to Alban with her quick smile, and held out her hand in its red woollen glove. It seemed to him that her smile faltered slightly as she looked at him, as though disappointed. As though she had expected someone more exciting.

75

He could only stare at her, stammering out correct greetings. She was so *foreign*. His aunt would not approve. The dark, creamy skin, the extraordinary, long-lashed oriental eyes. The barely perceptible French accent. She looked like an Arab girl.

'Are you related to the Baron Abderhazy, the financier?' he blurted.

A dimple appeared in either perfect cheek. 'So my mother told me – the Baroness Abderhazy. And one should always believe one's mama – is it not so?'

Alban went scarlet. She was laughing at him! But she relented and said, 'We've been having so much fun. Do you skate?'

'I'm afraid not,' he said stiffly, 'it is my first visit.'

'Mine too. I have been working at it very hard so I would not be a complete duffer when the boys arrived, and today I achieved a waltz turn!' she said triumphantly. 'You will excuse me?'

She was off to join the group round the table again. Alban turned angrily, nearly knocking into the eldest Shawcross girl, Violet, handsome in her lean, English county way. Tom shrugged and followed Rose to the table.

'Steady on, Alban,' Violet smiled placatingly, 'what on earth's the matter with you? You look like a thunder-cloud.'

'Who is that girl exactly – that Rose Abderhazy?'

'Oh, she's a cousin of Tom's. She's at school with Jane at Pendrill's. That is Tom's mother, her aunt. Madame Léon, the great London dressmaker.'

'A *dressmaker*?' he said incredulously.

'Oh, really, Alban! You are positively antediluvian. She is very famous. And her sister who died last year was the Baroness Abderhazy, a great beauty.'

'A touch of the tarbrush there,' he sneered, but he was watching Rose over Violet's shoulder.

'Well, Baron Abderhazy is Persian, I believe. It's all a bit of a mystery. She lives with Madame Léon, and Jane loves her. In fact the whole sixth form seem to have a crush on her. She is very attractive.'

'Violet,' he said abruptly, 'tell me where I can learn to skate and to ski? I suppose I must learn, even if I never come again.'

'Oh, of course,' she said pleasantly. She recommended a skating coach, and promised to take him to the nursery slopes in the morning. Tom, seeing Alban sliding splay-legged on the ice next day, felt quite relieved. All the Shawcross girls were good sports, and it looked as though the queer chap might have a good time after all.

It was the last night of the holidays – tomorrow they would all be driving down the winding mountain road to the station, the train to Berne, and the long railway journey back across France. There was a carnival on the ice, with fancy dress and coloured lanterns glowing everywhere. Later there would be a ball at the hotel, a bonfire on the mountainside, and fireworks.

People had changed into costume for the ball. Tom and Stephen were already in their Harlequin costumes. They would be difficult to tell apart when they wore their black dominoes, except for Stephen's limp. But on the ice he did not limp, nor on the dance floor. Light and graceful, he was a perfect partner.

Rose was dressed in a rose pink padded cossack coat, embroidered with gold and multi-coloured flowers, tiny mirrors sewn into the pattern that flashed in the lights as she turned in his arms. She wore her white fur cap, looped golden earrings and her hair loose, twirling round her like a long black veil. Her cheeks were flushed and her eyes brilliant – she was like an oriental princess from some exotic mythical country, straight out of the Thousand and One Nights.

It was splendid dancing with Stephen. He was better than Tom, lighter, very graceful, but his arm around her waist did not give her the same strong support, and his hand on hers was not so firm and steady, and her skin did not tingle or her senses melt at his touch. But he was fun to flirt with.

'Will you marry me, Rose?'

'What day were you considering, Stevie? One day soon?'

'Well, one day certainly.'

'Who knows what will happen one day? I haven't really thought what sort of man I wish to marry. How about Thursday?'

'You'd rather marry Tom,' he accused her with mock jealousy.

'Maybe I will marry a Persian prince, and sail away on a magic carpet.'

Rose knew it was a game, but it was a pleasant game. His desire for her was half pretence, half real, full of affection. He and Tom were nearly the same age, but Stephen was still a boy by comparison. He and Rose were childishly at ease together, enjoying the dancing, and the laughter, and the flirting.

'Tom won't marry for a long while,' said Stephen.

She gave him a searching look. '*Pourquoi pas*?'

'Because he thinks there is going to be a war.'

She swayed slightly, her skate veering off balance, and his hands were quick to right her. They stood together, the waltzing couples flying past them. The rhythm of the Strauss waltz seemed to beat in her brain.

'I don't want to dance any more – let's go back to the hotel.'

'Oh, Rose, come on – don't take it so seriously. A lot of people don't think it will happen.'

But she was skating slowly to the steps which led up from the lake, sitting down and beginning to unstrap her skates. Many people were leaving to change for the ball.

'Here, let me.' He took her slim ankle in one hand and began to take off the skate.

'Where will there be a war?'

'Haven't you heard? Don't they talk about it at school? Everyone is talking about it . . .'

'I haven't heard them. Aunt Margaret doesn't talk about it.'

'She does with Tom.'

'Who will be fighting?'

They walked slowly up the ice-clad road back towards the hotel, her arm through his.

'Germany and France – and if France fights, we shall have to fight. We are bound to France.'

'But this is a German village – everyone is very nice. Why should they fight us?'

'This is a German-speaking village in Switzerland, you little ignoramus! I'm talking about *Germany*. They have a huge army and are building a huge navy, and they want colonies. A place in the sun, they say. Tom goes out there on business and he says they are not buying our cloth. But the British Army is buying uniform cloth very heavily. He and Dad talk of nothing else now. How it will affect business if it happens – although at the same time it may never happen. I think that some people hope it will, for our district will make a lot of profit.'

'But why should this affect Tom? He's not a soldier?'

'He is in the Territorials. He was in the O.T.C. at school. I couldn't get in – I can't march!'

'But do you want to be a soldier?'

'Of course I want to! Tom is an officer in the Thornsby section of the West Riding Regiment. He would go straight away if ever war was declared. Chaps younger than me, straight from school, can get in. Any mill-hand's or miner's son can get in, but I can't because of this damned leg!'

'But I never notice it, Stevie . . . '

'Don't pretend! I try not to talk about it. I have a special shoe, a specially cut trouser leg, I have learned to disguise it. But I would never be accepted for military service. Mama,' he said grimly, 'is very pleased. She tells everyone how hard it is for me, and how bravely I bear it. But really she is happy that her darling is safe.'

'Of course she must be happy. I would be much more happy if Tom also had a limp.'

'Would you? Would you really? Would *he* be happy?'

She stared up at him. She had not looked at it like that.

'You know he would not be happy. Not Tom. He is a born leader of men. And I am not happy either because I want to go with him and do my duty like every Englishman should.'

She did not answer but thought, I must talk to Aunt Margaret.

As though she had spoken aloud and he was answering her, Stephen said, 'Don't speak to Tom's mother about it. She is only too aware of it. She'll not blackmail him with tears and sulks and hysterics. It's not her way. But she'll suffer – we all shall.'

They stood in the great cream and white foyer of the hotel beyond which, through swinging glass doors, they could see into the ballroom. The orchestra was already tuning up.

'I must change. I can see Tante Margaret sitting with Mrs Shawcross.' Rose smiled and said, 'She is very good to listen to all that chatter so patiently for my sake. Her own friends in London are so different.'

'I wish to God,' said Stephen, 'that she was my mother!'

Rose went up in the elaborate gilded cage of a lift to her room, washed her face, brushed her long black hair smooth and shining. In the ballroom the embroidered, fur-collared jacket would be too hot. She would have to improvise a costume – she had thought to spend the night on the ice and had not prepared one for inside.

She found a long purpose chiffon scarf of Margaret's and wound it tightly round her breasts and over one shoulder, securing it with a brooch of emerald green stones out of her collection of costume jewellery. Over the Christmas holiday season she had collected a box full of party favours. One, her paper crown, was just what she wanted. She added huge gilt earrings, like brass curtain rings, Margaret's green motoring veil and little eastern slippers with curved toes, and Margaret's golden harem trousers. In her sketching box there were coloured chalks. Rose rubbed her finger on a bright green and coloured her eyelids with it. She elongated her uptilting eyes with black, and rouged the palms of her hands and the soles of her feet with pink like the ballet girls in *Scherezade*. Like an Arab queen.

Margaret, trying to keep awake among the group of chattering matrons, saw her at once. There was an interval before the supper waltz. Rose stood quite still for a moment, and then came slowly forward, her beautiful bare arms undulating as she had seen the girls do in the ballet, her hips swaying seductively from side to side, her great eyes smiling above the borrowed motoring veil. She came to a halt in the circle of her school friends, brought her hands together and made a low, mocking salaam. If any of the English boys or girls thought she was unaware of the derogatory comments and prejudices about her – 'A touch of the tarbrush there,' 'You can't trust people of mixed blood,' and from one disapproving mama:

'Well, I mean, the girl's not even *white*!' – well, they knew now she was not. She was flaunting her difference, glorying in it, challenging their friendship.

Tom had just come in from the Kleinersee, looking for her. He began to clap, as did Stephen, until applause spread around the room.

The music for the supper waltz started up. Tom was at her side, and swung her out on to the floor in the waltz.

Stephen stood, applauding and laughing. Beside him Alban Stoneberry watched her intently but he neither laughed nor applauded.

'Your cousin Rose is quite an actress,' he said.

'She's a wonderful girl,' said Stephen, 'but she's not my cousin. She's Tom's. Come on, we're wasting time.' And he was off across the room, picking out one of the prettiest girls, dressed as a powder puff in pleated pale blue satin and marabout, sweeping her off on to the floor, leaving Alban standing by the door, conspicuously the only young person in formal evening dress – the only young person not dancing.

Rose Abderhazy was the only girl he wanted to dance with, and his longing for this was so painfully intense he felt that everyone must be aware of it. But she swept past in Tom's arms, with no eyes for anyone but him.

'I thought you were going to spend the whole evening down at the ice carnival,' Tom said. 'You were dancing with Stephen and then suddenly you vanished!'

'I felt cold, so we came up to the ballroom. How do you like my costume?'

'You look very seductive.'

'Well, houris are supposed to be seductive.'

'But well brought up young ladies from Lady Pendrill's College are not houris.'

'But tonight I *am* a houri, sent by Shaitan to dance in the dreams of men, so don't lecture me!'

She stopped dancing and walked away from him into the long glass-walled winter garden. It was warm there, filled with exotic climbing plants and flowers, but through the glass one could see the mighty panorama of snow-covered mountains, jagged against a moonlit sky. She turned to face him and said abruptly, 'Stephen says you are going off to be a soldier.'

He was startled by the fierce anger in her eyes.

'Well, I'm only playing at soldiers now!'

'Stephen says that you think there is going to be a war. You won't be playing if there is a war.'

'Oh, Rose,' he said indulgently, 'it may never happen.'

'But you think it might – and so does Stephen. And so, he says, does your father. Stephen says your father has been in consultation with the Government – about making material for uniforms.'

'Stephen has no business to tell you such a thing. And anyway we always do make material for uniforms. One part of the mill has always specialised in this. It is just a matter of bringing the department up to date, getting in new machinery. Don't fret about it – come and dance!'

'*Sale bête!*' She struck his hand down, jerking away like a furious kitten. 'Always you treat me as an idiot! As a child! You lecture me about how I behave. Why have you not written to me?'

'I told you, I rarely write. I have been very busy.'

'Busy preparing for this war which does not exist? Why have I always to plan and scheme to meet you? Why do you think I came here, and persuaded Tante Margaret to bring me? To be among schoolfriends? *Mon Dieu!* Such boring girls and their moon-faced brothers! I wish to talk with you. If there is a war you will be a soldier, and if you are a soldier you could be killed. What should I do if you were killed?'

'Rose . . .' He was shaken by her intensity, but she swept on in her anxiety for him, her passionate desire to make him understand touchingly childish and undisguised, all her guile and coquetry forgotten. 'I could not bear it, Tom. *I could not bear it!*'

She collapsed on to one of the arboured seats, burying her face in her hands, her golden-crowned head bent. A lost princess.

'I have thought a great deal about all the things you have said to me – about myself, about men, and how easy it can be to think oneself in love. But now I think love is quite different. I have thought who could I not bear to live without, and I know there is only you, Tante Margaret, Papa Léon, Respy – I've always known I would be without them one day, and so it does not hurt. I could not bear to be without you. All the foolish things I have said about being a great lady are just so much silliness – like all girls talk. Men and love, riches and marriage – I could not bear to be without *you*. I love you more than anyone, and I want you to love me.'

Dark eyes full of tears, and then sweet, smooth arms about his neck, and so he kissed her, for the second time, and then without thought, without caution, surrendering to the reality of her sweetness in his arms.

Against her lips he was giving her the answer she so naively, so desperately, demanded, and all the reasons why he should not were for the moment forgotten. And the moment was enchantment.

Presently they slipped back among the dancers, and Margaret, bored among the chaperones, watched their rapt faces and remembered when she and Tom's father broke all the rules and seized a brief happiness so many years ago.

How many years left? she was beginning to wonder. The holiday in Glockenschule had not been a real rest. When Rose was back at school for the spring term, perhaps she and Henry would steal some days together. She was middle-aged, and Henry, her once tireless lover, was an old man – though a fine man, still very much in command. But he was preoccupied with the great business of Grimshaw & Sons. How many years or days left? How many new anxieties creeping in? And now the shadow of a possible war.

Life resumed its pattern back at Lady Pendrill's College. Rose felt sometimes that the holiday at Glockenschule had never happened. Tom did not write, but now she did not worry. He knew she must finish her education. She was sure he loved her. And she had straightened her life out, or so she thought. Tom loved her and one day they would marry. They would be rich, because Tom was rich and she was too. She would not be a great lady, a society queen with many jewels, or use her beauty as her mother had – and all this seemed unimportant now. She would live only for Tom.

Margaret had promised her that she would not have to stay at school after she was eighteen, and that then she must decide for herself what she would like to do.

'Even if you just wish to follow your original idea of being a society queen, we shall have to work at it,' said Margaret, smiling. 'You'll have to come out. I think I could get you presented, but it wouldn't be easy. I'd even, God forbid, have to give a ball.'

'Unless there really is a war?'

'That we won't talk about,' said her aunt. 'Not unless we have to.' They were both thinking of Tom. But Rose did not say what had happened between them. Back at school, she sometimes wondered if it ever had. Better to wait and hope, and tell no one.

Just before Easter Margaret went away with Henry Grimshaw. In days past they had gone to Europe to continue their discreet but passionate friendship. Now, though the discretion was still there, their passion was like an ember that glowed steadily, rarely bursting into the old flame. They were secure in the depth of their tender affection and their deep, mutual liking. Lovers they had always been, but now they also knew what friendship really meant.

Margaret travelled alone by train along the Thames Valley in the early summer sunshine. Along the limpid green stretches where she and Henry had rowed and punted in contented silence beneath the hanging woods, brash new suburbs were being built. But as yet the small village in the upper reaches had not been engulfed in their remorseless embrace.

The old inn still stood there beyond the tow path, the pink brick façade reflected rosily in the glassy water above the weir where the yellow rain of the willow branches was breaking into bright green leaf. The wooden chairs and tables had been freshly painted for the season and set out on the rough lawn, and scarlet geraniums had been planted in tubs along the lawn.

Henry was sitting at one of the tables, bending over a newspaper with a gold rimmed eyeglass, reading the small

84

print assiduously. The headlines were large and full of warning, and there was a photograph of Lord Kitchener above the words "Be Prepared". A poster that would appear like a rash all over England in the great recruitment campaign which had seized the country.

And yet here it was so quiet. A few pleasure craft idled along, swift canoes and a swinging eight flashed by in rhythmic time, cutting an arrow in midstream; a group of punts with white-clad youngsters laughing and flirting, the gramophone trailing the beat of ragtime they went.

He heard the taxi and looked up and rose to his feet, and her heart kindled as it always had when she saw him; as it would, she knew, to her dying day.

His thick fair hair was white now, and he moved a little stiffly. The big shoulders were slightly bowed, but he still looked ten years younger than his age, and dressed in the cool summer suit and open-necked shirt, as immaculate as ever. He pleased her fastidious eyes, accustomed to elegance. The strong features, the clean-cut ruthless mouth which could smile for her – his qualities had been enhanced and tempered, not ruined, by age.

'Maggy!' His arms went round her. 'It's been such a long time, love.'

'Too long. Why? Have we only the energy for work now?'

He made a wry face. 'God knows there's enough of it.' He searched her face anxiously. 'Tom tells me you have not been well. Did you go to the specialist? What did he say?'

'He said I had been overdoing it.'

'Well, you always have.'

'Who's talking now!' she teased. 'I *am* tired. It's been a bumper season. It must be the beautiful weather. Every woman in London seems to have gone clothes crazy.'

They walked down to the water's edge, his arm about her, then turned and looked back at the old inn where they had spent so many happy secret days. It could only accommodate six guests and over the years had been a heaven and a haven to them, but it was primitive compared to the luxury they had become accustomed to on their annual longer trips abroad.

'Wishing we had gone to the Riviera?'

'No. You've only a few days, and it would have been too much bother to travel far for that, no matter how much I love you.' She did not tell him how wearying she had found the journey across to Switzerland with Rose in January. 'Shall we take a boat?'

'If you would like it.'

'So long as I don't have to row.'

There were several boats for hire tied up to the mooring. He handed her in, and she leaned back against the cushions while he took the oars and they went slowly up stream; occasionally he stopped, allowing the oars to drift, smiling at her, filled with happiness just to be with her. She took her hat off and shook out her short, curly hair.

'Do you like it?'

'It's pretty,' he said, 'but I miss it. It was so long, and used to burn like fire in the sunlight. I shall miss it tonight.' He had always loosened it, loving to see the wavy mass of bronze and gold tumble down over her slim bare shoulders.

'The red has nearly all gone. And I got so sick of it; all that combing and pinning, holding my arms above my head until they ached. I kept seeing those women from New York with their short hair, and thought how sensible it looked.' She saw a look of concern in his eyes and said quickly, 'How long have you got, my darling?'

'Just this weekend,' he said grimly. 'We're extraordinarily busy.'

'When I spoke to Tom last week, he said that you are turning both the Calder Beck Mill and the Britannia over to uniform cloth.'

'Yes. The War Department seem to be eating it. We started production in the spring. We're making very little else now. Britannia is making officers' material, Calder Mill the rankers, and the Water Meadows all Navy. We could do with more men, so many of our younger chaps are volunteering. But with our trade, and the iron and steel and coal they need, they'll have to keep some men at home for the mills and mines.'

'Then it is going to happen, this war?'

'Aye, love, I think it will. I was in Germany in the autumn and they talked of nothing else. I had contracts over there for

86

high class suiting and they've all been cancelled. But they will give me short term contracts for Army cloth. All the orders subject to instant cancellation. There was a touch of arrogance about them – I thanked them politely in my best German, and said I had firm contracts to execute at home, and we were stretched to our full capacity.'

'But what is it all about? Why do they want to fight?'

He shrugged. 'Why do nations ever want to fight? For power, for greed. The Prussians dream of their old European domination under Bismarck. They feel they have been outsmarted in the grabs for colonies. Someone will win, someone will lose, and for the majority it will be loss and pain, terror and hunger, and – for many – death.'

They were silent. It was still on the river. Henry plunged in the oar, turning the boat. 'Time we went back,' she said.

It was natural for them to talk about their work, especially Henry. Angela, his wife, had no interest in how his money was made. But they both knew that they were trying not to talk about the matter lacerating both their hearts. As they neared the inn the sunset was painting the high hanging woods below Cookham, and making the latticed panes gleam in gold.

'At the Club they say I should be proud of Tom,' Henry said suddenly. 'He *need* not go. His is a reserved occupation. But like me they really want their own boys to stay – at least until they see which way the cat jumps. You gave me a splendid son, Maggy, but he is only twenty-four, and I don't want to lose him. One of the grim things about war is that it is the young that fight and die. Tom's as useful in the business as I am, possibly more. But it's no use to whistle in the dark. If it's war, he'll go when he's called. I'm lucky to have young Stevie.'

They dined, and afterwards walked as they always did on fine nights a short way along the darkling river, their arms entwined, their hands locked. Usually they talked, with always so much to say, but this time they were silent, and after a short while Margaret felt the small pang of pain in her left side, and said she was tired, and maybe it would be nice to go early to bed.

In the low-ceilinged room which overlooked the weir sliding glassily over its fall in the moonlight, a tray had been set with champagne and glasses, a romantic custom over the years.

Henry opened the bottle, and poured two glasses.

She took one, saying, 'The landlady tells me they are retiring and the place is going to be modernised and extended. So this may be our last champagne under the eaves in the feather-bed.'

'You sound as though we have come to the end of everything.'

'I think we must have come to the end of something or why are we sitting here with all our clothes on talking, after so long apart?'

Margaret had never just yielded to him – which was what he had found beautiful in her. Even as a young girl she had always demanded the best from life and love. And that night, although her face was now softly wrinkled and the short curly hair was nearly grey, her thin body was, as always, sweet, frail, yet passionate. Her arms about him, and the eager entwining legs, the abandonment of caressing lips, roused him as though he was twenty years younger.

But afterwards, when they had slept, Margaret woke when dawn was showing pale chinks through the window shutters, and felt the sensation beneath her left breast which she had felt once or twice before, a feeling of terrible restriction which moved outward beneath her rib cage, a silent instrument of torture like a medieval Iron Maiden closing inexorably about her lungs, so that she sat upright, swinging her legs out of bed, and her breath became short, shallow and gasping, and she reached out blindly for something to grasp, something solid, something on which to pull herself upright.

Henry was awake and beside her instantly, his arms about her. 'Maggy – what is it, Maggy? For Christ's sake, speak to me!'

'My handbag . . . give me my handbag . . .' He looked around blindly, saw it on the dressing table and picked it up. She snatched it from him, and it dropped from her nerveless hands. He picked it up, snapped it open. 'What is it? What is it you want?'

'Tablets – white tablets . . .'

He found the little bottle, shook tablets out into his palm, took one between his fingers and put it into her gasping mouth. She dropped back on the bed, crouched over the pain in her chest, sounding like someone drowning, sinking, surfacing to gasp for breath, only to sink again.

Henry reached for his dressing gown. 'I'll ring and send for a doctor.'

'No.' Her voice steadied and the shallow panting began to subside, the strange gasping giving way to deeper, easier, more natural breaths. Her head fell back against his shoulder. The iron band slackened round her ribs. There were black rings round her eyes, although she was not visibly pale. 'It's all right. It's going. We don't want to wake everyone.'

'To hell with that,' he said roughly. 'If you need a doctor I'll rouse the whole damned village. Tom didn't tell me it was like this.'

'He has never seen me like this. The other attacks were very slight and passed quickly. I'll be all right. Perhaps I should not have come here with you.'

'You mean, we should not have made love?'

'Well, not perhaps like we did last night – it was like that first wonderful time.' Her pretty, three-cornered smile glittered a little wanly in the pale light of dawn. He lit the lamp by the bedside.

'How many of these attacks have you had? Be truthful, Maggy.'

'About three. But not so bad, or so long. I have these pills, and when it starts I put one under my tongue and then the iron band stops squeezing the breath out of me.' She wondered how long it would be before the iron band ignored the pill, and how long the gasping breath and struggling heart could stand against it. 'Sit here, and hold me upright. This is a lovely feeling. Like coming back to life again.'

He wrapped the fleecy white shawl she always wore instead of a bed jacket about her bare shoulders. So delicate and beautiful, she still had all the white, smooth, desirability which had always intoxicated him. There had never been any full-fleshed voluptuousness about Margaret. As a girl she had glowed like a white flame, and even now the flame was still there. But the fragility was frightening. She had been strong as a red kitten. He groaned audibly. 'I didn't know. I didn't think.'

'How could you? How could I? I've been tired and run down, but that's all. I've been tired before.'

'I'll find you the best heart specialist in the world. In Vienna perhaps – or Switzerland. We'll go to anywhere where we can get you well again.'

'If there is this war you talk of, we may not be able to go anywhere like that.'

She spoke so normally that his fears were assuaged. Perhaps it was a passing thing – not so serious as it had appeared. Her cheeks were quite pink now, the blind look gone from her eyes.

'You're looking better. Do you want to sleep again? Shall I ring, and get some tea?'

'No. I want to talk.' She saw his confidence returning. She was so many years younger than him, and had never ailed in her life until now. She must keep him thinking that way. But there were things she must say.

She lay with her head on his shoulder, wondering what to say or what not to say that might alarm him.

'Now, tell me exactly what the doctor said,' he pressed her.

'Nothing much. He gave me these pills for if my breathing got bad . . . mostly it was what not to do. Not to work too hard. To avoid rich meals and alcohol. He did not mention making love, and I did not mention you. I can just imagine what he would have said then!' She looked down her nose, mimicking her imposing doctor, ' "As you are a widow, Mrs Léon, I would have thought that kind of thing did not apply to you." '

He laughed as she had hoped he would, relaxing. 'You're a monkey, beloved. Supposing we act though as if he *had* warned against it. To keep you quiet?'

He was hoping it was some passing thing. But hope could lie. He remembered how when Stephen was born, for instance, how sure he had been the doctors could put it right – and they had done wonders, but his son's leg was not quite right, and never would be. And now Tom, his splendid boy, his right arm, Maggy's boy, would be a soldier. Henry was telling himself that it could not be serious, that he needed her now more than ever – her voice on the telephone, her occasional treasured presence and love – because he was growing old, and was afraid for Tom.

'I'm happy just to be with you. That is enough.'

'But we will find a specialist. And you must take care, and telephone me every week.'

'Oh, yes, yes, yes, I'll do all that! Don't fuss so, Henry. I won't go on a champagne fling. I want to talk about Rose. About Charmian's girl. If by any chance anything should happen to me, which is unlikely, you'll take care of her, won't you?'

He was silent – astonished. He had forgotten all about the girl whom Tom had told him of.

'You see she has found a family. Me – and Tom. And I love her. And she is in love with Tom, and I think he is in love with her.'

He frowned. 'But they are cousins!'

'Oh, what does it matter? People find their happiness where they can, if they're sensible. We're hardly ever together, but we have had more happiness than most people get in a lifetime of marriage. Rose is young and clever, and strange and beautiful to danger point.'

'Like her mother?' he asked dryly.

'No. Charmian was a danger to herself. She was self-destructive. Rose is not like that. She has found a home with me – cousins in Stephen and Tom. I want her to be happy. I don't want her to be without a family again.'

'She seems to have enchanted you.'

She smiled. 'Well, she's a potential enchantress. But it's not that. Until Ferdi died and left her his money, and made me her guardian, I did not even know she existed. I've found something very appealing about her. Her steely sense of self-preservation, I suppose. She's had a hard, bewildering childhood, but she's come out of it with her chin up.'

'She's got under your skin,' he said.

'I never wanted children, Henry, until I had Tom. I certainly did not want a daughter – perhaps because both my mother and sister were beautiful, self-deceiving fools. But this one is different. A daughter can be very special, Henry.

You can laugh with her about men. You can talk about women's things. If they like you, you can be understanding with their youth and they understand and are compassionate with your age.' She paused. 'I've left her money, of course. Tom has more than he needs now. I've named you as her guardian and executor – if she needs a home, will you take her into yours? You will do this for me, won't you? If the need arises?'

'The need will not arise, but I will do that.'

'I have your promise?'

'Of course. And stop talking like this. You're twenty years younger than me. We'll hire a car and drive back to London, and see the best man in the heart business to get you right.'

'Maybe I should have done what you wanted once – given up my business and made a home for you and Tom.'

'*Maggy* – At that time you could no more have given up that business than cut off your right arm.'

'No,' she gave a long sigh, 'So! Twenty-three years ago I swallowed my pride and bottled up my love and asked you and Angela to take Tom for me. And now I'm asking you to take Rose if ever I should be unable to make a home for her. Tom was nearly three. Rose is fifteen. She needs a home and a family.'

He kissed her forehead, and said, 'I promise, of course, if you wish – if it will set your mind at rest.'

'But – Angela? How will Angela accept it? I gather she is happier now that Tom has his own place, and only Stephen is at home. Will she accept it?'

'Angela will do as I wish,' he answered with certainty. 'She brought up the two boys. A girl should be little trouble.'

'This one could be a great deal of trouble – or a great blessing. If you can give her affection, something she has starved for since she was born. Charmian's doll-toy until she grew too big. Loyalty and devotion from her foster mother, but not affection. Cynical generosity from Ferdi. She is a mixture of passionate innocence and infinite sophistication.'

'I shall look forward to meeting her,' Henry said.

But Rose only met Henry Grimshaw the day after Margaret died.

She was summoned from the hockey pitch by her Form Mistress. A late practice before the season closed. Rose thought hockey idiotic. Pounding round after a little white ball in an extremely unbecoming dark green tunic, getting one's ankles and feet trodden on and hit, so when she was beckoned from the side lines by Miss Smythe, she ran willingly off the pitch. But one look at the form mistress's grave face released a fountain of apprehension. Something had happened. Something awful. What had she done? What had she said? What *had* happened?

'Will you come with me, Rose? The Head Mistress wishes to see you.'

'Most certainly, Miss Smythe.' They headed towards the main building. 'Have I done something wrong?'

'Oh, no, nothing like that, my dear child!' Miss Smythe, fortyish, nice, but plain, had long been enmeshed in Rose's charm. 'Your cousin Lieutenant Grimshaw is here.' She hesitated. 'I'm afraid it is bad news from home.'

The apprehension spread and engulfed Rose. She and Tom had written regularly since Glockenschule, and at Easter he had spent ten days of his holidays at Chelsea and taken her out a great deal. But he had, in schoolgirl parlance, cooled off. At Glockenschule, he said, maybe they had both taken too much champagne – but she knew perfectly well what stood between them. Her age, of course. She had turned fifteen in March. His letters were friendly and teasing. Hers were – like all letters from the school – vetted, but vetted tolerantly. ('My darling handsome lovely cousin, you will look *ravissant* in uniform, but I had rather you were not a soldier but remained a captain of industry. Cloth mills are so safe.') This had raised considerable amusement in the staff room, but no one took it seriously. Neither, apparently, had Tom.

Miss Smythe, her round plump face crimsoning with suppressed tears, suddenly embraced Rose and said, 'You must be a very brave girl.'

Rose had a hysterical desire to giggle. She was quite aware that Miss Smythe and several pupils at Pendrill's had some difficulty in restraining their affection for her and dry amusement and the black cloud of apprehension fused terrifyingly within her breast. Something dreadful *had* happened. There was already a war and Tom was going to fight? Or Margaret was ill? Like her Mama one morning, white among her satin and lace pillows, with the pills spilled across the side table, and the smell of alcohol and expensive perfume filling the room? Or Papa Léon – so thin and fragile, like a bundle of shrivelled brown sticks, being carried on to the Paris Express and never being seen again?

The Head was sitting at her desk and Tom was standing at the window, looking out across the gardens to the Downs. He was in uniform and the minute he turned and she saw the look in his eyes, she knew. She wanted to wail and tear her hair like the Arab women far back in her heredity, but he came across to her and put his arms about her, pressing her face against his breast, and she put her arms round him and his enveloping strength and warmth quietened the panic.

She raised her head and spoke to him in French and English, her two languages becoming ridiculously mixed.

'*Elle n'est pas morte? C'est impossible. Elle n'était pas malade!* A small *fatigue* . . . I have need of her, Tom, I have need of her. I am not prepared – I am not ready to be without her.'

'Neither am I,' he said. 'No one was. But it has happened. I have come to take you to London. And then home with me to Thornsby.'

She could feel his tears against her forehead. She felt lost – apart from him. In Margaret she had found a guiding star, serene and steady, and now the whole sky was empty and darkly grey and unbroken, like the long English winter. And Thornsby? What was Thornsby? A place in the north where there were many ugly factories and the skies were more grey than London – where nothing was ever clean and the sun never shone, and the people were as dull and grey as the skies. Or so her mother had said, once, when she had asked her where she had been born, and what it had been like. "A grey, dull place from which one only wanted to get away."

Chapter Five

Tom had driven down to Pendrill's in Margaret's car. He and
Rose left almost immediately for London. Miss Smythe asked
tenderly if Rose would like her to accompany them, but she,
very French, calm and practical, said this was quite unnecess-
ary. Her cousin and his father would advise her, and Mrs
Dyson, her aunt's housekeeper, would chaperone and care
for her.

Miss Smythe thought how hard she seemed; not a tear after
that first wild breakdown; but how beautiful. She even wept
beautifully. In the car Tom remarked that Miss Smythe
seemed very fond of her. Rose shrugged, and said indifferently, 'She is a sentimental woman.'

They travelled in silence for a while, winding through the
Sussex beach woods towards the high road for London.

It was a hot and brilliant summer. In the fields the corn was
already ripening and the June roses wilted in the cottage
gardens. Hardly a breath stirred the torrid summer air. But
Rose, whose dark creamy beauty glowed in the heat, looked
cool. Tom had taken off his uniform jacket and cap and put
them in the rear of the car. He glanced at her, sitting silently
beside him. She looked ridiculously young in her summer
school uniform of striped mauve and white cotton. She wore a
Panama hat with the Pendrill's shield on the mauve and green
hatband, and elastic under her chin. Her mauve blazer was
thrown in the back of the car with his jacket. She wore flat
summer sandals and white socks.

Ten years between them. When he was thirty, she would be

twenty. A big enough gap then – enormous now. Especially when she was wearing this ridiculous uniform.

But not when she had undulated bare shoulders beneath a transparent yashmak and glinted at him with her unfathomable eyes.

As though she knew what he was thinking she put her hand on his on the steering wheel, and the touch roused the desire made latent with grief, making him feel guilty and ashamed. He patted it consolingly, and she let it slip back into her lap.

'Tell me about it,' she said, 'tell me about what happened.'

'Heart failure. Did you know she had had several mild attacks? She did not tell me – or anyone until she had one when she was away with father!

He had taken her to an army of specialists. He was going to take her to Vienna to a world famous doctor. They all said it was an unpredictable thing. Quiet, rest, care – but you know what she was like. She still went in to that damned business twice a week.'

'I have never seen anyone die.'

'Neither had I – until yesterday.'

Her dark eyes widened apprehensively. 'It didn't hurt her? Tom – say it didn't hurt her?'

'Not at the end – she would take no drugs until my father came. He was in Yorkshire. Then the doctor gave her morphine. She died in Dad's arms as though she was going to sleep.'

He did not tell her of the agonising struggles for breath and the fierce bouts of pain, punctuated by furious anger. Her eyes blue slits in her white face. A cat caught in a trap, exasperated, struggling to get out.

'I'm so cross about this – making all this fuss!' she had gasped. 'I never could *stand* women who made a fuss!'

And then she was still with her head on Henry's shoulder, his face bent next to hers looking suddenly very old. Seventy-five and he looked older. Tom had always thought him indestructible.

She had been still so long that they had thought she was asleep. Then the pain-darkened lids had flickered open, and there was a shadow of her gay and brilliant smile, and hope absurdly lifted their hearts.

'Henry . . . ' she whispered, and then a little crossly, 'Don't cry. Kiss me.' He kissed her and she smiled up over his shoulder at Tom. 'You too, my darling.' Tom had bent and kissed her. Her lips were blue and cold. Then she said, very clearly, 'You'll both look after my girl, Rose, won't you? She will need looking after.' And her eyes closed, her dark lashes making small crescents on her pale cheeks. Behind them, Sarah Dyson, the housekeeper, had suddenly burst into noisy tears.

Tom pulled the car off the road into an open glade in the woods.

'Let's talk a little, Rose. Mama is still at Chelsea, in the flat, where she died. Would you rather go to an hotel – or have you any friends you might like to go to?'

She shook her head.

'No. I'll stay in Chelsea.'

'Tomorrow we will be taking her up to Danesfell, where all the Normanbys are buried.'

'Except Mama. I wonder if Respy still puts flowers on her grave?'

Grief suddenly overcame her. She began to struggle with a fierce paroxysm of tears as though she too was in pain.

'Don't,' he said. 'Don't, my darling . . .'

She thrust open the car door as though in need of air, and stood swaying with her hands over her face. He got out and ran round to her and caught her or she would have fallen. He lowered her on to the warm bracken, taking off her absurd school hat, carefully stretching the elastic over the smooth young chin, undoing the school tie, and gently wiped her face.

She lay motionless while he kneeled above her. He lifted her against him. It seemed a long while until she spoke.

'I'm back again, Tom. I'm back again where I was after Mama and Papa Léon died. Where I've always been. No-where. Belonging to nowhere and to no one. No one wanting me.'

'You have me. I want you.'

'You don't – you think I'm a baby. You always run away.'

She took his hand and laid it on her breast. Beneath the thin cotton of her summer dress he could feel her heart racing and the nipple hardening on the small, full breast. Her eyes were blazing up into his with a fierce and desperate yearning. She was waiting, watching him, expectant, her body like a flower opening its heart to receive the probing bee, every innocent force of nature within her willing him to take her. And he wanted to – she was so temptingly lovely, and it would be so easy when he loved her so.

He released his hand and lifted her closely and comfortingly against him, his lips pressed against her shining hair.

'You must not make things impossible for me, Rose. You are very young and life is a long time.' But he felt her lips lift against his throat.

'If there is a war, you will go away to fight. You have no right to go away and leave me! Tante Margaret had no right to die! I have a great need of you both – what will happen if I am left quite alone?'

'We promised her, my father and I, that we would always care for you.'

'But *now* – if you love me now, I think you will not go away? You are most honourable. I think you would then marry me, Tom, and then I would surely feel safe. And you would not go away.'

'You are an impossible child,' he said shortly. 'You think life is a box of bon-bons and you can pick and choose just what you want, or scoff the whole lot at once. My father and I are your guardians now – we control your money until you are twenty-one, we are responsible for you in every way. It would scarcely be what my mother wished for if I seduced you when you are still only fourteen.'

'Fifteen,' she corrected him, and he laughed.

'Fifteen then, you little idiot.'

She sat up straight-backed, brushing the leaves and country debris from her skirt. The small, neat head balanced on the slender neck reminded him irresistibly of his mother. She buttoned up her dress, and re-tied the school tie. 'When we get to Chelsea, I shall put on some nice clothes,' she said.

'You will have to get some mourning.'

Her mood changed. The grief returned.

'Oh, Tom, I am so silly because I am so unhappy. Inside here,' she pressed her hands against her chest, 'I ache for her. I cannot bear to think that she has gone.'

'Would you rather have stayed at school? I will take you back if you wish.'

'No!' She rose and went back to the car. She had made a bad mistake, she knew it. He was seeing her only as a child again, dangerously provocative and precocious, but still a child, unable to think clearly or control her instincts. She must get him back. Somehow she must get him back. He was all she had in the world.

The blinds were drawn in the Chelsea flat when they arrived. Margaret had always loved the light – and loved the curtains undrawn at night so that she could see the lights along the Embankment and on the shipping on the river. Truth, clarity and laughter were the qualities she lived by. In the hall one electric wall light was on and the heavy damask curtains drawn. It was hot, airless, cloyed with the scent of fading flowers.

When Rose had come home before she had always called out from the door: 'Tante Margaret – I'm home,' and the sweet, crisp voice had answered immediately.

The closeness, the dim light, the heavy silence and airlessness of the hot summer day, told her that bright presence was no longer waiting.

'She would have hated this!' she said, and went impulsively to the window and drew back the heavy curtain, letting in shafts of golden light. 'It's horrible. She loved the light. She would have *hated* this!' she cried.

The door of Margaret's bedroom opened and a tall old man stood there, a handsome man, Tom's father. His presence silenced her anger. He was like a great oak tree, hollow and empty, its heart burned out by lightning.

Mrs Dyson, red-eyed, nose congested with tears, came fussing in, shocked and disapproving.

'Now, Miss Rose, that's not seemly.' She went towards the windows to draw the curtains back again but Grimshaw said, 'She's right, Sarah, leave them be. She did love the sunlight. Pull them all back, except where she is sleeping.'

Startled, the housekeeper went into the drawing room and dining room, drawing back the blue damask curtains. Light flooded through into the hall, sunlight and leaf shadows dappling the blue walls.

'Will you get some fresh flowers?' Henry Grimshaw said. 'Flowers she liked in the vases where she always kept them.' He took out a notecase and gave the housekeeper some money. 'And then, please, prepare some lunch for us . . . Tom has driven a long way, and the young lady looks exhausted.'

Mrs Dyson hurried out to do his bidding. Henry Grimshaw stepped towards Rose, held out his hands and took hers.

'You are Charmian's girl?'

'Yes, M'sieur.' She bobbed the conventional little curtsey. 'You are Tom's father – and also Tante Margaret's *bon-ami*?'

He took her head between his big square hands and looked at her, turning her face as though searching for some likeness. He smiled, nodded, patted her cheek.

'I am not like my mother,' she said. 'Not at all. I am like my father, an oriental.' Her lips tightened defensively. ' "A touch of the tar brush," I hear you say here in England. A "milky", as the Memsahibs say in India.'

'They say that?' His eyes kindled, and she could see Tom in that aggressively protective gleam. 'A touch of glory would be more like it, Missy. You will be a very handsome lady one day. I was looking for a likeness to Maggy. And, yes . . .' He searched her face as though he longed for a resemblance to his dead love, and finally found it. He saw Margaret in the proud, imperious lift of the round chin, the firmness of the pretty mouth with its sweetly soft lower lip, the defiant set of the small head. He saw it in her wariness and touch of recklessness, recalling the young girl who had so defiantly set her cap at him all those years ago.

'Yes, you have a look of her. More like her than your mother. Much more like.'

'You knew Mama?' She was surprised.

'I saw her when they were small children. They were twins, you know, and Charmian was always her mother's favourite and the beauty.' He shook his head as though the memories were too much. 'And again briefly, when they were seventeen. She was extraordinarily lovely then, as was her mother with whom I was once in love – and she was the silliest woman I have ever known! You are not like either of them.

But somewhere, yes, I can see Maggy. I am to be your guardian, so I must be grateful for that small resemblance.'

He turned towards the bedroom door, and Tom saw the terrible desolation in his face.

'Are you all right, Dad?'

'Aye. I'll go back to her now.' He turned to ask Rose: 'Did you want to see her, child?'

She lost colour but said bravely, 'If you please, M'sieur.'

'Come.' He took her hand to lead her into the bedroom, and she felt Tom's strong, warm hand take her other arm.

She did not know what she expected, but when she saw Margaret she gave a little cry, wrung from the heart, for it looked like a young woman who lay there, asleep.

A soft silk rose-coloured gown reflected colour on to the white cheeks; the lashes were as they always had been – thick, short, dark, curled, slanting upwards – as though, like the mouth, with its straight firm upper lip, and soft sweet lower, always on the verge of a smile.

Henry let go her hand and went to the chair by the bedside. He looked up, smiled, and shook his head, and the emptiness crept back like frost into his eyes.

'Nay, lass, she'll not come back to us. Not any more. But you and Tom here have all your lives before you. Don't grieve too much.'

As Tom led her out, Rose turned and saw the old man bend his head until his lips touched the still cheek, and then draw his head back sharply, as though he too, for a moment, had thought that Margaret was only sleeping. She went back, quickly and quietly, and bent and kissed the cold still face. But for her Margaret was no longer there.

Tom said, 'D'you mind if I go back and sit with him?' She shook her head silently, and went into her own room.

The curtains had not been drawn there and the sunlight flooded on to the charming furnishings. Together she and Margaret had planned it, and she had been encouraged to make it very much her own, but she realised now how much Margaret had guided her taste. It was a sunshine-filled room, with simple fumed oak furniture and plain ivory walls, so that the bright cretonne curtains glowed in contrast. There was a cluster of drooping yellow roses in a thin crystal vase, and she guessed Margaret had put them there herself – not many hours ago – before it had happened. The sense of loss became insufferable. An aching pain gripped her.

She dropped down on her bed, clenching her hands, her face contorted, fighting the tears of loss and self-pity, thumping savagely at the pillows as though she was trying to beat her own feelings into silence.

'*Merde! Merde! Merde!*' she cried.

There was a tap on the door and Sarah Dyson looked in. 'Are you all right, miss?'

'Oh, yes, Sarah, thank you.' She had not realised she had cried aloud. 'I am so sorry. I knocked my hand against the bed rail.'

'Shall I bring something?'

'No, please. It is only a small bruise. It will be quite all right.'

'Very well, miss. I have made a cold luncheon for you and Mr Tom. Shall I serve it now?'

Rose realised with a shock that she was the woman of the house now. And the long wardrobe mirror showed an untidy crumpled object in a school uniform, a face distraught with sorrow and anger. She unclenched her fists and drew in a long, deep breath.

'Not just yet, Sarah. Will you draw me a bath, not too hot? I'll change, and then you can call Mr Tom and serve.'

'Right, miss.' She hesitated then said, 'Mr Tom asked me to travel up to Yorkshire with the family to attend the funeral. You've not heard any plans – about whether or not he intends to keep this place on?'

'No? Why?'

'Well, I've been with Madame ever since Miss Leck, her old housekeeper died. Madame said to me some time ago that she'd left me a bit, and said she'd arranged for me to stay here until I'd got settled again, or if Mr Tom wanted me to stay on, because it seems the place is his now – that is, the lease is. I told her not to talk so daft. But then, I never thought . . .'

'Oh, Sarah, none of us did.' Rose jumped up and put her arms round the distressed woman. She was thinking frantically, I've got to take Tante Margaret's place. For the present. They all expect it.

'Don't worry, please. Mr Grimshaw and Mr Tom are my guardians now – I know they will take care of you. Now I must change.'

It was the moment in which she grew up.

She stripped off the hated school uniform, the white socks, the loathed liberty bodice, the dark green cotton bloomers, and wrapped in the lavender silk kimono which Margaret had given her, went into the bathroom, and bathed and washed her hair free of its tight waves caused by the plaits. When Tom and his father came in for lunch she was wearing a summer dress of dark blue cotton, square-necked and with neat elbow-length sleeves, her mane of hair combed back and secured on the nape of her neck. She went forward and took Henry's arm and led him to the table. Tom was touched, knowing she was trying to do what Margaret would, but wondered as he so often did, whether she was consciously playing a part.

The meal was light and delicious. Henry ate as though it was a duty and he could taste nothing. Rose said suddenly: 'I shall go over to Hanover Street this afternoon. To the Salon.' They looked bewildered. 'The business,' she said. 'It was her life. Someone must go and speak to them personally. You have told them, yes?'

'Yes, I telephoned,' said Tom. 'Of course you are right. Someone should make a personal call.'

'I must go and speak with Mr Brinkley, and Miss Jenner the showroom manageress – they will both wish to travel up to the funeral. There are many people in London they should notify. At Papa Léon's funeral, all the salons along the Rue de la Paix had their blinds drawn. I think they should close for one day.'

A curious little twist of pain crossed Henry's face. 'Yes, of course,' he said. 'It is important. It was her life – and perhaps it killed her. But there are many loyal workers there.'

Rose went to Hanover Street early that afternoon and with Roy Brinkley, Margaret's Managing Director, visited every department and spoke personally to the employees.

'But Madame was *never* ill!' they said. Rose suggested they should close for the day of the funeral. Miss Jenner and Mr Brinkley and Rose Briggs, the Chief Workroom Hand, would travel up to Yorkshire to represent them. Mr Brinkley assured the staff that they had no need to worry – the firm would continue under his management.

Rose must look her best for this strange, sad arrival in Yorkshire. Margaret had been the transgressor – the mistress, the other woman – and she wondered about Henry's wife, Tom's mother by adoption. Would she really welcome her? How would she take this new presence? Another continual reminder of the past. How would she be received?

But she must go – she and Tom must both demonstrate their love and loyalty.

That night Henry insisted that Tom should take Rose out – tomorrow would be a great ordeal. She was too young to be overburdened with it all.

Tom chose a quiet restaurant in Sloane Square. Rose wore a black silk dress, and a close-fitting black straw hat trimmed with small black grapes. His mother herself might have chosen it.

'You look very chic,' he said.

'Tante Margaret would have expected me to,' Rose replied, 'she always said her customers were walking models for the business.'

'Yes, I remember.' He studied her face for signs of distress or grief. She had been overwhelmed at first but now she was quite calm.

'I have been taught to respect the wishes of my elders,' she said primly, as though she guessed his thoughts, 'and your father said we were to try to be happy tonight. That Tante Margaret would have wished it. So I am trying very hard to obey. Would you prefer that I should weep until my nose was red?'

'Ah, Rose,' he said, and took her hand. 'You are adorable.'

'Tell me about your other mother, Monsieur Henry's wife? The one you sometimes call Aunty Angel. Will she be there tomorrow – at the funeral?'

'Oh, yes, of course. It would spoil her reputation for long-suffering martyrdom if she was not.'

'You do not like her?'

'I wouldn't say that,' he said equably. 'I sympathise with her. In her world such things as affairs should be hidden and secret. But Father loves me as much as he loves Stevie, and Stevie and I love each other, and we both love him – she has forgiven Father but not me.' His blue Normanby eyes creased with amusement. 'Although I can scarcely be blamed. And he is taking Mama up to Danesfell to be buried among the Normanby family which will set every tongue in the dale wagging again. Dad will never be ashamed of his love for my mother. Angela need not attend – but she will.'

'That is brave of her. If I had been her, I would have killed Tante Margaret.'

'And if you had been my mother?'

'I would have taken no notice of Mrs Grimshaw at all – or, maybe, I would have killed her.'

He laughed, and beckoned for the bill. 'Two murders in one evening, my Rose? You are a dangerous woman. Come, we should leave. We have to leave very early tomorrow. I wish it had been a different sort of journey. Not so sad. I would have liked to show you Yorkshire for the first time without this grief. I want you to like it up there. It is my country.'

In Shaftesbury Avenue the theatres were beginning to empty and the streets were full of home-going people, a few limousines, many taxis, but there were still some horse drawn cabs, and a hansom, already becoming a curiosity, clopping along towards them.

'Let us take one of these old carriages,' she said. 'Oh, Tom, please?'

He signalled to the hansom. 'It will take us much longer.'

'But that will be nice. All the sorrow is at home.'

She was entranced when the apron was fastened and the cabby asked their destination through the small trap in the roof.

'It is fascinating. Mama used to tell me about riding in these cabs – driving with her lovers, hidden from the world. She was like the woman in that book, *Madame Bovary*.'

'Is that standard school reading?' he teased.

'No, of course not! I heard it was very wicked so I bought it, and it was very sad but very true.'

He was leaning back, watching her, his eyes both tender and amused.

'Shall we pretend that we are lovers, Tom? Would you not like that?'

'I would like that very much indeed.' She saw the flash of his white teeth as he smiled in the semi-darkness. 'But no. It would be better if you played no more games of let's pretend with me, *chérie*.'

'Is it because you are sad about your mama?' she asked ingenuously.

'No, although I am very sad. More sad than I ever believed I could be.'

'Oh, darling Tom, I too am sad . . .'

He folded his arms, and made no move towards her. 'You change like a windy sky, Rose. Sunny patches, dark and stormy patches, brilliant gleams of sunshine. Sweetness, mockery, mischief, sadness, and often outright provocative wickedness. Tell me – which is the real Rose?'

'Perhaps they are all bits of me, and all of them sincere.'

He laughed and took her small, tense hand and would not let her pull it away. 'Which is the real you? The one *you* wish to be?'

She was silent, the cab was turning off the King's Road towards the Embankment. 'Why is it that you do not wish to love me?'

'*Petite*, I do *not* wish to love you, but God help me, I do!'

'Ah . . .' She moved towards him.

'No, wait. Together with Father, I am your guardian – Mama asked us to do this before she died. It is a responsibility I have to honour. And there are other things. There is this threat of war. I am in the Army. And you are very young. If I made love to you now, Rose, we should both go up like straw – and where would that lead?'

'Why, to happiness.'

'I wonder how many times your poor, beautiful mother thought that, and how many times it brought her into fear and disaster?'

'Oh!' she exclaimed furiously. 'Why must you always be so bloody wise, Tom Grimshaw?'

He burst out laughing as she intended he should, but as they drove up to Riverside Apartments she drew comfort from the fact that he was still holding her hand.

At King's Cross it was a mixed group of mourners that accompanied Margaret Normanby back to the town where she was born, who waited until the casket, bearing a sheaf of red roses, was carried aboard the train.

Henry Grimshaw, his son Thomas, her niece Shareen Abderhazy, Mr Roy Brinkley, Miss Jenner the Showroom Manageress, Mr Briggs, the hall porter for twenty years, and his daughter Rose Briggs, the Chief Workroom Hand, together with a peacock group of distinguished friends and customers. Rose was touched but not surprised to see the heads of other fashion houses, wholesalers, two famous designers from Paris, and figures from society and the fashion world boarding the train.

On the journey she made it her business to go along the corridor with Mr Brinkley and speak to every one of them personally, moving easily from English to French, and Tom watched her and wondered at the woman she could so unexpectedly become. She asked Henry's permission to invite the representatives from the Salon to lunch with them in the dining car.

'They are her family, Mr Grimshaw. To her staff she was, in some sort of way, a mother. She was very stern but very kind, and sometimes she would laugh with them. And she always showed how much she valued work well done, and how much she despised carelessness.'

Something glinted in Henry's tired eyes – recognition of the qualities he had loved in the dead woman they were taking home. He said, of course they must be included.

Stephen came to meet them at Leeds and there was a fleet of cars waiting to take the southern mourners to their hotels. Henry's large limousine took the family and Mrs Dyson, whom they dropped off at her sister's little stone-built house. The cortège drove along the Bradford Road which was crammed with commercial carts and heavy drays loaded with bales of wool and shoddy, the trash material with which cheap woollens were made and which Grimshaws never touched.

Trams clashed and sparked. The stone-built mills towered behind their prison-like walls. The people in the streets seemed pale and wizened and shabby, the women aproned, their sleeves rolled up from bare raw arms, their hair tied in scarves. A group of colliers clattered clog-shod from a tram, their eyes ringed white like negro minstrels, lines of sweat streaking through the coal dust on their faces.

Tom saw the dismay in Rose's eyes. Nice, Paris, the West End of London . . . these were the places she understood. He knew how ugly, dirty and poor this northern manufacturing town must seem to this sophisticated child.

They were passing a group of three mills, each with a large entrance arch leading into inner loading yards.

Big, green facia boards bore the names "Britannia", "Calder Beck" and "Water Meadow Mills", and above, "Henry Grimshaw & Sons (Thornsby) Ltd. MANUFACTURERS OF FINE CLOTHS".

Rose looked questioningly at Tom and then at Stephen, who said mockingly, 'Behold our Kingdom. *C'est vrai, chérie. C'est notre royaume.* It's where t'brass is made, lass.'

'Brass?' she repeated.

'Money,' said Tom, 'that's where we work. That's our place!'

Her shoulders shot up. '*Mon dieu, c'est incroyable!*'

'Not hereabouts,' Tom said drily. 'In the West Riding the manufacture of woollens is the breath of life. It is our world. We love it.'

'Speak for yourself, old boy,' said Stephen. 'I think there are other places and other worlds I want to know.'

The car drew up at Cliffs Edge House. Tom, Stephen and Rose got out, but Henry said briefly, 'I'm going on to Danesfell Church with her. Tell your mother I'll be home for dinner,' and the chauffeur turned the car and drove off up the main road, following the hearse. The funeral was to be on the following day in the small parish church which stood in the grounds of Danesfell Abbey. Tom and Stephen glanced at each other, and with a little shrug Stephen ran up the steps. The door opened and a tall, rather stout lady dressed in deep mourning came out and held out her arms to him as though he had been away on a long journey.

She kissed him and said, 'Where's your father?'

'Oh, he thought he would go on to the church. Just to see if everything is all right for tomorrow.'

She put her handkerchief to her eyes and turned away, but he held her arm. 'Now, Mother, I want you to meet Tom's cousin, Rose. His ward.'

Angela held on to his arm as though she might fall and looked at Rose with wary eyes in which there was no welcome. To this woman she would always be an alien. Because of her foreign blood, because of Margaret. Like Tom, she was a resented intruder.

At dinner there was little conversation. Only Stephen pluckily tried to restore some kind of normality. Rose loved him for it. Even a funeral could not suppress his irreverent charm. But then Margaret had not been his dearest protector and friend, nor his mother. Margaret – Angela's invincible rival. The woman whom her husband would love until his death.

Both Tom and his father were still in shock from their loss, and their sorrow kept them apart. Between Stephen and his mother there seemed to be an uneasy affection, tolerant and a little derisive on his part, on hers watchful with intense possessiveness. Edgy little scenes continually flared between them, and Rose guessed they must often explode into anger.

Henry had, very courteously, suggested to Angela that if she did not wish to attend the funeral, he and Tom and everyone would understand. But as Tom had foretold, she was doggedly determined to defend and justify her presence. It was her duty. She had, she hoped, never shirked any real duty.

Tom was, after all, her adopted son. It was only right that she should support him. But, she said sharply, there was no need for Stephen to attend, and she could not understand why he should wish to do so.

'Oh, come on, Mama,' Stephen said good-naturedly. 'I want to support old Tom too. Besides, Madame Léon was a ripping lady – I met her in Switzerland, and she was jolly nice and good fun. She knew so many interesting people in London, and some of her yarns about them made us die laughing. She *was* Tom's mother.'

'But no relative of yours. You will do as you like. You always do. You never have any consideration for my feelings or those of my family. I am always willing to do my best for Tom, but there is no need . . .' Her voice, which had been rising hysterically, shook and stopped as she became aware of the deep, patient boredom of the three men.

It was obvious they had listened to these complaints for years. Henry looked very tired – the bones seemed to show through his skin, there were shadows beneath his eyes, and hollows beneath his cheekbones. Margaret had once said of him, "He's like a Red Indian Chief, carved in a rock-face." Now he was a tired old man.

He put down his table napkin. They had only just reached the entrée. His voice was as it always was when he spoke to his wife: patient, kind and distant. Tom rose too, but his father's hand pressed him back into his seat.

'I'm afraid that old scandal will never die down while Tom lives in Thornsby. He is too large and healthy a reminder of it. If you will excuse me, my dear?' He turned to the butler, 'Botham, tell them to bring the car out again.'

'You are going out?' said Angela. 'To the club?'

'No,' said Henry. 'Not to the club tonight.'

Tom rose and went to his side. They were both beyond pretence. He could not spare his stepmother's feelings in his anxiety for his father.

'Dad,' he said, 'let me come with you. You can't keep watch all night.'

'Nay, I'll be back, lad. There are things to see to. You stay.' He smiled at Rose. 'Make the little girl feel at home. It is a different world to the one she knows.'

Rose felt tears rush to her eyes. Henry went out and they heard the car draw up to the door and then drive away.

Tom sat down, pushing his plate away, momentarily covering his eyes. 'He's grown so old,' he said. 'In a few days he has become an old man. As though his youth died with her.'

There was a long and painful silence, and then he looked up and went to Angela's side. 'I'm sorry, Aunt Angela. Don't be hurt, please.' He would have taken her hand but she thrust him away. Her large eyes were full of tears – tears of angry self-pity.

110

'There are times, Tom, when I could expect some sensitivity, even from you! Stephen, come to me.' Dramatically, she stretched out a hand to her own son, who rose with a shrug and went to her side. She leaned against him, crying, 'My boy – my beloved boy!'

Rose could not stand her. If Angela had been an angry shrew and showed some genuine fury, that she could have understood. But what man on earth could stand this self-pitying, whining, perpetual reproach? She thought of her own mother going down so recklessly into destruction. She seemed splendid in comparison.

Angela rose, turned from Stephen and went out, her eyes buried in a handkerchief. Tom rose, saying apologetically, 'It was a damn fool thing to say. I'll go and eat dust.'

Stephen sat down at the table again and filled Rose's glass and his own. 'I'm sorry about that, Rose. Have a drink. I'm sorry for Mama too – it is a difficult occasion. It would be so much better if she would try to put the whole thing in the past but she seems to insist on these scenes. We're all so used to them now, that they've ceased to hurt. I sometimes think . . . well, perhaps if she had really forgiven and forgotten, Margaret and Dad would never have taken up again. But she would never let it rest. She could never stop reminding him, and reminding Tom that he was only here on sufferance.'

'You mean,' Rose said faintly, 'your mama is *always* like so? It is not just this special occasion which is so very sensitive?'

'Lord, no! It's been better lately since Tom moved out into a place of his own. Like the elephant, Mama never forgets. For instance, she is mortally hurt if one member of the household forgets her birthday. Every year Dad wracks his brains for some treat, some wonderful thing to do on their anniversary, and then on the day she is indisposed, and feels she cannot go. Let me help you to some of this delicious lamb stew. I'm so hungry! Dad has wonderful kitchen gardens. New potatoes, lifted today. I find food a great comfort in times of stress. I shall be enormous by the time I am thirty.'

Rose began to smile. 'You are making me laugh, Stephen, and to laugh on such occasions is not correct. But I think Tante Margaret would like to see us laughing.'

111

'I'm quite sure she would,' Tom said as he came back and took his place again. 'Your mother's coming down, Stevie. I beat my breast. But it was unforgivable to say what I did. I'm so sorry.'

'Think nothing of it, old chap,' said his brother airily. 'If it hadn't been that it would have been something else. Have some ragoût – it's splendid. And *I* should have run to comfort her, so now I expect I'm in the wrong too.' He spoke so comically that they all laughed, unfortunately at the moment Angela returned. She took her place, glanced round at the three young faces, and the meal was finished in silence, except for Stephen who courageously talked nonsense until even he was defeated by his mother's icy disapproval.

Angela signalled to Rose, as though she was hosting a large dinner-party, and led the way into the drawing room. Rose had been schooled in these English social niceties at Pendrill's and found them faintly absurd.

The drawing room was long and fine with three large bay windows overlooking the gardens and the moorland. The town of Thornsby lay concealed in a deep valley, only the perpetual smoke haze and the flare of factory chimney stacks could be seen, but now, although it was high summer, Angela had had the heavy brocade curtains drawn. On every shelf space there was a photograph of Stephen, from earliest babyhood until the present day, all framed expensively in silver. There were no photographs of Tom.

Angela opened her workbox and took out some embroidery, adjusted her pince-nez and began to work, still in silence.

Presently Botham brought in a silver tray set with tiny cups and saucers and an elaborate silver coffee set, all of which he set on the table beside her. She put down her work and poured out two cups, one of which she passed to Botham who passed it to Rose.

'Sugar?' asked Angela.

'If you please,' replied Rose, 'and no milk.' Botham attended to that.

'That will be all, Botham, thank you,' said Angela, and silence once more descended. Rose felt stifled. In a moment she would run from the room. But she must not. She was in a battle of wills, and she wondered how often these tactics had been deployed against the young Tom.

'This is a very fine house,' she ventured. 'So spacious and convenient. Did Mr Grimshaw have it built?'

'No. It was built by Mr Thomas Jagger who originally owned the Britannia Mill. My husband bought it from his widow.' She paused, as though the subject held little interest for her, then said, 'His daughter married Sir Richard Normanby, Baronet, the owner of Danesfell Abbey. That is where the Stoneberrys live now. I believe that Sir Richard and Lady Normanby were your maternal grandparents?'

At last there was something to talk about with this difficult woman.

'Oh, yes, my mama was always most proud about being his daughter. My poor mama adored such things – it was, how do you say? *Snobisme*? Yes, it meant a great deal to her. But Tante Margaret always said that her father, this Sir Richard, was a well-bred old rogue and gambler, and her mother was as silly as mine. Tante Margaret was very clever, but Mama was not. She was a beautiful fool – but both Mama and Tante Margaret had great style.'

'You show little respect for your mother,' Angela said severely.

'Yes, it is not possible,' Rose agreed. 'My mama was not respected. She was loved by many men, but mostly by the wrong ones. She was very much loved – indeed, to distraction by some – but she was not respected.'

Angela was astounded. She had never known Charmian Normanby, and her reputation was not known locally. But she could see Margaret in Rose. The whole air of this girl suggested her, although there was no actual physical resemblance. Margaret had been red-haired and fair-skinned, whereas Rose was eastern, dark, exotic. But her neat, finely proportioned body and direct, uncompromising manner, her elegance and style, all recalled her aunt. She was wearing a diaphanous black evening dress, with an under slip of dark purple and elbow-length sleeves through which the creamy young arms gleamed. Her luxuriant dark hair was drawn severely back, and she wore small pearl earrings and one

113

magnificent strand of pearls. All so modestly suitable, all so well-chosen and attractive.

To Angela it brought back vividly to mind Margaret, the young saleswoman from the shop in Leeds who had chosen her trousseau, and whose judgement had made her feel almost beautiful on her own wedding day. The girl who had been so fiercely ambitious. Who had waited in the porch of the church for her to arrive, who had arranged her train and veil and headdress, and sent her on her way down the aisle to where Henry was waiting: Tom's mother Margaret who had never been out of Henry's mind and heart, and who one day had stolen his love from Angela forever. Margaret who had so shamelessly borne Tom, whom Henry had loved more than anyone on earth. Angela hated even to think of her. Even though she was dead, in Rose Margaret had returned, bringing back the old scandal and humiliation.

Tom and Stephen came in and Angela poured coffee for them.

'Your father did go out?' she asked.

'Yes, Mother.'

'Tom – you did not accompany him?'

'No.'

'And may I ask why not?'

'He wanted to go alone,' said Tom, 'You heard him, Aunt Angela, he wanted me to stay with Rose.'

The big room was lit by electric chandeliers and the heavy brocade curtains were drawn tight against the summer night. Angela stitched in silence, making no further attempt at conversation.

This is an awful house, Rose thought. I think I could not bear to live here with this woman. Tom and Stephen talked, but chiefly about the business and their anxiety for their father.

Rose thought of Margaret lying in the church at Danesfell, and the handsome old man keeping his vigil beside her, and shivered. On an impulse she stepped between the curtains and pushed open the French windows to the summer night. The west was still lemon-streaked with sunset and a tired yellow moon dragging itself up from the smoke and mist from the hidden town.

114

Angela stopped stitching as Tom and Stephen sprang to their feet.

'Would you like to take a turn outside, Rose?' asked Stephen. 'Tom and I often take a walk after dinner and it is a lovely night.'

Angela put her work down, her plump hands shaking. She said stiffly, 'Miss Abderhazy is in mourning. I think you should stay.' But it was Stephen she wanted to keep by her side.

'Oh, Mama, don't be so stuffy,' he exclaimed impatiently. 'It's so hot. It's like a furnace with the curtains drawn. We won't be long. No one means any disrespect to anyone. You come too.'

'You would do anything rather than spend ten minutes with your mother. No sooner does Tom, or anyone else, come to this house then you want to go.' She rose, shifting her attack. 'And, Tom, don't you think that you should sit here quietly, with your mother not yet in her grave?'

Tom's voice was exactly like his father's: courteous, patient, ironic. An indifferent tolerance acquired over many years.

'If I sit here in unhappy silence it is not going to bring her back, Aunt Angela, and she would not care. She did not enjoy suffering. Come with us, if you wish.'

'You know I do not.'

'Well, we shall not be long. Just up to the ridge and back. How about it, Rose?'

'Oh, please, yes, if you will permit me to go, Madame?'

Tom knew she would come – knew the respect was devious, that she was longing to get away.

'I am wasting my breath,' Angela said. She was weeping now. 'The boys, like their father, will do whatever they wish, whenever they wish! It is the Grimshaw way. My wishes count for nothing.'

She rose as though to go out of the room, then went to Stephen, straightening his collar, pushing back a lock of hair from his forehead, straightening his tie as though he were a five year old on his first day at school.

'You ought to have a scarf . . .' she began.

115

'Mama, for heaven's sake! It's a hot night.' He jerked his head free, pulled his tie and collar loose, and pushed the French window wide to the summer night. Then, suddenly, he ran out into the moonlight.

Tom caught Rose's hand and they followed. Stephen was racing ahead, through the rose garden, out through the wicket that lead on to the open moor. Rose bent down and kicked off her high-heeled shoes and they ran after him, leaving Angela standing at the lighted window, watching until they were out of sight.

It was some inner compulsion she had to drive people from her – people whom Stephen liked – as though she could not bear to share him, to see him happy in the company of others. She had been happy when Tom had left home. She thought she would have Stephen and Henry to herself forever. Instead she saw less of them both. They had begun to build a life without her, with many friends she did not even know.

She drew the curtains again, leaving the window open. She went to the sideboard and unlocked the old-fashioned tantalus, pouring a glass of brandy which she slowly drank down. Its head was fiery and comforting, running through her veins. She wiped the glass and put it back and replaced the heavy cut-glass decanter, locking the case and returning the miniature key to its place. Then she went upstairs to her room and rang for her maid. It would be a long while before Henry came – he was keeping watch beside his one true beloved.

When her maid came to help her undress, she asked for hot milk and some brandy to be brought to her room, and the curtains to be drawn against the brilliant night.

The yellow moon had turned to silver as it climbed the sky, silvering the grey tile roof of Cliffs Edge House, lighting the high moorland outcrops with facets of black and white as the shadows moved. Stephen, far ahead, his bright hair flying, had a magpie-pierrot look in his black and white evening dress.

He reached the brow of the hill and took off his jacket, swinging it over his head like a banner, then leaped over the boulders like a stag. His limp gave him a curious uneven

116

bounding movement, not ungraceful, as he lept downwards and disappeared from sight.

Tom and Rose followed him. The tiny grass thistles and small loose stones hurt her feet but she did not complain. Her hand was warm in Tom's, and they were out in the fresh air, under the free sailing moon. The air smelled of sage, and the day's heat rose from the stone as they finally sank down on a low outcrop on the crest of the ridge. Stephen was nowhere in sight.

'He'll be all right,' said Tom. 'It's something we've always done when Aunt Angela gets too much for everyone. Dad started it – not quite so dramatically. He used to put his table napkin down and ask very politely if Aunt Angela would like to walk with us on the moor. Sometimes we had the horses out and rode, but she would never come, although she was once the best lady rider to hounds in the country.'

'Poor lady,' said Rose. 'To lose love must be terrible – but one should not throw away one's life.' She shrugged. 'But she is jealous. Mama was jealous, even of men she did not want. Tante Margaret did not know what jealousy meant. I do not think I am like that. I could be jealous too.'

The moor fell gently away from the ridge into a wooded valley where a narrow stream ran through meadows and coverts and they could see the twinkling lights of distant farms. Grazing sheep made white patches on the open moors. And beyond the stream, surrounded by fine trees and open parkland, stood a great house like a palace, built in three wings round a formal entrance of steps beneath a wide pedimented frontage, supported with pillars painted white by the moonlight.

Lights gleamed in the windows, and there were some carriages standing in the drive. A short distance from the house stood a small church, dwarfed by the great house and the ancient abbey ruins. Lights shone there too – Henry Grimshaw keeping vigil beside his love.

'Is that Danesfell Abbey?'

'Yes. It is also part of our kingdom.'

Her eyes widened disbelievingly. 'That *grand palais*? How can that be?'

'It was left to my Aunt Mildred, Dad's sister, by her husband who was an American millionaire.'

'So you and Stephen, you also are millionaires?'

Tom laughed. 'Well, I suppose if you added up all our assets it would amount to that!'

'But do you not wish to live there?'

'It is not Dad's style. Nor ours.'

'And you both work – you all work? You could be gentlemen and not work at all?'

'Yes. Well, Dad and I want to work, and Stevie tries – when he does he is very able indeed. But I don't think he is made for the trade.'

'But why do you work so?'

He shrugged. 'We play a great deal as well. But in a great industrial family like ours – wool men for generations – the family have to work. It's traditional. Or maybe we don't really want to be what are called "gentlemen".'

'And you despise them a little, yes? People like Alban Stoneberry?'

He smiled at her perception. 'Yes, perhaps we do. It is our defence.'

'And that is where he lives – in that great house?'

'Yes. His aunt and uncle lease it from us. He is their nephew and heir. He is still at Oxford – although he is at home now, of course.'

'And you have never lived there?'

'No, and as I said, never wanted to. Sometimes Stevie has had ambitions of being Lord of the Manor, but only fleetingly. His mind is too active for that sort of life.'

'I would like to live there and be a great lady,' she said naively.

'Then you will have to find a husband who is a nobleman. How about Alban?'

'I think of you,' she said. 'You are the lord of my heart.'

'Rose,' he said roughly, 'the time for dreaming is over. Tomorrow I go away. Back to camp. Everyone has been recalled.'

'But you cannot leave me here alone with that terrible lady, who does not want me. You cannot! I *cannot* live here.'

'I'm afraid you must. As I had to. Where else will you go? You will go back to school, of course, and finish your education. You are only fifteen.'

'And then – in the long summer – what shall I do? We, Tante Margaret and I, were going to Italy. Why cannot I live in the flat at Chelsea?'

'You are too young. You cannot live alone in London.'

'I should have Mrs Dyson.'

'It is impossible. Neither Dad nor I could permit it. And you will find it pleasant enough here. Stevie will be around and he has many friends. There is the Shawcross family – you're at school with Jane, and you know her brothers. There will be dances and tennis parties. Walking, climbing, riding if you wish to learn. There's an awful lot to do up here.'

She said unexpectedly, 'Who is this Arthur Sykes you and Stevie talk about so much?'

'Oh, he's my right hand man. What the workmen call "the gaffer", down at Britannia Mill. We must get someone to take over if I go away and he's the obvious choice. He is young and capable and knows the business from the ground up.' He saw the panic rise in her eyes and went on, 'Stevie is a splendid salesman and has an excellent eye for design. But Dad is failing – and this loss has struck him a blow. We want a chap who knows everything, like Dad does.'

'And you do?'

'Yes. A man who can manage men, who can cost and assess, a man who knows *our* business, not someone from outside. Nor an old chap with set ideas. So we have decided to offer Arthur my job – Managing Director.'

'I see.' Her attention switched away. Men's talk, out of her experience. The business of fashion – Margaret's business – she understood. Not the grubby, oil-smelling business of the factory.

She said thoughtfully, 'So that great house is where Alban Stoneberry lives?'

'Yes. Rumour has it they are trying to find him a wife.'

'He is someone I do not care to know. He has eyes like a . . .' She made ears of her forefingers and sniffled her nose, so that he started to laugh. '*Une belette.*'

'A weasel? Yet he is thought to be very handsome.'

'I do not think so. He looks at you only when he thinks you do not know. Tell me, Tom, where do you live?'

He pointed across the sweeping dale beyond the big house and the parkland to the rising tree-clad slopes beyond. Lights from one or two small villages shone brightly.

'Over there. It is a small farmhouse which I had converted. It is one of those white patches that stand out in the moonlight.'

'Can you take me there?'

'Not now – it is over ten miles away! Rose, be serious. Be good to my father while I am away. He has lost half his life now – and I shall not be here. I know Aunt Angela will resent you, and I know what that can mean. But he is very much alone.'

Her eyes filled with tears. She wanted, so passionately, to make him stay. She could not bear to think that he might meet with any danger. But like a good child, she said, 'I will try, Tom, I will try.'

He kissed her cheek gently. 'Bless you, darling. You'll charm her, as you charm everyone when you wish it.' He cupped his hands and called loudly, 'Steve!!' A shrill whistle came in reply from behind a granite outcrop, and Stephen appeared and plodded up towards them. 'I think we should go back, old chap,' said Tom, lifting Rose's hand. 'Rose will stay on – you'll have to look after each other.'

She smiled at Stephen. 'We don't have much choice, do we?'

'Well, that's fine,' Stephen said delightedly. 'I'll have someone while you're away, Tom. Someone who can be jolly.' He threw up his arms suddenly. 'Oh, God!' He put his arms around his brother and hugged him. 'I wish I was going with you, Tommy. Two Grimshaws would terrify the Kaiser. But at least I'll have Rose.' He hugged her too, and caught her other hand. 'Come on, let's run back to the mausoleum.'

The three of them raced down the hill full tilt, linked together, the two boys lifting Rose in flying leaps over stones and tussocks until they came to the wicket, when Tom took her shoes out of his pocket and put them on for her, and Stephen buttoned his collar and tied his black tie. Then they crossed the garden, where the roses were wilting and the

120

night-scented stocks and tobacco flowers perfumed the air, and went quietly back into the house.

Chapter Six

The following day Margaret was buried near her father and mother in the small church at Danesfell.

When Rose stepped out of the car and, with Tom and Stephen, followed Henry and Angela through the lych gate, she was astounded to see how many people were lining the pathway to the church porch, and how eagerly they leaned forward to catch a glimpse of the mourners driving up outside. Who were they wanting to see? The family – or the distinguished guests from London?

'Who are all these people waiting for?' she whispered to Tom.

'A funeral is an event here,' he replied. 'Especially this one. The old scandal surfacing again. To see how Stevie's mother is taking it. To see Mama's West End and Parisian friends. And to see you, my love. You are almost as much of a shock as I was twenty-five years ago.'

Henry glanced round at the watching faces with a nod of acknowledgement, removing his hat. He put his hand on Angela's with a brief protective gesture.

'Oh, he is a love!' Rose exclaimed, seeing Angela's spaniel glance of loving gratitude. For the first time she realised the deep loyalties on which this marriage had been built, and a sense of sadness filled her. Life seemed too big, too sad, and too puzzling to her. She felt Tom's hand close on her arm, and glanced at him with swift gratitude.

They walked along the aisle between the avenue of curious faces and she realised that she was the centre of attention. She heard the little murmur of surprise and knew it was not at her elegance or beauty but her foreign, eastern look, her dark skin, long black hair and almond-shaped eyes.

She was conscious of speculative eyes weighing her up. She could hear the question in their minds, especially those of the older people who could remember Lady Normanby's twin girls, Margaret and Charmian.

'So that's young Charmy's daughter,' they would be saying. 'I wonder who t'feyther was?'

She felt more alien in Thornsby than she had ever felt in her life. How could she possibly live here? She would be perpetually reminded of her own foreignness among these fair, grey-eyed, broad-speaking folk.

She felt an impulse to rise and flee. But where to?

Looking round frantically she met Sarah Dyson's faded blue eyes and loving smile, and the rising panic simmered and died. Her fingers tightened on each strong forearm, and both Tom and Stephen put their free hands reassuringly over hers. She gave a long shivering sigh. It *would* be all right. She *must* try. She must face this new life with courage and no antagonism.

The small coffin set on a carpet of red roses did not touch her, for her Margaret was no longer there. Her bright and steadfast spirit had vanished, flown away somewhere, never to return.

After it was all over, and the family stood in a conventional group with the Vicar, Rose was introduced to many people who had known her mother as a girl; who had known her grand-parents too, Sir Richard and Lady Normanby. 'She were the prettiest bride ever seen in these parts,' one old woman said. As Tom had said, the old scandal had revived and was buzzing among them, but there was also a genuine kindness and Rose was beginning to feel different. One side of her belonged here. Her mother's forebears had lived here for generations, and this was where she must now make her home – for she had nowhere else to go.

Sarah Dyson introduced her sister, saying, 'Daisy, this is my Miss Rose,' so proudly that Rose leaned forward and kissed her when she thanked her for coming.

A tall, ruddy-faced young man with a pronounced West Riding accent and a handshake like a vice was introduced to her. He was accompanied by a pleasant girl called Pamela – Mr and Mrs Arthur Sykes. The girl's greeting was a little wary, but Arthur said, 'I didn't know Tom's mother, Miss Abderhazy, but my folk did and they say she was a right grand girl. Mr Tom, what can I say? I'm right sorry. I'll be seeing you and Mr Stephen at t'mill tomorrow. We'll have to look after your old chap now. I know he set great store by your mother.'

'Thank you, Arthur,' Tom said, 'I'm lucky to have him still.'

A wave of desolation swept over Rose again and that was what frightened her. That Tom would not be there.

He left that week to rejoin his regiment and, a short while after, Rose returned to school.

Miss Smythe met her at Waterloo, taking over from Mrs Dyson, recalling the time when she had the feeling of being handed over from one person to another and sent anywhere they wished, like a parcel. But school, when she got back, was consolingly familiar and there was a real welcome for her.

Jane Shawcross, Head Girl now, said, 'I'm frightfully sorry about your aunt, Abderhazy,' and unexpectedly hugged her. 'She was such a ripping sport when we were all at Glockenschule.'

And little Marian Palmer had tears in her eyes and offered invitations for holiday visits and condolences from her family. For the first time Rose felt a sense of belonging. Here at last she had real friends.

The long lease of the flat at Riverside Mansions belonged to Tom now and Sarah Dyson agreed to stay on, because both Tom and Stephen would use it on their frequent trips to London. Apart from the lease and bequests to the staff and to personal friends, Margaret had left everything to Rose. Tom, she said, already had all the money he would ever need. Her assets amounted to something near fifty thousand pounds. Mr Brinkley was to continue to keep the business going until Rose was of age. He was Managing Director and owned a third of the shares. Miss Jenner also held a few shares – but the majority was left to Rose. Henry and Thomas Grimshaw were her guardians and held everything in trust for her until she was of age, when some decision would be made as to the

124

future of the business. If she wished to dispose of her interest in it, Mr Brinkley and Miss Jenner were to be offered the first opportunity of buying. She was now a rich young woman.

Rose worked hard that summer term, passing her exams and acquiring all the social skills she could. She wrote regularly to Tom and to Stephen, and small dutiful notes to Angela. A secretarial course had been started at Pendrill's and she took that too, with some vague idea that she might be able to help Angela in her charity work during the holidays.

In mid-July she once again travelled up to Thornsby for the summer holidays. She had done well at school. Her reports, duly sent to Henry, said that Rose had shown a welcome new sense of responsibility and a surprising talent for organisation. She wrote to Tom, tongue in cheek, saying it was all very boring and quite easy, it was just a matter of doing the best one could. And, please, did he still love her?

Stephen welcomed her home with open arms. The summer round of parties and tennis, flannel dances and picnics, was well under way.

A cousin, Stephen told her, especially a pretty one, was a useful asset as ready-made partner to protect him from predatory mothers with marriageable daughters.

But the rumours of war became a reality. On the 4th August 1914 England declared war, and the "invincible" German Army began its great sweep through Belgium towards the French Channel ports. Tom, who had a commission in the Yorkshire Light Infantry now, came home on embarkation leave. He would be in Thornsby for ten days, and Rose waited for his arrival with a painful mixture of joy and fear. He had changed. Before he had been a boy, although he had been a businessman too, accustomed to making decisions and handling men. But he was a trained soldier now, an officer, preoccupied, older – indeed, it seemed that in the few months since she had seen him, he had moved a generation away from her.

He spent most of his time at the Mill with Stephen, his father and Arthur Sykes, holding meetings, planning and discussing management for the future when he would be out of England.

He seemed remote from the social life that she and Stephen still shared. The county life and summer amusements went on among the big pleasant houses outside the busy, toiling town. Stephen had been teaching her to ride. She bought a fine bay mare and Angela, once a splendid horsewoman, was mollified by the presence of horses in the stables again, and acquired a trap and pony for short journeys when the threatened petrol shortages took effect.

Young men who had joined the yeomanry were being called up, but there were plenty of undergraduates and schoolboys in their senior terms – all of them fervently anxious to "Get in to it all before it's too late". Everyone said it would be over before Christmas. The German Army was personified in the press by two characters: "Kaiser Bill", a ferocious figure with a waxed moustache and spiked helmet, threatening the world, and "Little Willi", the Crown Prince of Germany, a weak reluctant figure trembling in his father's shadow. A joke enemy who could not possibly defeat the Allies.

Once the British Expeditionary Force got underway, then they would see! They were all so anxious that they would miss military service, these boys, and lifted on the waves of patriotism, the minute they were of age, they volunteered. The rich middle-class boys with whom Rose flirted and danced, the farmers' sons, young miners, mill hands and workmen of the town, left their jobs to become soldiers.

The local girls gazed at them with worshipful eyes. They had yearned after theatre and cinema heroes, but now the boys they had grown up with had become potential warriors.

Rose thought they were all mad, an unpopular opinion which she kept to herself or only spoke about with Stephen.

'Men!' she said witheringly. 'Are they all crazy? Why should they be so eager to meet death? They only have to wait, and he will come!'

Stephen was very close to her these days. He was suffering from a sense of inferiority caused by the patronising sympathy of his friends. 'Hard luck, old chap. It's rotten about that foot of yours. Still, your dad will need you at the Mill. Keep the home fires burning, eh?'

Which was true enough. Age was beginning to gnaw at Henry. His great vitality was wearing thin and he needed all the help he could get. Men at machines and first-rate management. But, most of all, he needed Tom.

During his embarkation leave, Tom was constantly at his father's side. In the evenings the three Grimshaws went to the club, talking with other men about the Germans' swift advance. The day before Tom left for France he spent at home, and so did Henry and Stephen. There was a constriction on everyone. Even Stephen seemed to have grown up over the past two weeks and was really getting to grips with his responsibilities. But that evening Henry could not disguise his anxiety and distress. He loved Stephen, but not as he loved Tom. He could not take his eyes from him. Angela managed to contain her jealous resentment. At least her boy was safe.

After dinner Tom took Rose's hand and without any preliminaries said, 'Let's go out and look at the moors again,' making it plain that he wanted to speak with her alone.

It was hot in the garden. The moon was only a thin silver nail paring, rising from the haze of Thornsby valley.

They sat in the rose garden on a seat which overlooked the smoky valley.

Tom had brought two jewellery boxes with him. He gave them to her. Rose opened them wonderingly. First a long string of pearls, identical to the string she had inherited from Margaret.

'Your mother's pearls,' he said. 'Old Papa Léon said they were to be given to you when you were old enough. He did not stipulate how old. I think you are old enough now. Certainly lovely enough.' He smiled. 'And these.' He opened the second case. 'I bought them at the sale of your mother's possessions.'

The cluster of thin bangles of chased yellow gold, studded with jewels forming minute flowers. Tom gave a shrug as though not quite understanding his own impulse. 'I wanted to buy something for you – although then I did not realise who you were. "Little Miss Nobody", I called you. I asked Papa Léon to give them to you, but he said it was not permissible at

127

your age. I told him to keep them until it was. I think it is now, don't you?'

She held out her arm and he slipped them one by one over her fine-boned hand. The ten circlets clinked musically together. She turned her wrists so that the stones glittered in the faint light. He saw tears, too, glittering on her cheeks.

'I remember sitting on Mama's bed playing with them,' said Rose, 'slipping them on her arm, then on my skinny little ones, and crying because they fell off. And she said, "But one day they will suit you best, *ma belle Arabe*." But there were twenty?'

'I only managed to buy these,' he said, 'I had a limited amount of money with me. I wanted to give them to you before I went back to England. You were such a funny little thing then, though it is not so long ago. I can remember you in that black hat and dress, and your hair in long plaits, saying, "I'm nobody – just someone who lives with Madame Respigny." You're beginning to bloom now, my Rosebud.'

She looked up at him pleadingly, and very tenderly he put his arms round her and kissed her.

'Tom – stay! Don't go back tonight. Stay just a little while longer.'

He drew the soft arms from around his neck, saying, 'When this war is over, Rose then I'll ask you many things . . . if you still want to hear them.'

'But, Tom, I want to hear them now. You may not return for ages.' She thought, but could not face the thought, Perhaps never, and hurried on again, 'It's not fair.'

He smiled. 'That is the reason why. I don't know when I shall be home. I must say goodbye to the family before I go. I have to catch the night express from Leeds, and Dad's car is going to take me there.'

They went back into the drawing-room, taking her mother's necklace and the ten thin Persian bangles, explaining Margaret's bequest and Tom's impulsive gift. The first things of her mother's Rose had ever possessed.

Then the car came round and they all went out while the chauffeur loaded Tom's case into the boot. And he stood there, tall in his new uniform, and embraced them one by one, his father closest and last. They stood on the step and

128

watched the car go down the drive and turn left towards the station and the train – to London, and the boat train, and so to France.

In 1916 Rose was eighteen. The war which was to end so soon now seemed to go on for ever. This term would be her last at Lady Pendrill's College. Like many girls of her age, she would once have left and gone to finishing school or to university but the war prevented that. There was a great deal of knitting of scarves and balaclavas and mittens and gloves for "our brave boys in Flanders", and first aid classes. Rose found these less boring than games or embroidery, and during her commercial classes found she had inherited Margaret's gift for organisation. The Head Mistress, an academic with feminist sympathies, suggested that after she had matriculated she might go on to university.

Rose looked at the grey-haired woman in her unexceptional tailored suit, and shook her head with a smile.

'Think about it, Rose. It seems you can do most things you set your mind to. Women today need every weapon they can get.'

'*Bien sûr*, Madame, but there are other weapons that I need which I cannot learn at school.'

The Head Mistress saw the mockery in the velvet eyes, and said, 'Quite.' She coughed – she was a travelled woman and had heard of the Baroness Abderhazy. 'So you have decided to leave at the end of the summer term?'

'Yes, Madame. I believe my guardian, Mr Grimshaw, has written to you?'

'Yes. I have had a letter today from Captain Grimshaw. He is your younger guardian?'

The colour rose and fell in Rose's cheeks.

'He is in England?'

'Yes. He is coming to see you the day after tomorrow. He has asked permission to take you out before he returns to France.'

So far he had written only combined letters to her and Stephen who had sent them on to her. They were irregular and uninformative. At first she wrote every week, and then every month, and then as irregularly as his replies. What was there to tell about school? All she wanted to tell him was to stay alive because she loved him.

The knowledge that he was alive, and in a few hours she would see him, made her tremble. She was glad to get away and run upstairs to the dormitory where she could sit alone until she could control her passionate relief and joy.

He had been staying in Chelsea for the past few days and drove down in Stephen's new car. He called for her just before noon. She was not in school uniform.

She ran out of the main door and stood looking down at him, vibrant with fear and delight. She came flying into his arms like a young swallow and he kissed her decorously, as a guardian should, gently on each cheek, then smiled as he helped her into the car.

It was a warm May day, with wild blue skies. In the gardens the blossom and spring flowers were out, and as they drove towards the downs and the coast, the young beech woods were flushed with the first pink buds that held the new green leaves.

Rose wore a dress by Margaret Normanby. A coat dress of a violet and grey tweed, her hair tied severely back with a large grey bow, and a purple beret pulled on to her neat smooth head. She wore a small collar of pale grey fur which framed her face deliciously. She sat with her hands folded, stealing covert glances at Tom, a handsome stranger with a clipped moustache. He kept his eyes on the road before him, not turning and laughing down at her, nor reaching for her hand.

They had lunch at an hotel near Arundel. She spoke of school, told him of her successes and her decision to leave this term. She heard herself gabbling home news. Jane Shawcross had joined the V.A.D.s and her two elder brothers were already in France.

'I have been in Yorkshire for ten days,' he said. 'The eldest Shawcross boy, Val, was killed.'

'Oh!' Her hands came up to her mouth. 'So soon?'

'Boys in command can die very soon out there,' he said. 'There was a service at Danesfell, and I went. Jane sent her love.'

130

He had two graven lines in his forehead now, like his father. He had changed. He was so much older. Thin and taut, drawn tight as a bow-string.

'*Val*?' she cried. 'I can't believe it! I saw him – at Christmas. He was in uniform for the first time. He was commissioned early, like you were. He was so proud and happy to go.'

'They are all proud and happy to go.'

'Were you?'

For the first time the blue eyes kindled. 'Not really. I just knew I had to.'

They did not speak a great deal over lunch. He ate hungrily, as though food – or perhaps good food – was a rarity. She tried to eat.

Afterwards he asked, 'What shall we do? Go somewhere? Perhaps there is a matinée at the theatre? Or there's sure to be a tea dance.'

'Which would you prefer? I can do any of those things at home.'

For the first time, he really smiled. 'I'm glad to hear you feel that Thornsby is home now. Come, let's drive up on to the downs and look at the sea.'

He drove fast and skilfully up the lanes, through the beech woods until they came to the downs and took the winding lane up to the top where he stopped the car. They could look down on the Channel, and the grey warships creeping in and out of a harbour far below. 'It's good to see trees with leaves on, and grass that's green. I came back through France after dark, so did not see any unscarred country until next morning – England seems like heaven.'

'Tell me about Val,' she said.

'There's nothing much to tell – he was in my command by pure coincidence, delighted to be with a Yorkshire regiment. When I came home I brought his things, the C.O. asked me to. Bits and bobs. The wrist watch the family gave him when he joined up. Family photos – two of his girl friend. Dad, Angela, Stevie and I were all at the Memorial Service. The Stoneberrys asked them to have it at Danesfell. The Vicar said he was our first local hero . . . Poor kid! He didn't have time to be heroic – a sniper got him on his first patrol. He died

131

in my arms – quickly, I'm glad to say.' He was silent for a long moment, then said, 'I got the sniper at dawn, creeping back from his post. I saw his body the next day – a youngster about the same age as Val, just as blond, could have been brothers.'

She was frozen with horror. All the newspapers, the speeches, the flag-waving, and fund-raising seemed irrelevant. This was the reality. She remembered Val with whom she had skated and snowballed at Glockenschule, with whom she had ridden and played tennis last year. At Christmas she had admired his uniform and teased him about his almost invisible moustache. Tom was so enraged by this terrible war. Tom, whom she loved, had killed a man, perhaps many men, had ordered his men to kill. Tom, who could not bear to see any living thing mistreated.

She gave a long shudder and suddenly put her arms about him and her head down on his shoulder, shaking from head to foot. His arms closed about her. She felt his lips against her hair.

'At home no one could understand,' he said, bitterly, 'except Father, and perhaps Stevie in a way. He has been humiliated by his exemption. This war is making us, as a family, richer than ever before. Everyone up there in Thornsby is filled with pride and patriotism – or greed. It's like some mad dream.'

'But you were so patriotic when it started. And I did not want you to go.'

'No. I never felt like that, Rose. I knew it was inevitable, and that we would have to face it, and the better equipped I was, the better I could do the job. It is what keeps us going in the trenches, the Germans as well. Both sides know they *have* to win, even at this terrible cost. We cannot withdraw. Neither can they.'

'Where do you go for short leaves?'

'To Paris.'

'Ah, tell me about Paris now. Is it still so beautiful?'

'It is a queer oasis, full of men who do not have to fight, and men who have to be back at the front in a few hours. Men who have staff jobs and never go up to the line, and men who have escaped for a few days from the filth and the eternal noise of gunfire and the stench of death. Or men being shifted in bloody train loads into hospital trains, or back to the line after repair. Cabarets are still going, drink still flowing, girls still laughing and men dancing with them. There are many men there hiding like rats, men who have run away from it all, who will get shot if they are caught, and are called cowards. Why? They've just come to the end of their endurance – I don't blame them. There are different limits to what men can endure. They want helping, not killing.'

'Why don't you run away? Your father and Stevie would hide you? We would never give you away. You have given it three years. It is surely enough?'

He laughed and stroked her hair, 'Baby! You are still a baby.'

She said hopelessly, 'Alban Stoneberry only enlisted in December, just before conscription came in. His aunt and uncle were pressing him to go.'

'I know,' he said bitterly, 'they would, the flag-wavers! I heard a chap last week make a crack at Arthur Sykes. He is in a reserved occupation. He works all hours, and so do my father and Stevie and every man-jack in the mills to keep those machines turning out the stuff they need. Every now and then Arthur cracks and wants to chuck the job in and enlist, and Dad tells him that it is the easiest thing in the world to get shot, if that's what he wants, but to keep those mills going needs a different kind of courage. And Stevie . . . people don't notice his foot. It is so slight a deformity. Girls ask him why he isn't in uniform. Fellows who are in uniform patronise him, even if they have safe blighty jobs. They make me sick.'

'Yet you will go back, Tom. When?'

'Tonight. So let's enjoy this day. Let's walk, Rose. I can't see enough of it all – come along. To see it with you, still safe and sweet, makes it worthwhile.'

They walked to Cissbury Ring and then climbed to the top of that ancient fortress, looking down over the roofs of the town below. From far away, like a tremble in the air, could be heard the distant sound of heavy guns. Tom stood shielding his eyes against the summer light. Rose searched his face and saw with anguished tenderness that there were already touches of grey in the thick fair hair above his temples. It

133

seemed to her that he was surrounded by an army of ghosts. Boys who had put on uniform and disappeared into France, never to return. She pulled off her beret and the ribbon from her hair, and shook it loose so that it blew and coiled about them, the long tendrils flicking across his face.

'Tom,' she said seriously, 'we are here alone on the top of the world – quite alone. Will you not love me here, while you can, before you go away? I am not a child now, Tom, and I want this so much.'

He remembered when he had first seen her, that small sea-nymph swimming in the blue Mediterranean waters, with the black hair floating about her like sea weed, entangling his heart and imagination.

'You are a witch, Rose,' he said. 'You think if that happened I would never go back. You must not try to put spells on me. Now I must take you back to school, and be on my way.'

He drove her back to Pendrill's and she sprang out of the car stricken beyond words, feeling as though her heart was being torn from her breast. She ran up the steps and stood in the porch above him, frantically twisting the violet beret in her hands.

'I cannot say goodbye to you,' she said.

He came slowly up the steps until he stood just below her, and then reached up and took her face in his hands, kissing, or trying to kiss, the fear from her eyes before he kissed her lips.

'We won't say goodbye. Say *au revoir*. You have said that to me so often. I will come back when I can, and when the fighting is finished we will talk again, about ourselves. I love you so much. You love me now but you are very young. Don't build your dreams on me, my Rose. Don't feel you belong to me. Do not believe that I am the only man you could love. Now, just say *au revoir*.'

She said it. The tears were pouring down her face and he could taste their salt as he kissed her once again. Then he ran down the steps and turned the car towards London, on his way to France, and the long, troop-crowded journey across the Channel towards the pounding guns.

Rose ran straight upstairs into the dormitory, throwing herself on her bed, covering her ears with a pillow so she could not hear him drive away.

July and the end of term came at last, and Prize Day with its traditional procession of the whole school, garbed in maidenly white, flowing down the wide staircase into the main hall.

Younger fathers and elder brothers were conspicuously absent this year, but Stephen came down and it was a delight to see his bonny fair hair in the front row when Rose went up to take her certificates and prizes.

At tea afterwards she introduced him to all her friends, and their eyes lit up at the sight of an eligible young man, even if he was not in uniform. Little dark-haired Marian Palmer, who was also leaving this term, went pink and speechless when he took her hands and Stephen, true to form, was particularly charming to her. Rose was accustomed to his subtle handling of women – he made the plain ones feel pretty, and the pretty ones feel beautiful.

The afternoon was given over to the annual Garden Party in aid of the Red Cross. Stephen spent a lot of money at the stalls on items which he gave back for re-sale, and left early for London.

'One night of fun,' he said. 'A theatre, dinner, then back to Thornsby and toil. I wish you could come back and spend it with me.'

She laughed and said, 'You won't spend it alone, I know, darling Stevie. But I'll be back at the end of the week. If you're staying at Chelsea, give Sarah my love and tell her I will be there quite early.'

'She's not there – she's home with her sister on holiday.'

On her way north she spent some hours in London. She had planned to do some shopping and have a light lunch at one of the Regent Street stores. Halfway down she met Alban Stoneberry, a lieutenant's pip on his shoulder. His strange pale eyes lit with pleasure at the sight of her. As though, she thought, I am some kind of bon-bon for which he has a particular taste.

'Mademoiselle Abderhazy,' he saluted punctiliously, 'how nice to see you. And what are you doing alone in London on this fine morning?'

'Looking at the shop windows like the rest of the women.'
A mischievous impulse to tease him made her add, 'And you,
M'sieur – or should I say Lieutenant Stoneberry – what are
you doing alone in London?'

'I am on my way home – ten days' leave.'

In Yorkshire she was always surrounded by friends and
admirers, and he knew she avoided him. In her flowered pink
and blue summer dress, and plain straw hat with one large
rose, she looked exquisite, the essential English freshness of
her clothes accentuating her dark beauty.

She had grown tall and slim and graceful now. He remembered her at that first meeting at Glockenschule when she had
been so very young, but even then so precocious and so
desirable, and how he had dreamed of monopolising her so
that the other boys would envy him. He had wondered if Tom
Grimshaw had been her lover? Surely she had been too
young. But even then she had been a temptress, with none of
the shy self-consciousness of the English girls. There was a
mixture of innocence and mockery about her that made anger
buzz in his mind like a hornet, and yet filled him with desire.
To see her again so unexpectedly – and alone – filled him
with excitement.

Listening to older men round his uncle's dinner table after
the ladies had retired, and more recently in the Officers'
Mess, he had heard men say that a man could always tell when
a woman was available. But now, confronted with Rose, he
was at a loss. He did not know how to take her, and she knew
this. He could see the laughter in her eyes. It made him stiff
with self-consciousness.

'And what are your plans for today, Miss Abderhazy?'

'Oh, do not be so formal, Alban. We have known each
other a long time now.' Her head tilted charmingly. The
unfathomable dark eyes met his. She certainly had not included Alban Stoneberry in her plans. But he was in uniform
now, and she remembered Val Shawcross, shot down on his
first patrol, and thought that even if she did not like Alban, he
too would soon be going to France. So she said gently, 'Well, I
have just bought some perfume, and I was going into a tea-
shop or store for a sandwich and some coffee before going on
to Thornsby.'

'Then – will you lunch with me?' he said eagerly.

'Why not? That would be very nice.'

'Where would you like to go? Anywhere. The Ritz? The Savoy?'

'Oh, no! Those grand places are not fun. I like to go to the bohemian and interesting places where Tante Margaret went with her friends – or where I go with Stephen and Tom when they are in London. "Customer's chop-shops" they call the grand places, because they take customers there. How about the Café Royal? You see all the painters and writers there . . . or the Criterion? Or the Monico?'

'The Monico?' He was horrified. 'It has a terrible reputation!'

'Has it?' she asked innocently. 'But the food is very good indeed. And, anyway, there are heaps of little places in Soho. I love Italian cooking. How about Pinoli's?'

She was enjoying herself. She knew perfectly well that Alban's aunt and uncle would think that no well-bred young lady would go to any of these places, or certainly not without a chaperone. But Sir Miles and Lady Stoneberry were what Stephen and Tom called "Country stuffies", and had made Alban one too.

His face darkened. He said shortly, 'Wherever you please.'

She relented. 'Let us go to the Trocadero. It is considered very respectable now.'

So they went to the Trocadero and had a splendid lunch among the cream paint, gilt and palms, the officers and theatre girls. Alban ordered champagne at once and after two glasses was talking more freely and becoming a little more suggestive in his manner. Rose, barely touching her wine, listened to him with a gravely attentive face, her siren's eyes glinting her concealed laughter. Disliking him, yet sorry for him.

He suggested oysters.

'But are they not an aphrodisiac?' she said innocently. 'Do you intend to take me to bed after lunch?'

He was shocked and startled. But the champagne still talked. No good girl, he thought, would say such a thing.

137

'I would like to,' he said crazily. 'You drive me mad, Rose. You always have. Tell me – have you ever – ?' He foundered, realising too late that she had been teasing him and he was now in impossible depths. He went scarlet and began to rise to his feet, then became conscious that people were watching him.

She caught his arm, laughing at him, shaking her head. She made him feel a young idiot – as though he was years younger than herself, instead of five years older.

'Alban, you want to know too much. Do you suppose that any girl of my age would tell you such things, even if they were true? You must learn to laugh. Let us choose. It is very hot, and I am not hungry. I will have half a lobster with some mayonnaise and a small salad. That will be delicious. Then we will have raspberries. They are in season, and they are fruit from God's garden. And the Turkish coffee here is very good. That will be a lovely lunch.'

The rest of the meal passed happily enough. Rose did not tease and managed to keep him talking about himself, which she found excessively boring as it was mostly about his aunt and uncle and their tight-fisted refusal to give him an adequate allowance, until now. Neither at school nor university had they given him a decent allowance. To her, the meeting was a waste of an afternoon. She was sorry for him, as she was sorry for all young soldiers.

But to Alban her cosmopolitan charm and sophistication, the elegance of her clothes and the exotic beauty of her face and ripening young body went to his head like wine. He thought, as he had thought at their first meeting, that to possess such a girl would be to possess the world.

He tried to delay her, keep her with him. He implored her to come to a matinée or to the cinema. Would she like to go up the river to tea?

'You must. It is my last day in England,' he said.

'You are going to France?'

For the first time her eyes were not teasing but genuinely concerned and kind. The newspapers had proclaimed an Italian victory, but she knew that it was a minor triumph and they were using it to disguise the appalling stalemate on the Western Front. Battles where one side or the other gained or lost a little ground, losing hundreds of men for a trivial advance. And Tom was out there again. It was a nightmare – she was never free of it.

She said compassionately, 'I am very sorry. You will be in great danger. I will think of you, and pray for you.'

His face filled with delight. 'Will you write to me?'

She shook her head. 'No, I would rather not. I have many things to do when I get back to Cliffs Edge – I write many letters for my aunt, and for wounded men in hospital, when I am home and of course I write to Tom every week. I cannot write more letters.'

Outside, as she stood drawing on her gloves, he still tried to detain her. She signalled to the doorman to call her a taxi, declined once more his pressing offer to escort her anywhere she wished, and gave him her hand.

'Goodbye, Alban. Perhaps we shall meet at Thornsby one day. Let us hope the war will be soon be over. I wish you a safe return. *Au revoir.*'

She left him staring after her taxi and thought, He is a fool, poor boy. I do not like him. I wish him well, but I do not want him in my life.

She decided to go up to Thornsby the following day. She had left her shopping and luggage at Hanover Street, and taken a cab to Chelsea. She had never stayed at the flat alone, and it seemed quite exciting to do so. She was just eighteen now and quite used to travelling alone. Sarah might be cross if she heard, but she could easily get round Sarah. One day more in London? Or why not two? She could go to some galleries and perhaps a matinée. It would be fun. She would telephone Stephen at the office and tell him not to expect her until the day after tomorrow.

At Riverside Mansions no smart uniformed porter hurried out to meet her and take her parcels. He had been called up some time ago. An ancient man in an equally ancient uniform came in, sorted out the newspapers and letters, swept the hall and made a pretence of polishing the front brass. He locked the outer door at eight o'clock. An unknown individual came in to stoke the boilers and at least the bathwater was still moderately hot – in the winter Sarah managed to get a ration of coal delivered. Riverside Mansions was acquiring a wartime look. Its tenants were just as distinguished and its address as prestigious, but like the ancient man in the hall a little the worse for wear.

Rose walked up to the first floor, not wanting to burden the ancient with her parcels by asking him to operate the lift.

She let herself into the flat, and went into the drawing room to set down her parcels. The blinds were drawn against the sun, but she could see that Sarah had left everything as pristine as ever. She went back into the hall and then froze, aware of another presence, of Tom's bedroom door ajar, and of a faint but pervasive smell of whisky, dirt and sweat. She thrust the door open and switched on the light.

He was asleep in bed and did not stir when the light went on. Above the sheet his arms and splendid shoulders were naked. He slept heavily, snoring a little like a drugged man, his eyes sunk into dark shadows of weariness. His clothes and kit were thrown into an untidy heap on the floor. She lifted the crumpled jacket, automatically straightening it, and went to the side of the bed. She bent and stroked the thick fair hair from his forehead, and kissed his dry lips.

'Tom,' she whispered. '*Mon pauvre bien aimé.*'

He stirred irritably, caught her hand without opening his eyes or turning his head, saying irritably, '*Toni?* Shut up. *J'ai besoin de dormir.*'

She clapped her hand across her mouth, stifling the spurt of laughter. Toni? Some pretty Parisienne whore? Rose hoped she had given him some hours of peace and pleasure.

'*Bien sûr,*' she whispered again. '*Dormez bien, Tom, mon amour.*'

She flew back to her room, pulled off her pretty hat and threw it down. Then with deft fingers she undid her clothes – everything – silken underwear, silk stockings, shoes, until she stood like an ivory statue. Then she raised her arms, undoing her long black hair. She went back into Tom's room and slid down between the sheets, winding her arms around him.

'*Dors, dors, mon petit soldat.*'

He groaned and turned, sweaty and smelling of whisky, and Rose drew him close into her arms and held his sleeping head against her breast.

140

Chapter Seven

Tom smiled without opening his eyes, stretched a heavy arm across her, stroked her breasts and was asleep again in seconds. She lay trembling with delight, in the hot, darkened room, watching the afternoon sunlight making pencils of light through the curtain chinks and creeping slowly across the floor and walls.

She woke up about seven o'clock but it was another hour before he stirred and began to caress her, his lips moving across her breasts from nipple to nipple until she was roused unbearably, crying out with desire. Almost automatically he took her, murmuring, caressing, grumbling absurdly and wearily, until he remained motionless in her arms, instantly asleep again. It had been agonising but it had been glorious. She silently blessed the unknown Toni who must have sometimes helped him forget the thunder of the guns.

She could feel the wetness between her thighs. In the dawn, she rose. She saw the tell-tale red stain beneath, and drew the upper sheet high across Tom. She rose and bathed, put on a silk kimono, and when she returned to the bedroom Tom was lying awake, his blue eyes puzzled, still half-asleep, the two graven frown lines deep in his forehead.

He had been alarmed by the silence – no sound of distant gunfire or smell of Paris in the dawn – and then he recognised his room in Chelsea, and sat up with a start, remembering the sweet warm female presence in his arms last night.

It had not been the illusion of an over-weary brain, or the three neat whiskies taken at Victoria Station before climbing into a taxi, falling asleep until it stopped outside Riverside

Mansions. He got in at the flat door with the help of the driver, stumbling in, dropping his kit on the floor, finding his bed, stripping and falling flat on his face, instantly asleep. But the night presence had been so vivid. He could still smell the girl's scent and warm clean skin. He sat on the edge of the bed and twitched back the covers and saw the small, telltale red stain upon the sheet.

The door opened softly and Rose stood there, pale and heartbreakingly lovely in a silk kimono, her long black hair loose about her, dark eyes glowing with love.

'Oh, Christ!' He held out his arms and she flew into them. 'Rose, my darling, my darling, what have I done?'

She leaned back, linking her arms about his neck, smiling.

'Ah, what indeed, my friend, my Tom, my love? You have loved me most painfully, and most beautifully, and now I am always yours for ever.' She kissed his bare breast, slow, loving kisses, lifted her lips to his mouth, then said, 'I was as good, I hope, as this Toni, for whom you seemed to mistake me? *Une Parisienne, n'est ce pas?*'

He began to speak, but she put her hands imperiously across his lips. '*Fut!* I am not jealous of this Toni, or any other lady in your past, or anyone before me. What you have done with them has taught you much – you are a man and this is what I love. So do not look at me so! This is our wedding morning!' He held her very close, serious, still unsmiling. 'What is the matter? You are not angry with me because I have tricked you into loving me?'

'I am not angry,' he said, 'I am caught in a trap. I got in from France last night straight from H.Q. I've been recalled and I don't know why as yet.' He looked quickly at his watch, relieved when he saw how early it was. 'I might have slept through the morning. I have an appointment at the War Office today, and was out to the world. I thought I was dreaming. But you are here, my love. And so is this.' He flipped back the upper sheet, exposing the small red stain. Rose's cheeks burned, but she was not ashamed. 'This is not a dream, is it, Rosebud?'

'I do not like this word "trap"!' she blazed. 'Am I a trap? I am here and I love you, and I am sure you love me. Last night we were very happy. At least, I thought, we will belong to

142

each other before you go back to those hellish guns. It is enough for me – is it not enough for you?'

'If that was all, it would be so easy. But I'm not on leave. We cannot rush up to Yorkshire and get Dad's blessing and a special licence. I can tell you a little of what's in store for me. My C.O. thinks I would be the right man for a certain job. It is to organise something which has not yet begun. He put my name forward. If I am chosen, I shall have to leave at once. If not I shall go back to France tonight. Either way, I have scarcely twenty-four hours.'

Her eyes were tragic. Her mouth trembled like a child's and he held her tenderly as though, indeed, she was a beloved child.

'I thought,' she said, 'that we should have ten days together before you went back and I would be afraid for you again. But,' her eyes lit up, 'maybe you are not going back to that terrible Western Front. At least that is something.'

'I don't know yet where I shall be sent. Perhaps, if I'm given the job, I shan't be able to tell you where!'

She folded her arms across her breasts like a French marketwoman. 'So! Like all the women in this war, I must wait and hope and pray! You men are so clever with your games of war. And power – and making money. But you *never* learn!' Her arms went round him again, 'But you will write to me?'

'As soon as I can, I promise. Perhaps by the New Year I shall be home again. But you will say nothing at home about this? They must not know I was in England.'

'I promise.'

'I must get dressed. My appointment is at eleven.'

'I will get coffee for you. There is no food in the place because Sarah is away. But when you return I will have something ready. I am very hungry myself.'

There was coffee and some tinned milk, a tin of biscottes from Fortnum and Mason and a jar of honey. She brought the tray to the bedside table.

'It is delicious,' he said. He adored her. She was so very French, so practical, so very touching, so young.

'As delicious as the breakfast that Toni gave you?' she asked wickedly.

143

He kissed her honey-smeared lips. 'Much better – and for free!' which made her laugh.

It was very strange. Remembered words came back to him – "Hold to the here, the now, through which all futures hurry to the past." He caught her up against him, burying his face against her, kissing below her chin and down to the small breasts beneath the pale silk, feeling her instant shivering response of abandonment. 'You are a devil child, my darling. Without conscience or shame and with a gift for love.'

'And are you ashamed?'

'No – I'm guilty. I'm not a lad of nineteen. I am twenty-seven. But, God knows, it was heaven, and I cannot wish it any different. I only wish we had had more time to think.'

'If we had thought, it would not have happened, and it might not have been so wonderful.'

'Oh, you babe!' He rose. 'I must go. But you will be here when I return?'

'*Bien sûr.*'

He bathed and changed into a civilian suit. When he had gone she dressed and took his uniform to a local valet service for brushing and pressing, and polished his brown boots until they shone. She had her ration book with her and bought bread and butter, an expensive unrationed pheasant, some new potatoes and young peas. She had not cooked since she had left Respy's flat in Nice, but she knew how.

She took a good bottle of Montrachet from the store cupboard. She would leave a note for Sarah saying she had friends to lunch. She telephoned Stephen, telling him not to expect her until the following afternoon.

Tom came back in the mid-afternoon. He could smell the roast as soon as he put his key in the door. In the dining-room Margaret's pretty octagonal table was set with flowers and silver, and a bowl of peaches. There was a fresh green salad waiting to be dressed and served. Rose had made a home-coming party for him.

She came out of the kitchen, her face flushed from the heat of the oven, and knew immediately she met his eyes that he had been accepted for the mission. And he saw for the first time yet another facet of this diamond-cut girl. Not the siren,

144

not the petulant, imperious child, but a woman who loved him completely.

'I have to go tonight,' he said.

'We have a little time – we must use every minute.' They ate and talked and laughed as though time went on forever. The afternoon sped through its remaining hours. When Tom rose to put on his uniform and go and catch his train, he asked her not to come to Victoria with him. 'There will be many troops leaving, *chérie*, and nowadays stations are full of tragic goodbyes.'

He left at seven. She went to a front window and watched him walk away with that quick, swinging walk. He stopped a taxi and in a second had gone.

She went back to the tumbled bed. At least he had not gone into that muddy hell in France. He had gone to some unknown destination, mysterious and unpredictable as the moorland mist above Cliffs Edge.

Presently, she rose and dressed. She poured coffee over the blood stain on the sheet. She made up Tom's bed with fresh linen, leaving his razor, tooth brush, dressing gown and the things he always kept there.

Then she went to her own room and rumpled the bed slightly before she made it up, and tossed the coffee-stained sheet into the laundry basket. She wrote a note to Sarah apologising for spilling her morning coffee on the bed. She washed the dishes and put them away, scraped the remains of the meal into the bin and put it out on the fire staircase.

She lay awake for a long while, thinking how strange and wonderful that day had been – a lifetime of love condensed into a few hours.

That afternoon they had rested together in his room, and had made love again, and she learned how different it could be from the previous night, when she had only been a comfort in the darkness, a night's release from the murdering guns.

This time it had been bright and clear and full of a shimmering delight, and she had thought that every time of loving in the future would be like this.

Before he left her, he had said, 'You could be pregnant, Rose. It is possible. If that should happen, go to my father and Stevie and tell them everything.'

145

'You mean – if you should not come back?'

'Yes.'

'But you will come back. I will not think of anything else.'

He smiled, and touched her cheek. 'When I come back' – he could not bring himself to say "if", or blur her wonderful, childish confidence in any way – 'we will get married. And, dearest love, please get out of London. Don't sleep here alone. There are too many raids.'

'It does not worry me,' she said, 'all I want in this whole world is that you should come back to me.'

He held her close and kissed her, then without another word picked up his kit and was gone. It felt to Rose as though a part of her heart went with him.

There was a raid that night and Rose lay awake listening to the distant explosions, watching the searchlights sweep across the sky. In the morning she took a cab to King's Cross, and as she followed the porter along the platform saw Alban Stoneberry.

He was in uniform, standing by the entrance to a first-class carriage.

His face lit up when he saw her and he came straight forward to meet her.

'You did not tell me you were travelling north today?'

'I did not know myself,' Rose shrugged. His persistence was becoming irksome. 'I decided to stay at the flat overnight and travel today.'

'You will allow me to accompany you to Leeds?'

She thought, *Merde*! But she said politely, 'No, thank you.' And searching for an excuse, saw to her delight and relief her schoolfriend, Marian Palmer, standing with her family and a load of luggage further along the platform.

'I am sorry, Alban, I do not think it would be proper. And I am travelling up with Marian Palmer, my friend, so you will excuse me.' She ran off towards the family group, waving her hand, and Marian, delighted, ran forward to meet her.

'Are you travelling to Leeds?' asked Rose.

'Yes. How wonderful!' Marian cried, as they embraced. 'We're all going up to Yorkshire. Daddy wants us all to be out of London because of the raids, especially now the aeroplanes are coming. I said it would be nice to be near you and the

146

Shawcross family who are my friends. At least I should know someone. Daddy has taken a furnished house near Danesfell village.'

Marian looked extremely pretty in a dress of amber-coloured shantung and a summery hat trimmed with buttercups.

'How smart you look,' cried Rose. 'And did you go to Margaret Normanby?'

'Yes,' Marian glowed, 'I took your card as you suggested. It was frantically expensive but Mama is very pleased with me. In fact, she let me have two more dresses. Now, come and meet my father – you met Mummy and the others at Glockenschule.'

Mr Palmer was not travelling with the family, but said he hoped to visit them on occasional weekends. He smiled approvingly at Rose as he greeted her.

'The charming Miss Abderhazy of whom I hear so much. How do you do, my dear?'

Rose smiled, gave him the little French courtesy bob – old-fashioned but delightful.

'May I please travel up with your family? I have no booking and Alban Stoneberry wants to take charge of me.' She pulled an expressive little face. 'Imagine trying to make conversation with Alban all the way to Leeds. *Mon dieu*, I do not fancy that! And I do not think Mrs Grimshaw, my guardian's wife, would approve at all.' She added appealingly, 'He is rather persistent, as you know.'

'Of course, my dear, we shall be delighted to have you,' said Mrs Palmer. 'We have plenty of room, and will be glad of your company. Where is your luggage?'

'Over there. The school trunk. And I've been doing quite a lot of shopping in London. Alban seems to be keeping guard over it.'

'Daddy, please . . .' Mrs Palmer said to her husband, who laughed, walked smartly up to Alban, introduced himself, shook hands briefly and took charge of Rose's luggage, summoning a porter to see it aboard the train.

'What joy!' Marian said. 'This is the last time we have to travel with those beastly school trunks!'

147

They settled into the first-class carriage, Mrs Palmer, Marian, three schoolboy Palmers, and Marian's fox terrier. Around them were strewn a luncheon basket, sewing bags, magazines, books, Mrs Palmer's knitting bag, various treasured tennis racquets, and even a cricket bat belonging to the boys.

'Jack always assumes that every carriage we travel in is exclusively ours,' Mrs Palmer said, patting the terrier who sat aggressively on guard near the platform window. 'It's very useful. See, here comes Daddy. He had to be back at the House this afternoon or he would have travelled up with us.'

Mr Palmer came into the carriage, kissed his family affectionately, patted Jack the terrier, shook Rose's hand, promised to come up and see them as soon as possible, and stepped down as the guard's whistle sounded and the train moved out of the station.

'Have you met this young Mr Stoneberry, Marian?' Mrs Palmer asked.

'Yes, and so have you. Don't you remember, at Glockenschule? When Rose was there with her aunt, Madame Léon?' Marian giggled. 'He was frightfully sweet on you, Rose. He used to trail about after you with a hopeful expression.'

'Like old Jack when there's a lady dog around,' said one of the boys, and all three of them collapsed with laughter.

Switzerland seemed such a long time ago now – a fairytale dream when they had all been so young, and there had been no war, and she had waltzed in Tom's arms through a magic world of starshine, a glittering world of snow and ice and coloured lanterns and laughter. Where she had still been a child in heart and mind and Tom still a boy, a young man but still a boy, not a strong experienced man, sickened by slaughter, weighted with the responsibility for other men's lives.

Mrs Palmer watched Rose thoughtfully, remembering her as an alluring young thing, provocative and over-sophisticated, daringly playing the accepted role of film vamp, with all the boys buzzing around her like intoxicated bees. She had been a child who already knew the power of her exotic beauty and delighted in exploiting it. The chatter between the two girls now was the usual schoolgirl exchange,

148

and yet – Rose had changed. There was something quite different about her. A maturity. It was as though she was talking to Marian and the boys in a language she had forgotten.

She was, as always, beautifully dressed. She had put up her hair, wearing it coiled on the nape of her slender neck like a girl from the Russian ballet – and in the lavender marocain dress and severely chic hat trimmed with one large pink rose, Mrs Palmer saw the stamp of Madame Léon's taste in everything about her.

'I was very sorry to hear about your aunt's passing, Rose. She was so young – and such a brilliant woman.'

Rose looked up with one of her rare gleams of limpid sincerity. 'She was very kind and wise, and I did not have her long enough. We had just learned to love each other very much.'

There was a small pause in the chatter, then she turned to Marian and asked, 'Who looked after you at the salon? Miss Jennings?'

'Oh, no – she was far too grand for me. She always seemed to be looking after Duchesses and such. It was a small, rather pretty girl with a Cockney accent. Known, I believe, as third sales.'

'Betty Briggs?' Rose said in surprise. 'She certainly advised you very well.'

'I found her excellent,' said Mrs Palmer. 'At first I thought her rather a common little thing for such a place. But she picked exactly the right styles for Marian, and for me. I was tempted, and treated myself to two dresses.'

'I'm so glad.'

'And she suggested some alterations – that hidden pleat for instance.' Mrs Palmer, delighted that her shy little duckling was showing signs of developing into a pretty little swan, indicated a clever insertion which made Marian's fashionable tight skirt easy to walk in. 'She made clever little sketches showing us how it would look.'

There was a tap at the window and they all looked up. Alban Stoneberry slid the door open and saluted smartly. Jack bustled across, with lifted lip, and growled warningly. The three schoolboys stared with round eyes.

'Lieutenant Stoneberry?' Mrs Palmer said questioningly.

He asked if he could order them some coffee. Mrs Palmer thanked him but said they had ample provisions. He hesitated, then asked Rose if she would care to lunch with him in the dining room. Rose said gently that Mrs Palmer had brought a luncheon basket, and that she was rather hot and tired after all her shopping, and hoped to get a little rest during the afternoon. Alban's narrow-set eyes flickered – a curious, rapid glance, like the dart of a snake's tongue – and he coloured, almost as though her refusal had been an insult, and said, 'Perhaps some other time?', before closing the door and going towards the dining car.

All the Palmer children burst out laughing.

'Marian! Boys!' exclaimed Mrs Palmer, 'Really!'

'He's still absolutely swoony about Rose,' said Marian.

'Poor Alban,' said Rose, 'I don't like him a bit. But all the boys I know seem to be disappearing into this dreadful war, and since I learned about poor Val Shawcross, I can't be horrid to any of them.'

Mrs Palmer, whose eldest boy had just enlisted straight from school, agreed. 'But there's no immediate worry about Alban,' she said. 'My husband knows his uncle quite well. Apparently Alban is going to a junior staff position in Paris.'

'Oh.' Rose was silent, then smiled, 'I didn't ask where he was going – I just assumed that it would be to France. Which, of course, it is.'

'Yes,' Mrs Palmer said dryly, 'Paris *is* in France. And Alban's uncle, Sir Miles, has friends at the Ministry of Defence.'

'He was a dreadful funk on the ski slopes,' said the eldest Palmer boy, a gangling twelve year old, 'and someone told me he was a pig of a bully at school when he was a prefect.'

'Johnny! You really must not repeat school gossip.'

'Well, I remember he wouldn't go up on the ski lift,' Johnny said defiantly. 'I did when I was only a kid, and came down with Daddy holding my hand.'

'You are still only a kid,' said Marian. 'But it's true, Alban *was* pretty hopeless in Switzerland.'

150

'Some people cannot stand heights,' Mrs Palmer said, 'That's quite understandable. And quite enough of this subject.'

Presently they had lunch from the ample luncheon basket, and afterwards Rose took off her pretty hat and put it on the rack, curled up in the corner and tried to sleep. But she did not sleep. She thought about Tom.

One by one the chattering children fell quiet, and Marian and Mrs Palmer repacked the basket and followed Rose's example. But they were really asleep. Rose wanted to turn and toss, but kept still, not wanting to waken them. She thought of Alban Stoneberry going to a "cushy job" in Paris. And where was Tom going? To some unknown place which might or might not be dangerous. When she had found him in the flat she had been so overwhelmed that he was safe and with her, even for a few hours, that she had been able to think only of their immediate happiness; their entwined bodies lying in the darkened bedroom through all that summer afternoon, and being lifted out of the world as he guided her through rising waves of pleasure into an ecstatic climax of love. She smiled slowly to herself, drifting into a light sleep.

She was wakened abruptly by the slight shudder of the train as it slowed down at some village halt, and the growl of the watchful terrier. She felt she was being watched, glanced up and saw Alban staring down at her through the corridor window. Instantly she pretended to be sleeping again. She was frightened by something in the way he was looking at her, intense and predatory. The terrier burst into a volley of indignant barking, the train jerked as the signals were changed, everyone began to wake up. Jack went grumbling back to his seat and curled up again. Alban had vanished.

'What on earth was the matter with Jack?' asked Mrs Palmer. She looked at Rose's pale face, 'What happened?'

'Nothing really.' She stretched as she sat up. 'The train stopped and I woke suddenly. Someone was standing in the corridor watching me as I slept. What you call a Peeping Tom, no? Anyhow, he has gone.'

'My dear, how horrid! We should have pulled down all the blinds.' They busied themselves packing and tidying, and presently Mrs Palmer looked out and said, 'Well, it looks as though we are running into Leeds at last. Mill chimneys, and factories, and rows of little houses.'

They pulled on gloves and adjusted hats and when Rose looked through the window, Stephen was there on the platform waiting for her, and she felt a strange sense of relief. She did not see Alban when they all got out but she had the feeling that somewhere he was still standing, watching her.

Stephen, as always, was completely charming, taking the whole party under his wing, finding porters, getting their luggage together, and managing to flirt gently with Marian whose undisguised admiration amused and flattered him. He saw the Palmers into the hired car waiting for them, and said how glad he was that they would be living so near, and they must come over to Cliffs Edge soon while the weather was good enough for tennis and croquet.

He had brought his own car, a smart dark red saloon, and when he was in the driving seat he put both his arms round Rose.

'*Ma chère jolie cousine!*' he exclaimed. 'You have come at last to stay and help me, because I'm bored to death by the young ladies who, although they would admire me more if I was in uniform, are glad to find any chap who is young, presentable and unmarried.'

She kissed him sympathetically, accustomed to the touch of bitterness in his voice, for she knew he had taken a good deal of unpleasantness from the insensitive and unobservant. The two inch shortness of one leg was so well concealed by his boot makers and tailor that it was barely visible. 'And *why* aren't you in the forces, Mr Grimshaw?' he mocked as they drove through the main square heading towards the road leading northwest to the moors. 'I meet it from every new partner at every dance. What the devil do they want me to do? Go around with a placard round my neck? "Disabled"? "Two inch leg shortage"? "C3"?'

'Stevie, don't fret,' she said gently. 'To work as you do every day in that awful factory, smelling of raw wool and machine oil, and to travel like you do, up and down the country, and sometimes to France to see government departments and military tailors, is just as useful as going out and getting shot.'

'Thank you, *chérie*, I will try and believe you. Poor Arthur Sykes is a young, strong, fit man. Without him, I do not think Grimshaw & Sons could continue. But because he is reserved, he has to take a lot more than I do.

Even his wife has had white feathers sent through the post – and his kids too have to take it at school. You know the kind of thing, "Our dad says your dad's a right shirker." He's nearly cracked and joined up once or twice, but the authorities wouldn't hear of it. It's a little better now. Every family has lost someone and every man who comes home tells them what it's really like – now people know that dying for one's country may mean drowning in the stinking mud before Ypres.' He was silent for a minute.

Rose wanted to tell him that Tom was, for the present, safe. She remained silent as they drove through the busy mill-lined streets, then said, 'And how's Aunt Angela?'

'Mummy's fine. Up to her eyes in warwork and loving every minute of it. She's in with all the local nobs. She's looking forward to your being home permanently!'

Rose raised her eyebrows.

'Oh, yes. When we read your last school report she bought you a typewriter. Says your organising ability will be of great use to her fund-raising.'

They both laughed.

'The hospital at Danesfell Abbey is always full now. She and Lady Stoneberry work all the time, raising money. So if you don't make eyes at me over the dinner table, all will go merry as a marriage bell. But why *don't* you marry me, Rosebud? Mummy would get used to it in time. Just to protect me from these hordes of girls. I'm the only bachelor in the county who still has a good chance of being alive when the fighting stops.'

'Oh, Stephen, don't make me laugh. Anyway, you are very attractive and eligible, civilian or not.'

'Thank you. By the way, that Marian friend of yours is a sweet little thing. I rather go for her.'

'She is, and don't you tease her. Her father is a very influential M.P. But she will go potty with delight if you ask her over to play tennis.'

'Then I certainly shall. Have you heard from old Tom?'

153

'No, I haven't had a letter,' she said steadily.

'It's a month since we heard. Dad's getting a bit edgy, though he should know that Tom must be all right or we would have heard. So what about my proposal?'

'Stevie, you are silly. You know we should make a terrible match.'

'All right. I know you belong to Tom.'

Tears filled her eyes. She wanted so badly to talk about Tom, to tell Stevie about him, and about what had happened between them. All the chatter with the Palmers and this foolish fencing with him seemed so trivial. As though he knew, Stephen patted her hand reassuringly.

'Don't look like that, *chérie*. He will come back. But shield me from the other girls just the same.'

'And you shield me – from persistent bores.'

'Like Alban Stoneberry?' he said quickly.

She laughed and said yes.

He gave her hand a quick squeeze of reassurance and they drove on to Cliffs Edge.

She was glad to be free of school and back at Cliffs Edge. During the war years the edge of Angela's resentment had been blunted. At first it had been Stephen's tact and inconspicuous influence that had made it so. Now Angela needed Rose.

She did write to Mr Brinkley at Hanover Street, telling him about Betty Briggs and her success with the Palmers.

"Have a look at her sketches," she wrote, "and watch her sales – she seems to be doing very well."

Her interest in Margaret's business was not because it was a source of income to herself, but because it had been her aunt's great creation and she wanted it to continue.

Rose was very busy that autumn. The Stoneberrys had opened the side wings of Danesfell, each containing two great reception rooms, as a convalescent hospital for local wounded. Lady Stoneberry, whose suggestion it was, had wanted it to be for officers only, but Henry, to whom she and Angela had turned for financial support, would not hear of it. All ranks or no money, he said bluntly.

So they had to be content to put the officers in the right wing and other ranks on the left. Her Ladyship was surprised to find that as soon as they were mobile the officers would go in to see the men they had commanded, and the men, keeping up a formal "with permission", went in to talk to the "Old Man", some of whom were boys still in their twenties.

Henry was responsible for the general finance for all the basic funds, and tactfully lowered the rent for the rooms still occupied by the Stoneberrys. Though the patients were from all parts of Yorkshire, it was near enough for their families to visit them.

Angela and Lady Stoneberry were leading fund-raisers, and had plunged into the work with great enthusiasm. They were both talented organisers – and socially it was very prestigious. Angela was meeting people she would never have had the chance to meet before the war.

Rose worked at the hospital three days a week, and the rest of her time was spent working as Angela's secretary at Cliffs Edge, attending to the running of the big house, doing the work Angela was now too busy to attend to. At the hospital she did ward work on her own account, reading and writing letters for the men who could not see or use their hands.

She became accustomed to the horror and pain of torn and burned flesh. She fed men who could not hold knives and forks, shopped for their small personal wants, chose greetings cards for them to send, found small gifts for their children's birthdays, listened to them talk – the ones who told of the horror they had experienced, and the cheerful liars who bravely and facetiously pretended it had been nothing but fun and comradeship. All the small duties that she could take off the nurses' hands, she did.

The men waited for her. If they could not see, they recognised the sharp sweet scent she wore or listened for her light voice with its faint French accent. They laughed when sometimes she exclaimed, '*Merde!*'

They called her by Tom's name for her: *Chérie*. Angela and Lady Stoneberry disapproved at first, but as at school Rose's charm and tact smoothed so much red-tape away. Here overworked V.A.D.s, over-strained doctors and martinet

155

ward sisters were sweetened into laughing approval at her audacity.

Henry was her great ally, so that Rose was able to wheedle and wangle liberties and sidestep obstructions or routines, easing life for everyone without anyone quite knowing how.

Angela was blooming – her charity fund-raising for the wounded had given her a career. Her engagement book was always full. She drew raffle tickets, made excellent speeches which Stephen wrote for her, opened fêtes and garden parties, and received bouquets and votes of thanks and praise. For the first time in her life she was really being noticed. She even sought Rose's advice on what she should wear, achieving a new and gracious chic which Henry noticed and approved of. The agonising, suppressed jealousy that had boiled up at Margaret's funeral was forgotten. Henry's great love was dead and he was growing old. He was always courteous, always supportive and helpful and unstintingly generous, and for the first time they had a cause in common: the care of the wounded men. But there was a frailty about him which Angela chose to dismiss as overwork; she was always pressing him to retire. But he was at the mills every day and worked like a man possessed.

'He's working for Tom,' Stephen said, 'to keep the whole thing running for him when he comes back. They're both bred and born wool men, their hearts are in the business. But he knows, when all this mess is over, I won't stay.'

'What will you do?' Rose asked.

'Well, I've been talking to Marian Palmer's old man – when he comes up to see them – and he's taken me to lunch at the House once or twice when I've been in London. I showed him some of the speeches I've written for Mummy and Sir Miles and Lady Stoneberry, and he was tickled pink. He says I've managed to make them talk sense without knowing it.'

Rose propped her chin on her hands and said, 'Go on. Tell me.'

'He thinks and so do I, that after the war the people will need younger men to represent them, men bred and born in certain localities, who know the needs and difficulties of that community. I haven't liked working in the mills, but I've learned a great deal about the trade and the men who work in it. West Riding men in particular. They are honest, hard-working, humorous, stubborn, and proud as the devil. Like Dad and Tom. They ignore class barriers. They know how to create understanding between all ranks. They make good workmen, good bosses, and good soldiers. It seems to me Tom thinks the quality of the troops is not so good in the army.'

'It is a little different,' she said drily, 'to ask men to work or ask them to die.'

'I'm not so sure. Men will work and die for someone they really respect, and who respects them and a cause they believe in. Sometimes I think snobbery is a sort of sickness in this country. There is an enormous difference between Mummy's lot, who take service for granted, and Dad's, where both the labourer and the boss should be worthy of their hire. Mr Palmer thinks only a local man could understand local conditions, and so do I. What do London people know about the North?'

She clapped her hands. 'Well done!' He bowed as though he were standing on a platform.

'Thanks for your support. But seriously, *Chérie*, one day I should like to try for a seat up here. Mr Palmer would help me. He says I ought to think of being a parliamentary secretary for a few years. After all, I'm young, I'm rich, and very clever. And the war will be over one day.'

'And beneath all your foolishness, you are very, very sincere.'

He was not smiling. 'Yes, Rose. With you I can always be sincere. Not with everyone.'

Their eyes held for a long moment, then she said, retreating into their habitual affectionate badinage: 'I think you will make an excellent politician. And you must then find a nice, suitable, helpful wife, with the right background and connections.' She tilted her head back, smiling at him. 'Like Marian who fits the part like a glove and so obviously adores you.'

He changed colour, and his eyes were no longer laughing.

'I haven't any hopes with you then, *Chérie*?'

'No, Stevie.'

At the end of September they received their first letters from
Tom. He was in Cairo attached to Allenby's army. It was the
usual uninformative letter. He was very busy, which he liked,
but not in the intense Egyptian heat. He sent a snap of himself
in drill shorts with his sleeves rolled up, riding on a donkey
with the Pyramids in the background. He had grown a
moustache, looked lean, alert and very brown, and quite
different from the battle-worn man Rose had loved through
that night and day in Chelsea. He did not say exactly what he
was doing so they presumed it was to do with transport. Both
Henry and Stephen thought that an army would be sent
against the Turks in the Middle East. They were all delighted
to see Tom looking so well and so far from the stinking hell of
the Western Front.

That year the pressure was on the cotton towns in a demand
for tropical materials, and the woollen towns were less busy.
Nevertheless, some families of mill owners had indulged in an
orgy of spending, new houses, new motorcars, new clothes.

'Dad and I feel that the war will end before the year is out,
and like an old chap at the Watergate Mill said the other day:
"Us'll need all we've got, brains and savings, and some'll wish
they'd not been so free then." It'll take time to change back to
peacetime trade. Dad says we ought to start thinking of
turning another floor back to it, and get out some new
samples. Money's going to be tight. And that's when he'll
need Tom, and I'm not him. I only pray that they'll release
him soon.'

It was September when Rose suspected she might be
pregnant. At first she did not worry. She was young and rich;
if Tom was a long time coming home, she could wait. What
did she care about scandal? She could go and live in Chelsea
with Sarah. No one here need know.

"Go to Stevie and Dad and tell them everything," he had
said, but she was not ready to do that yet.

They had another letter saying things were on the move,
and that he was fine. The papers were carrying jubilant
headlines about the Turkish retreat and then came the Arab

158

victories at Damascus and the Turkish capitulation. There was a feeling of victory in their hearts. Tom was with Allenby and the war there was won. Surely he would be coming home soon.

Chapter Eight

Rose had worked a long morning in the wards. The usual tiring but rewarding day, going from bed to bed, attending to each man's individual wants, trying to smile and laugh, and flirt a little to make them forget their pain, and reassure them of the existence of families who were waiting anxiously for them to come home. She always took a wad of letters home to write and would being them the following day for signature.

It was a fine autumn day as she walked across the moors towards Cliffs Edge along the path where she and Tom had so often walked together. The heather was purple now and in the slopes down to the stony becks the bracken was already rusty red.

It was along this bridle path he had taught her to ride. Here he had once kissed her, the controlled and smiling kiss of a responsible boy who was not going to allow either of them to slide away into abandonment.

Love at that time had been like the little beck she was crossing now by large, flat stepping stones – clear and playful, tumbling into small, deep pools, then rushing onwards again.

The last meeting in the flat in Chelsea had been a plunge into the maelstrom. They had swept down together into an overpowering current, down into depths, and then away, helplessly, into a beautiful calm sea of love.

Like many of the staff at the hospital she kept an autograph book, and when a patient left, well enough to be sent home, she always asked them to write in it. When the war was over she wanted to have a record of these men who had taught her so much of courage, the facing up to fear, the all-conquering endurance.

There was every kind of entry. Trite and abrupt, hackneyed, witty, suggestive, romantic. All of them were subconsciously tragic. Even if their bodies healed, these men would carry the scars of the war within them for ever.

She sat at her desk reading the ones that had been written for her that morning.

"Many thanks for your kindness, J. Smythe, Gunner 7th Yorkshire Light Infantry."

The old school ploy, "By hook or by crook I'll be last in this book." A farming lad from Wharfedale – he had lost a leg just below the knee and beamed when she said he would be able to ride to a meet again.

There were sketches, copies of Bairns father cartoons. Old Bill in his Better 'Ole. Naughty ladies from La Vie Parisienne.

Another from one of the few colonials:

You'll find them in their glory
If you only take a run,
Up the Strand, that's the land
Of the Overseas son.

"Love and thanks to Miss Cherie. Jim Dawson. See you down-under one of these days."

A pawky long-chinned chap, with a big smile, here because of his Yorkshire family. He had been patched up to be sent back overseas. She had hated to see him go.

Another poem by a private in Tom's regiment. It made her shiver, clumsy and original:

Across no-man's land is sweeping
Through the rapid leaden rain,
Telling the khaki, crawling, leaping,
Grinning death is reaping, reaping,
What matter? If we win the trench
His reaping is in vain!

She shut the book and shut her eyes. The picture was so vivid. This man would neither creep nor crawl, nor leap again. He had lost both his feet.

161

She came to the last entry. He was a grey-haired white-faced officer, with gentle eyes. He had been curious about what he had called her Arabian Nights' beauty. He knew the Middle East well, and teased her: 'West Riding and Persian? That's a formidable heritage, *Chérie*. Which predominates?'

'I think I'm all West Riding inside and all Arabian outside.'

He had asked her if she had anyone she cared for "out there" and she told him, guardedly, about Tom. 'He is no longer in France, thank God! He is with Allenby in Palestine.'

'That's a different kind of war. I think it will soon be over. Turks are terrible fighters, terrible enemies, but inefficient. Don't worry, child. He will soon be back with you.'

She kissed him goodbye when he left, thinking what a handsome gallant soldier he must have been. He had written in her book,

Lovely kind and kindly lovely
Such a mind is worth the moving:
Truly fair and fairly true –
Where are all these but in you?
Wisely kind and kindly wise,
Blessed life where such love lies.
Wise and kind and fair and true,
Lovely live all these in you.
Sweetly dear and dearly sweet,
Blessed where these blessing meet,
Sweet, fair, wise, kind, blessed and true,
Blessed be all these in you.

She shut the book with a little snap. She was not like that at all. She was tenacious, single-minded and determined to make life give her what she desired. But life was not being like that. It was like water – you could feel it, but it ran away from your grasp.

There was a nervous tap at the door and Elsie the house-maid came in. She stood with her hands behind her back, staring down at Rose. Her face was white and frightened. Rose sprang to her feet, thinking the girl must have received some bad news. But Elsie suddenly brought her hand out from behind her back and thrust a telegram towards Rose.

'Happen it's all right,' she stammered. 'Happen it's nowt that matters. It's for the Meister.'

Rose was suddenly terrified.

'It's for Mr Grimshaw? Should you open it? Should I call Madame?'

Rose took the envelope and tore it open and heard herself say: 'It says, missing, believed dead.' She looked up at Elsie. 'They say that sometimes when it's all right, don't they?'

'Yes, miss, often! There's lads in Thornsby that turn up after all.'

Rose reeled, caught at the back of her chair, and sat down.

The white-haired officer had said, "The Turks are terrible enemies," and then he had told her not to worry, and she had known he wished he had not said it. Turks maltreated their enemies, and mutilated their prisoners. She clapped her hands across her mouth to stop her lips from trembling, her teeth from chattering.

Let him be dead if it means torture and pain. Please God, let him be safe or dead. No thirst or horror, no lingering in the burning sun.

There was a bustling sound of footsteps in the hall, and Angela's voice calling Elsie.

'There's Madam. She's off to open that grand do over at Danesfell with a countess coming, and all kind of theatre folk from London. She'll never go now.'

'Don't say anything, Elsie. Don't tell her. She musn't know yet. It's important that Tom's father knows first. I must go down to the Mill and tell Mr Stephen. Let Mrs Grimshaw go to Danesfell.' The girl stared, confused and unsure.

'It's important that they raise a lot of money for the wounded. Mr Stephen will tell her tonight. *Mon Dieu*, don't you see? Mr Grimshaw *must* know first – this is not *her* son.'

'Oh, yes, miss, just what you think.'

Angela came in looking very smart in a new plum-coloured silk dress and a dashing little hat trimmed with black and plum ruching. She was flushed and excited, looking forward to a triumphant afternoon.

'Are you ready, Rose?'

'No, Aunt Angela. I can't manage today. I have such a lot to catch up with here, many letters for you, and you have all your notes.'

'Well, do as you wish. How do I look?'

'You look magnificent.'

Angela smiled and asked Elsie if the car was ready.

'Yes, Madam, it's waiting out front.'

'Good.' She glowed. She had done very well in obtaining the Countess of Manston this weekend. The Countess was a society woman, a middle-aged beauty with a passion for the theatre and theatre people, and she had a house-party to entertain the stars of a company on a northern tour and had promised to bring them along to the fund-raising fête. It was a pity that Rose chose to stay at home, she was very helpful, but she always attracted a lot of attention, especially among the men. Angela particularly wanted the Countess and Lady Stoneberry to be the central figures.

'Well, I'll be getting along then.' Rose helped drape the sable stole about her shoulders, handed her a small case and her speech for today, and all her notes, and she sailed out to the car, anticipating a triumphant afternoon among the elite of the county.

The two girls drew in great breaths of relief as the car drew away. Rose stood watching it out of sight. She felt extraordinary. Her terror was so intense that she appeared stonily calm. It did not matter that Angela who had never loved him did not learn of this until later. But she must go to Stephen and to Tom's father. Tom was missing, *only* missing. They did not *know* he was dead.

'What'll you do, miss?' asked Elsie.

She could not bear to think of the grand old man fighting to keep his kingdom for his son. And now there was no son – no Tom. The big, ornate grandfather clock in the hall ticked loudly in rhythm with her agony. No Tom – no Tom – no Tom! She went across to the sideboard and poured brandy into a glass and drank it down, felt the firey spirit scald her throat and shock her back into action, poured another glass.

'Elsie, for you . . . ?'

'Eh, no Miss, I daren't. I'm chapel.'

'*Mon dieu! Drink it! We need it!*'

Elsie drank obediently, spluttering and choking, her pale face going red, and gasped, 'I don't know how folk can *like* this!' She sat down, gasping, and cried out aloud, 'Nay, Miss Rose, don't look like that!' And, forgetting her position, rose and put her arms round her young lady, the tears running down her face. 'You've got to cry, miss, you've got to – it's only natural.'

'Elsie, I must tell Mr Grimshaw. I'll telephone Mr Stephen first.' But when she called Stephen's office at the Mill she was told he had an appointment in Leeds, but should be back within the hour.

'Tell them to hitch up the pony trap, Elsie.'

'You're niver going to tek that pony into Thornsby?'

'Yes, yes. It's my only way. Go and tell them now – hurry!'

All the menservants about the house now were either very old or very young, and it was a boy of fifteen who led the trap out to the door. He stared at the white-faced girl who ran down the steps, sprang into the trap and took up the reins. She was not dressed for driving, hatless and in an afternoon dress, her long black hair blowing loose in the moorland breeze. She was not pale as other girls were pale; her usual glowing golden skin looked greenish and her beautiful dark eyes burned fiercely, as though she wanted to destroy something or someone, fierce and witchlike. Like all the staff at Cliffs Edge he was her devoted slave, but now he was afraid of her. He had never seen despair before.

'D'you think you should tek t'pony into Thornsby, Miss Rose? He's not used to trams and drays.'

'He'll be all right.'

'Shall I drive then, miss?'

'No, I'll drive.'

She cracked the whip over the tough little animal, and it scrabbled on the gravel and started off at a spanking pace. The boy clung to the sides as the trap heeled out of the gate and swung down the steep hill towards the town. He put on the brake, and she steadied the pony. No point in killing the boy, the pony or herself. The shock eased as the brandy settled her. Now she was one solid ache. Her fury at the idiocy of war ebbed away. If the boy had not acted quickly they might have been thrown into the ditch.

'Thank you, Toby. I'm sorry. I will be more careful now.'

She concentrated on driving. Tom had taught her, and she had loved it, but the pony was only used to country roads and quiet villages, and when they drove through the newly built suburbs into the narrow crowded streets of the town it took all her will and skill. When she finally turned into the big cobbled yard of Calder Mill, Stephen had just arrived back from Leeds. He came across to her at once, astonished to see her there.

'What the devil, Rose?' he began, saw her face and knew at once. 'It's Tom?'

She took the telegram out of her pocket and thrust it towards him. 'I telephoned, but you were out. I couldn't tell your father over the phone.'

'No.' He looked up, his face nearly as white as her own. 'Does Mother know?'

'No. I didn't tell her. She has this big day at Danesfell. I thought I would not tell her. She would have felt it her duty to cancel, and what good would that have done? You have to tell your father, Stevie. He must know first. I think you should tell him.'

'Yes.' Her colour frightened him. He stretched out his hand. 'Come with me, Rose. We'll go together.'

She pressed her hands against her eyes. 'Stevie – I cannot weep.'

'Nor me,' he said, pushing his thick fair hair away from his forehead with a gesture so like Tom's that she felt a sharp, physical pain shoot through her.

He put his arm about her. 'I can't believe it,' he said. 'It can't be *our* Tom. He can't be dead.'

'It says missing,' she said frantically. 'It only says missing – not dead. They have been wrong. Elsie said, here in the town, this mistake has been made. It is only missing.'

'Come with me, please *Chérie*. Hold my hand. Come.'

But they had not to tell him – when they went in hand in hand, like two white-faced children who have seen something terrifying beyond their ken, Henry looked up and read the news in their eyes. He stood up and gave a great cry of denial, then pitched forward and fell at their feet.

He was unconscious for an hour and by that time Stephen had driven him home, and telephoned the Doctor who arrived a few minutes after they had carried him to his bed. Henry was breathing in quick, hard stentorous breaths. The Doctor gave him an injection and presently the breathing slowed down and he appeared to sleep quite naturally. Stephen, the Doctor, and Henry's middle-aged chauffeur undressed him and got him into bed.

'It is his heart,' the Doctor said. 'It was a sharp attack but not too severe. I warned him recently against working at his present pitch. But he's always been a stubborn man, and a very strong one.'

'He seemed to ease up when Tom was sent to the Middle-East. In France we always expected the worst, everyone does. But out in Egypt we thought he was safe.'

'It is happening to so many families now,' said the Doctor. 'Some good men have been sent out there. At least the Palestine campaign has been a success. There seems no chance of any immediate cease fire on the Western Front.'

When he had gone, promising to return later to see Angela, Stephen and Rose sat by the bed for a long while, holding hands, watching the colour return slowly to the old man's face, and the blue shadows fade about his sunken eyes.

They heard the sound of wheels on the gravel and went downstairs, meeting Angela, all flushed from the triumphant success of her afternoon.

Stephen told her quite bluntly what had happened. There was no other way. Aghast, all her simmering suspicions and fears of the past rose. Dropping her bouquet, flower heads shooting across the parquet, she hurried upstairs to Henry's side.

Angela bloomed in a new and curious way during the next few weeks. For once she had Henry entirely to herself. Not the magnificent, powerful gentleman who had treated her with respect, courtesy and great tenderness, but never with passionate love. The man who had never even tried to hide his love for another woman from her, and had idolised their son. This was an old, sick, broken man, like a great oak tree struck by lightning. But it was still Henry Grimshaw.

167

Now at last he needed her and she would not tolerate any interference with her care of him. It was difficult to get private nurses in wartime but she managed to find two retired nursing sisters who were anxious to earn some extra money, and she paid them well. She shared the watching in their off-duty hours, supervised everything in the sick man's room, and kept a guardian watch on visitors. Even Stephen was only allowed a daily fifteen minutes. Rose, hardly anything at all. No one from the works was admitted. Particularly not Arthur Sykes, the man with the most responsibility at the Mills, and the man Henry most wished to see.

'He is not to be worried with business. He has to have complete rest. When he is strong enough I shall take him away to Bournemouth or Torquay and he will gradually regain his strength. He has been over-working for years, doing the work of ten men, and this is the consequence. I am surprised at you, Stephen, and at Mr Sykes – surely you could see what was happening.'

'What caused it was the news from Palestine,' Stephen said patiently. 'Has anyone, ever, been able to stop him working? Do you imagine he will let you imprison him in a sick room like this, if and when he's better?'

'We will see about that when the time comes.'

'But, Mummy, he's bored! Every time I go into his room he asks to see Arthur, and begins to quiz me about various orders we're dealing with.'

'Well, you must not tell him. His mind is shocked and exhausted.'

'His mind is sharp as a razor.'

'That's enough,' Angela said fiercely, 'let me hear no more about it. Until he is quite better, you will do as I say.'

Stephen gave Rose a helpless glance. When his mother had gone from the room, he said, 'At his age it is unlikely he will get quite better. The specialist told me. The mills have been his life for over fifty years. Can't she see what she is doing to him?'

Rose shook her head. Angela was in full control for the first time in her whole married life and she would not relinquish her power now. But under her care Henry did not mend.

Then one day, when Angela was out, the day nurse came down, visibly shaken.

'May I telephone the doctor, Miss Rose?'

Rose sprang up anxiously. 'Is Mr Grimshaw worse?'

'I don't think so, but it's getting beyond me. When I'm alone with him he keeps on telling me to get you, or Mr Stephen, or Mr Arthur Sykes. He says he has to see you all. There are things he must talk about. I can't calm him. If I try to give him a sleeping draught, he knocks it out of my hand. I have had strict orders from Mrs Grimshaw that he must have no callers while she is out.'

'I will telephone the Doctor, if you wish,' Rose said gravely, 'but I do not think he will be at the surgery. At this time he is usually on his rounds.'

'I'm at my wits end with him today!' The nurse suddenly sat down and folded her arms, as though she was giving up the whole matter.

'Well, I'll go up to him now and see if I can soothe him,' said Rose. 'Do not agitate yourself, Nurse Bradshaw. I will take all the blame. Go and tell him I am coming. I will not be many minutes.'

As soon as the nurse had gone upstairs, Rose telephoned Stephen.

'Stevie, I think you should come. Your mother will be away for at least two hours, and your father is giving the poor nurse merry hell. He is asking for you and Mr Sykes.'

'I'll bet he is,' Stevie said grimly. 'I'll be with you soon, and I'll bring Arthur and the books along with me.'

Henry was sitting up in bed when she went into his room and for a second she thought he was really well again, his face was so pink and his eyes so clear. He was cleanly shaved, his thick silver hair brushed slickly back like a good little boy. Before his collapse he had been pale. But she knew through working at Danesfell that his colour was too high and his eyes too bright; that men were like that sometimes before a relapse.

She went to his side, bent and kissed him, and he smiled, keeping her hand in his.

'What is it, Uncle Henry? Miss Bradshaw tells me you want to see me.'

'Little Rose – little *Chérie,* you smell like a spring flower.'
The hand that trembled slightly on hers tightened its grip.

'Tell that woman to get out of here!'

Rose smiled at the anxious nurse, exerting all her charm.
'I'll make certain he will not overtire himself, Miss
Bradshaw, and will take any blame. I think it would help him
to speak with me alone.'

In the hospital she had seen men near death but she had
never seen this strange detachment he had had since the loss
of Margaret. He had been shattered by the news of Tom's
death, but now he was not grieving. His strong grasp cut into
her wrist. She gently stroked his hand and he looked down
and released her, the old, tolerant, courteous smile flickering
back into his eyes.

'I'm hurting you, child, I'm sorry. I'm planning my escape.
My poor Angela thinks she is going to wrap the Old Man in
cotton wool and have him wheeled about Bournemouth for
the rest of his life.'

She began to laugh helplessly; he was so like Tom, and she
loved him too.

'Bend down, flower,' he said, and when she did so he took
her face between his hands, searching her deep dark eyes,
then held her hand closely against his heart.

'You must not despair. When I am well – and I shall never
get well cooped up like a baby in a cot – I will go back to
work. I know Tom will be all right. I must have everything
waiting for him when he returns.'

She felt her heart tighten with apprehension.

'Uncle Henry, you must rest too.'

'There's no time to rest. You must not worry about me.
Send for Steve and Arthur Sykes.'

'I have already done so, Uncle Henry. They are coming.
But you must be quiet and calm, or Aunt Angela will roast me
alive.' That raised a smile in the tense old face. 'And I will stay
with you until they come.'

Steve and Arthur Sykes arrived shortly afterwards. Henry
had been sitting up, listening, and when he heard the car he
looked at her anxiously. She went to the window. 'It is all
right. It is them.'

He lay back, relaxed, the over-bright eyes fixed on the door, and when they came in asked them tetchily to put an extra pillow behind him, and bring up a small table to the bed. And where the devil had that idiot of a woman put his glasses?

Rose did all this, quietly and quickly, and the two young men sat down. It was a board meeting and there was no doubt who was Chairman. It was over before a second car was heard in the drive and Angela came storming up the stairs, red-faced, furious and speechless with distress.

Henry smiled up at her, his charming, bland, mischievous smile, and held out his hand to her.

'Angela, my dear, how nice. We've just finished,' he said urbanely. 'I'm glad. Now I can rest. You boys get all this stuff back to the office. I've set them up with enough to see to for a few days. Come now and sit by me, and don't be cross with Rose or poor Miss Bradshaw, because I frightened them to death.'

They rose. Steve kissed his father, Arthur shook his hand. Henry drew Rose down to him, smiling and whispering, 'Courage, flower. *Missing*, remember. Only missing.'

Angela was silent throughout dinner. Henry had broken her domination and reminded her who was master at Cliffs Edge. It was not until after they had gone into the drawing-room that she said reluctantly, 'He has said that I must allow you to come to him twice a week. I telephoned Doctor Granger, and he says he thinks it might do some good. Henry also says that Stephen and Arthur Sykes must telephone him if anything important arises, must let him know at once. He also says you must bring him his letters every morning, Rose – they will be sent up from the office, and he wants you to work for him for an hour. I will say now that I think you are wickedly wrong, and so is Dr Granger. I think he needs complete rest and seclusion from any worry, but I have learned not to expect anyone here to share my anxiety, or try to understand.'

For a month it seemed that the Doctor was right. Henry

seemed to mend apace. He sat up in his wheelchair conducting his affairs by telephone, holding his bi-weekly meetings, and occasionally seeing important customers.

On warm afternoons he liked to be wheeled through the gardens or driven out in the trap, and he liked Rose, as well as Angela, to be with him. He encouraged his wife to go back to her charity work. She would see, he said, how much one's real work helped. She fumed and fretted, but she knew he was right. It was much more pleasant to be making speeches and receiving bouquets than riding out with a silent, preoccupied man or fussing about his rugs and shawls. He had escaped from her smothering love, and he could not conceal his impatience with it.

Then one morning Rose came in and found him staring at the papers before him in a bewildered way. The top page was filled with a feeble, slanting, meaningless scribble quite unlike his firm, decisive script.

He looked up in a puzzled way and said, 'It's rubbish, Rose. Why can I only write rubbish? Rose, why is it so dark? Hold my hand, *Chérie,* I can't see . . . ' She held his shaking hand and rang for the nurse who telephoned the Doctor and called Angela. But he was unconscious before the Doctor came. That evening he died. He was in his seventy-ninth year.

That night the domestic routine of Cliffs Edge continued like a well-oiled machine, although Angela stayed in her room and Elsie could be heard sniffing audibly as she served dinner. But Stephen and Rose ate very little. They sat in the drawing-room together, and he held her hand, and they spoke only occasionally. She thought of Tom, and the baby that she knew now she was carrying. "Tell Henry and Steve," he had said. But she had been unable to tell either of them. Tom's death seemed trouble enough. She was relieved when Pamela and Arthur Sykes called.

Pamela, like many young Thornsby matrons, had regarded Rose with wary eyes, admiring and even liking her but finding her beauty too compelling for real peace of mind.

But Pamela also worked at the hospital and had come to respect her devotion to the wounded men, and realised what an asset her charm could be, how she used it both generously and deviously when she was trying to cut through red tape to make things easier for everyone.

Tonight she looked as perfect as ever in a simple, black dress, with elbow-length sleeves, but her pallor was masklike, and she looked both frightened and bereft, and seemed to be holding herself under an iron control. She looked almost more beautiful, but Tom's death had etched into the bloom of her youth. The almond-shaped eyes seemed too big, the high cheek-bones making shadows in the greenish pallor of her skin. She looked so fragile, the sleek dark head drooped like a flower. She rose courteously to greet them, but went back at once to Stephen's side. He put his arm around her protectively. Impulsively Pamela put her arms about her, and her hand on Stephen's.

'Rose – Steve, perhaps we shouldn't have come? Old Mr Grimshaw was such a grand man – everyone in t'valley thought so. He lost Tom's mother who meant so much to him, and then Tom. It's like a trap none of us can get out of – all these deaths. All the young men. First young Shawcross and now Tom – and everywhere you go in the town you hear the same thing. You look at them, and I know they resent that I haven't a father or husband out there – or they used to. But we can understand why they feel bitter.'

Arthur sat beside Stephen. 'I know that your mother doesn't welcome us, Stevie. But I've worked for your dad all my life and known you since we were kids. We just had to come.'

'I'm glad you did. He thought the world of you, Arthur. And I'll need you more than ever now.'

'How's your mother taken it?'

'Badly. She won't see anyone – not even me tonight.'

They all turned at the sound of the opening door. Angela was dressed in stiff black silk. She had not worn black since she had turned to Rose for advice about her clothes, and this was an old dress she had kept for funerals. It made her look older, and her long pale face was puffy and red with tears – of anger as well as grief. When she spoke, her voice was a little slurred. They all realised she had been drinking and had probably not eaten all day. Both Rose and Stephen rose and went towards her, but she thrust out a trembling hand.

173

'Don't touch me! Don't speak to me. I blame you all. You should have kept it from him. You should not have allowed him to work as he has since Tom went away. He was a strong man, with many years before him.'

'Mummy darling, you must not be like this,' Stephen said, and this time she allowed him to put his arms about her, and leaned against him weeping noisily into his shoulder. Presently she said loudly, 'Most of all I blame Tom. He was brought here as a child, always reminding me of that woman . . .'

'Mama, Tom was only a baby then. He had no choice but to come.'

But she railed on at him, bitterness welling out of her like a poisoned stream. 'Why did he go away, breaking his father's heart? He had to show off, to be a hero, he always did. Always wanting to show he could be better than you.'

'Mummy, Tom wasn't like that. He just *was* good at everything. He was a splendid fellow.'

'He could have been reserved and let Arthur Sykes go instead. He could have stayed and been a comfort to his father. But not him! He had to join before anyone, and he broke Henry's heart, and now it's killed him. It's Tom's fault. All of it. All our lives went wrong when he came to Cliffs Edge . . .'

'Mummy, don't go on. It does no good to anyone. And even it it were true, Tom has paid for it with his life.'

For a moment her head rested on his shoulder, then she raised her head and glared madly at Rose.

'I would rather Stephen had been able to go and die for his country than that he should ever marry you. Don't think you can have him now that Tom has gone. Don't think I don't know what goes on when I am not present. A whore's child, with a father no one knows about except that he was black.'

Rose did not move. She said quietly, 'I'm so sorry, Pamela and Arthur. Madame Grimshaw is very upset, as we all are. She is suffering very much. Please don't be hurt, but I think you should go.'

She went to the door with them, staunch friends, she knew they would not repeat what they had heard. When she got back to the drawing room, she sat waiting in the flickering firelight until Stephen returned. He flopped down at her feet, dropping his fair head against her knee as he so often did. She put her hand gently on his hair. It was so like Tom's, thick and fair. He reached up and drew her hand down against his lips.

'What's got into her? I thought she was glad Tom had gone away.'

'She is *désolée* – a little crazy with grief – I know. Your father has gone from her and she knows that his heart never belonged to her. And she feels guilty because she could never love Tom.'

'You're a wise old *Chérie*. Have I told you – she wants me to marry Marian Palmer?'

'And what do you want? Marian is in love with you – how do you feel? You like her, don't you?'

'Yes.'

'But you don't love her?'

He made an irritated little gesture. 'Not as she would want me to – as she deserves to be loved. She's such an innocent.' He turned, crossed his arms on her lap, his boyish, handsome face turned up to hers. So like Tom, a weaker, finer, self-indulgent Tom, slender in body and in character. 'Rose, this is not the time to say it – so soon. But perhaps both you and I needed his strength, perhaps together . . . ?'

'No.' She rose so sharply that he had to catch at the settee to regain his balance. 'No. Please don't speak about this, Stevie. Not even in fun. I do not know what I shall do – I must follow my own star and you must follow yours. I could not even think of another man while there is the smallest chance that somewhere he is still alive. What would *I* have for anyone else?'

'Your beauty and your charm – and – oh, everything about you.' He drew the curtain impatiently.

'Mind the light, Stevie!'

'Oh, damn the lights! When shall we throw back the curtains and finish all this? I can't breathe in this room tonight. It's like a prison built of sorrow.'

He turned out the lights and drew the curtains wide, looking out into the early winter night. 'Come out for a walk. It is moonlight again – like the first evening you came and we went up to the fell with Tom.'

It was very cold and clear with the first frost. She put on her warm cossack coat, embroidered and cuffed and collared with white fur, and Stephen put on one of the shooting coats that were hanging in the hall. They walked in silence to the edge of the fell and stood looking down across the moon-illuminated valley. A siren wailed in the far distance, and there was a spatter of anti-aircraft fire in the direction of Leeds. But the drone of aircraft moved northwards and silence fell again. Far away she could see Tom's little white-walled cottage. It had been shut up since he had left. It seemed lonely. Waiting – like they all waited.

As she looked she felt a little stir in her belly, faint but distinct like the velvet thud of a moth against the window pane, and cried out, so that he said in concern, 'What is it? Are you all right?'

'I caught my foot against a stone,' she lied. 'Let's go back to the fire. It is cold out here.'

But she was not cold. It was sudden, stark fear that engulfed her. It was the unborn announcing its presence. Tom's child, a separate entity for which she was responsible – and until that moment had scarcely thought about, pushing the reality away. Tom would come back – maybe late, but he would come back – and what did they care about a ripple of scandal? Tom was missing, she must believe that, only presumed dead. She shivered but not with cold.

In the warm drawing-room, she said, 'Would you like a drink? Or shall I get some coffee?'

'A good idea. I had better go up and see Mother. I'd ask her to come down, but I don't think she will.'

As he opened the door, she caught his arm. 'Stevie, tell your mother you are very fond of Marian. It is true, I know, and it will put her mind at rest. Remind her Tom is only missing.'

He cupped her smooth dusky face. There were shadows beneath her eyes but the frost had brought a flush to her cheeks. 'You mean, persuade her that I would become engaged to anyone so long as it wasn't you? Is that what you're saying?' She gave a little half-smile and he said, 'I'll do that, sweet sister. And to tell the truth, pretty Marian is the only other girl I have ever considered.' He grinned, a gleam of his old mischief surfacing, and went out of the room.

That night when she changed into her nightdress she sat on the edge of her bed and felt her abdomen and breasts like a woman searching for a malignancy. She had scarcely thought about her condition before. She had not been surprised, terrified or overwhelmed with joy. She had convinced herself that Tom would come back to her. She could go away. She could tell Angela that Respy was ill and needed her, and as soon as he returned they would get married quietly, probably down in the South of France.

But now everything had changed. "Tell Dad," Tom had said, "tell Stevie if you want any help." But Henry was dead, and Stevie, she was sure, would one day marry Marian Palmer and enter the world that had begun to attract him. The great world of politics, of which through Mr Palmer, he had already learned such a lot.

She did not want Stephen offering quixotic and generous suggestions of marriage, although she had always known there was a serious vein underlying his facetious proposals. He had feigned frivolity because he had always known she belonged to Tom.

Henry's funeral was not in the small parish church of Danesfell but at the large, cathedral edifice in the heart of the town where all the Thornsby worthies were interred. It was near the Market Square and the ornate Town Hall, and the funeral was held with all the pomp and panoply due to a great local figure, reminding her of Papa Léon's funeral. But Rose knew Henry would have liked to lie beside Margaret, his only love.

Here it was the Mayor, the town councillors, the local Members of Parliament, the grandees of the wool trade in force. At Papa Léon's funeral the fashion houses along the Rue de la Paix had drawn their blinds; at Henry Grimshaw's the great mills were run on skeleton staff for the two hours during which the procession passed through the town. The women were in their best hats, the men in their Sunday suits, snow white scarves about their throats. 'He were a good old lad,' they said, 'he were a right grand meister.'

Angela did not invite any of them to the house afterwards. She graciously shook a few hands, and thanked some of the overseers for coming. Then she drove away with Sir Giles and Lady Stoneberry and the Mayor to the necessary baked meats, laid out with splendour at Cliffs Edge.

But Stephen stayed behind and thanked his father's men. The following day Tom's possessions were returned and there was a letter to Henry from his Commanding Officer.

Stephen read it. Angela turned away, her handkerchief pressed tightly to her mouth. Rose sat motionless and silent.

It was a formal expression of deep sympathy, sincerely and personally expressed. A sad loss to the regiment of a brilliant and popular officer, with great gifts of organisation and leadership. Major Grimshaw had been specially chosen for some difficult work. He had been sent with a small party of men scouting ahead of the general advance which had led to the recent victories in Palestine. The patrol had been ambushed and there had been no survivors. The C.O. said he hoped to get a clearer picture of what had happened later. Major Grimshaw's body, his identity disc and his papers remained to be found. The possessions sent were those which he had left at headquarters in Cairo. A clean uniform, underwear, a box of family letters. That was all.

Stephen held out a bundle of letters to Tom from his father. 'D'you want these, Mummy?'

Angela turned frightened eyes towards him, and said, 'No!'

She stood up and stretched an imploring hand to him, and he rose at once and took her arm. 'Mummy, you've got to try and get over losing Dad. He was a very old man, and very tired. Today hundreds of young men are being killed. You've done so much to help the wounded and their families. Try to go back to it. Think of them.'

'Yes,' she said, then turned stiffly to Rose. 'Have I any engagements tomorrow?'

'Yes. You were going to Leeds to speak to the Ladies Guild about the hospital at Danesfell. I was going to ask if you wished to cancel?'

'Will you come with me?'

'Of course, if you wish me to.'

'We will go.' Angela paused and said, 'Thank you for your support and help this week. If I have said anything to offend you, I'm sorry.'

'You did not offend,' Rose said, 'I understood what you felt.'

'Come, Stevie.' Angela put her hand in his arm, and with a resigned glance at Rose he went with her.

Sitting alone in the room, Rose pressed her palms into her eyes. What could she do? What should she do for the best for Tom's baby? Her own parentage was questionable and Tom's had been a scandal. Did she want that for Tom's child?

Autumn had turned to winter. In spite of the dreary dragging anxiety of that fourth year of war, at Upper Thornsby and Danesfell there was a different and more hectic social life. Now the large army bases about the county were filled with American troops all bound for the Western Front, and Angela and Lady Stoneberry were deeply involved in organising entertainments and hospitality, as her ladyship said, 'For our brave Allies who are training to help us destroy the German beast.' And now curiously the Stoneberrys were eager to include Rose in all their invitations, and she received a tactfully worded letter from Alban from Paris. She was surprised – she remembered then that although the Grimshaw boys had never been close friends with him, Tom had felt vaguely sorry for the lonely, self-conscious boy and had done his best to make that memorable holiday at Gluckenschule a success for him. Alban wrote saying how distressed he had been to hear about Tom – and he said he expected to be due for leave and would be home for Christmas, when he hoped to see her.

She wrote a polite note of thanks. While she posted it, she remembered looking up through the carriage window coming from school that last time, and finding him standing looking down at her while he thought she was sleeping, and how she had felt absurdly frightened and pulled down the blind, trying to shut that strange, hungry face out of her mind.

Chapter Nine

Angela, who was now Lady Stoneberry's second-in-command, took up her war work again with the fervour of a crusader.

The two ladies travelled about the West Riding to open fêtes, speak at meetings or give prizes at garden parties, accepting every request for their services to raise money for the wounded at Danesfell Hospital for Convalescent Soldiers.

Angela traded unashamedly on the general sympathy for her newly widowed state and the loss of the fine young man whom everyone believed she had loved as her own son. Rose sometimes wondered what these two ladies would do to fill in their time when the war was over.

Christmas was drawing near and a determined but artificial cheerfulness blurred the prevailing sadness, for there was scarcely a family in the district free from mourning.

Lady Stoneberry had decided to mark the New Year with a ball at Danesfell Abbey, opening the magnificent ballroom for the occasion. The proceeds would go to wards equipping this imposing room as a new ward. Everyone, she said, must try and put aside their personal grief. They must make everyone welcome, especially their new allies, the Americans. They must show them that Yorkshire still held its head up high and there was no question of spirits getting low.

The tickets would, of course, be expensive, ensuring that only the right members of the community would attend. By "right", she meant of course the rich. Officers only would be invited guests, although American troops were paid so much that no doubt many of their other ranks would attend. The tickets would be £5 each. There would be all the usual money-raising side shows: tombola, stalls, raffles, spot-prizes – and they would persuade the local tradesmen to donate really worthwhile prizes. It was to be the event of the season, a splendid evening in a truly worthy cause.

Rose worked at the hospital in the morning and devoted the afternoons to secretarial work for Angela which at the moment was all to do with the great New Year's Ball.

'Alban Stoneberry is coming home on leave and will be here over Christmas,' Angela told her. 'His aunt was saying how very fond he is of you. He is extremely anxious that you should attend the ball. You must have some relaxation, Rose. You're beginning to look quite thin and pale.'

'Well, I shall certainly be at the ball. I wouldn't miss it for anything. And I'm glad for Lady Stoneberry that Alban is coming home and is quite safe. But I don't think that he is seriously interested in me.'

'Oh, come now, Rose,' Angela sounded quite cross, 'you know he is! Sir Miles himself told me that in his last letter from Paris, Alban particularly asked if you would be there. It is so silly and affected to be coy about it. You know perfectly well that he has always been attracted to you.'

'We shall meet some time, no doubt. I do hope the ball will make a great success, Madame, and make much money for the hospital. We need more room for more beds and the state ballroom will make a splendid ward.'

'It will be. Everyone in the county will be there, and I believe Mr Palmer will be able to get away from Westminster for the night. Nearly all the American officers have accepted so there should be plenty of partners for you girls.'

'I hope the noise won't keep the patients awake.'

Angela never quite knew when Rose was secretly laughing at her.

'You are so absurd! They may hear a little music, but the patients who are fit enough will be allowed to sit in the gallery with the nurses. And,' she glanced triumphantly at Rose, 'I am hoping to announce Stephen's engagement to Marian Palmer.'

181

Throughout December, Rose's baby had been making its presence felt, the first faint, mothlike movements changing into positive little blows that she could not ignore. It was a living presence within her.

What to do? How should she plan her future? Still clinging to the word "missing", she dreamed that of course Tom was alive and would come back to her. But if he did not, how to plan? Should she ignore conventions and brazen it out as an unmarried mother? She would by no means be the only one in Thornsby Vale. But she could not do that to Angela.

Or should she go right away, take on the status of a young war widow and surround herself and her child with a web of lies? What if she moved far away to some distant town, or even perhaps a different country? She hoped the baby would be a girl not a manchild. Men made wars, went out to fight them, dragging heartbreak and despair in their wake.

Her mirror told her her body was still slender apart from a slight thickening of her narrow waist. The fashionable clothes, falling in straight lines from shoulder to hem, were concealing. But for how long? She could no longer ignore the impatient movements within her. It was as though the child, impetuous as herself, was beginning to feel bored within its warm, dark prison. Sometimes she found herself talking to it softly, sometimes fiercely, sometimes pleading.

'Oh, baby, *ma petite*, lie still and wait. I have not yet made plans for us. Tom is still only missing. We have to cope alone, you and I. With him beside us there would be no fears.'

She had had many fears through the dark winter days, but no regrets. And when she talked, the child would be still, as though it heard and understood, and for a brief while she would forget.

Then, on the morning of the great ball, the morning of New Year's Eve, just as she was sorting out the post, Stephen telephoned and asked her to meet him on the Ridgeway, the rough track across the moors that lead to Danesfell.

It was a clear day with snow on the high ground. She pulled on a warm coat and took the trap to drive out to meet him. On the High Moor above Thornsby Dale she saw him standing by his car, his slim figure muffled in a heavy coat collared with fur. His hands were thrust deeply into his pockets as he paced up and down watching for her. As she drew up he came slowly towards her, and then stopped. She dropped the reins and sat frozen with horror at what she read in his eyes.

'Tell me what has happened, whatever it is. Please tell me, Stevie.'

The suppressed fear rose, and Stephen opened the door of the pony trap and lifted her out, holding her against him.

'It's all right,' she said, 'I'm not going to faint.'

He thrust his hand into a pocket and held out a buff-coloured letter and a metal disc.

'It came this morning,' he said, 'Tom's identity card and another letter from his Commanding Officer, confirming his death.'

'I can't read it. I don't want to touch it. Just tell me quickly what it says.'

'Wait until later . . .'

'No. Tell me now. Everything!'

'Well, this is all they know. Tom was leading a scouting patrol. It was just before the Turkish collapse after the fall of Goriza. They were well ahead of the general advance. When they did not return it was assumed they met a group of the retreating Turks – they must have been travelling fast and not taking prisoners. The British have no facts. They found only eight bodies, although some twenty men went out. They had been stripped and robbed. Later they found the identity disc thrown away with some other worthless possessions. Tom was known to have been one of that party.' He drew a deep breath and said, 'All the bodies were unrecognisable.'

'How do you mean? How could that be?'

He pressed her head into his shoulder so he could not see her eyes. 'Rose . . . in the desert there are scavenging beasts, hawks and insects. It is very hot and it must have been days before they found them. Only the men whose discs were found can be listed as dead. The rest of the poor devils were probably thrown down holes or dragged away by animals.'

'For God's sake, don't!' she cried in anguish, and for a moment could not speak. 'Now Tom is really dead?'

'What else can we believe?' He did not tell her that the bodies were mutilated, or that desert robbers would cut off a man's hand for a watch or bracelet, or slice off fingers to get at the rings.

'In my heart I will never believe it. How can I, when for me he will always live?'

They clung together, their minds locked in horror at the thought of that arid place, and the naked bodies scorching in the sun, thrown like garbage into a hole in the ground while the kites hung in the air above, high up in the blue sky, waiting to tear at the torn carcasses.

'It would be better to believe it now,' he said, 'I'd go crazy if I thought he was alive somewhere in that hell.'

It was crisp and clean under the winter sun. They grieved like children, clinging together, and like children they wept.

'It's all such a damned waste,' Stephen said bitterly. 'Tom was always the best. I tried so hard to be as good and never could. Dad always loved him the best – and I loved him more than anyone in the world. What use shall I be to Grimshaw's now? I'm not a businessman and I have never wanted to be one. I only stayed for Dad's sake, and for Tom's, to keep it in the family until he came back. And now they have both gone – what's the point of it all?'

She stood back, drying her eyes then pushing her long black hair back from her face.

'We must not tell anyone else about this, Stevie. Not today. Your mother told me she is hoping to announce your engagement to Marian tonight at Cliffs Edge, after dinner. And there is the great ball.'

He looked at her blankly, not understanding.

'Tonight is the ball, Stevie. Everyone has worked so hard. We must not let them be disappointed. If we tell your mother, she will feel it is her duty not to go. Everyone has already accepted that Tom is dead – except you and me. I do not suppose I am the only one she has told of your engagement to Marian. I hope it is true. I would hate for Marian to be disappointed and humiliated. Tell me – is it?'

'Chérie,' he said with a little smile, 'I won't hurt your friend. She is a very sweet girl and I'm fond of her. She is everything I need in a wife. But I don't feel for her as I have felt for you.'

Rose began to walk back to the trap where the patient pony was cropping the moorland grass, she stepped up into the driving seat looking hopelessly down at him.

'You know that I love you,' he said.

No vestige of his easy, facile charm showed now. His eyes were full of pain. Full, too, of self-doubt.

'Stevie darling, we have always loved one another,' she replied, 'but not as I loved Tom and he loved me. Not as you should love the girl you marry. I know how well you have played the flirting game. I have too – but I shall never play it again. One can do such thoughtless harm. I do not want Marian hurt, or your mother, or have this great affair tonight spoiled or saddened in any way.'

He stood by the trap, looking up at her.

'If it had been any other fellow but Tom I'd have made a fight of it – but from the very start I knew, from that time in Switzerland when you were just a kid, how it would be between you two. Maybe before you knew yourselves.' He smiled, although his eyes were still red from tears. 'I knew he was only waiting for you to grow up.'

'Thank God I did not let him wait too long! At least we loved each other before he went away.' She bent and kissed him again, on both cheeks, like a sister. 'Tonight we must not cry, Stevie. We must keep our flags flying.'

'Wait – there are things we shall have to talk about. Practical things. Tom made a new will before he went to France. He wrote to Father. Now they are both dead, your guardianship devolves to me. Can you imagine *me* your guardian, Rose? Tom left his shares in the firm between me and Arthur Sykes. I have the larger interest. But he left all his investments and property to you.'

'Property?'

'Yes. The cottage on High Moor, the long Crown lease of the flat in Chelsea, and a half interest with me in the Danesfell Abbey Estate.'

'That great house!' she exclaimed, appalled. 'But I do not need any of this.'

'That great house, yes, and all its land, its parkland, cottages and mineral rights – you now own half of it, with me. The Stoneberrys are only short lease tenants of the house, the gardens and a small amount of parkland. The rest we administer and draw an income from. Don't you remember the first time that you were up here from school, how we told you about it? It was left to us by our Aunt Mildred who was my father's sister. We are Lords of the Manor of Danesfell, as Mummy will not let anyone forget. Tom left this to you as he would have left it to his wife.'

For a moment she sat there, pale and motionless, then with a familiar impatient gesture, pushed back her black hair, blowing in the moorland wind, and took up the reins. A wistful little smile touched her lips. 'When I was a child, and penniless, I used to daydream about being the châtelaine of a great house and a queen of society. Well, I met my lord, but I did not dream that I would love him so much that I would willingly throw all this away just to have him with me, warm and safe again. I think *le Bon Dieu* has played a little trick with me – I shall now have everything I once wished for, and it means nothing.'

'You will find it will matter a great deal to other folk,' said Stephen drily, 'the Stoneberrys, for instance.'

'Do not let us talk about it. Not now! Not *yet*. Do not let us talk about Tom – when I hear his name it tears me apart and I do not want anyone to see me break down. Perhaps one day I will forget a little – I hope so. I could not endure this pain forever!'

She turned the pony back towards Cliffs Edge. He stood watching her until she was hidden by a bend in the track towards Thornsby.

As she drove her hands fell into her lap and the wise pony, given a free head, trotted slowly back towards his warm stable.

There was still the baby. She had not told Stephen about it, and that but for its presence she would have seen no reason for living. All the money in the world would not make her child legitimate. It would be for this baby as it had been for her. And for Tom. At school he had been called Grimshaw's bastard – as a child, he had been known through the valley as Grimshaw's bonny little bastard. He had carried this latter

186

easily, because it was usually said with affection, and at school he had been big and strong enough to stop their mouths. But his adoption had been a scandal that still lived and had roused bitter resentment and jealousy in his stepmother that she would harbour all her life. But he had been greatly loved by both his parents, and they were united by love if not by marriage.

It had been different for her, whose mother had rejected her. She had known what it was to be truly base born, prey to the covert glances and snide whispers at her first school. "Everyone knows who her mother was, but God knows whether Abderhazy was really the father." "He certainly gave her a name, but then to these rich, rich Arabs a European involvement does not count. After all, they can have four legal wives if they wish." "But it was probably one of the grooms or Persian servants Abderhazy always brought over with him." A meaning glance and sniff. "The Baroness always had a penchant for dark, good-looking men!"

She could not give her child any name but her own. What kind of man would offer her the protection of marriage? What kind of man would want a wife with a fatherless child? God knew this was happening every day in this wartime world. A world of sudden passion and sudden partings.

Who did she know who cared enough for her to do this? Only Stephen – her dear friend and brother – and marriage between them would be quite wrong. Almost like incest. The man she sought would have to love her with utter devotion and complete generosity. With patience and kindness. Or perhaps, she thought cynically, there might be a man who would love the fortune she brought with her.

Respy had said to her a long time ago: "It is difficult for a girl in your position to marry without a *dot*."

Well, now she had this *dot* of money and property, and what kind of man would take on another man's child without love? The answer was, a man who could be bought.

She looked up and found the trap was at the entrance to Cliffs Edge House, the pony eating the grass near the hedge. She got down and caught his bridle to lead him through the gate. The big square house shone with clean paint and polished windows, untouched by war shortages. It was no

187

longer her home now that Tom was dead. But for the child's sake, somehow, she must find a way.

That evening Marian arrived looking radiantly happy, wearing an apple blossom of a dress and a fine diamond on her engagement finger. She stood with Stephen and his mother to greet the dinner guests. There were young friends of Stephen's, a clutch of Thornsby notables, Marian's parents, and Sir Miles and Lady Stoneberry, accompanied by a very different Alban.

He had arrived the week before Christmas, and was no longer brusque and awkward. His aunt and uncle were obviously delighted with this well-mannered young officer who seemed a most presentable heir. They congratulated themselves on their wisdom in getting him the Paris posting.

Rose had stayed in her room until the last minute, drained of energy, until Elsie knocked to tell her it was time to dress. The terrible finality of Tom's death washed over her in a great wave of despair.

'You're not ill are you, miss?'

'No, but I won't hurry. There's no need for me to be on the reception line tonight.'

Angela did not like her to stand in the family reception line. Rose had learned not to mind – she understood very well why Angela would not accept her as family. Henry had always insisted on her taking her place with them and so did Stephen. But to Rose it was unimportant, so now she lingered over her dressing.

She chose one of the evening dresses she had had made for her at the Salon. It struck a provocative line between modesty and daring with its high cowled neckline and long, tight-fitting sleeves; but the back was cut low, almost to the waist. Every line spoke of *haute couture*, and Rose wore it with the same bravado with which she had dressed up as an Arabian dancing girl when she was still a schoolgirl. The fabric was layers of black chiffon over pale pink taffeta, giving a tantalising suggestion of bare limbs when she moved under the lights. She had a feeling Margaret would not quite have approved of it, nor Papa Léon. She could almost hear him saying: "A

188

dress for an actress – *not* a young lady!" She had not worn it before, but tonight she would have to act.

She dressed her black hair high, and wound one of her pearl necklaces into its shining coils, the other round her neck. Her golden bracelets tinkled on each wrist. If she was up for sale, she would dress the window well. She knew there was no other girl in Thornsby who would, or could, wear such a dress.

The hall was almost empty as she came down the staircase. Most of the dinner guests had already arrived and were in the drawing room. But Alban Stoneberry was waiting for her.

He had been present at every house to which she had been invited that week. When she drove the trap down to the hospital in the morning, she always met him out riding. He came to meet her, and rode back with her to Danesfell. He frequently sent her flowers. She thanked him, afterwards taking them down to the hospital. And now here he was, waiting for her, patient and courteous, as though his only wish was to serve her; offering his arm, saying, 'I've been told we are dinner partners?' as though it was a favour he had hoped for but had not thought to receive.

She was quite aware of the glances and raised brows when they entered the drawing-room together, but she had not expected Lady Stoneberry to swoop across to greet her with a new and fulsome affection, kissing her on both cheeks. Rose felt she was in some ridiculous nightmare world where people seemed to be behaving curiously out of character, and the only truth was that Tom was really dead, and that she and all these chattering, smiling people were as meaningless as marionettes.

What on earth was this woman saying to her? Something about being so glad that she and Alban were really friends at last.

She met Stephen's eyes across the room, and looked away. She could see her own agony painfully reflected in them. Only the two of them knew about those stripped and naked bodies rotting under the torrid desert sun. Stephen did not look towards her again. He and Marian were surrounded by congratulating friends, the girls exclaiming enviously at the size and beauty of her ring.

It was as though she and Stephen were isolated in their grief. All they really wanted was to cling together and weep for Tom as they had done that morning on the moorland road.

She and Alban followed the parade of guests into the dining room, and found they were placed immediately opposite Stephen and Marian.

Angela, a flushed and triumphant hostess, sat with Sir Miles and Lady Stoneberry.

Alban drew back her chair for her.

'Did you do the place names, Rose?'

'Yes.'

'I was hoping we would be together. Thank you.'

'No need,' Rose smiled, 'Aunt Angela planned the seating. I simply followed her list. So you should really thank her.'

She looked down the long table where the guests were now all seated. It looked splendid, decorated with berries and green leaves, and pink and white Christmas roses, arranged between Angela's splendid silver. She remembered being a child in Nice, listening to Papa Léon's shrewd and worldly lectures on what she should do with her life. She had imagined herself a grand and beautiful lady like her mother, but respected too. "A married woman with beauty and intelligence is a queen," he had said. Aunt Margaret had teased her about it.

Were the Stoneberrys really offering her that child's foolish dream? Did they really want her to make a match with Alban? Was she being invited to queen it over Danesfell Abbey one day? Was she suddenly no longer "that Arab girl"? Of course, the Arab girl was now a very rich girl and was half-owner of the great house in which they took such pride . . .

Suddenly she saw it all as inexpressibly funny, and laughed aloud. Meeting Alban's surprised and puzzled eyes, she said, 'I'm sorry. It was just something that came into my mind.'

'Won't you share the joke with me?'

'It's nothing – just a silly thought.'

Angela and Lady Stoneberry would, no doubt, see this match as a very good thing for her. The engagement of Stephen and Marian was also a very good thing. And she could see why they thought so. Anything must be good that brought money and property together. She was now a lucrative asset – enough to make Barbara Stoneberry forget, for the moment at least, the colour of her skin.

If she was putting herself up for sale, she reasoned, it would be easier to bargain with a man she did not care for rather than to take advantage of a dear friend and brother. Stephen must not know about Tom's baby. She did not want him to rush forward with a quixotic offer that would break Marian's heart.

The whole idea of marriage with Alban seemed impossible. Yet, impossible or not, she could not put it out of her mind. When she smiled at him, she was surprised at the delighted response in his eyes. There was already something possessive in the way he bent his head to speak to her. She knew that he had always desired her, and that he had never accepted her mocking rejections, although they had sometimes been thoughtlessly unkind.

Did he really care for her or was this to please his aunt and uncle who, until lately, had found him a disappointing burden? Or was it because she was part owner of Danesfell? And yet, she thought not. For the first time she was taking him seriously, and she had begun to believe he was sincere.

Her mind seemed to be detached from her heart. She was coldly examining her assets. She would be an excellent hostess, as good as any who had lived at Danesfell. This dinner party had been Angela's idea, but it had been *her* creation. She had planned it completely. She had driven over the moorlands to distant farms to buy game and fish and eggs. She had managed to recruit extra help to serve. She was well dressed, well educated, she spoke two languages, she even had Normanby blood. Oh, she was certainly a very good thing if one discounted her velvety dark eyes and smooth olive skin. What she had always been in Thornsby – an alien in their midst.

She found herself recklessly enjoying this game. She glowed and sparkled, charming everyone she spoke to, her performance dulling the knowledge that beat like a terrible clock . . . Tom is dead . . . Tom is dead.

191

Beneath her silks and chiffons Tom's baby stirred rest-lessly, its soft, mothlike movements reminding her of its presence within her.

People were watching her as they would watch an actress playing a part: Stephen, whose glance she could not meet, and Alban Stoneberry, burning to touch her golden skin, triumphant that at last he was the man by her side.

When the champagne was served, Marian's father rose and announced the engagement, and wished Stephen and his daughter all happiness. He made amusing references to Step-hen's rise in local politics and his great ability in that sphere, saying he hoped to see him representing Thornsby at the next election, even if he did belong to the wrong party. Mr Palmer was a Tory, and Stephen had just accepted the Chairmanship of the local Liberal Party following Henry's death.

Stephen rose to reply, flashing his brilliant smile around the table, and gracefully made the right kind of speech, brief and to the point. He gave the conventional thanks to his mother and to his future father-in-law whose interest and encourage-ment had helped him so much in his parliamentary career. He knew every one would work hard tonight at the ball to raise money for Danesfell Hospital. He referred fleetingly to Tom's death and told them that Lady Stoneberry had gra-ciously asked him if they could call tonight's efforts the Thomas Grimshaw Memorial Appeal, and name the new ward for Tom. After tonight the great ballroom at Danesfell would be equipped as another ward and would not be seen as a ballroom until hostilities had ceased. But tonight was not a night for remembering sadness and pain, which almost every family in the district was sharing, but for rejoicing that victory was at last in sight.

Under Mr Palmer's tuition Stephen had learned very fast and his delivery was very easy and professional. He took Marian's hand and kissed it, and the beautiful diamond ring flashed in the candlelight. Trust Stephen to do everything in style once his mind was made up! But he still could not meet Rose's eyes. Beneath the tablecloth her hands twisted tightly together. She knew that in spite of his slick brave words, Stephen was suffering as she was suffering.

The table rose, not waiting for the ritual port and the ladies' gossip in the drawing-room. Instead they hurried into wraps and coats for the drive across the moors to Danesfell.

There had been no night raids recently, only sporadic warnings in the distance. The Germans had abandoned the Zeppelin as too vulnerable an aircraft, and their fighter planes were all needed on their Western Front. As they drove, Rose watched the great dark mass of Danesfell loom until it seemed to blot out the sky. She and Stephen owned it and everything as far as she could see: the pits in the north, the forest parkland where the fallow deer grazed. It was unbelievable. Half dream, half nightmare. And when they went into the marble-tiled hallway it was like stepping into another world. A world that had vanished with the declaration of war.

Although Rose had worked for the past month organising this ball, she had never seen the state rooms of the great house dressed for entertaining, with the chandeliers alight, flowers and greenery banked in the curve of the elaborate stairway. She heard the sound of music from the ballroom, already crowded with brightly dressed women and many uniformed men. It was as though the great house had come to life again. Only a coiffed nurse crossing the hall towards a ward, and a group of patients in the blue flannel uniform of the wounded, making their way up to the gallery where they could sit and watch the dancing, were reminders that the leaden rain of machine gun fire was still raking the cold mud of France and men were still being killed in thousands.

The organisers had planned an old-fashioned, formal ball. There were dance programmes, and a fine military band from the American Camp already beating out a march. The dancers formed two great chains, making concentric circles, men on the inside, girls on the outside, and when the music stopped one had to dance with the person who stood opposite.

Rose and Marian had been besieged with requests for dances and their cards were filled within a few minutes of their entry into the ballroom. A handsome young American lieutenant wanted to write his name against half their dances, bewailing that the American custom of cutting in was not accepted in England. Nevertheless, when the music stopped he did cut in very smartly, sweeping Rose from Alban's outstretched arms with a flashing grin of mock apology.

'I guess your beau was real put out, ma'am.'

'I guess you're right,' she said. 'He is a man who always likes to win.'

'Don't we all, ma'am?'

The American boy's name was John Damian and he danced like a dream. He was also bubbling with patriotic enthusiasm.

'Yes, ma'am. We all want to get into this war and get it over. We'll clean up the Boche in no time at all for you.' He began to sing the popular song: "We won't give over 'til it's over over there."

'You will be going to France soon, yes?'

'I certainly hope so. I don't want to miss the real fighting. I come from a southern family, and we southerners are real keen soldiers. I've been training until I'm trained stiff. I want to see some action.'

She smiled at him and his boy's heart was shaken by the slow lift of her beautiful eyes, her glance of pity soft and compassionate. She had heard all this from so many partners, and so many of them had never returned.

'*Mon pauvre petit*,' she said. 'You will be there soon enough. Do not be in such a hurry.'

'You are French, ma'am?'

'I was born and brought up in Nice, so in a way I am a southerner too.' She had wondered if her dark skin would rouse his southern prejudices, but he showed no evidence of it. 'I pray God will keep you safe.'

'Thank you, ma'am. May I have another dance?'

'I am so sorry but my card is full. Would you have me lose all my friends? Let me introduce you to a friend of mine who has been over there – right up at the front line. She is a nurse and can tell you what it is really like.'

She introduced him to Jane Shawcross who was home on leave. She had finished a stint at a front line dressing station, and was going back to a British hospital on the outskirts of Paris. Her sandy good-looks and crisp manner had not

194

changed since their schooldays. Rose was glad to see her, and that she had a dance or two left for the American boy.

Rose could not remember whom she danced with that night. So many dancers – so many partners. So many light and meaningless flirtations, many with boys she had not seen before and would not see again. Alban danced only with her. He stood and watched her as she swung past in other partners' arms, and smiled at him as she passed. She was the centre of the ball. A beautiful young girl, beautifully dressed. Who could really believe she had been in love with Tom Grimshaw when she could smile, could flirt and laugh, like this?

He had booked her for the supper dance and claimed her as the band swung into the bars of the interval waltz, saying, 'Shall we sit this one out, Rose? It is so hot and you have danced so much.'

'I shall be glad to,' she said gratefully.

'Come into the Winter Garden. We could not light it, of course, but it is brilliant moonlight tonight, and the stephanotis is in bloom. My aunt is very proud of it.'

'You are all very proud of this wonderful house.'

'Yes. Although the upkeep is very heavy, and it entails a great deal of responsibility, we would hate to leave it now.'

He followed her through the heavily curtained door into the large conservatory. 'Your family were the original owners, I believe?'

'The Normanby family, my great-grandparents. And my grandfather, Sir Richard Normanby, was the last male heir.' She shrugged. 'But I never think of myself as belonging here, or feel anything about it. Except admiration.'

She knew the Winter Garden well. She sat here so often writing letters for injured men or reading them aloud for those who could no longer see. There were only a few couples lingering there and they went back into the ballroom when they heard the supper waltz strike up. The moonlight glittered on the fountain in the lily pond, and the stephanotis was in bloom. She would always remember its sweet cloying scent and the white glitter of this night when a man she did not care for asked her to marry him. She sat down on a marble bench and he stood nearby, looking down at her. The look in his eyes brought her to her feet.

'It's the Merry Widow Waltz,' she said. 'I like it. Let's go back and dance.'

'No,' he said shortly, and then, more quietly, 'wait. I must speak to you, Rose.' Her brows rose teasingly at his insistence. She saw his shaking hands and was sorry for him. He seemed to have slipped back into the gauche and awkward boy he had once been, eager, over bold, desperately shy. 'Rose, for pity's sake listen to me! Just for once take me seriously. There is something I must say to you.'

'But we can talk while we are waltzing, Alban.'

'No. Please listen now. I heard when I was in Paris – about Tom Grimshaw.'

She put her hands over her ears. 'I will not talk about Tom! Not with you or anyone. If you talk about him, I shall go away.'

'Don't be such a child, Rose! I do not want to intrude upon your grief, but I must try and make you understand.'

He moved in front of her, barring her way to the exit, an agonised furrow between his brows, his arms held stiffly by his sides, fists clenched so tightly that the white knuckle bones showed. She found his anxiety touchingly sincere, though she had a sense of danger, as though she was about to make a life or death decision. She wondered if the boys she had known who had died in France felt like this in the minutes before an attack.

She was quite aware of his obsession, that he had always admired and desired her, but had felt that in some curious way he despised himself for doing so, and had thought it must be because of her mixed blood or her mother's reputation. She knew he had always been influenced by his aunt and uncle, afraid of their disapproval, afraid to take any step which might offend them. But tonight he seemed to be quite different, as though some thread of control had broken and his real feelings could no longer be held in check.

'Alban, please let us go and dance and then go down to supper. And, please, I beg of you, never speak of Tom again.'

'I wish *you* would neither speak nor think of him! I wish you would think of *me*. In a short time now I shall have to return to Paris. Before I go I must know: will you marry me?'

She stared at him incredulously, began to laugh and stopped, realising how difficult it had been for him. She said slowly, 'Are you serious, Alban?'

'Haven't I always been serious with you?'

'I did not think so.'

Words began to tumble from him. 'Because you have always laughed at me! Don't laugh now. I know I should have given you more time. I know you have suffered a great loss. But before I go back I must know if I have a chance?'

She said quickly, 'If it is the renewal of the lease, please forget it. Steve and I would not dream of being difficult.'

'How can you think that? It's Grimshaw. I would have spoken before, but his memory stands between us. But now I must speak because I have so little time. And there are other difficulties. You are rich and I am comparatively poor. You must not laugh at me. I have wanted you as long as he did. From that time in Glockenschule, when you were just a schoolgirl. I was a clumsy oaf then, but in my heart I always wanted you for my wife!'

'Alban – did your aunt and uncle know that you were going to speak to me tonight?'

'Hasn't Mrs Grimshaw told you my aunt's wishes? Didn't she tell you?'

She shrugged eloquently. 'She did say something but I do not believe all the things she says. I thought maybe you were flirting, to fill in your leave before you returned to France . . .'

'No. You and I are grown up now. I love you very much. I want you to marry me.'

'Is it that your aunt has learned that Stephen and I now own the entire Danesfell estate? And that your lease is getting very short? You see, I know all about these business matters.'

'Of course that has influenced her. But she has also known what my feelings are, and what they have always been, since I first met you.'

'It is strange that you should remember that – someone else spoke of it to me.' She looked at him gravely, troubled and thoughtful. 'Until now I had no idea that you were thinking of marriage. Or that your people would actually give their consent.' She smiled. 'This seems to me to be a very

French situation, and I was brought up as a French girl, and French girls expect their parents to bargain on their behalf. What are you offering me? Besides your devoted love? That one day I shall be chatelaine of Danesfell when you are Sir Alban Stoneberry? A great position in the county – and I am flattered that you think I can fill it. But I already own a half share in the property. What else can I offer you? Well, besides my looks, and I think good taste,' her eyes were mischievous, 'I have a small cottage property locally, and a flat in Chelsea, also shared with Stephen, I am afraid, but there is also my considerable invested capital and the yearly income from my aunt's business, a very profitable concern. So, you see, I have quite a considerable *dot* – what do you think?'

He had relaxed a little. 'Rose, – please, don't tease now.' He gave a sudden, harsh little laugh but said quite gently, '*I* think you are a bargain – the grandest in the world, if you want to tease me like that. But let me know before I go back.'

'You say you love me, Alban? But I do not love you.'

'I had not expected that. Not so soon after . . .'

She put her hand quickly over his mouth. He turned it over and kissed it passionately. 'Well, I will bargain,' she said, forcing her voice to remain calm. 'But I believe in honest bargaining. I can bring you all those things I spoke of – except virginity. I am not a virgin, Alban.'

She heard the hiss of his indrawn breath and added, with passionate sincerity, 'And I am pregnant with Tom Grimshaw's child. This is why I want most urgently to marry. You would be doing me a great service, one that very few men would offer. Now you know my secret, shall we continue to talk or shall we go back to the ballroom and forget everything we have said? If you never speak to me again, I shall understand!'

The veins stood out in his forehead. His eyes were bright with fury. He raised his hand as though he would strike her, but she did not shrink. She was unashamed but she understood his anger. His arm fell to his side and he strode across to the curtained doorway as though he would leave her, then stopped abruptly, covering his face with his hands, his head swinging from side to side, fighting for self-control.

'So! Do not distress yourself. I ask too much.' Her hand went to the curtain, but he caught her wrist.

'*No*! Rose, wait! he said explosively. 'Don't go. I must think.' He took out a handkerchief and wiped his lips. His hands were shaking. 'I do not wish to withdraw my offer. I am willing to make a bargain. Grimshaw is dead, and whatever has happened, he can never take you from me now. I have always wanted you. I want to marry you more than I have ever wanted anything in my life.'

She was astounded. She had not believed he had any real, deep feelings for her. But then, when had she ever thought of him until tonight? He had been a tiresome boy who had pursued her and, recently, a disturbing but attractive man whom she could not love.

Then, fleetingly, she remembered that last journey from school when she had travelled up to Yorkshire with Marian and her family to avoid him, and how she had wakened to find him standing in the corridor, looking down on her with that strange, devouring look, and how, a little frightened, she had pulled down the blind.

'I did not think you were sincere,' she faltered. 'Although I knew you wanted me, a woman always does. I was wrong. I'm sorry. I know what pain it can be to fall in love.'

She was trembling now, quite different from the confident elegant young beauty whom he had pursued for so long. She was vulnerable, needing protection, afraid.

'I do not think your people really approve of me. I have mixed blood. Perhaps you too think like this?'

'Rose, that does not matter to me. I cannot help my aunt's stupid prejudices.'

'There is one thing more about our marriage – if I accept you. Until after the child is born, I will not . . . I do not wish to sleep with you.'

'I agree,' he said quickly. 'I too would rather it was like that.'

'That is very generous of you, Alban.' They stood facing each other in silence. 'So? Should we both consider it then?' She tilted her head charmingly like a kitten, a gesture he knew so well. Beneath her confident charm he glimpsed a very young, very frightened girl, frantically searching for a haven and hiding place.

'I do not need to consider. I know what I want. I always have known.'

She gave a long, shuddering sigh, and slowly held out her hand. 'Then I will marry you, Alban, and I will do everything in my power to make you happy. To be the kind of wife you need in every way. We have made our bargain. I promise, if you keep your side, so will I.'

He did not take her hand but gripped her arms, drawing her close to him, and as his lips closed on hers his strong fingers bit hard into her soft flesh.

'Alban,' she leaned away, 'you're hurting me!'

He had scarcely touched her lips. He let her go as though the brief contact had burned him. 'I'm sorry. I sometimes think it is possible to love someone too much. You must teach me to be kind and gentle, Rose.' He lifted her hands and raised them to his lips. 'You won't regret this, I promise you.' He kissed her then, very gently, and for a moment she felt happy and confident. Then he said eagerly, 'May I tell my aunt and uncle tonight? I know it will please them.'

'But we must not tell them the reason. Promise me that? It is our secret now. And everything must be done quickly, so I can go back with you to France and no one need know about the child. Then I shall be safe.'

His close-set grey eyes flickered. He seemed to be looking over her shoulder, as she had often noticed him do when they were younger, as he stammered out in his eagerness.

'Of course not.' He would have kissed her again, but involuntarily she moved her head so his lips touched her cheek. 'You are right. If we could be married immediately, you could travel back to Paris with me. Come – let us tell them now.'

She gave him her lips, deliberately trying not to think about, or even face up to, what she was doing.

The Stoneberrys were predictably delighted. And Sir Miles insisted on immediately announcing, 'This happy event, the engagement of my nephew Alban to Rose, the daughter of Baron and Baroness Abderhazy.'

Barbara Stoneberry and Angela glanced at each other. Lady Stoneberry's long face was flushed with relief. A few eyebrows were raised among the older women, and then there was a spontaneous and good-hearted rush of congratulations from Rose's younger friends. Only Marian and Stephen hung back a little, and the young American who had danced with Rose said in his laconic drawl, 'Guess this guy Stoneberry is the luckiest man in the room.' He was with Jane Shawcross, just going in to supper, and was startled by the incredulous disbelief in her eyes.

The ball was over. The last waltz had been played, and the National Anthem sung, facing the Allied Flags draped along the balcony. Marian caught up with Rose as she left the cloakroom. Her cheeks were as pink as the flowers in her dress but with indignation.

'What on earth are you up to, Rose?' she exclaimed. 'You've always disliked Alban. I thought he was a real wolf-oaf, and you did too!' Rose laughed. Wolf-oaf! She had invented the name to describe the well-spoken young boys who were invited from a nearby public school to the monthly dances at Pendrill's, over-eager and painfully shy.

'You're not really going to marry him?'

'I most certainly intend to,' she said airily. 'One has to be practical. I am sick and tired of living with Aunt Angela, and it is quite obvious she is sick and tired of me. It is time I was settled in life. There is no London Season now to put me in the marriage market, and no Aunt Margaret to arrange it all if there was. Alban has most honourably asked me to marry him. I have said yes. We want to get married immediately so I can return with him to live in France. I shall be a great lady one day and, as you know, I have always wanted to be.'

'I don't believe you really love him. And that great lady stuff was just silly schoolgirl talk. You remember, before I met Stevie I was going to marry the Prince of Wales?'

'Well, if you haven't got the Prince of Wales, you've got the prince of your heart – and a prince of this district. Once you saw him he was the only one, and you were lucky. I dreamed of being a great lady and living in a great mansion, but you would live in a mud hut with Stephen.'

'And you would, if Tom . . .'

'*Don't!*' Rose cried. The colour left her face. 'I have had to compromise.'

Marian was trembling with distress, but Rose put her hand gently against her cheek, her eyes very sad. 'Hush! What must be must be.'

Stephen came up to wish her goodnight. He took Marian's arm. His eyes met Rose's, angry and questioning. But she just kissed his cheek, and bade them both goodnight.

On the way home Angela chatted triumphantly. The ball had been a great success, and she was *so* happy about Stephen's engagement.

'She is such a charming girl, and they make such a lovely couple! Her family are so friendly, and Mr Palmer has really taken Stephen under his wing.'

'Yes, indeed, Madame.' Since their brief conversation as to how she should address Angela, Rose had always used the formal French term. 'It is indeed a very good thing.'

'And now you too, Rose,' Angela said graciously. 'I am so glad you have found happiness. You have been so helpful to me in recent months, but I must not be selfish. It has been a sad and difficult year for us all, and I shall miss you very much.'

She could not see Rose's ironic little smile in the darkness of the car, only her exquisite profile silhouetted against the white, frost-bound fields. These enigmatic silences ruffled Angela. One could never quite know what Rose was thinking. She had not seen her shed a tear over Tom's death. It was, of course, her oriental blood, and then there was that impossible mother. Angela's prejudices burned. She would not feel that Stephen was really safe while Rose was still at Cliffs Edge. She had tried, of course, to warn Barbara Stoneberry against this match, but there it was. Tom's will had radically changed the girl's position. She had been comfortably off when she first came to Cliffs Edge – now she was extremely rich. But one had to be loyal to one's friends. The Stoneberrys were important people in the county but they could not afford to keep up that great house. She had helped them to make this match although she really thought Tom most unfair. Rose was not really family, and Tom should have left everything to Stephen. Still, she would do her duty.

On the drive home Angela said to Rose, 'I think we should have a really splendid wedding. Barbara Stoneberry' – Angela had only just achieved first name status with that lady – 'will expect it. Early in the New Year, perhaps. Alban will surely be granted leave for it, and you both have so many friends. It will be a great advantage that you have the connection with the shop in London for your trousseau. Have you thought about your bridesmaids?'

The silvered profile turned, and the moonlight, shifting as the car turned a sharp corner, shone full on the beautiful face. Angela caught the gleam of amusement in the dark eyes. She was conscious of the pride and power in the girl and, as always, resented it.

'That will not be necessary,' Rose said calmly. 'Alban has to return to Paris very shortly and I wish to go back with him. I do not need clothes. I have plenty. We will have a small wedding with only our families and our good friends. I have no family but you and Stephen. I hope you will both come.'

Rose wished passionately that Margaret was still alive to be with her now. A woman who had loved her and whom she had learned to love. Someone to share her grief and to mourn with her, someone to whom she could tell everything in her heart, who would not be shocked or care what people thought. But then, she would not have agreed to marry Alban if Margaret was still here.

'But what will people think?'

Rose shrugged indifferently, the furs sliding from her shoulders.

'Is it important what people think? You are afraid they may look badly upon it? Foolish people often think bad things. We will suit ourselves, and it is our wish to be married as soon as possible and go back to France.'

'But is it safe? The war is so near in France.'

'It is quite near here – except in Paris, I have been told, they can hear the guns. I am not afraid of the guns, and I like Paris very much. And this way I will not need to worry you with my presence, Madame, for which I am sure you will be grateful. I shall have a home of my own.'

They travelled the rest of the way to Cliffs Edge in silence.

Chapter Ten

John Alban Stoneberry and Shareen Florence Abderhazy were married in the small parish church at Danesfell Abbey, which stood within the park of the great house. Its ancient grey spire was dwarfed by the towering Gothic arches of the ruined abbey from which the manor house took its name.

Afterwards Angela, long-suffering about this hole-in-the-corner affair, gave a luncheon for them at Cliffs Edge.

She had put herself out, even baking and icing the cake herself with whorls of silvered leaves and roses. The champagne had been the best from the Cliffs Edge cellars, and both the church and the luncheon table were decorated with spring flowers forced into early bloom in her fine greenhouse. No one, Angela thought, could say she had not done her duty.

Elsie, who had helped Rose to dress, was serving at table, and when her eyes met her young mistress's they were filled with tears. Elsie and Stephen were the only people there who really knew what Rose felt. They had seen her paralysed by the first shock of Tom's death; they alone had known her long-drawn-out hope that perhaps he would be found, and the bitter emptiness of her final acceptance that all hope had gone.

Elsie supposed that any decent chap would do if you could not have the one you had set your heart on. And Mr Tom had been such a lovely man.

Rose had asked Elsie to come to Paris with her, but she, just turned eighteen, much to Angela's indignation had just signed on for the Land Army.

Angela and Lady Stoneberry, who like everyone who lived in a large house were feeling the acute shortage of domestic help, bemoaned the ingratitude of the departing servants over the wedding cake.

'One takes these girls straight from school, trains them in superior domestic service, and as soon as they reach eighteen they rush off to the factories or farming or into the armed services. Girls in the army – it's ridiculous! I can't understand why their mothers don't protest.'

'I suppose,' sighed Lady Stoneberry, 'that we shall have to go to the orphanage again. All the people from the agencies are old and unreliable. The girls from the orphanage are quick and willing, but they are only fourteen and much too young to take any responsibility.'

The Matron of Danesfell Hospital, spurred on by Elsie's affronted face, and forgetting the deference she was supposed to owe these two important ladies, said, 'Well, I for one am grateful to all my volunteers. We couldn't manage without our auxiliaries, could we, Rose?'

'Indeed we couldn't,' she replied. 'And farming is very important too. The girls work for a very low wage, and often far from home.'

Stephen glanced at his watch and rose to his feet, lifting his glass. He spoke briefly, apologising that he had to cut the party short, but Rose and Alban had a train to catch, the night express from Leeds.

'However, before they escape, I ask you to join me in drinking their health. To my dear friend and sister Rose, and her husband Alban, the luckiest chap alive, who will, I know, care for her and love her as she deserves. To Alban and Rose!'

The guests drank the toast, and then Alban rose rather stiffly to reply, his hand tightening on Rose's almost as though he feared she might run away. She looked up and smiled reassuringly, and he pressed on with his formal thanks to Angela for the wedding luncheon, and to his aunt and uncle for their many kindnesses. As he sat down he did not kiss Rose but raised her hand to his lips.

Stephen and Marian drove them to Leeds, accompanied by two more cars crowded with their young friends, and they all walked up the platform in the customary wedding flurry of laughter and confetti.

Alban and Rose stood together at the carriage door. He was silent and watchful, while she was animated, laughing and talking. They're all *my* friends, she thought unhappily, mine and Stephen's. They know Alban but are not his friends. He has no friends. He never has had.

Alban knew what they were all thinking. He could see it in their eyes. They did not think it a good match for her. They knew how deeply in love with Tom Grimshaw she had been. His hand tightened on her waist. Rose was his wife now and no one could take her away from him.

It was nearly time to say goodbye. Rose stepped down from the carriage and moved among her friends, kissing many of them and taking everyone's hand in turn, thanking them all for their good wishes. Alban stood alone on the carriage steps, his eyes following her, then glancing impatiently at his watch.

'Be happy!' they cried. 'Write to us. Come back soon!'

'I will, I will,' Rose tossed her bouquet and Marian caught it.

She could not see Stephen. Anxiously she looked around, and then, typically, he was pushing towards her at the last moment, a great cluster of Parma violets in his hands. She jumped down and went to him. The guard was whistling his first warning. He thrust the flowers into her hands, put his arms about her and whispered frantically, 'I don't know why you are doing this, *Chérie*, but I swear I'll kill him if he doesn't make you happy.'

'Silly! If I'm not, it will be my own fault. Goodbye, darling Stevie.' She kissed him on both cheeks and fled back into Alban's waiting arms. He lifted her inside the compartment and shut the door as the train began to move.

'God, I thought you'd miss it! I was getting frantic.'

'I'm sorry.' She smiled apologetically.

He closed the window, pulling down the blind. The train jolted across junction lines. It was blackout time, and all the blinds had been drawn. The grim industrial suburbs of Leeds slid by unseen. Hundreds of mills were beginning the nightshift, their stacks belching smoke and sparks, working all out to supply the Allied armies.

Rose took off her hat and grey fur coat, and sat with Stephen's flowers on her knee. Alban sat down opposite her.

'It's strange,' she said, talking for the sake of talking, 'when I first came up here from school, I hated it. I never went into Thornsby town where the mills and factories were. I think I was afraid of it. I knew no one. The people seemed strange and rough-spoken, and Angela did not want me. But gradually I got to know the Grimshaw boys' friends, and Cliffs Edge became home. I've lived in Nice and London and Thornsby – now I am to live in Paris. It seems that the moment I settle down anywhere, I have to move on. I wonder, shall I like living in Paris?'

'I am sure you will like it very much.'

'Do you have many friends, Alban?'

He hesitated and said, 'Well, the fellows at H.Q. – but they are not really friends. There's one, Count Adolphe Bridault – a Frenchman I have met.'

'He is in the Army?'

'No. He's not fit. He's a useful chap, though. Knows Paris very well.'

'I hope I shall meet him.'

'I expect you will.'

He spoke no more of this aristocratic friend and they fell silent. The reserved compartment seemed a strange place in which to spend the first night of one's honeymoon.

He said suddenly, 'Do you mind if I smoke?'

'No, of course not.' He took out a golden engraved cigarette case and an expensive gold lighter. She had noticed these small extravagant personal possessions, silk monogrammed handkerchiefs and leather travelling bags, and supposed these niceties had been learned in Paris. His uniform was well tailored, the overcoat an expensive British Warm, which he put up in the rack with his service cap and sat down again, drawing the cigarette smoke down into his lungs. He did not know what to say to her. He did not attempt to touch her.

There was a feeling of withdrawal about him which she did not understand.

'What did Stephen say to you?' he demanded suddenly.

'Stephen? When?'

'Just now, when he gave you those flowers. When he kissed you.'

'Oh, Stevie is a very affectionate person! He just wished me happiness.'

'You seem to have been affectionate to both brothers. I have been told they customarily shared everything?'

She felt a great flame of anger sweeping over her, and for the first time he smiled.

'You are very beautiful when you are angry, Rose.'

'I shall be irresistible by the time we reach Paris if you make that sort of joke!' Her anger receded and she said more calmly, 'I am sorry, Alban, but I think you wish to quarrel with me. Stephen was as he always is, charming and thoughtful. He brought me flowers, as he often does!' She buried her face in the cluster of pale mauve flowers. They felt cold, and like many southern flowers had no scent. But they were very pretty.

'He thinks, as does all of Thornsby, that you are crazy to marry me. A lieutenant, living on his meagre army pay and a ridiculous allowance.'

He rose, snatched the flowers from her hand and thrust them out of the carriage window into the frost-bound night. And then, without a word, he sat beside her, put his arms about her and buried his face in her neck.

She found she was patting his shoulder comfortingly as though he were a child. 'You must help me, Rose,' he said.

She rose, closed the window and drew the blind, then asked gently, 'Alban, sometimes you look at me as though you want to hurt me. Why?'

He was silent for a moment, then said lightly, making it sound like a joke, 'Sometimes, when you tease me, I could spank you. I'm not used to being teased. Come, *Chérie*, let us go and eat.'

Before she could stop herself, she said, 'I would rather you called me Rose.' She bit her lip, angry that she had so thoughtlessly reminded him of something he wanted to forget. It was Tom who had first called her *Chérie*.

'Very well,' he said coldly, 'if that is what you wish. We must avoid reviving painful memories. I quite understand. I'm sorry.'

He helped her into her jacket punctiliously, and they went along the corridor towards the dining-room.

He went ahead of her, opening doors and steadying her against the jolt of the train. The third-class carriages were full of soldiers, men from the North returning to France. At Leeds there had been many anxious families, mostly smiling bravely as they bade their loved ones goodbye, but some openly in tears.

The corridor smelled of tobacco, sweat and khaki – she wondered if Alban was the only serviceman on the train not returning to the mud and blood and noise of gunfire. Once, when she looked at him, she caught a brief, unexpected glimpse of that strange expression she had seen before. But the next moment he smiled and, reassured, she went before him as he opened the door of the dining carriage.

'Why did you look at me like that?' he demanded. 'As though you were afraid of me.'

'I heard the siren. There!' Faintly, above the sound of the train, they could hear the warning wail. 'It must be quite near.'

He shook his head. 'We are travelling fast, and it is not so near. Come, Rose, we are holding people up.'

The dining carriage was the warmest and best lit compartment on the train. There were many officers at the tables and Alban did not miss their admiring glances as Rose passed them by. He was fiercely proud and yet at the same time could scarcely bear the admiration in other men's eyes. But now she was with *him*, and he knew that every man who saw her envied him. He put his arm possessively about her shoulders, displaying his ownership.

The waiter pulled out their chairs and they sat facing each other across the small table.

'I think every man here envies me,' he said.

Her smile teased him a little. 'They are only young boys, and I think they will be going back to the front.'

He was instantly on the defensive. 'You'd prefer that I should be on active service?'

'Oh, no!' she cried. 'You must never think that. I hate to hear of anyone going out there. Never think *that!*'

Neither of them were hungry. Rose gave the excuses that it was not long since they had eaten Angela's fine luncheon and that wartime food was not particularly appetising. They did not talk much, and she felt that they were both covertly trying to anticipate their next move. She knew of his moods. They were the reason for his unpopularity with the gay young set in Thornsby. The realisation of what she had so recklessly done swept over her. It was a trap which she herself had helped to set, and now they were both caught. Two people who had nothing in common, who did not really know each other, and there was no possibility of escape.

He ordered champagne and filled their glasses, and she drank, smiling across at him, feeling again that the smile was a mask which she could not afford to let slip.

'How filthy the food is,' he said, dropping his knife and fork with a gesture of disgust. 'Thank God the wine is not rationed. Let us order another bottle.'

'Not for me,' she smiled. 'I will have some coffee and then go back. I am very tired, and as you said we have a long day before us tomorrow. They will have made up the beds now, I should think.'

'Of course. Go when you wish.'

But he ordered another bottle of wine, and when the coffee came, ordered brandy as well.

'You must have something to take away the taste of this meal?'

'No, thank you. The champagne was enough. That, at least, was delicious. I will say goodnight now, in case I am asleep when you come. Give me time to change.'

'Of course. I will stay here for a while and have a cigar. Goodnight, Rose.'

As she left she heard him summon the waiter and tell him to bring the brandy bottle to the table.

A middle-aged couple sitting at a nearby table smiled sympathetically as she passed, and four of the young officers rose and saluted. She nodded, wondering if she had confetti in her hair and hoping it would not make Alban angry again.

When she reached the compartment she shut the door and stood pressing her palms to her eyes, holding back the tears. She must *not* weep. He must *not* see her weeping. She had made her bargain and she must keep it.

She undressed quickly and changed into a pale rose-coloured nightdress and a wrap of fleecy wool. She climbed into her bunk, put out the main light and picked up her book. In a few minutes she was fast asleep. She was awakened by a fierce grip on her shoulder. The bed light was still on, her shoulder and right breast were naked, her open book slipped to the floor.

Alban was bending over her, gripping her shoulder.

'What is it? What's happened?' She sat up, half awake, pulling her wrap over her shoulder. Alban's hand fell to his side.

'The train jolted,' he said. 'You would have fallen.' He stood back, and she could see he was trembling. She stretched out a hand reassuringly. She could smell the brandy on his breath, but he ignored her hand and turned angrily away, speaking to her over his shoulder.

'Did you think I couldn't see the terror in your eyes all through dinner? Was it fear? Or was it disgust? You needn't worry, I won't touch you. I will keep my side of the bargain. I won't trouble you tonight or any night while you are carrying Grimshaw's bastard.'

He pulled the door open and stumbled into the corridor, shutting it loudly behind him.

She felt weak with relief. How long had he been there, gazing down at her? She was too tired to think or care. She could not plague her mind any more. She turned the light out and pulled up the blanket. She knew he would not return.

She woke early. The opposite bunk had not been used. She looked at her shoulder and saw a purple bruise with four dark patches, like print stains on her skin.

The steward came, calling that he had brought her breakfast, and handed in a tray with coffee and rolls, butter and jam.

'The gentleman told me he is having his coffee in the dining car. He said to ask you to join him when you are ready.'

She tipped him and asked him to tell the gentleman she would be with him directly. The night before was a jumble of dreams and reality. It was still dark although it was early morning, they were running through the northern suburbs of London to Kings Cross, and from there would go to Victoria to catch the boat train.

She drank a hurried cup of coffee, rinsed her hands and dressed, moving quickly within the small space as she packed her travelling case, adjusted her hat, picked up her gloves and fur jacket and went to the dining car.

Alban was there already, anxiously watching the door. She stood for a second, looking at him through the glass door. Her husband, who was not her lover, who was still a stranger. She wondered where he had spent the night and what mood he was in this morning. But when she smiled, he rose quickly and opened the door for her.

'Did you sleep well?'

'Yes, very well. And you?'

'I have been so worried – I only just caught you, you were about to fall out of the bunk. Afterwards I came back here and fell asleep at the table. The porter woke me and found me an empty bunk in which to finish the night. I didn't want to disturb you.' He put his hand on her shoulder very gently and said, 'Does it still hurt you? I didn't mean to hurt you.'

'It is nothing. May I have a cup of coffee, please, if it is not too late?'

'Of course.' He ordered a cup of coffee for her and they sat in silence, looking out into a grey, muggy morning. Nothing will be said, she thought. Perhaps they had both been apprehensive on that strange first night together. He had been drinking. People who drank too much could remember nothing of what they had said when they were sober. *In vino veritas* – the Latin tag caught her memory, how awful if he were speaking the truth.

She drank her coffee, and started to talk about the next part of their journey. She asked him what kind of an apartment she should look for? Something small, she suggested, and near his headquarters.

213

'Not too small,' he said positively, 'somewhere with at least one large reception room. Somewhere where we can entertain at least forty people. I owe a good deal of hospitality, particularly among the top brass. They know about Danesfell. We mustn't be too cheeseparing.'

'I have never shopped for a home before,' she said, 'and I find the prospect most exciting. There are some lovely things there for me to buy. I am sure that Monsieur Raymond, Papa Léon's *avocat* over there, will advise me where to go.' She thought, and the thought was like a prayer, that Alban would like the home she was creating for them, and everything would be all right.

They arrived at the Hôtel Ventura Royale in the early evening. It was old-fashioned compared to the new palace hotels which had sprung up just before the war, but was still famous for its opulence and Edwardian comfort. It was the hotel in which Rose and Respy had stayed on their first momentous journey from Nice to London, and where, later, she had stayed with Margaret. It gave her a sense of stability. They had been given a drawing-room and two bedrooms, and there were flowers to greet them. She could not believe that the Western Front was so near – not until she heard, for the first time, the distant thunder of the heavy guns.

'That cannot be thunder!' she exclaimed. 'It is too cold.'

Alban's eyes flickered. A vestige of alarm, quickly concealed, showed in his face.

'It is the guns,' he said. 'They seem worse as night falls. But you will hear them, on and off, all the time. They have yet to make their great final attack.'

'They? Who? The Allies? Or the Germans?'

'Who knows. They are both playing a waiting game, like chess. It drives one crazy, wishing they would start and finish the whole disgusting thing. Both trying to find the other's weakness. Life is cheap to the Generals – but they're not in the front line.'

'Well, I'm glad you are not there either.'

'If I was sent out there, I think . . .' He did not finish the sentence but laughed shortly and said, 'It's no use talking about it. But I think it would be a good idea if I dropped in on H.Q. tonight to let them know I'm back, and find out what's happening.' He saw the disappointment in her eyes, and said quickly, 'After we've been out, of course. I will not wake you when I return. Will you be frightened if you are an hour or two in the hotel alone?'

He was looking at her with a strange, speculative glance, as though he was about to tell her some secret. It made her feel as though they were walking on thin ice, wondering if it would bear their combined weight.

'I want to introduce you to some of the fellows as soon as possible.' He grinned boyishly. 'I want them all to see what a beautiful bird I've captured. And I want a gorgeous cage to show her in.'

She understood at once and it made her smile. He had always wanted to be important, even as a boy. He had boasted of Danesfell and his uncle's position in the county. It had made him unpopular at school, a butt for teasing. And now it was so childish it was almost touching.

'I will find you something very impressive,' she promised, smiling indulgently. 'It may be difficult to find exactly what we want. Paris is extraordinarily crowded . . . I had not expected that. But there must be someone I know who will help me.'

'Who?' he asked suspiciously. 'Who do you know in Paris?'

'Well, friends and customers of my Aunt Margaret. And Papa Léon's solicitor. I am sure Monsieur Raymond will help me.'

He gave a tight-lipped little smile, the covert withdrawal that she was beginning to dread. It was so instantaneous, it frightened her. His moods changed so quickly.

'And friends of your mother? Gentlemen friends?'

She ignored the covert little sneer. In Thornsby her mother's name was scarcely known. To them the Baroness Abderhazy had been just a glamorous personality, read about in the yellowing newspapers of a decade ago. She supposed in Paris everyone would have heard of Charmian.

'My mother,' she said, 'knew some very interesting and influential people. And you would be right in thinking they were all men. But *I* am not my mother.'

The ugly flush died and his handsome face was lit by a smile that did not quite touch his eyes. She realised she had never heard him laugh.

'I was teasing,' he said. 'I am sure you will find somewhere splendid, and I will like anything you choose.' He bent forward and touched her shoulder, just above her breast, and she flinched a little. 'Does it still hurt?'

'Not really. It is nothing. When will you be back? They tell me that Parisian night-life still goes on in spite of the guns. You must know your way around by now. I have never been to Maxim's.'

'We cannot dine at Maxim's,' he said, 'unless you want to see the fashionable whores.' The hand on her shoulder twitched.

Her beautiful dark eyes met his steadfastly. 'Why not? I understand that nowadays many great ladies go there too.'

'But not young ladies of good family,' he said stiffly.

'Married young ladies with their husbands, Alban! It is wartime. Young ladies can go anywhere – or almost anywhere. They even work just behind the Front at dressing stations. Jane Shawcross does. She is nursing over here now and she writes to me, and she has often been to Maxim's when she's staying in Paris on short leave.'

The colour burned in his face. His hand fell from her shoulder. He turned away, saying furiously, 'I'll be ready to go out at nine.'

He went into his room and shut the door. She heard the key turn in the lock and gave a weary little shrug. She knew how sensitive he was about his position, and that most of his fellow officers were much older and had let him know that they thought any man of his age, with no specialised training, should be at the front. Sometimes they were aggressive, sometimes they were merely teasing him, but they never let an opportunity slip by. They guessed Sir Miles Stoneberry had used his influence to get Alban into a "cushy billet". She could only try not to say anything that would make him feel ashamed or guilty, but she was not going to tap on his door and apologise. She too went into her room, and tired and travel-worn, enjoyed the comfort of a long hot bath and a sleep on the bed afterwards. She asked the desk to call her at seven-thirty so she would have plenty of time to dress.

She put on her dark blue velvet dress, with a long evening cloak padded with rose-coloured silk and collared with sable.

216

She wore her pearls and her golden bracelets. When Alban came from his room, shaved and affable, attentive and courteous, ordering champagne to drink in the room before they started, she understood that nothing more was to be said about their disagreement.

She twirled before him like a mannequin to display her dress. It was ankle-length and had a full skirt. The movement showed her long, slender legs with their elegant, fine-boned ankles.

'Well, what do you think?'

'I think you look very beautiful, but then you always do. I have always thought you the most beautiful girl I have ever seen.'

'*Merci bien, M'sieur.*' He caught her hand and drew her against him, but he kissed her cheek not her lips.

They went to Maxim's, he insisted, and the restaurant lived up to its reputation for beautiful, elegant women and good food. Nearly all the men were in uniform, and there were many Americans.

Afterwards, they went to a cabaret, where the noise and chatter and gaiety were just as hectic and the songs full of patriotic defiance. It was below street level, a very large place, and although a red light flashed an air raid warning, no one left or seemed to heed it.

Voices were lulled for a second, and then rose again in the endless chatter and laughter. The dance band did not miss a beat.

Rose put her hand on Alban's arm and said gently, 'Would you like to dance with me?'

He rose and they went on to the dance floor. He held her as he always did, stiffly and a little away from him, as though close contact disturbed him.

He said suddenly, 'Once I thought you would never, ever dance with me.'

'Alban!' she cried remorsefully. 'Was I really so horrible – so cruel and thoughtless?'

'Yes,' he said, and smiled and held her close, and she felt his lips against her forehead. 'But you're my wife now, and everything will be all right.' She lifted her lips to his and he kissed her, and for the first time she felt a new warmth and

217

tenderness between them. Yes, perhaps it was going to be all right after all.

They left at one o'clock. As they waited for a taxi, gunfire could be heard plainly in the clear night air, bringing the war even closer. The bravado of the cabaret seemed almost pitiful.

In the foyer of the hotel Alban kissed her hand and said he thought he would now drop in to H.Q. and report his return.

Rose went up to their rooms alone.

During the night she sat up, startled. The sound of the guns seemed almost to be in the city. The monotonous thud and rumble like distant thunder and the rattle throughout the building set the chandelier tinkling and shook petals from the elaborately arranged flowers.

She did not return to sleep for a while. The room was a luxurious bridal suite suitable for a rich young couple, but lying there alone it was not a bridegroom she wanted but a friend. In the early hours of the morning she heard the door open, and knew Alban was standing looking in on her. She shrank down beneath the covers. Finally she heard him stumble across to his room. It was an hour before she fell asleep again.

Alban had been greeted with a new warmth when he went into H.Q.. News of his marriage had reached his brother officers and he was greeted with congratulations. Even the C.O. condescended to ask when they were to meet the new Mrs Stoneberry.

'We are looking for an apartment near here, Sir,' Alban said, 'then you will be able to meet my wife.'

The Colonel looked surprised. An apartment in this district would be pretty expensive, and he had always understood that Stoneberry was short of cash.

'Your little Missis must be a very plucky young woman!'

'I was hoping things might have settled down.'

'Didn't we all,' said the Colonel dourly. 'I've tried to make my wife go home, but she's an old campaigner and wouldn't hear of it. Your Missis is young, I suppose?'

'She'll be nineteen this year. What is happening, Sir? I seem to have been away for ages.'

'Nothing much, except for the usual straffing, both trying to find the weak spots. We're waiting for the Yanks to get up the line in strength. Won't your little girl be frightened on her own?'

'I don't think so. I'm not on duty tonight. I shall move my things out of here as soon as we get a place of our own.'

'I wish you luck. Paris is crowded these days. Everyone is scrambling back as though the war was already over, and it's not by any means. We may have to move our stuff out of here and get back ourselves. You get back to the little woman while you can.'

Alban did not want to go back to the hotel. Rose's sleeping presence in the next room would not let him rest. He left the Mess and went out into the darkened streets, wandering idly towards the river. The talk in the Mess had been of women, and they had chaffed him a little, accusing him of being a dark horse, not telling them about this whirlwind romance.

He decided to go to a gambling club which he had recently joined on Adolphe Bridault's introduction. He had discovered that gambling gave him a sense of high excitement he had never known before. It was like the sexual excitement men felt for women, but which he had never experienced. He had thought to find it with Rose. Her exotic beauty filled him with dreams of ecstatic conquest. And now he had her – only to find that she had already given herself to Tom Grimshaw. He still wanted her, but the thought of the child she carried revolted him. When that was over, then perhaps it would all be different. The memory of Tom Grimshaw's handsome face and smiling blue eyes haunted him: the boy who had everything, whom everyone loved.

He went to a famous brothel, where he might find Bridault. The days of its flamboyant heyday were long past and there was a musty air of decay about the tarnished gilt furniture and red velvet banquettes. Like an empty stage set when the curtain was down. The naked and half-naked women were neither very young nor very beautiful. But he set a table and bought them drinks until, as he'd hoped, Comte Adolphe

Bridault arrived. They greeted each other eagerly, like old friends.

Bridault was older than Alban by about ten years, in his thirties but looking older. They had met shortly after Alban's arrival, falling into conversation at an all-night café near H.Q.. Bridault was a night creature. Elegant, pale, languid, and apparently always hard up. But he was as near a man friend as Alban had ever known, and had introduced the English officer into many dark avenues of pleasure.

He was a very clever man from a great family, and his degradation made Alban feel superior. A man of title and position, once heir to great possessions and a proud name, begging for a few hundred francs to buy the drugs that kept him going, or pay entrance to strange and often sleazy places of pleasure.

But he could still exert a cool charm and had the assurance and confidence of the born aristocrat. But Bridault was a sly and secretive man behind his delightful bonhomie, exploiting the unwary.

There was one room in the establishment where a client could sit at his ease looking through a concealed window, watching the girls plying their sordid trade.

That night Bridault told Alban about it, laughing as though at a joke, and when Alban pressed him, arranged an hour of amusement for them. Both the wine and the hour were expensive. Alban could now afford to pay. Bridault made a show of protesting.

'My dear fellow, of course I must pay, and I will, but at the moment I am exceedingly short.'

'I insist,' said Alban firmly, he had taken quite a deal of drink, 'and now I can afford it.'

The bewigged and raddled Madame exchanged understanding glances with the Frenchman as she led the way. *Chacun à son goût*, she thought, and behind Alban's back paid Bridault his cut for the introduction. The two men spent an enjoyable hour there, Alban laughing immoderately at Bridault's comments and criticisms.

He felt quite sure that none of his fellow officers knew Paris like this. Inwardly he was shocked and embarrassed, and

ashamed that the woman's degradation should disturb him
so.

He would have stayed, but Bridault was bored and restless
and insisted that they go on somewhere else.

It was after three o'clock. Bridault suggested a small gambling club he knew, exclusive and privately owned, where the
stakes were very high and only the big gamblers played.
There was no need to play, of course, but it was interesting to
stand and watch. Alban said he must not be too late as he was
on duty in the morning.

Bridault laughed. 'On duty? Where? H.Q.? Or with your
wife?'

They both roared, and Bridault slapped Alban on the
shoulder and promised to get him back before dawn. He was
thinking there were more possibilities in this boring, provincial English boy than he had first thought. He was staying at
the Ventura Royale, so there must be money somewhere.
The new wife, of course. Alban had always pleaded poverty
before. Bridault saw to it that he was back at the hotel in the
early hours.

Alban went to his room and stumbled into bed. But he
dreamt. He dreamt that he was watching the Montmartre
prostitute through the mirror, and felt the excitement growing within him. But suddenly she turned and looked back at
him and the face was pale and pure, framed in long shining
black hair. It was Rose.

He woke, sweating, feeling the coldly violent anger he had
felt when she had told him of Tom Grimshaw's child. He
turned his face into the pillow but did not sleep again. He had
bathed and dressed and left for H.Q. before Rose was awake.

As soon as she had finished breakfast, she telephoned Jane
Shawcross at the British Hospital. Jane was delighted to hear
her voice, and as she had twenty-four hours' leave they
arranged to dine together that evening.

She arrived at the hotel promptly and the two girls decided
to dine in the hotel restaurant rather than venture out into the
black-out and the dark Paris streets. Rose asked Jane to stay
overnight.

'Alban had to report to headquarters, and now he is on
duty,' she explained, perhaps a little too glibly.

221

Jane's sandy brows went up. 'On his honeymoon?'

Rose met her eyes, but felt they were back at school again and that she was giving feeble excuses to a prefect.

They had been given a corner table. The restaurant was full in spite of the food restrictions. The majority of the men present were in uniform and the women of Paris seemed to be as elegant as ever.

Jane had changed out of uniform and was wearing a simple black evening dress, still in mourning for her brother. But Rose's dark blue velvet, with its big rose-lined hip bow catching the draping of the skirt, made Jane feel distinctly provincial. She sighed and grumbled good-naturedly, 'How is it you always look so . . . I don't know how to describe it. It's not just well dressed. Even your shoes match the satin lining of your dress! At school you always looked better than anyone, however rich they were.'

'It's the training,' Rose said laughingly, 'I had the advantage of being Margaret Normanby's niece, the great Madame Léon. She was not strict with me except when it came to my clothes. I don't think she ever sold a dress that she did not think was exactly right for that particular customer. To be badly dressed would be to let down the Salon.'

'You speak as though you own the business.'

'Well, in a way I do. At least, I own a lot of the shares.' She picked up the menu. 'Come, let's order, then we can talk.'

When they had ordered Rose said, 'But now you tell me about yourself. Tell me about your work over here.'

'I'd rather not talk about it. It's good to get away from it for a while. At first I was at a dressing station up the line. After that, everything else seemed a piece of cake. Let's forget it. How long will you be in Paris?'

'Oh, quite a while. First I have to find an apartment near Alban's headquarters. I may be going down to Nice later to see Respy. Is there any sort of voluntary work I could do at your hospital, like the work I did at Danesfell? I would have time once I find us somewhere to live.'

'I should think you could be very useful. The patients are all British, of course, and so are most of the nursing staff. But we do have many French auxiliaries. You speak both languages.

Come over and see us when you are ready, and I'll introduce you to the Matron and Superintendent.'

'I should be most grateful, for I must have something to do when Alban is on duty. I don't want to play around being a smart lady.'

'Who is this Respy you are going to see?'

'My foster mother, Madame Respigny. She looked after me when my mother died – well, really from the time I was born.'

Jane said unexpectedly, 'Is that the only reason that you are going to Nice, to see this Madame Respigny?' Rose glanced up into Jane's clear grey eyes. No-nonsense Yorkshire eyes. There was no point in being evasive with her.

'Does it really show?'

'Barely. My professional eye, I suppose. But you're only just married?'

'It is why I got married. Are you very shocked?'

'Good Lord, no!' said Jane, and her face crinkled with amusement. 'The war and nursing have rendered me shockproof. The truth is, I always thought you disliked Alban. Well, none of us liked him, let's face it.'

Rose took a flower out of the vase on the table and began to pull off its innocent petals, her long dark lashes hiding her unfathomable eyes.

'It isn't his baby, is it?' Jane said bluntly. 'Is it Tom Grimshaw's?'

They seemed to be isolated in a little pool of silence in the crowded, chattering room. 'They say he's dead,' said Rose, 'but somewhere inside me I still don't believe it. But they say there's no doubt now.'

'Say?' repeated Jane. 'Has there been no confirmation?'

'His body has never been found, only his identity disc. That confirms it, doesn't it?'

'It usually does,' said Jane grimly. 'Does Alban know?'

'Yes. I told him when he asked me to marry him. It was part of our bargain. He wanted me anyhow – he said. He had wanted me for a long time, and I needed a husband.'

'But why Alban?'

'It was my only offer,' said Rose simply, and smiled. 'I had no time to shop around.'

223

'That's not difficult to believe. There can't be many men of marriageable age left in Thornsby now. Right – let's get this straight. I don't blame you for that. I was in love with Tom once. All the girls in Thornsby were. He was very special. But of course none of us had a look-in when you appeared. So why didn't he marry you? He was in love with you, wasn't he?'

'There was no time. He was only passing through London. He had an appointment at the War Office, and left the following evening. I happened to go into the Chelsea flat and there he was, fast asleep and filthy from travelling. We had one night and most of the following day, and I never saw him again. It just happened. I made it happen. I think we both felt we might never meet again. But I'm glad we had that night. When I had realised the baby was on its way, I heard that Tom was missing. I didn't know what to do. I just kept hoping he was only missing. Then, just before Christmas, they sent the identity disc.'

'You never thought of an abortion?'

'No,' said Rose, looking puzzled. 'It never entered my head. It is Tom's baby. I want it.'

'But what in heaven's name made you marry Alban Stoneberry? You have plenty of money. For the sake of respectability? I don't believe that.'

'You don't know what it is to be treated like a bastard, Jane. My mother was married to Baron Abderhazy, but she had many lovers. No one knew which of them was my father. It could not have been the Baron. He sent her money, but never a *sou* for me. My mother was notorious in Nice. It was gossiped that even she did not know who my father was except that he was of Eastern blood. When she died, no one came forward to claim me. Papa Léon, my Aunt Margaret's husband, was my guardian, but even he did not know the truth. Aunt Margaret only learned of my existence from his solicitors after his death. She sent for me at once. And so I was brought to her in London. For a short while, until she died, I had someone who loved me. She died too soon. With her, for the first time in my life I had a real home. She was even proud of me. But then, Tom too was a bastard. He was my cousin, you know.'

'Everyone knew about Tom,' said Jane, 'but everyone loved him. It made no difference. There wasn't a girl among us that wouldn't have given her eye teeth to have married him.'

'Ah, but Tom was rich, and handsome, and a man. Supposing this baby is a girl? Why do you think the Stoneberrys have only recently pressed Alban to marry me? Would they have done so if I hadn't inherited half ownership of Danesfell Abbey? They are very proud of it but they are only tenants, and their lease is running out. And remember that Tom suffered as a child, because Henry Grimshaw forced his wife to accept him and she never forgave either of them for it. I want none of this for my baby. To be illegitimate is to be a target for malice. So you see, the Stoneberrys wanted the use of my fortune, and Alban wanted me, and I wanted a husband. We made a bargain.'

'It is a devil's bargain, Rose. And will you really be able to keep it?'

'Of course. If he keeps to his word, I will keep to mine. If he breaks it, then I shall break it too. But even if he does, I shall still be Mrs Alban Stoneberry – a Married Lady. And my child will be legitimate. And I am French enough not to be a fool over money. Stephen is my guardian now, and he has made Alban a very generous allowance, but the capital and property will still belong to me.'

'I see.' Jane looked grave. 'No one else knows about the baby?'

'No.'

'Not even Stephen?'

'Particularly not Stephen!' Rose said fiercely. 'He would have insisted on marrying me himself, and Marian's heart would have been broken. And I could not make such an agreement with anyone as close to me as he is. Now, that's that. Let us not talk about it any more. It's done and cannot be undone.'

Jane shook her head doubtfully.

'Tomorrow I must start looking for an apartment. Then one day this week I will come out to the hospital, and see if they will let me work there two days each week until I go away. It will probably be in March or early April. Alban says we need a large place because he wants to entertain. You know he loves to display me – but I don't think he will if I get too enormous, so I shall tactfully slip away then. What do you think of my plans?'

'I think you are a dreadful girl, Shareen Abderhazy, and how do you propose to set about finding an apartment?'

'I shall go to Papa Léon's solicitors who arranged for me to be delivered to Aunt Margaret. There was a very nice young man there, Paul Raymond, who looked after Respy and me when we came from Nice. I am quite sure he will help me if I ask him. I am calling at their office tomorrow – who knows, he may like me even better now I am grown up?'

For the first time that evening her eyes twinkled with mischief.

'Not so grown up as you think,' said Jane, laughing. 'As I said, you are a dreadful girl, and not only dreadful but incorrigible. But then, you always were.'

Rose could not see Monsieur Paul Raymond when she contacted her solicitors because he had been called to his regiment early in the war and was still at the front. Instead she saw his father, the head of the firm, Monsieur Jean Raymond, an important-looking gentleman with a small Imperial beard and pointed moustache. He had a very gallant manner and told her his son had always said what an enchanting little girl Monsieur Léon's ward was, but that he was quite unprepared for Madame Stoneberry's radiant beauty.

Having got these preliminaries satisfactorily settled, he proved to be both businesslike and kind. He had already been instructed to open a bank account for her in Paris, so that her allowance and that of her husband could be paid into their accounts in Paris. He had the papers here for her to sign. Mr Stephen Grimshaw, her guardian, had also said that if she needed extra money, she was to be allowed to overdraw. But *not* Lieutenant Stoneberry.

She nodded her agreement, smiling a little at Stephen's Yorkshire caution.

Now as to the matter of the apartment – he would of course be delighted to help her if he could. In fact, he knew of a place belonging to a friend of his son's who was also away in the army, a Captain Frossart, who was finding his Army pay a little insufficient, and could do with extra money. He would arrange for her to see it that afternoon.

'It is very old,' he said, 'Eighteenth-century, I understand. But very romantic. Just the place for newlyweds.'

Monsieur Raymond was looking forward to meeting Lieutenant Stoneberry who was a very fortunate young man. He imagined that the Englishman must be very prepossessing too, and a satisfactory husband, for there was in the beautiful oriental face of his young client the look of a woman who has experienced an overwhelming passion. True to his promise, Rose received the keys that afternoon at the hotel where she was lunching with Jane, who had not to return to the hospital until early evening.

They found the Place de Maréchal, an old square near the Invalides. There was a railed central garden with paths and trees surrounded by four-storey houses on an arched arcade running round the four sides.

'Eighteenth-century, did he say?' asked Jane. 'It must have been here before the Revolution. It's a bit creepy, don't you think?'

'Romantic,' said Rose firmly. 'He said it was very nice inside.'

The street level was faced with little shops beneath the shelter of the arcade. Map makers, booksellers, print sellers, stamp vendors, one running through into a sunlit picture gallery, and several antique dealers. Between every four shops there was a large arched entrance leading to the apartments above. The concierge's apartment with the usual little curtained window was on the right. They went up the wide shallow stone stairway and unlocked the large oak door with an enormous key. The door opened into a small foyer with a faded Persian rug, leading into a large beautiful salon.

Gilded furniture glimmered, shadowy portraits looked down, thin pencils of daylight showed behind the closed shutters. Rose went across the room and unfastened the shutters. Dust showered everywhere as she threw them open, and afterwards the windows which gave on to a large courtyard at the rear of the building. The room filled with afternoon sunlight. It was panelled in cream with gilded mouldings which concealed doors leading to smaller rooms beyond. Captain Frossart had inherited it from his parents and, apart from modernisation of the kitchen and two bathrooms, it was as his parents had left it.

The beautiful old carved and gilded furniture was upholstered in a faded brocade in rose and green. Curtains of the same pale material hung at the windows. High quality Persian rugs were strewn on the parquet floor, and the two large glass chandeliers were muffled in linen dustbags. There were fine walnut cabinets with serpentine fronts and a handsome desk under the tall windows to catch the light.

'I shall feel like Violette in *Traviata*,' cried Rose, bursting into the waltz song from the opera. 'I ought to wear a crinoline if I live here.'

'Well, they are very concealing,' said Jane. 'You don't look like a consumptive heroine. But then few operatic heroines do. It's very big – the room, not you.'

'It's beautiful,' said Rose. 'Alban wants to entertain and this place is built for it. It could take fifty people for a really big party.'

'D'you think he will like it?'

'Oh, yes. All the Stoneberrys love grandeur. They couldn't live at Danesfell otherwise.'

They giggled together like the schoolgirls they had been such a short while ago. In this unexpectedly renewed friendship they were finding some of the girlhood the war had stolen from them.

There were two doors on the inner side of the room, almost invisible in the elaborately carved panelling, for the knob handles formed part of large carved flowers. Rose opened them in turn. Behind the first there was a fair-sized bedroom and a small bathroom. It had obviously been Lieutenant Frossart's room, for there were photographs of school classes and sports teams, and a rack containing a saddle, a row of hunting whips, and a brass horn, which they both tried to blow and had another attack of laughter over when neither could raise a sound.

'This will be Alban's room,' said Rose.

The other opened on to a fairly wide corridor, off which lay a large bedroom and small bathroom, and the kitchen.

Still another door opened from the kitchen, behind which was a circular iron staircase going down to the ground floor below. Rose switched on a light and peered down. Dark and dusty, it contained an empty wine rank, some old bits of furniture, and there was a door opening on to the centre courtyard at the back of the house. It smelled of stale wine and the staircase was grey with dust. Rose hurriedly came back and locked the kitchen door.

'There's no dining room,' said Jane. 'That's odd, considering the size of this room.'

'It's one of these great old Parisian mansions cut into two,' said Rose. There was an octagonal table with four chairs at the street end of the room. She stood back, her eyes shining, looking round the room.

'It's beautiful. So big, you could swing a cat – several cats, in fact. I shall take down and store the most repulsive of the Frossart ancestors. The Lieutenant seems to have collected a few good paintings which you saw in his bedroom. I shall hang these in their place. And fill those great Chinese vases with flowers, and there's a great big bed in the back room which you can share with me when you stay the night, Jane, and you can come whenever you like. Of course, everything needs a good cleaning. It will look wonderful.'

She paused for breath, and Jane said, 'It certainly does need cleaning. There's a terrible smell of stale tobacco.'

'Come, let us find the concierge and see if she can help me with the cleaning.'

The concierge was a sharp-eyed little woman with a rolling Parisian accent. She accepted the large tip which Rose gave her and apologised for the state of the apartment. It had only been cleaned once a month since Monsieur Frossart was in the Army. Yes, she would start on it straight away, and she knew of a girl who would come in every day to cook and clean.

'Well, that's all settled then,' Rose said triumphantly. 'In one day I have been successful. I think I shall make an excellent wife.'

They hailed a taxi to drive Rose back to the hôtel and drop Jane at the station.

'Thank you for the offer of a bed,' she said. 'I shall certainly come whenever I have leave.'

'Jane, please come whenever you want to. Do not bother to telephone. I shall give you a key and you must make it your home in Paris. And bring your friends. There are many people here who will come and enjoy themselves, I hope, and forget about the sound of guns for a while. I am so glad to have found you. It is like having a little bit of home here.'

She sounded so wistful that Jane hugged her. It was so easy to forget how very young she was.

'I needn't go for an hour yet,' she said. 'Let us have a coffee first.'

They went to a pavement café.

'Wouldn't it have been easier,' Jane said, 'to stay in Chelsea? Or even at Cliffs Edge – and let Alban return to France alone?'

'No, I wanted to come, and he wanted me to come too. If I had stayed, I would have had to tell all sorts of lies to everyone. To the Stoneberrys, to Aunt Angela. And everyone would count on their fingers and watch me get fat. No one would have believed the baby was Alban's. This way I think they will. I shall go down to Nice to be with Respy when the baby comes, and stay on for a while, then no one will know the exact date of its arrival. I should have liked to go to Chelsea and live there alone, but not with Alban.'

She fell silent, thinking of the light, lovely rooms and seeing her aunt's slight figure resting in the lounge chair in the window, watching the Thames barges sail past. She remembered that first and last time with Tom. How she had slipped into his half-conscious embrace, and his muttered French endearments as the siren wailed and the guns barked in the south-east suburbs. 'Chelsea is my home really, I'm glad it belongs to me now. But I will never live there with anyone but Tom.'

She gave a long, shuddering sigh, the sound a child makes after it has been crying.

Jane shook her head. 'I think you made a mistake. I . . .' She hesitated. 'I feel I ought to tell you something. I don't know if it is true or just a malicious rumour. In fact, I don't know whether I should be saying this.'

'About Alban? Please tell me,' Rose said.

'Well, it is kitchen gossip. One of the maids at home told me that she knew a girl who had been working for the Stoneberrys at Danesfell, who went out with Alban and had been meeting him outside the house. When his aunt and uncle found out, she was sacked immediately but her father went up to the house and made trouble. She had told him that Alban had pestered her and threatened her with dismissal unless she met him, and had abused her in a very cruel way. The girl's shoulders were terribly bruised. The Stoneberrys found her a job down south and gave her a good reference. The father never said another word about it. It was assumed he had been paid off. I don't know how much truth there is in the story. It is unpleasant but I thought you should know.'

Rose's face had set into an expressionless mask.

'I know the Stoneberrys kept him on a tight rein, forbidding him to know anyone they did not approve of. Which meant only the rich. Perhaps the father had beaten the girl himself?'

'Perhaps.'

'It would be an excellent blackmail plan.'

'Very clever,' said Jane. Then, 'You just don't want to believe it.'

'No. He has made a great sacrifice for me. But he does have a fierce and unpredictable temper which is very difficult for him to control. I think – I hope – I can help him to control it. I think he trusts me. He has always been rejected. His parents sent him home from India as a very small boy, and the Stoneberrys disliked the responsibility of bringing him up.' She picked up her cup and drank her coffee quickly. 'But I'm glad you told me.'

'You're not angry?'

'No.' She put her hand into Jane's and smiled, 'Friends?'

'Of course,' Jane said warmly. 'Of course we're still friends.'

'I'm glad. I need friends. We've got to make the world right for Tom's baby.'

'Well, it's a queer sort of world just now,' Jane replied, 'but we'll try.'

Chapter Eleven

During the two months before Rose was due to leave Paris for Nice and Respy, the Stoneberry marriage appeared to be a great success. Rose possessed all the qualities Alban had dreamed of in a wife and hostess. She was beautiful, perfectly dressed, charming and capable, but most of all she was fun and drew people to her like a magnet.

She went twice a week to the British Military Hospital where Jane worked and her work there was appreciated, as it had been at Danesfell. The patients were all just down from the line, and were being treated until they were strong enough to be entrained for England, where they would get more specialised help. She was just as popular, adaptable and hardworking as she had been at Danesfell. Sometimes she felt tired, but she was careful not to let Alban see this.

They established a pattern of bi-weekly parties. All Alban's colleagues from Headquarters admired her very much, and quite a few fell in love with her, which she handled with charm and discretion. Alban seemed to become more confident and at peace with himself, and Rose was happy for him.

At their parties the Americans introduced some new dances – the fox-trot and the turkey trot – and the French tangoed romantically, cheek-to-cheek. The Stoneberrys' evenings became a welcome refuge for men and women far from home and loved ones, and a place to meet and make friends.

It was to Mrs Winterton, the C.O.'s wife, that Rose skilfully leaked the news of her pregnancy, one afternoon when she dropped in to tea. She knew word would filter through and become general knowledge in the Mess. She wanted to save Alban the embarrassment of having to make an announcement himself. Her pregnancy had not been spoken of between them since they had moved into the apartment in the Place de Maréchal.

'I'm not running away by going to Nice for the birth, Mrs Winterton,' she said, smiling, 'but I'm not a long standing soldier's wife like yourself. I don't really want the sound of gunfire to be the first thing my baby hears.'

'My dear, I sympathise. Having a baby under siege is not a good idea. I have experienced it so I do know. You go down into the sunshine, and perhaps after the baby arrives you might stay on for a while? Or you could return and leave the baby with your friend.'

'No,' Rose said positively. 'Nothing is going to separate me from my baby. Not even war. Oh, I'm sorry. It's just that I know very well what it is to be left with strangers when you are small. For a child not to know to whom it really belongs is terrible. If I come back to Paris, I shall bring the baby with me.'

'Well, let us hope the war will be over by then. Things are looking hopeful now. As the wife of a regular officer, I'm afraid I often did not have the luxury of having my children with me. And I must say I think you are quite right, we never quite got to know our eldest, and it is better for you and Alban to be together. But don't forget, husbands are queer cattle. Left alone for too long, they soon jump over the fences.'

'I asked her not to say anything just yet,' Rose told Jane later, 'but of course she will, and that will save Alban from having to make an announcement, which I know he would hate. Now no one will worry about how long I stay there and start counting the months. With these guns pounding all the time, I have every reason not to stay. I didn't know I was such an actress.'

'Well, I did,' said Jane. 'I remember when we were at school how you had everyone, including the teaching staff, on a string. We used to call you the Snake Charmer.'

'I had a very good tutor in charm – my mother.'

'Madame Léon's pretty sister? My mother and grandmother still talk about her. She was world famous at one time.'

233

'Well, everyone had heard of her in Paris. And she wasn't just pretty. She was a great beauty and a famous whore. And,' Rose's voice was suddenly tense, 'Alban sometimes reminds me of this. I think it is one of the reasons for his jealousy. Like mother like child, or so people say.'

'That's horrid,' Jane said anxiously. 'He doesn't ill treat you, though?'

'Oh, no! He likes to – well, take me down. I don't think he really *likes* women. And perhaps I did, as I said, learn a great deal from my mother, watching her when I was a child.'

'But I don't think you're like that, Rose. You have a sort of ingenuous charm. Not at all a *grande horizontale*.'

She waited while Rose skimmed through her post.

'Oh, a letter from Stevie! He and Marian are getting married in March. It will be a great affair, it seems. Angela will really let herself go. The reception will be given at Cliffs Edge as the Palmers have only a small rented house now. He wants me to go, but of course I shall be in the South with Respy in Menton. She has moved there since her husband died. Will you go?'

'If I can get leave. I'm glad. I like little Marian. You certainly helped her – knowing you has given her assurance. I often wondered what made you so friendly. You were so different.'

'At first, selfishness,' Rose said frankly. 'As it was with everyone. I used to cultivate girls who might be useful friends. But neither you nor Marian was devious. Neither was Respy, nor Aunt Margaret, nor Tom. They taught me to value people for themselves. I'm glad they did – I'd have been impossible otherwise. I think she and Stevie will be very happy.'

It was one of the days when she went with Jane to the British Hospital. They would travel to Chantilly together where Rose worked until five, and Jane would go on duty at midday after lunch.

'I think,' Rose said, putting on her coat, 'I'll keep up the open parties until the beginning of March. I've applied for a travel permit, and then I'll go south. Who knows? Perhaps when I return, the war will be over.'

234

These days she was beginning to feel like a marathon runner. Every morning, dreading the day's long effort, she longed to rest and lie in the sun with her feet up. There would be open house again tomorrow night. Today she must go to the hospital. Tomorrow she must work all day preparing for the party. Then the soldiers and the girls, British, French and American, the fashion people, the nurses and the theatre folk, friends of Jane, Mess mates of Alban's, would all come. The gramophone would play, the rugs would come up, the young ones would dance. All except Alban.

He would talk to his fellow officers, play cards if anyone wished to play, and all the time he would be watching her. Watching her talk and dance with other men. Some of them, particularly the French boys, would flirt, and no matter how adroitly she kept them at arm's length she would see him stiffen, see that strange look come into his eyes. It was a little frightening. His need for her seemed to have become a torture of frustration which she could neither comfort nor understand. Their moments of tenderness were becoming rare, and the startling fluctuations in his moods more frequent. She tried. She wanted them to be happy. She told herself that after the baby was born it would be different. It had to be, if they were to survive.

Her beautiful eyes were beginning to look too large and a little shadowy beneath those high cheek-bones. Her face was thin, its shadows had deepened. She danced less, her lithe body was thickening visibly now, and however carefully she chose her clothes, her condition was becoming obvious.

Alban hated her pregnancy. It disgusted him. Every thought of it was an insult. He had longed for a peerless beauty whom all men desired but who belonged only to him. Now it seemed to him his dream woman was turning into a mother-creature who longed only to get away.

On the first of March Rose gave her last evening salon before she left for Menton, and many people came to bid her good luck and *au revoir*. Many people brought her flowers. Mrs Winterton brought her gifts for her layette, and to Rose the small, beautifully knitted garments were a shock. They made the baby a reality. A small person who would have to be dressed and washed and cared for, not just a part of Tom within her that must be treasured for his memory.

Everything was just a little hectic that night. In the short while they had been in Paris, their big old-fashioned apartment had become a haven of comfort and gaiety to many people, especially to men returning from the front; some who came once or twice would never return.

Lieutenant John Damian was there tonight. He often came with Jane. His regiment was stationed near Paris waiting to be sent up the line. He was still the boyish optimist she had danced with in Thornsby.

'I'm glad you are going away, Ma'am,' he said, 'the war is getting far too close for comfort. But you can bet your life they won't get any closer once our boys get up the line. I'm surprised that Alban let you stay so long. It's common knowledge that Jerry's going to hot things up soon. There's going to be a big push. Then – whoopee! – you'll see the balloon go up!'

'Everyone talks about the big push, but no one seems to know anything about when and why and who,' she said lightly. 'I suspect that Colonel Winterton knows, and some others at Alban's H.Q. But one general wants to do one thing, and another something else, and meanwhile men go on being killed. I'm glad Alban doesn't really know about it. Our parties would be full of spies if he did. Every week there are new faces here whom I never see again.'

'Yeah, I've noticed. And for Pete's sake, who is that oddball with your husband? Looks as though he runs a funeral parlour.'

Rose looked over her shoulder and saw Count Adolphe Bridault. He had been to one or two parties, never before midnight and Alban had always left with him shortly after he arrived. Meeting her eyes he bowed courteously.

She knew Alban liked him. Or that he liked his impeccable lineage. In the few brief conversations between them she had gained no further knowledge of the man other than he was a drawling aristocrat, very certain of his breeding and with the confidence of centuries of privilege. When he had taken her hand he had raised it to an inch away from his lips and pecked the air; she had noticed his thin, greasy hair and felt his chill, lifeless fingers and had instantly thought of slugs, sliding across the wet cold mud of early spring.

'He's an acquaintance of Alban's, apparently not fit enough to join up. His name is Count Adolphe Bridault. *Very St Germain*, I believe.'

'That means old aristocracy, doesn't it? Before Napoleon? Direct descendants of Louis XIV and all that? Does Alban play cards with him? I'd sooner play cards with a rattle snake.'

Rose smiled. She was longing for tomorrow. To get away from Paris, and the sound of guns, and Alban's watchful eyes. He made her feel as though she was serving a life sentence. What did he suspect of her? Didn't he want her to go away? Or was he longing to see her go? She did not blame him. She had thought hopefully, that it was going well between them. But as the time for her departure approached, the old unease crept back.

But tomorrow she would be going away. The thought made her colour return and her eyes brighten with renewed hope.

Alban stayed to the end and was by Rose's side as she bade her guests goodnight and goodbye. Jane was leaving with John Damian – he was sharing a staff car and giving her a lift back to the hospital.

'Goodbye, goodbye, and thanks once more for these lovely evenings. A good journey to the South,' said Jane, 'and good luck with the baby. I wish I could come down and look after you. Everyone from the hospital asked me to give you their love.'

Rose thanked her and kissed her. Alban shook Jane's hand and John Damian said, 'Goodbye, Mrs Stoneberry, it was a pleasure to have met you again.'

'For me too. Take care, and good luck when that big push really starts.'

He still had her hand and she impulsively kissed him on the cheek. Alban bowed without speaking, and did not offer his hand which did not disconcert the American in the least. Paris was silent now, but earlier in the evening the sound of gunfire had scarcely ceased and during the day there had been the continual crackle of fighter planes in the distance. She knew that in a short while Damian and his men would be thrown against the German salient, like so many men she had known and never seen again.

'We'll be back soon,' she said to the last guest, 'all of us. And it will be over, you'll see. Goodnight, and for the present goodbye.'

She was about to turn away when Alban caught her arm.

'There's still my friend.' And she realised that Bridault had just put down his glass, and was approaching them.

She felt her hand tremble a little as he took it and bent to give his usual formal salute. He murmured some compliment on the evening. His grey face looked almost feverish tonight and his eyes bright.

Alban took his hand warmly. 'My dear Adolphe,' he said, 'wait for me in the foyer. I'll send you some champagne. I just want to speak with Rose before she starts for the South early tomorrow. I won't be long.'

'I will wait, of course, with pleasure. But could it not be brandy? One has had enough of champagne.'

'Of course.' Alban signalled to one of the hired waiters whom the concierge recruited for these evenings from the middle-aged, the rejects, and those as yet too young for active service.

'Thank you,' said Bridault, 'for your charming hospitality, Madame. And my best wishes for the future. *Au revoir.*'

'*Merci, M'sieur le Comte, et bonne nuit.*'

He went into the foyer, and Alban, charging his own glass with brandy, followed Rose through into her small boudoir. She had a desk there where she kept the accounts and all the household correspondence, and there was a small safe where they kept jewellery and such cash as might be needed.

'What time will you be leaving tomorrow?'

'The train goes mid-morning.' She sat down at her desk. 'I have arranged with M'sieur Raymond that all the household bills and wages will be paid from his office. If you wish to entertain, do – just initial the bills and send them to his office.'

'I suppose you thought I could not manage these things?'

'You have little time, and I did not think you could be bothered.' She waited, expecting one of his outbursts of resentment, but he was apparently mollified.

238

'No, you're right. Especially with this offensive due to start at any moment – we are very busy.'

And, as though some malicious spirit had heard him, there came the familiar thump and shudder of heavy guns, the chandeliers tinkling uneasily as though touched by a poltergeist.

Alban lifted his head sharply and she saw the naked fear in his eyes. 'They're so damned near,' he said. 'When the devil will they start this offensive? It's becoming unbearable!'

'You know better than I,' she said unhappily. 'I suppose more men will be killed. These young Americans we have met lately. They are so eager, and I wonder if they realise what it will be like.'

Suddenly, he flamed with anger. 'I suppose that is your reason for being so affectionate towards Damian?'

'But he's an old acquaintance! We met him at home, in Danesfell. He came to your mother's great ball.'

'It is very important how you behave in France. I will not tolerate gossip. It gets back to the Mess – I don't want your behaviour to become the subject of talk there. It was not part of our bargain that you should flirt!'

'It was not, and I have not.'

He was standing behind her. Suddenly he put his hands on her shoulders. There was a mirror on the wall before them and Rose saw his burning eyes reflected there. She sat quite still. She would not let him see she was afraid. His hand slid round her throat, grasping the link of pearls and twisting them until the iridescent globes bit into her skin. He bent her head back and put his mouth down on hers. His lips were rough. She felt his teeth biting and stiffened with disgust. He dropped the pearls and turned away, laughing.

'You must not think, Rose, that because I have to wait for you I don't want you!' He flicked the pearls. 'Who paid for these? Tom Grimshaw?'

She knew he was trying to make a quarrel, because he hated to have to ask her for money. But he had to have it.

'Alban,' she said, 'please don't be cross. When we first came here, we were both trying to make each other happy. But now everything is slowly being worn away. It's not because you are so often away from home – you cannot help that.' She stood up, put her hands upon his shoulders, forcing him to look into her eyes. His glance seemed to slide away. 'Is it my fault?' she persisted. 'If so, tell me what I have done?'

To her surprise, his arms closed round her and there were tears in his eyes. 'Nothing,' he said, then touched her bracelets. 'And yet everything. You wear his jewellery, not mine.'

'That was thoughtless of me. I'm sorry. The jewels your aunt gave me were too valuable to bring away. I won't wear these if you dislike them.' The Stoneberry jewels had been family heirlooms, heavy and ugly but extremely valuable, and she had never liked them. 'These don't matter, so long as we can be friends.'

'It's not enough,' he said. 'Every time I look at you now, I remember it's his child not mine. It is *his* child you want. And after it is born, will you ever want a child of mine?'

'One day, I promise you, we will have one of our own. Would that make you happy?'

'I don't know. Perhaps I shall never know. Perhaps we shall find the answer when you return. I hope so.' He glanced at his watch and looked anxious. 'Bridault is waiting. I must go.'

'Shall I see you before I leave tomorrow?'

'No. I shall sleep at H.Q. tonight.' Then, brusquely, 'Can I have the money?'

'Of course, I'm sorry. How much do you want?'

'Three hundred pounds.' She looked up, startled. He had never asked for so much before. Immediately the blustering fury flared in his eyes.

'Don't look at me like one of those bloody French shopkeepers, sitting up at a desk with their noses into the family money. I have debts – my Mess bill, for instance. I haven't paid it since I went home at Christmas. I owe Bridault money, and I have some card debts I must settle. Our pay has been held up – something to do with the railways which are loaded with troops.'

'You don't have to explain, Alban. Of course you can have it.'

She opened the safe and took the notes out of the cash box. It was money drawn for her journey to Menton.

240

He stuffed it carelessly into his pocket and said, 'Well, I suppose this is goodbye,' and looked at her with an expression that made her go up to him and put her arms round him again.

He caught her up against him and kissed her on the lips, so fiercely that she caught her breath as he let her go.

'It is not goodbye, Alban. When I come back, all will be well again.' She said gently, 'Don't look so cross. I am coming back.'

'Don't ever leave me, Rose,' he said, pleadingly. And then threateningly, 'Don't ever try to leave me. I won't let you.' He turned and went abruptly away, and she heard him speak to Bridault in the foyer and then the sound of the front door closing behind them.

She felt her lip and found blood on her fingers. She felt violated. It was though in some strange way Alban did not want to love her. He wanted to destroy his love. He was ashamed of his weakness in ever loving her. She realised that it was not a bargain she had made but a trap, and that they were both caught in it. And that Paris had changed him, and she knew nothing of his life outside their home.

Alban and Bridault walked in silence towards the river then the Frenchman said, gently, 'Well?'

Alban took out his wallet. He peeled off half the notes and gave them to his companion.

Bridault counted the notes carefully before pocketing them.

'Was it difficult?'

'No,' Alban said, 'why should it be? And there's plenty more where that came from. God, what an awful evening! All those silly devils, dancing away the night as though tomorrow will never come. Tomorrow, like as not, they'll be cringing in their dugouts, up to their stupid necks in that mess out there.' The air trembled to another barrage as he spoke. 'What will you do, Adolphe, if they take Paris?'

Bridault gave one of his rasping laughs.

'Run away, of course! I should be little use to anyone in a besieged city, and I have no taste for stewed rat.'

'But where? Where would you go?'

241

'Where?' The Frenchman shrugged. 'Who knows? Perhaps to Spain. A fine country where people still know their places and families like mine command respect. The poor remain poor and are apparently content, very sensibly, because they always will be. Madrid is a city where life does not begin until midnight, and when it does it can be most amusing.'

'I wish I could go with you.'

'Well, why not? We could slip over the frontier.'

'Desert? You're crazy!'

'Well, perhaps that would be a little extreme, because we should need money, of course, and I have no money.'

'You have devilish luck at cards.'

'Sometimes. Tell me, do you know anything about this big push, if that's what they call it? I mean about the strength of the man-power, and when and where the troops will be deployed?'

'Not really,' Alban said indifferently, stopping and scanning the road for a taxi. 'All the big planning is done at Versailles. We're a very boring set-up. Just supplies. Yards and yards of requisitions for blankets, and chits for uniforms and puttees and hats, and God knows what. Nothing but paperwork.'

'So! My friend, I see a taxi. Shall we take it and drive somewhere for a pick-me-up to start the evening? Just while we decide what to do? We could join a small school of baccarat. You've played? Of course you have. It is the most interesting game of all.'

The taxi stopped and Bridault opened the door, waiting courteously for Alban to get in, noticing that he stumbled slightly. There had been plenty of champagne, and the brandy just before they left. Alban would be in a very suggestible mood, and it was time to put to him that even scraps of information about supplies could be very valuable – for where supplies are sent, men would follow. Bridault knew very well where he could sell such information, it was just one of his more secret activities. It was all a question of contacts – just as he knew where spirits could be purchased at a price, and where the drugs he depended upon could still be bought.

Rose left well before her train time the following morning, to see her lawyer, Monsieur Raymond, before going on to the station. The old man was delighted to see her, and she apologised for her early visit.

'I am off this morning, escaping to the South, M'sieur, to visit my old governess, Madame Respigny, for a long visit until my baby is safely born. I have a train to catch and she is meeting me at Nice. That is my reason for calling so early.'

Monsieur Raymond responded that a visit from a lady so charming was a pleasure at any time, and had she obtained her travel permit?

'Oh, yes. I have everything.' She told him that she wanted to make arrangements about the flat while she was away and give him her address in Menton. She had already arranged with him to pay the rent and household expenses. She did not know if Lieutenant Stoneberry would be entertaining when he was off duty but if he did, he would apply to Monsieur Raymond for the necessary cash.

'His allowance from home is paid to his account, but if he should need another hundred pounds a month, I would be glad if you would let him have it.'

'A very generous allowance for a young officer.'

She smiled. 'So now I have taken care of everything.' Her big dark eyes smiled at him above the shadowed cheek-bones, but it was a mirthless little smile. He knew that she had not come to the real reason for her visit. He thought she looked very tired and very beautiful. But there was a steel core beneath the charm that he well remembered in her Aunt, Madame Léon. 'I wonder,' she said lightly, 'if you have heard of a Count Adolphe Bridault?'

The old lawyer's face sharpened. 'Indeed, yes, Madame. He is very well known in gambling circles in the city. A man who has brought disgrace on a fine old family. Surely you don't receive him?'

'He has visited us twice, I think. My husband has brought him. I understand they play cards together. At his club.'

Raymond hesitated, wondering how much she knew. Bridault would not be accepted by any reputable club. He would be a dangerous companion for a bored young officer. Again he was aware of some unspoken plea.

243

'Well, you have my address in the South,' she said, rising. 'And you have my husband's account number? I do not think he will need any more. Certainly not any large sums. Now I really must go.'

He accompanied her to the street, opening the taxi door for her, bowing as she gave him her hand. She was wearing a loose blue coat with a white fur collar and her small, white fur cossack cap. He kissed her hand with all the gallantry of an old *boulevardier*.

'To the South, *mon enfant*, to the South! Have your baby in safety. Then the roses will come back to your cheeks. I have heard all about the work you have been doing for the hospital, and the entertaining you have done for your husband's colleagues and friends. You must be tired. Give my regards to Madame Respigny. *Bon voyage et bon accouchement*. Do not fear – I will look after your interests.'

'Goodbye.' She hesitated a moment longer. 'If you should have any queries, write to me. Don't bother to contact my guardian, Mr Stephen Grimshaw.'

'Of course not.'

Now he knew. She feared for her husband, but did not want her family in England to know. If young Stoneberry was fool enough to gamble with a rat like Bridault, he might be in serious trouble. Raymond would certainly see that her capital was not touched, and understood why she did not want her family to know. He imagined that this young Stoneberry must be one of these feckless aristocrats whom women become infatuated with, one of those charmers who aroused their maternal instincts. No foundation for a good marriage. He shook his head anxiously as her taxi drew away.

At the Gâre de Lyon, Jane Shawcross and John Damian were waiting to see Rose off, a lovely surprise. They saw her safely into her reserved seat in a first-class carriage. Less fortunate passengers were standing along the corridors.

'Take off your coat,' whispered Jane, 'and look as pregnant as you possibly can. People will stop shoving. The French are very thoughtful towards mothers-to-be.'

244

Rose did as she was told and found that it worked miraculously. Everyone suddenly became very solicitous. Rumours of a big battle to come were causing a fresh exodus from all the districts north-east of Paris and when she saw the crowd besieging the second and third classes she was grateful that she had not to join them.

She stood at the window and looked down at her two friends and was struck by the likeness between them. Both tall, strong-boned, sandy fair and level-eyed. Nordic blood somewhere in each of them. John was from the American South, yet she had never felt alien with him. They had both been to her evenings whenever they had short leave and a friendship had grown steadily between them. Rose knew they did not think about the future. The deaths of Jane's brother Val and Tom Grimshaw were too vividly remembered, specially now when John was waiting his first posting to the front line. But they promised to write – to each other and to Rose.

She waved to them until the platform was out of sight. At the last moment a man's figure caught her attention. A British officer, turning away. Something about his quick, stiff movement was familiar. Alban? Watching her? Why had he not come openly to the train?

She shrugged the thought away. As she took her seat and they were finally out of Paris, she felt a great wave of relief sweep over her, and a sense of freedom. It was the sensation a bird must feel when released from its cage.

It was nearly five years since she had left Nice for London, just before the outbreak of war. And now, going back, it seemed like yesterday.

But it was no longer home – home was the high, windy uplands of Thornsby Manor. Home was most specially that flat in Chelsea, lying in Tom's arms with the afternoon sunshine slotting golden shafts between the curtains. Home was where Tom had lived and loved her.

But Tom was nowhere. A lost skeleton in a desert wadi, small desert plants growing between his bones, and she was married to a man she had never loved but thought she had come to understand. A man whom she had once mocked a little, flirted with only to tease, not meaning to be cruel but exasperated by his persistence. But she had come to believe, with all his pretensions, Alban did really love her; that if she could make him happy, then he would control his dangerous, touchy temper which swung so easily to acts of cruelty. She had tried to believe that they might work out a happy future together. Now she was not sure. Had she really seen him at the station? And if she had, why was he spying on her? Was he making certain no other man accompanied her? Or had he come bearing flowers as Stephen had once dared to? What was he, this man who could not bear to see her pregnancy, or be alone in her presence, and yet was fiercely jealous of her? A man who understood the conquest of a woman but not tenderness or affection? A man who perhaps could pretend devotion, like baiting a fish hook?

The train stopped and shunted on to a siding to let a troop train pass towards Paris. It was loaded with men in field uniform and tin hats, as they called the steel helmets, and heavy packs. They were standing along the corridors, and grinned and waved at the sight of a young or pretty face. When the troop transport had passed, their southbound train shunted back on to the main line and continued on its slow journey.

At the large stations in the north they had to wait for further troop trains to pass. On one occasion the permanent way had been bombed and reduced to a single track and there was more than an hour's delay. But as they went further south the delays gradually became less frequent and there was a pleasant feeling of escape. For every mile they travelled the day seemed warmer, the skies clearer, the mountains greener, and when the train stopped the cicadas could be heard fiddling their frenetic love song. In the fields Rose saw women in straw hats and sun bonnets, working among the ranks of vines which spread as far as the horizon. At last they were beyond Lyon and could see the snow on the high mountains that lay between them and the sea. The train passed small towns with sleepy squares lined with plane trees, and ochre coloured farmhouses with roofs of orange tiles standing among the young green maize, and market gardens sheltered by high windbreaks of bamboo. When she opened the window, above the station smells of smoke, Gauloises, urine, coffee and engine oil, there was the sweet, unmistakable smell of the south.

As Jane had predicted, Rose's fellow passengers, two battle-weary French officers going on leave and a middle-aged couple with a young niece, tended to coddle her.

She was young, beautiful, and in that magic condition *enceinte*. The words '*Ne vous derangez pas, je vous emprie, Madame,*' whirled about her. The lady insisted on covering her with a shawl during the night, treating her as though she was the same age as her schoolgirl niece. At Toulouse the two officers leapt out and brought back hot coffee and the morning papers.

'The news is much the same,' they said after scanning their own newspapers. 'It depends on how long either side can hold out.'

'Someone said that to me last summer,' said Rose, 'exactly that, and here we are still saying it.'

'If we get reinforcements up quickly, and already the Americans and Australians are in transit, we shall win.'

'They have already been in action out in the East. Compared to what our lot have had, the fighting out there must seem a piece of cake,' said the other man.

'Someone I knew was killed out there,' said Rose, 'after being on the Western Front since the very beginning. On the Somme nothing touched him. Then he was killed on patrol outside Jerusalem.'

There was a silence. The woman ventured, 'Your husband, Madame?'

Rose smiled, but her lips trembled as she said to these friendly strangers, 'Yes.'

There was a long silence. Then the lady opened her large basket of provisions and brought out some fresh *croissants,* a bottle of milk and some treasured sugar. 'It makes this station coffee a little more bearable,' she said apologetically to the officers. 'I have plenty of milk for all.'

At last they were over the mountains, winding down through the woods to Nice and the real South, where Respy would be waiting for her, and they would take the local train to Menton where she now lived.

Respy was still as spry, a little plump, and decidedly prosperous-looking in her good English suit with a high-necked, spotless blouse and immaculate gloves, her gold-rimmed pince-nez secured to fine gold chain.

They embraced in a rush of deep affection, no longer governess and pupil but old friends, smiling and talking as the local train ran along the coast towards Italy, linking the small Riviera towns.

'I was sad for you when you wrote to me of M'sieur's death,' said Rose. 'I could not come, of course, because I was still in England, and with the war it would have been so difficult to get a permit.'

'It is no matter. I did not expect it.' They spoke in English together, as they always had.

Respy took off her pince-nez and began to polish them. 'He was a good man. I sold the *boulangerie*, as you know, which gave me sufficient capital to move to Menton.'

Respy had never really been happy in the small apartment in the harbour quarter over the baker's shop, with its ever present smell of freshly baked bread and the luscious perfume of the rich pastries.

'Menton is a very English town,' she said. 'I have both French and English pupils. I run no classes, you understand? Only private lessons.'

Respy always liked life to be neat and orderly. Remembering the tumultuous disarray of her mother's apartment on the *Promenade des Anglais*, Rose took Respy's hand and pressed it. Charmian, Baroness Abderhazy, must have been everything she disapproved of in a woman, but she had been faithful to her until the very end.

'My income now is very adequate,' Respy said, a little complacently. 'Besides the capital from the shop I have my small annuity from Monsieur Léon. Your Aunt Margaret also left me a legacy. I belong to the British Residents' Club. I like it very much.'

Respy had spoken French for so long now that her phrasing, if not her accent, was influenced by it.

'After Nice with my mother, it must be heaven!' Rose could not help laughing.

'Madame Abderhazy was very difficult,' conceded Respy, 'but she was beautiful and a very great lady.'

They travelled for a few minutes in silence, and then Rose asked impulsively, 'How did you come to marry M'sieur Respigny? I have never dared to ask you before.'

'It never occurred to me that you would be interested, my dear. And, anyway, you were too young for me to talk about such things with you. The truth is, I was abandoned in Nice and Monsieur Respigny came to my rescue.'

'How could you be abandoned? By whom?'

'I came out here with an Austrian family, a young couple with two little girls. I answered their advertisement in England. I did not know he was a gambler. They simply left one day. They sent me out shopping and when I returned they had gone. I had nothing. No salary – they had not paid me. No friends. No money. The apartment was rented furnished, but the rent had never been paid. I was terrified. I ran back to the *boulangerie*. I knew they owed Monsieur Respigny a great deal because I was always told to charge the purchases. I was very distressed and he let me stay in the little flat above his shop. He was very calm about the whole thing. He offered to pay my fare back to England, but I had nowhere to go. I had no parents or relations. Then he asked me to marry him. It seemed the only thing I could do. So we were married. He was always very kind to me. And then I was put in touch with the Baroness and you came to live with us when you were a very tiny girl. She did not care for a baby in her life.'

'But what on earth made you take me on?'

'I was paid well, and I always *was* paid. I was the only one she always paid. I was better off as a nursery governess than serving in the *boulangerie*. I had not the temperament for that kind of work.'

Rose remembered the pretty young assistants who had served at the pâtisserie counter, and began to understand Respy's marriage a lot better than she had at fourteen. She respected her husband and he had been proud of her, but no doubt younger and more responsive young ladies also shared his life.

The train was slowing down at Menton. The sea was brilliant blue and up on the rocky cliffs at the back of the town early blossom was already breaking. The sun was warm with the promise of summer and Rose was too hot in her loose blue coat. They took one of the *fiacres* waiting outside the station and drove up to the high ground to the attractive centre of the old town, perched on its rock like a miniature Parthenon.

The carriage drew up at an old cream-painted villa overlooking gardens facing the sea. Respy led the way to a side entrance. Her apartment on the ground floor was small but the three rooms were spacious and there was a pleasant terrace facing the sun and sea.

Rose looked round. 'It's lovely here! Lovely to be away from the cold and the sound of guns.'

'It must be dreadful, the war so near. Sometimes here we forget there is a war on French soil. Your husband was wise to send you away. You will miss him?'

Rose began to speak impulsively. 'Respy – I must tell you: Alban is not the father of my baby.'

There was silence for a moment. Rose waited, and then Respy whipped off her pince-nez and polished them fiercely, before replacing them with trembling fingers. Rose put her arms round her.

'Respy, I *had* to tell you. I'm not going to turn out like my mother,' she said gently, 'but I want you to know the truth. I had to make a decision and I did. Perhaps not a very brave one. My baby's father was Tom Grimshaw.'

'Your cousin? Madame Léon's boy? But he was such a gentleman!'

'Yes. He was killed out in Palestine or we would be married. Alban wanted to marry me and he was willing to accept the baby. Respy, I could not bear that my baby should be looked upon as a bastard. It was a wonderful thing for Alban to do.'

'I understand,' said Respy, suppressing all the questions she wanted to ask, 'it is a situation becoming commonplace in the war. Is he a nice man? Are you happy?'

But of course the child was not happy – one only had to look into her great, sad eyes. Rose shrugged the question away.

'I was not looking for happiness. I was grateful – I still am grateful. I just want to make Alban happy, if I can, and be a good wife to him. It was a bargain and I will keep it.'

Respy did not speak for a minute, then she rose and said, 'You would like some coffee? Or tea?'

'Tea, please.'

Rose followed her into the kitchen. It was small and, of course, immaculate. A place for everything and everything in its place.

'I have the ground floor to myself. The owners have the rest of the house. Two English ladies. They are good but not familiar neighbours, and very quiet and respectable.'

Rose's eyes sparkled with mischief.

'I promise you, Respy, that not a word of this will reach your good neighbours. I mean about Tom and me. It is for me, also, a matter of discretion. Alban's family would never understand and must never know.'

They carried their tea out on to the terrace because it was warm enough to sit outside in the sunshine. The small harbour below bristled with naval craft, the sea shimmered like silver fish scales, and far away, beyond the horizon, was Africa, where Tom had died.

Rose looked at Respy, this kind, conventional, inhibited woman who had brought her up, and wondered what would have become of the small Shareen Abderhazy without her.

Within a short while she received letters from Jane and one from England from Marian and Stephen. Jane had just been able to get home to Thornsby for their wedding and back to Paris before all leave was cancelled. It had been a quiet but lovely wedding, she said. Stephen wrote to say that they hoped to find a suitable house on the other side of Thornsby because Angela, he added wryly, was already proving to be a *very* attentive mother-in-law.

Jane had gone straight back through Paris to join her unit at the hospital and said it was absolute hell now, the guns never ceasing and casualties pouring in. She had not stopped in Paris and heard nothing of Alban. The newspapers were full of the battles on the Western Front and the Germans' three-pronged attack. John Damian had survived Château Thierry, and was still on the Front Line. But the feeling in Paris, Jane said, was high with hope. Both Paris and Thornsby seemed very far away from Rose.

She wrote regularly to Alban, telling him of the ordinary things that a husband would expect to hear. About the nursing home where she had booked a bed, and the gynaecologist to whom her Parisian doctor had recommended her. The weather which was getting warmer every day. She ended with a scrawled "love from". But she was ashamed of her letter. It should have been full of real love and affection but it was not. It was dull and prosaic. She could not make herself express a love she did not feel. She remembered the letters she had written to Tom, many of which he had never received. Alban did not write in reply.

In May her baby was born without any difficulty. Sitting with her in the nursing home, Respy remembered the baby Rose who had been handed over to her care so many years ago.

When Tom's baby was put into her arms, Rose looked down at her with wonder and tenderness. Tom's daughter, as fair as she was dark, cleansed and pink and smelling of that strange, lovely baby scent of newness and freshness, filling her heart with unexpected hope. She was overcome with pride and tenderness.

She was so glad she had a girl. If Tom had lived perhaps she might have wanted a boy, but boys grew up to be men and men went away to war. And she would not have wanted Tom's boy to be brought up at Danesfell. She would not have wanted Alban to bring up Tom's boy. A girl was safer.

'I am going to call her Stella,' she said, 'a star of hope. I do hope her eyes are blue.' And when, in the weeks that followed, the tightly folded, newly born bud began to unfurl its petals, the eyes were the deep violet blue of the Normanbys, and the wispy black hair rubbed off to be replaced with golden down.

A letter came from Tom's solicitors in Thornsby. There had been an unexpected hold-up in the probate of Captain Thomas Grimshaw's estate. The War Office was investigating some new information about the authenticity of the death report and until it was settled they could not proceed. Hope rose again within her, and with the renewal of hope an appalling realisation of the trap she had set for herself. Whatever Alban was he had made a bargain with her, at her suggestion and in all good faith, and because in his own way he loved her. Now her child was born he would expect her to return to him and truly become his wife.

Chapter Twelve

When Father Bosanquet's patient recovered, and physically he recovered rapidly, his tall, white-bearded, white-haired figure became familiar about the hospital. But he could not speak in spite of the priest's patient efforts to help him. There was no physical reason for this muteness; his mouth and throat had not been wounded and were perfectly healthy. It was as though he lacked the will to make sounds. He mouthed words silently like a deaf man, but he was not deaf.

He wore a cream serge Arab burnous. The other patients and the nursing sisters all thought he was a dumb lay-brother and called him Brother Sebastian. The full sleeves of the burnous covered the ugly stump just below the elbow of his left arm. The healed wound gave him great pain at times. Despite this he became very useful to Father Bosanquet, running the office for him and when he was asked if he had been in business before the war, he smiled and nodded, but made no attempt to tell how or where.

He helped in the wards, doing porter's work, easily lifting the patients with his strong right arm and supporting them on the crook of the injured one. He wheeled trolleys, swabbed wards, and did everything he was asked with silent willingness.

But he could not or would not remember his name or anything about his past. Bosanquet decided it was a severe case of amnesia but when he suggested he should inform the military authorities and ask for their help, fear came into his patient's eyes, so the priest kept him at the hospital and the weeks slipped by.

Then, as the spring came and Allenby's victorious armies began to withdraw after the Turkish surrender, the priest began to worry. Somewhere a family and friends were mourning this fine young man. It was Father Bosanquet's duty to remind the British Authorities that he was still here in Jerusalem.

Then came a day when the dry summer heat of Palestine had really set in when a patient came to the clinic with an abcess under a tooth which was giving him great pain. Father Bosanquet decided to lance and clean the place before sending him on to a dentist and asked Tom to assist him. Tom watched him closely as he prepared the man and injected an anaesthetic.

'Just bring the basin here with the towel. *Bon*! Now hold the basin closely under his chin. There is going to be a great deal of discharge.'

The priest reached for a scalpel and dropped it to the floor as Tom screamed a horrified protest, seized his shoulders and dragged him away from the now terrified patient.

'Don't! For Christ's sake have mercy on him!' He was on his knees, clasping Father Bosanquet's legs. He shouted in a queer harsh voice, in English, then in a smattering of Arabic. Bosanquet raised him to his feet, shaking him gently as though waking him. Looking into the blue, staring, sleepwalker's eyes, he said, 'Go into my office and wait for me there.'

He called one of the nursing sisters, reassured the patient, opened the abcess, drained it, cleaned and dressed the incision, and then went to his office.

Tom was sitting in a chair shivering, feeling his own mouth with trembling fingers, but the mad, dazed look had gone from his eyes. He looked at Bosanquet uncertainly as though he was wakening from a nightmare. Bosanquet dragged forward a chair to sit down opposite him.

'Tell me what you thought I was going to do to him? Come now, whoever you are, tell me about yourself. Tell me.' He saw no answering spark in the dull eyes. 'For God's sake, man, answer me! You can now. I heard you speak. What happened out there in the desert? Take a deep breath, and tell me.'

Tom began to speak in a queer rusty voice and soon the words came tumbling out of him in a mixture of English, French and Arabic. He dropped on his knees again, and Bosanquet took his hand and slowly caught the gist of what he was saying. He slowed down the tumult of jumbled words. '*No*, speak slowly! Tell me and then I will help you.'

'They slit their tongues, the ones who were still alive. They sliced off their genitals, my men, and they did not wait for them to die. My men, there in the sun. Some did not die all day. I could not help them. I tried to speak to them but no voice came. I struggled to stop my arm from bleeding. I thought if I could reach a gun I would shoot them rather than let the pain go on. But I could not move. Then the creatures came dropping from the sky, and creeping towards them, and afterwards I do not know what happened . . . I woke up here. Why didn't they do it to me?' Something seemed to click behind the blue eyes, and the terror went from them. Sanity returned like a flash. He said incredulously, 'Have I been thinking all this time that my tongue had been split? All these months?'

'Some part of your brain had, my friend,' said Father Bosanquet. 'Perhaps now you will tell me who you are?'

'My name is Thomas Grimshaw, Captain. I come from Yorkshire in England.'

'And why did you point to the picture of St Sebastian when I first asked your name?'

'I can't remember . . . unless he was naked and bleeding as I must have been when you found me.'

'You have not been identified yet, or the Army would have been here. The looters must have thrown away all the identity discs; they would only keep the things they could sell. All the bodies I saw were dead and unidentifiable. I counted eight. Their families must still be hoping that they will return to them. Your own people too. You must let me speak to the army authorities now.'

'Of course,' said Tom. His voice was becoming stronger. 'Of course. I told you – I am Captain Thomas Grimshaw, Third West Yorkshire Fusiliers, and I live in Thornsby in the West Riding of Yorkshire, at a house called Cliffs Edge. But I would like to write to my brother now, because I would like

256

him to know first of all . . . before he gets the official telegram from the War Office telling them I have been found. There are people who must be prepared.' He pulled up the sleeve on his left arm, showing the ugly red scarred stump below the elbow. 'Father, I have a confession to make. I did know my name. I thought I was one-armed and dumb and I did not want to go back home in that state. But I am only one-armed. I am not dumb, and I am still alive, and now I have things to do. I must return to my life again.'

'It is a miracle,' said Father Bosanquet.

'A miracle *you* performed. How can I ever thank you?' They stood looking into each other's eyes. Tom embraced the priest with his good right arm.

'Thank you,' he said again. 'Thank you – for my life.'

'And you have people to go back to?'

'Yes. I have my family.'

'I am sure they will welcome you. But take care. Things will have changed. It will be a great shock to your parents, as well as a great joy.'

'Yes, to my father who is old now . . . my mother died before I left England.'

'Yes. I understand.'

Tom did not speak of Rose, but his mind was full of the thought of her. Standing in his room in Chelsea with the sunlight slotting through a chink in the curtains behind her, and all the melting beauty of her glorious youth about her like a shining garment, no doubt in her heart that he would come back safely as he had before from the inferno of the Western Front. He rubbed his maimed left arm. He was a different man to the one who had loved her through that wonderful day. She was not yet twenty, and he had aged, God knows how much, in that day of death in the desert. Would she love him now?

Stephen and Marian had rented a furnished house across the valley from Cliffs Edge. At first they had lived with Angela and she had been overwhelmed with delight and triumph that, in spite of his marriage, she had managed to keep Stephen close to her.

But as the year went by, they knew they would have to escape. Marian was Stephen's political secretary and Angela expected her to take on all Rose's duties too.

Summer came and the German retreat, beginning as a trickle towards the frontiers, had slowly increased to a torrent; a desperate army, short of food and exhausted, reeling back before the renewed Allied might. The smell of victory was already in the air. Marian found her time more than full. What party would govern in the aftermath? Stephen had been nominated as Liberal candidate for the constituency of Highwick Moor on the opposite side of the valley to Cliffs Edge. They found and rented a comfortable, unassuming house there, so that they were living in his prospective constituency as well as nearer the centre of Thornsby and his duties at the mill.

Angela protested every inch of the way until they actually moved out, and insisted on driving over to the new house on the removal day, advising, supervising, criticising. She would have taken everything out of Marian's hands until Stephen insisted that she leave them to themselves, which she eventually did, very huffily.

They watched her depart with groans of relief, and Stephen produced a bottle of whisky and poured them both a drink, saying, 'For God's sake, let's go to the local and get some bread and cheese, then come back and go to bed. Do you think we should have the telephone put in? Mother will wear the lines out sending us instructions.'

'Don't worry,' said Marian, 'I'm here to protect you now. And we will have our first meal alone together, here in our own house.'

She made a cold meal, with some tinned soup, and they opened a bottle of champagne and celebrated their first night in a home of their own.

It was a warm evening. The house was high and surrounded by open land, and the west wind blew from the Pennines, cool in spite of the summer. They lay in their bed in the half-furnished room, watching the stars move across the dark blue sky. Her head was on his shoulder, his arms closely about her.

'This is the first time I've felt really married, Stevie,' she

258

said, 'I was always afraid we never would be. I was always afraid you really wanted Rose. You were in love with her?'

'Yes, I was, I suppose,' he said slowly. 'But then, weren't we all? In one way or another. Jane Shawcross told me that at school she even charmed the teaching staff when she wanted her own way.'

'Yes, at school she was like a magnet to everyone. She was so beautiful. There were many pretty girls but she was so exotic, like an Arabian Nights princess. And if she set herself to charm people, she was irresistible. I was very shy and silly and she was kind to me. I think she was only kind from force of habit, but later we became true friends.'

'Yes. I think she was like that with everyone except Tom, and to him she was just a wonderful kid who was far too much in love with him. She once said to me that we were far too much alike ever to be really in love. And she was right.' He bent and kissed the warm sweet hollow between her breasts. 'But you, my love, have your own impact. It is gentler but just as wonderful.'

She smiled, rubbing the top of his curly fair head. 'I know exactly what she meant – your being alike.'

'But, you know, there came a time when no other man in the world mattered to her but Tom. When he was at the front she seemed to stop breathing when a letter came, waiting to open it. To know he was still all right. She worked for Mother and the hospital, at parties she danced and flirted and laughed, but she was not really *with* people. She thought of nothing but his safety. And when he was killed, I thought she would die. I'll always love her, darling, but not like I love you. I once thought I would, but it was just because I was always competing with Tom. I never could, of course. So, my darling little second-best,' his arms closed round her, 'let's make the best of this lovely night. Tomorrow is one of those days . . . morning at the Mill, Party work afterwards, and I shall want you by my side. And tomorrow evening there's a meeting I must attend and you will be left alone. We must get a nice dog to protect you when I am out. We are domestic creatures now, my sweet, and I never thought that would happen to me. No more gallivanting!'

259

He shook his head dolefully, and she laughed as she slipped her arms about his neck.

In the morning Stephen drove straight down to the Mill where he shared a room with Arthur Sykes in the new office buildings overlooking the Water Meadows, after which the Mill had been named. His father had never allowed the meadows to be built over and there was a view across the moors towards Cliffs Edge. Business was still pouring in. It had not yet slumped as they had expected. The firm had never made so much profit as it had in these years of war, and only one shed in the three mills was still producing civilian cloth. But everyone in the industry knew that the German Army had fought itself to a standstill and for the first time a general retreat had started. When the fighting stopped, the orders would cease and they would have to start organising for peace.

The old main office was just as his father had left it. No one worked there now: the small general office with its tall Dickensian desks, the inner sanctum with its brass nameplate, "Henry Grimshaw, Managing Director". It marked the end of an era.

Arthur had already sorted out the post when Stephen arrived that morning. His pile was on the desk waiting for him. They had formed a partnership after Henry's death and worked well together. Their wives had become good friends.

'How's Pamela?'

'Grand. How's Marian?'

'Up to her eyes with the new house. Pamela is going to help her today, apparently. And help keep Mother at bay!'

He drew the pile of letters towards him and began to sort them out into separate piles, the business letters from the ones addressed to him personally. One bore an Egyptian stamp and was unmistakably in Tom's handwriting.

Arthur sprang to his feet as he saw the blood drain slowly from Stephen's face.

'For God's sake, what is it?'

Stephen had not opened the envelope.

'It's Tom's writing.'

'Yes, I saw it. It must be an old one. What's the date on the stamp?'

Stephen stared. King Fouad's moustached face seemed to fade mistily and he shook his head to clear it. 'Hang on . . . I can't see . . . This year, 1918 . . . I can't make out the exact date.'

Arthur took it from him and said, 'Two weeks ago!' He picked up the paper knife and slit the envelope, thrusting the letter into Stephen's shaking hands.

Stephen sat back, scanning the familiar strong slanting handwriting. He read it through, then read it again slowly, the colour rushing back into his face and his eyes full of joy. Finally he jumped to his feet, seizing Arthur's hands and shouting: 'He's alive! He's alive, Arthur! He's had some sort of shock and been in hospital all this time. We shall be getting the official confirmation shortly. He does not want anyone else to know yet.' He hugged Arthur again. 'Tom's all right! He's coming home! My God, now I've got a reason for sticking it out here. Now everything will be all right. The bloody war is nearly over, and Tom's alive and coming home!'

Excitedly he began to reckon out the sailing time from Alexandria. Tom might be on a troopship already. How long would it take? Where would he land? Liverpool? Or would they ship him to Marseilles and across France by train? A month? More?

Arthur had not spoken. He still held Stephen's arms in a tight grip.

'Have you forgotten? There's still Rose.'

'My God, Arthur – what shall I do? I was going to send her a telegram. I had not thought it out. I shall have to tell him she is married to Stoneberry.'

Rose and Respy were sitting out on the terrace in the sunshine. The baby lay in a hired perambulator while they had their breakfast. The beds around the terrace were already a riot of colour; roses were breaking their buds on the walls, and purple bouganvillaea creeping up round the windows of the house.

Respy had insisted on travelling back to Paris with Rose when she returned, although she protested that she was quite able to manage alone.

'Nonsense! You cannot, and I will not allow you to undertake such a journey with a baby.'

'Respy,' Rose said, folding the daily newspaper, 'the Germans are still very near to Paris, in spite of the retreat.'

'That front is static now,' said Respy, 'I put my pins in the map every day. They've missed their chance, you'll see. In a month the Allies will drive them back through Belgium. I am not afraid of the sound of gunfire. But there's no need for you to go back for at least another month.'

'I am a little worried. I have had no word from Alban. But I suppose it might be better if I did not go just yet.'

A bell sounded from the gateway. 'I expect it is the post,' said Respy. 'I hope there is a letter for you at last.'

The sound of heavy feet on the gravel bought them to their feet, a little alarmed. Two Gendarmes came round the corner of the house, and seeing the two women saluted politely.

'Madame Stoneberry?' asked one of the officers.

Rose went forward. She wore a flowered wrap and her long black hair was plaited like a schoolgirl's. She looked slender, beautiful, and very young.

'I am Madame Stoneberry.'

'I regret having to disturb you, Madame, but we have been instructed by the Military Authorities in Paris to enquire whether you have heard from your husband, Lieutenant Alban Stoneberry? Or if he has visited you lately? Or if he is here?'

'No.' Rose was obviously astonished. 'I have not seen him since I left Paris two months ago. And he has not written. He is in Paris, of course, at Headquarters.'

'It appears not, Madame. He has not been there for some time.'

'But, M'sieur, I assure you he is working there. He is in the British Army. At the Supply Headquarters. He has not been here.'

'Were you not surprised not to hear from him?'

'Indeed, M'sieur, I am very worried. I was thinking of returning earlier than I had planned.'

262

The two men hesitated. 'You know a Count Adolphe Bridault?'

'Why do you ask?'

'This gentleman, too, has disappeared.'

Rose looked at Respy, who was visibly bristling with indignation, and laid a restraining hand upon her arm.

'It's no use becoming angry, Respy. It is not the officer's fault that he has to make enquiries. We must tell him everything we know, which I'm afraid is very little. Count Adolphe Bridault I have met once or twice; he is a friend of my husband's. I know he is a great gambler, and that he certainly is not here. If he came, I would not receive him.'

The sergeant smiled for the first time. 'We know a great deal about that gentleman! Do you know where he used to play in Paris?'

'No. I only know he gambled because my husband told me he owed him money, and I remitted him the amount before I left to have my baby here, in Menton. Could my husband have met with an accident?'

'And the Count also?' said the sergeant sceptically. 'It is doubtful, Madame, though perhaps not impossible.' He shrugged. 'May we search the apartment?'

'If Madame Respigny will permit it. I am only a visitor here.' She looked at Respy imploringly, seeing indignation in every line of her usually calm face.

'Certainly,' said Respy in a stifled voice, and moved towards the door. 'You will forgive our disarray,' she added ironically. 'It is early and we have done no housework. But go where you wish.'

The two men glanced at each other and the sergeant said to Rose, 'Thank you, Madame. Today it will not be necessary. If we need to know anything else, we will call again.'

'But I must return to Paris at once! If my husband has met with an accident, I should be there.'

'Let us hope it is only an accident. You will keep me informed as to your movements. You have your permit to return?'

'Oh, yes. Thank you. Good day to you.'

'Good day.' They saluted and went on their way. The bell

jangled as they opened and closed the gate. Respy exploded furiously in English, utterly outraged.

'Search my flat? Whoever heard of such a thing? How dare they? What on earth was he suggesting?'

'That we might be harbouring a deserter, Respy.'

'You mean that Alban has deserted? But why should he?'

Rose kissed Respy's worried face, and said gently, 'We shall know when we get to Paris. And, Respy, I am truly sorry I should bring you all this worry. Believe me, I had not dreamed that such a thing could happen. I must go back to Paris at once. And, Respy, I should be so grateful if you would come with me.'

She had known he was afraid, but not to this extent. She remembered with sudden vividness hearing Marian's young schoolboy brother when they were all at King's Cross Station, boarding their train for Yorkshire. The end of their last term at school. How confident she had been then, and how she had teased Alban's importune approaches.

"He was a dreadful funk on the ski slopes," the boy had said, "and he was a pig of a bully at school." And how the boys had giggled when Mrs Palmer reproved them. And she remembered now, as she had then, the magic world of snow and frost, of lanterns shining on the ice, and learning to dance in the safe circle of Tom's arms.

Alban had been horribly afraid of the ski lifts, refusing to go on them and to high slopes above. He had been afraid then, and he had been afraid in Paris. And he had been afraid at home – of his aunt and uncle. It seemed to her, thinking back, that he had been afraid all his life.

They managed to get a first-class sleeper on the Paris train three days later. Reservations were easier to obtain than on the downward journey. Many people had left Paris but few were going back. Rose was grateful for Respy's efficient help, even though she made it quite clear that she thought it foolhardy for a young mother so recently confined to make such a long journey.

The trip was long, arduous, and very hot. But the presence of little Stella evoked kindness and assistance from their fellow passengers who, being French, were not in the least embarrassed to see Rose breast feeding her baby.

The long day and short summer night passed as, anxious and impatient, they longed to reach their destination. The beautiful panorama of central France went by unnoticed.

As she sat with her baby in her arms, Rose felt more like a refugee than a rich young woman going home to her husband. Ironically she longed to see him, as a woman might long to see her beloved.

If he had been found? If it were a mistake or an accident? If there had been some logical explanation for his absence? But if he *had* deserted . . . ? The thought of this and what it would mean terrified her. Her terror was not like the abyss of despair into which she had fallen on Tom's death, for she did not love Alban. But the finality of what he had done, and the terrible penalty he would have to pay if he were caught! The disgrace to his family! The Stoneberrys would suffer more than if he had been killed in action. They were elderly now, proud, and steeped in the prejudices of their class, hanging on to their old-fashioned conventions. They had worked hard to build up their position at Danesfell, and were inordinately proud of the historic house which they could not really afford.

Once Respy said, 'You need not stay in Paris. We could go straight on to England.'

The temptation to wash her hands of the whole sordid business, the whole tragic hopeless muddle, and go back to England, to Stephen and Marian, her friends, was almost irresistible.

But she could not go. She must try to find Alban. She was all he had – all he had ever had.

Rose shook her head. 'I must see if he has been found. If he has, I must visit him. There may be some way – though I don't know how – that I could help him. Once he asked me to help him, and I did not really understand. I think now he wanted me to help him to be brave.'

She held her baby close, the small, warm presence bringing her comfort. Whatever happened, she had Stella now.

They reached Paris just as the city was gilded with the light of early morning. There was the usual struggle to find a

265

porter, their ranks thinned since the outbreak of war, followed by an equal struggle to obtain a taxi. The French, she had long since discovered, had no scruples about queue-jumping, although to be young and pretty, and to have a baby in your arms, was a great help. They eventually managed to drive to the Place de Maréchal.

Placards holding messages of hope blazed from every corner kiosk. Ludendorf Held! The Tide Has Turned! Germans In Full Retreat!

'There!' cried Respy triumphantly, 'what did I tell you? They have stretched their forces too far.'

There was an air of festivity about the city. Groups of people stood about, talking excitedly, flags were flying from windows, and when they arrived at the old square it seemed oddly quiet with only the distant rumble of traffic and no underlying thud and tremor of guns.

Rose knocked at the concierge's window and asked Madame Dubois for the keys. She emerged from her den in a fluster, and as she handed them over burst into a tide of information without appearing to draw breath. Monsieur had gone away without surrendering his keys, and then the police had been here, and the Army, asking all sorts of questions. But before that there had been so many comings and goings in the evenings, dancing, shouting, gaming, and sometimes fighting . . .

Rose turned away to the stairs, but Madame Dubois began to follow them. Rose tipped the driver and asked him to take their luggage up to the first floor – Madame Dubois was now apologising for the condition of the flat. With all this happening, Madame Stoneberry would understand it had been difficult . . . and the concierge had not expected her to return so soon . . .

As she finally paused for breath, Rose thrust a banknote into her hand and said firmly, 'Thank you very much, Madame, the keys will be all we require now. We will call you if we want you.' She turned her back resolutely on Madame Dubois and went up the stairs to the entrance door.

'Whew!' she said as they entered the apartment. She gave Stella to Respy and leaned against the door. 'I wonder how

266

much that woman knows? Whatever she does, and a lot she doesn't, will have gone all round the neighbourhood.'

She crossed the small entrance foyer and went into the grand salon. *'Mon dieu!'* she exclaimed. 'There have certainly been some parties!'

The room was in chaos. Empty and half empty bottles of wine and spirits were thrown about the floor. There were spillage stains and dark liquor rings on the fine pale wood of the furniture, and what looked like wine and dried vomit on the beautiful rugs. Small pieces of furniture had been over-turned, some broken, and bits of glass and china were ground into the floor. The ashtrays were filled with cigarette and cigar butts, rotting scraps of food on silver serving plates, playing cards strewn about the floor.

Rose drew the curtains and thrust the windows wide. As the light and warm air flooded into the room, there was a sudden buzzing of flies.

'My God, Respy, what has been happening? It smells like a brothel.'

'I have never smelled a brothel.' Respy was white-faced and stiff with disgust. 'I hope you have not either. But we must clean the worst of this before that woman sees it.'

'Yes.'

'Is there anywhere clean we can put this child?'

'I hope so. Come.' Rose led the way through the door in the carved panelling. Thankfully, nothing in her bedroom had been disturbed. They laid Stella down on the bed and then went from room to room. It was not just the dirt and confusion. Rose realised that someone had been here, methodically searching the place. Every drawer and cupboard was opened and turned out. Papers, bills and letters had been thrown out on the floor. Only Alban's bedroom was tidy, apart from a scatter of face powder on the rumpled bed, a corsage of dead flowers.

They went back to her room, the only tidy place. The baby stirred and stretched and began a fretful little grumble. Rose picked her up.

'What will you do?' asked Respy. 'Will you go to Head-quarters to see his Commanding Officer?'

'I will let them know I am back. But first I will clean the worst of this up, and pick up and sort out the papers. Then I'll get the concierge to arrange for the flat to be thoroughly cleaned.'

'And then?'

'I don't know. I *must* wait a while. If he is hiding in Paris, and learns that I am here, he may come to me. Then there may be some way in which I can help him. We will wait for a few days.' She looked at Respy, who was obviously trying to suppress her anxiety. 'Respy,' she said, with pleading eyes, 'forgive me. If you cannot bear the situation here and would like to go home now, I understand.'

Her old governess did not reply, so Rose tried again. 'Or, if you would rather take Stella on to Thornsby, I will wire Stephen and get them to meet you at Victoria. I'm sure they would take her back with them, and you could go home . . . but, for the present, I must stay here. Please try to understand. I owe it to him.'

Respy stood silently for a moment, and then seemed to give herself a little shake.

'Don't talk such ridiculous nonsense! Of course I shall stay with you as long as you need me, but don't expect me to understand all this because I don't and never will! And now you had better feed and make this child clean and comfortable, while I make us both some coffee.'

'Oh, Respy darling, bless you!'

'Come now, no tears!' Respy said with some asperity. 'Here are Stella's things.' She patted Rose affectionately, set her glasses firmly on the bridge of her nose, and sailed off into the kitchen. Rose dried her eyes, a smile warring with the tears. She had half expected Respy to wipe her eyes and blow her nose for her, as she had done years ago.

She unpacked the baby clothes, made the baby clean and comfortable, sat down in an armchair and gave the small warm creature her breast. In the weeks since her birth, Stella had altered. The bud-like crumple of her pink skin had unfurled into firm roundness, and the eyelashes had unfolded into soft golden brown fringes. The eyes, instead of being the indeterminate slaty-blue of the newborn, were already the

268

deep, brilliant blue of the Normanbys. She was Tom's daughter, that was plain.

It was quiet in the room. A dim light filtered through the great plane tree in the courtyard outside. Thankfully the bedroom was only dusty with disuse, with none of the sordid disarray of the grand salon. It was peaceful enough and yet Rose felt imprisoned by it.

She put Stella in her basket cot in the centre of the bed, and went into the kitchen where coffee was waiting, black and strong and sweet. Respy was already attacking the stack of dishes in the sink.

Rose picked up all the scattered papers that the searchers had left, and stacked and clipped them on her desk to sort through later. There were no letters except one from the Credit Lyonnaise to notify her of the money which had been paid into her account. All the household bills had been paid. She noticed a monthly withdrawal of one hundred pounds in Alban's name. Poor Alban. He could have written to her, and she would have authorised Monsieur Raymond to give him more.

Rose and Respy set to and cleared away the more unpleasant remains of Alban's bachelor entertainments until they were exhausted. Afterwards they washed their hands and sat back in the two easy chairs in the bedroom. They seemed to have settled in there as though the rest of the apartment was no longer Rose's home.

She thought she would write to Stephen and tell him what had happened, and sat down at the desk in her room, drawing some notepaper out of the rack.

"I am short of money – tomorrow I will go to the bank," she wrote, "and I think I will go and see Monsieur Raymond. He must have heard the rumours. He will advise me . . ." She stopped, pen in hand. 'What is that?'

Beyond the door leading to the great salon, they heard footsteps.

Both women rose and automatically stepped before the sleeping child.

'Someone is there,' Respy whispered. 'Who can it be? Who has a key beside the concierge?'

'No one. Except Alban.' Rose's hand gripped Respy's wrist. 'Hush!'

They heard the door into the corridor open and footsteps cross to the bedroom door. They both knew who it was. They stood hand in hand, frozen.

He thrust the door open and stood there looking at them in silence, a haggard wreck of the man Rose had left in Paris three months ago. He was clad grotesquely in a workman's blue overall, a beret pulled down over his unkempt hair. He was unshaven, his eyes ringed with shadows.

He carried a revolver in his hand. He made a gesture with it towards Rose and she felt Respy's grip tighten.

'Alban.' Rose dropped Respy's hand and started towards him.

He raised the gun, 'Stop there.' He spoke in a quiet, hissing tone, afraid that Madame Dubois' sharp ears might catch his voice. 'Don't come near me! Go into the salon. This woman is to stay here and keep the child away from us!' He jerked his head.

Rose glanced at Respy and then went past him into the big room. He followed her, shutting the door silently behind him, watching her the whole time like a tethered dog. He dropped wearily into a chair on the far side of the elaborate desk.

'Listen to me,' he said. 'You'll have to be very careful. They searched but could not find me. I started for the frontier, but I hadn't enough money so came back. Now they think I've escaped. You *have* to help me. You must do exactly as I tell you. If you don't, I'll kill you and that bastard of Grimshaw's.'

'Alban,' she said, 'I won't give you away. I've come back to see how I can help you. You're not well . . . If we went to Colonel Winterton and spoke to him, surely he would listen?'

He started to laugh quietly, but his eyes were wild with panic. 'You're a fool,' he said, 'and you could have helped me by now – if you had left more money! Bridault was helping me. He said we would get money. I must have it!'

'I can get you money, but then what can you do?'

'They do not know where I am. Bridault left me some days ago. We were to meet and he was to bring the money. We won a great deal gambling one night. But he did not show up. I had to come back. What can you draw from the bank without causing suspicion?'

'I don't know – five hundred pounds. Perhaps more.'

'Get as much as you can,' he said, 'and hurry! And bring some food back, I'm starving. And a bottle of the good Rhône.'

All her anxiety for him in his appalling position drained away. Rose showed no flicker of feeling.

'I will do this, and be as quick as I possibly can. I will bring you food as soon as I return.'

He looked at her and said in a strange, envious voice, 'You're not afraid of anything, are you, Rose?' She did not reply and he reached across the desk and grabbed her hand. 'Answer me! *Why* don't you answer me when I speak to you?'

His fingers bit into her flesh and he twisted her wrist until she cried out with pain.

'If you break my wrist, Alban, I shan't be able to help you. If you want me to hurry, then I must go at once. And you know that you *are* frightening me. I came back hoping I could help you, but you will not let me. But I will do everything you say.'

He dropped her wrist. The pain from twisted muscles and bruised flesh was agonising.

'Get out then, and be quick! Tell that woman with the child not to come in here. And to keep it quiet. I must get rest.'

'I must get a hat and basket. Madame Dubois must not notice anything amiss.'

He made no reply and Rose went quickly into the bedroom. Respy was waiting anxiously for her. Mercifully, the baby was fast asleep.

'I have to go and get money for him,' explained Rose, 'and provisions. You must stay here with the baby. We must be very careful. I think he is quite mad. I hardly recognised him.' She put on a hat and found a shopping basket in the kitchen.

'How did he get in?'

'I don't know. He would not dare pass the concierge's window – she misses nothing, and she must know he is wanted. But these old houses are full of hidden doors and passages. I imagine he came in through the wine cellar. But

271

we must do as he says. He looks so strange, and not just in his appearance. He is a different person. A very dangerous one.'

'What shall we do?'

'You must stay here with the baby. We must not provoke him. Look.' There were some oranges on the table which they had brought from Menton. 'Squeeze one of these. Wait a minute . . .' She went over to a small medicine cupboard and took out a blue glass bottle. 'Here – it's some stuff Alban had when he could not sleep. Give her the smallest drop in the orange juice if she gets restless or cries.'

Respy looked horrified.

'You must,' Rose said sharply. 'We are his hostages, you and I and the baby. I must go alone and you must stay here and wait.' She gave a tight little smile and pressed Respy's hand. 'Believe me, when I asked you to come back with me, I never expected anything like this.'

She went out through the salon. Alban was still seated at the desk, sprawled across it, his arms outstretched, face down. The gun was lying close to his hand. He heard her enter. His fingers closed tightly upon the gun and he stared up at her with those mad, dark-ringed eyes. He looked as though he had not slept for days.

'Wait!' he said. Rose stopped obediently.

'When you have the money, go to this address. It is not difficult to find – up near the Marais. The apartment is on the first floor. The name is André Bretagne. Ask him for a packet left in my name, and pay for it – he will not hand it over without the cash.'

Rose wanted to plead with him, to go down on her knees and implore him at least to let Respy and the baby go, but she knew it would be useless. There had been a time when, in spite of his unprovoked jealousy, his rapid changes of mood and occasional outbursts of rage, she had felt that she could get close to him, pitying the helplessness and fear that lay beneath the surface. She knew that he would never learn to trust her completely, but this was even worse. It was as though all that was left of Alban was an animal fear and an instinct to escape at any cost.

Rose went to the bank and withdrew the money. It was not difficult. She then took a cab to the Bastille and walked until she had found the address.

The house, when she found it, was a crumbling, once magnificent mansion, its stone frontage defaced with small modern shop fronts. The wide entrance steps led to a massive hall and stairway with magnificent wrought iron bannisters. Every doorway, though scratched and chipped by local children and used by local cats for more intimate purposes, had a splendid stone pediment surmounted by a carved coat of arms. She went up to the first floor and rang the bell of the number Alban had given her.

As she stood waiting, she became aware of a strange, sweet, heavy smell. She waited for a short while, then rang again. Then she head the sound of slow, dragging footsteps, as though a very old person was coming to open the door. But when it finally opened a young man stood before her. He was still in a dressing gown, and his good-looking face was pale and unshaven. His eyes were darkly ringed with the same sunken shadows that she had seen in Alban's face.

He started at Rose's fresh beauty and at the elegance of her clothes as though he were seeing a ghost. He drew the collar of his shabby brocade dressing gown closer, and said, 'Madame?'

'I have called for a packet for Lieutenant Stoneberry.'

'Stoneberry?' He looked surprised. 'Did he give you this address?'

She held out the envelope. 'This is correct, is it not? You are André Bretagne?'

'What is left of him, Madame,' he said wryly. 'And you are Madame Stoneberry. I have been at one of your charming soirées. I understood you to be in Nice?'

'I have just returned.'

He smiled, 'I will not be so tactless as to enquire where Alban is.'

'Have you what he asked for?' she said impatiently.

'Of course. Anything for a friend in need. If you will wait a moment, Madame?'

She waited by the open door. She could glimpse the dirty untidy hallway inside, and, stronger than ever, could smell the heavy sweetish odour which hung about the place. He came back shortly with a sealed packet.

'I was told to pay for it. What do I owe you, M'sieur?'

He told her. It was more than she had expected, and he was obviously amused by her surprise. 'I am sorry, Madame. Needs must when the devil drives. And Alban will need the devil's luck now if he is still in Paris.'

'You know about him?'

'Of course. Everyone knows. The police have been here and it created a small awkwardness for me. And indeed for all his friends. You are very loyal, Madame.'

She gave a little nod. 'As you say, M'sieur, needs must when the devil drives.' She paid him and he took the money with a bow. 'Neither of us has seen the other,' he said, 'if the police should call again. And good luck to Monsieur Stoneberry.'

Rose thrust the package deep into her handbag and hurried down the stairs. Now she had only to buy the food and go home.

She stopped at a market and bought cold meats and charcuterie, butter and cheese, salad, fruit and milk. Then she caught a taxi back to the Place de Maréchal.

She asked the driver to carry her heavy basket upstairs. She let herself into the apartment and stood listening, but everything was silent. Her instinct was to run straight across to the opposite door to see that Respy and Stella were safe. She drew in a deep breath and instead opened the salon door.

Alban was stretched out on the settee, his eyes closed, but as she moved forward they opened and he sat up, holding the gun in his hand.

She put down the heavy basket.

'I have got what you wanted.'

'Put it on the desk.'

She took the packet out of her bag, and the wad of money, and put them down on the desk.

'Now get me some food – and a decent bottle of wine!'

She knew what the packet contained. She had so often seen her Mother waiting in an agony of impatience for her little yellow-skinned doctor to come, bringing her a similar package. Afterwards she had seen Charmian's tired blue eyes

274

begin to sparkle as though life had returned, and she would call her maid and rise to dress for the evening's pleasure.

When she had fed the baby, Rose went to the wine cellar which was beneath the kitchen, via iron stairs in a spiral curve. The cellar was not below ground but on the courtyard level, a large windowless place smelling of horses and leather and stored wine. But it was also foul with a smell of open drains. Rose had not been down here since she had first viewed the apartment, but could not recall noticing such a smell before.

A little light filtered round the edges of a large heavy door leading into the rear courtyard. She found a light switch and pressed it down. A row of unshaded bulbs hanging above the wine racks against the wall sprang into light. She turned on the other switches.

The floor and walls were all built of stone. The roof arched to bear the weight of the old building above. She tried the heavy door but it was locked. She guessed that Alban must have the key. She walked along the rows, peering at the labels in the poor light, and found there were many empty spaces. She remembered the bottles she and Respy had cleared away and knew that Alban and his friends had been using the stock without replenishing it.

She found the Rhône in the last rack. Next to it there was a narrow space between the end of the rack and the wall. There was no light here and the foul smell was disgusting.

She heard an unpleasant scuttle of mice or rats behind the wine racks, but went on. She saw there were wooden partitions and remembered that they were the old horse stalls, and that the place had once been a stable.

But there must be another entrance here somewhere. She was certain there was another way besides the stone steps she had just descended. She stepped gingerly forward and began to feel along the wooden wainscoting. She went along the surface of the wall, pressing and probing, and then, on the back wall, she found it. She pressed gently and a low narrow door swung back into the darkness beyond. The smell of urine and excrement nearly choked her.

275

She hung on to the door, a handkerchief across her mouth and nose, as her eyes became accustomed to the semi-darkness. Straw on the floor, a discarded British uniform, a grubby blanket, and on the back wall a narrow flight of rickety iron steps leading up to a trap in the floor. The stink came from a drain, such as she had seen in any horse stall, from which the iron grid had been taken. There was a broom beside it, filthy as the drain, all smelling foul, and as she moved a sudden buzz of flies.

This was where he had been hiding for the last few days, since he had had to come back to Paris. A place in which you would not put a dog. Creeping out at night to buy food, and across to the stable entrance where there was a water faucet. Not daring to go up into the room above in case Madame Dubois heard.

She stepped gingerly across to the foot of the rusty iron stairway and crept cautiously up to the trap at the top. She pressed it and it opened smoothly, as though the hinges had been oiled. She pulled herself up into a small dark place. The only light was through a knothole in the wooden wall facing her through which came a brilliant pencil of light. She realised she was behind the elaborately carved panelling of the salon.

She stepped forward and looked through the peep-hole – and started back, nearly crying aloud. Alban was so near that she felt she could reach out and touch him. He was still seated at the desk, his head down on his arms, the gun just beside his relaxed hand, fast asleep.

She felt gently down the wooden panelling and found the spring lock.

She knew there were several of these concealed places in the old house, the tenants' boltholes when the Terror ruled. The door opposite, leading to the bedrooms and kitchen quarters, was similar, but the concealed locks had been replaced by bronze handles.

Alban stirred and groaned in his sleep, felt the gun beside his hand and relaxed again. Rose hoped he was too tired for hunger to rouse him. She waited, holding her breath until he was quite still, and then crept down the stairs, pulled down the trap, closed the door on the foul-smelling hovel, picked

276

up her bottle of wine and raced up the steps which led to the kitchen.

Respy had prepared hot soup, and a cold meal of salad and the charcuterie Rose had brought in.

'Why were you so long?' she asked anxiously. 'I was terrified that he would call again.'

'I have found out where he is hiding. Is the food ready? I must take it in now. Wait . . . I will tell you when I come back.'

She picked up the tray and carried it through to the salon. When she opened the door, Alban was already awake.

She set the tray down on the desk. 'Is there anything else you want?' He did not speak. 'May I go now?' she said.

A curious smile twisted his lips. He indicated the bottle.

'Open it, for God's sake, and pour me a glass.'

He started to eat and drink, watching her all the time, the curious smile on his face as though he enjoyed seeing her standing there, silently waiting for his permission like a servant. She opened the wine and poured him a glass.

She knew she must not make a false move. His eyes were like those of a wild animal, ready to attack at the slightest threat to his safety.

'Leave your keys,' he said.

She paused in surprise, and he hit the desk with the palm of his hand.

'Keys?' she said.

'Of course, you fool. Don't think I shall let you creep out of here behind my back – or send that woman of yours out with the baby.'

She put the keys on the desk without speaking. She had hoped for a minute that Respy would be able to get out with Stella. She could face him alone. Now there was no chance of that.

He jerked his head towards the door behind her.

'You can go now. And keep that brat quiet! I want to get some sleep. I don't want to see or hear it. Or you. I'll call if I need anything. If you have to go out for me, you go out one at a time, and don't attempt to take the child. If anyone rings the doorbell or the telephone, answer it at once. You must keep out any callers, particularly the woman Dubois, until I can hide. Do not attempt to contact the police or Army Head-quarters. If you betray me, I swear I will kill all three of you before they get me. I will go as soon as it is dark. Tell them whatever you like when you get to Yorkshire . . . better tell them I am dead. Bring me a razor and water, a dark suit, shirt, and a dark scarf – if you can find one. And a hat.'

'You wish me to bring these things now?'

'Yes, now, get on with it!'

She went to his bedroom, selected the things he had asked for and took them back into the salon.

'Shall I bring the hot water now?'

'No. I'll call. Leave me now.' He picked up the razor case and looked at the seven gleaming blades. 'My father left me these. I can just remember the Indian servant shaving him before he went on duty.' He picked up one of the blades and tested it with his thumb, then looked up at her again with the same strange smile. 'Get out now! Don't look so anxious. I wouldn't use a knife . . . Get out!'

She went out, silently closing the door and leaning against it, covering her face with her hands. She was breathing fast, as though she had been running. When her heartbeat began to slow, she dropped her hands and went into the kitchen.

Respy looked at her, and she shook her head. The baby was still fast asleep in her basket. 'Did he say anything about going?'

'He said he is going tonight, as soon as it is dark.'

'I gave the baby what you said.' Respy looked anxiously at Stella. 'Only the smallest drop. But we cannot go on doing that – it would be harmful.'

'I don't think we shall have to.' She told Respy about the stinking lair in the cellar. 'It seems that the Gendarmes and some army people searched the apartment when he had made his escape to the frontier. But Bridault did not meet him, and he had to turn back because he had no money. He was here when they searched again, lying hidden behind the panelling, and until we came he dare not come out in case Madame Dubois heard footsteps or any noise. He has all the keys now. We could not get out if we tried. I had thought you might take Stella away through the cellar. But not now.'

278

'Tradesmen and refuse men come through the courtyard. Could we not call to them or drop a message?'

'No! I daren't risk it. In his present mood he could do anything.'

'But then he too would be killed.'

'He faces death whichever way he turns. Poor Alban! He will be lucky if he is given a long imprisonment. He is a deserter. I tried to persuade him that it would be better to give himself up at Headquarters. He does not even listen. He only wants to run away, like a little boy wants to run away from home. He wants to run from the sound of the guns, away from war and death, and away from me – away from his own thoughts of when his family will learn of this, and how bitterly humiliated they will be. He needs courage and he has none.'

'You sound sorry for him?'

'Yes, I think I am.'

'I cannot understand you. If he escapes from France, where would he go?'

'Who knows? He wants to run to safety, and there is no safety anywhere for him now.'

They looked at each other helplessly. The day had already seemed interminably long and a longer night stretched before them. What could they do?

On an impulse Rose went to the salon door and opened it. Instantly Alban was on his feet.

'Please talk to me, Alban,' she said. 'There must be something or someone who could help you . . .'

'I told you not to come in here unless I called! Do you want me to treat you as you deserve?' On the wall behind him there was a display of hunting trophies. He snatched up a small riding whip and went across to her. As she stepped back he slashed at her, catching her upraised arm. 'Do you want more or will you obey me?'

She went back into the bedroom, closing the door behind her.

'We just have to wait,' she said. Tears were rising in great, shuddering sobs, and she sank upon the floor by Respy, burying her face in her lap, comforted by the gentle hand that stroked her head.

'There now, there now . . . we will wait, and he will go without harming us.'

'Oh, Respy,' Rose cried, and black despair seemed to close about her, 'what have I brought you into?'

Chapter Thirteen

So the long summer day went by. Through the courtyard window came the muffled noise of traffic, the smell of petrol, the sound of street cries. They seemed to come from another world. The women spoke in whispers. If the baby made the slightest sound, they jumped up to quieten her. They made a scrappy lunch, barely tasting what they ate, and washed the dishes, worrying in case Alban should hear the tinkle of the crockery as they stacked it to dry.

The baby did wake at midday and Rose changed and fed her. To their relief Stella put her thumb in her mouth and settled down to sleep again.

They sorted out their clothes and packed two light suitcases as through they were quite sure that they would be travelling on to London the following day. Each minute seemed like an hour, and the slightest sound from the salon brought them to their feet, alert, dreading Alban's next move. Sometimes they lay down on the bed and tried to sleep but could only snatch uneasy minutes, filled with anxious dreams.

Late in the afternoon the sound of the doorbell brought them to their feet and they almost ran into the salon together.

Alban had shaved and dressed in the clothes Rose had brought him. His face looked thin and haggard without the straggling beard, his eyes wild and desperate. He snatched the gun from the desk.

'You,' he pointed to Respy, 'answer that!' Then he went to the panelling behind him and pressed the hidden catch in the centre of an elaborately carved flower. The door slid silently open.

'Wait!' Rose cried. She whipped up the dirty workmen's clothing he had discarded, ran across to the open panel and threw it inside. 'Now the tray.' She collected the china and remnants of his meal on to the tray and thrust it after the clothes. 'If it is the police outside, they'll certainly search the house!'

He stood watching her. For a second she thought he was going to thank her, but he turned away and stepped into the hiding place and the panel slid to behind him.

Respy looked at her pleadingly, but Rose shook her head and mouthed silently, 'Not yet . . . not *yet*! Go and answer the door.'

Respy hesitated then went steadfastly out of the big room across the foyer to the door.

But it was only Madame Dubois, demanding loudly in her raw Parisian accent if they required anything? Would they like her to clean the salon or do some shopping for them? Should she take up the rugs tomorrow and beat them in the courtyard? If only they had let her know in advance, she would have prepared everything for them.

Then Respy's voice, speaking French with her irrepressible English accent, thanking her coldly and refusing her offers, concluding crushingly, 'Madame has been awake since the early hours of the morning. We had a most exhausting journey. She is trying to get some rest for our journey tomorrow and I would like to do the same. You have just awakened her and the baby. It is *very* inconsiderate of you!'

Madame Dubois apologised and withdrew, still insisting that they had only to ask her and she would be glad to do anything.

The door in the panelling slid silently open, and Alban came back into the room. Rose wondered what he would do now. Where would he go? Would he hide somewhere in Paris? No one he knew would take him in. If he managed to get out of Paris, where would he get the drugs or money? Supposing he did not go? She felt a cold sweat break out on her forehead. She must not think of that. She must listen and watch and wait.

'Double lock the door,' he said. 'That woman has a key.'

Respy went back and did as she was bid, and put the keys on the desk.

'I want to speak to my wife alone.'

'If you maltreat her,' Respy said shakily, 'I will throw open the windows in the bedroom and scream for help.'

'Do as I say.' He spoke as though he had not heard her. Rose looked at Respy with frantic appeal, and she went out, pale with suppressed anger. Alban threw the bunch of keys at Rose's feet. 'Lock the other doors.'

Like an obedient servant, Rose locked the doors leading into the bedrooms then dropped the keys into his hand. He stood watching her silently for a long minute, but his eyes were frightened, as though he expected her to make an attack upon him.

'I cannot trust you,' he said savagely, 'I never could. You made a bargain with me which you had no intention of keeping. You knew what Danesfell meant to me, but you did not tell me that you could not dispose of any part of it without Grimshaw's consent. You knew that until you were of age, we should have to go running to them, cap in hand.'

'But I have plenty of money of my own, Alban! And in any case the solicitors have held up probate again. They have no real confirmation of Tom's death.'

'Yet you wanted to keep the power of your inheritance when you came pleading for me to marry you. Do you deny you have always hoped that he will return?'

'Yes, I hoped to see him again. I loved him. I could not forget him. But I made an honest bargain with you, and I mean to keep it.'

'If he did come back – would you keep it then?'

She did not answer, there was no answer, and the pain of her loss filled her face with despair.

He looked at her and laughed. 'Of course you would not! You lie like the whore you are, like the whore your mother was before you. Did you think I married you because I was hopelessly in love with you?'

She gave a small, eloquent gesture. 'You said you loved me, and I believed you. You had never said it before. You did want me, you always have, and I came to believe you really cared for me. When you said you would marry me in spite of the baby, I was grateful. I made a mistake. Perhaps we both did.'

'Oh, I wanted you all right. I wanted you to look at. To possess. I wanted to have you on my arm so that all the other men would envy me. I wanted you to be my wife at Danesfell, so the whole county would envy me. But all you wanted was that I should give my name – *my name* – to Grimshaw's child! You are no better than the girls I have watched in the brothels of Montmartre. That is all one wants from such women – to give a performance. So put on a performance for me now, like you did then, to trap me. Let me have that at least before I go!'

For a moment Rose did not move. He wanted to humiliate her as she had unwittingly humiliated him. He wanted to despise her as he despised the women of the brothels, and perhaps himself.

Her heart was torn with pity for him. She made an involuntary gesture towards him and he could see the compassion in her eyes.

The whip was still on the desk. He struck at her hand so that she exclaimed, and put it to her mouth to staunch the blood. He caught her shoulder and swung her round to face him, tearing her blouse from her.

'Take that off!'

Without a word she undid the small pearl buttons at her neck and wrists, slipped the blouse off and stood before him in her skirt and white satin camisole. The material emphasised the golden glow of her beautiful skin.

'And that thing.'

The little whip darted, stinging her shoulders, leaving a thin red weal. He flicked the lace of her camisole. 'Take it off! You were never modest before Grimshaw, I imagine! I am your husband.' He was circling her like a wild animal, the little whip darting snakelike, stinging wherever it touched.

She did not wince or cry out but lifted the pretty garment up over her head and laid it by her blouse. She made no attempt to cover her breasts but stood before him, waiting.

'Where shall I mark you now?' She did not move and the whip cut viciously across her shoulders with the full force of his arm. She swayed under the impact but made no attempt to run or cry out.

'Look at me, damn you!'

She raised her eyes, meeting his frenzied, frightened face. Frightened of what he was doing. Frightened of everything.

'Why are you never afraid? Aren't you afraid for your beauty? I could mark you for the rest of your life. Aren't you afraid for your life? If I have to, I will not hesitate to destroy you before I go.'

She raised her arm but the whip cut across it and struck her face. The telephone rang. Alban stood transfixed, staring at the blood dripping down her face.

'Answer it!'

It was Colonel Winterton.

'Mrs Stoneberry?'

She answered in French. 'Oh, yes, Monsieur Raymond, we arrived back this morning. I was going to get in touch with you.'

'You are not alone?'

'No, I have brought Madame Respigny and the baby with me to Paris. We are on our way to England tomorrow, I hope.'

'I understand. He is there. You are going to be all right, I promise. For God's sake, hold on, my dear.'

'Thank you so much, Monsieur. *Au revoir*.'

She replaced the receiver. 'I wrote to Monsieur Raymond before I left Nice. He only telephoned to see if we had arrived.'

They stood silently. Rose became aware that her cheek was throbbing and touched it, glancing down at the blood on her fingers impersonally as though she had not felt the cut of the lash.

'Take your things and get out of my sight. Here!' Alban threw the keys at her feet.

She picked them up, took her clothes, unlocked the door then put the keys on the desk and went out.

Respy was standing just outside. She was trembling.

'My God, child, what has he done to you?'

'He hasn't killed me. For a moment I thought he might. But, thank God indeed, he is too frightened.'

'The telephone?'

'It was Colonel Winterton. He understood. He said – hold on. We must keep our nerve, Respy. We must wait and hope.' Rose looked down at the ugly lacerations on her breast and arms and said, 'I came back here because I felt I owed him so much.'

'You owe him nothing now,' Respy said savagely.

'I don't know. I did not realise . . .' Rose stopped. She had never realised on what a tightrope Alban had walked, between his desire for her and his crazy jealousy of Tom. She knew that it was Stella who was most at risk. 'We must keep our heads, Respy. We can do nothing but wait. They will come.'

Respy gently washed and dressed the ugly little lacerations. The one on Rose's face was now surrounded by a purple bruise. Would the scar last all her life as Alban had intended? Would she remember this day all her life? But it seemed unimportant. All that mattered was that somehow they must escape.

The day dragged on interminably. Once she ventured to open the salon door and saw that Alban was asleep on the settee, the gun on the carpet just below his hand.

It infuriated Respy when she told her.

'Could we not rush in, one of us snatching the gun?'

'No!' Rose insisted. 'We cannot take any risks. We *must* wait. He will not go until it is dark. Let us get a meal. I brought some eggs this morning. You will make one of your beautiful omelettes.' Respy turned away, her lips tight, tension in her once kindly face. She had aged in the past few hours. They both had.

'Respy, try and forgive me for all this. It will pass. One day the war will be over and I will bring Stella to Menton, if you will have us, and we will take her to one of those little coves like the ones along the coast where you taught me to swim. Where the sun warms the rocks and sand, and the pines grow right down to the beach, and the water is like pale green crystal. We will spend many days there. We will forget all this. You will help to teach Stella to swim, and I shall want you to help me be wise and show me how to live peacefully, alone. Because Aunt Margaret and Tom are both gone, and I have no one but you to help me now.' Respy relaxed and smiled, and Rose added, 'I have never told you how much I love you.'

Respy went very pink, and took off her pince-nez to wipe her eyes. She polished them fiercely and re-fixed them firmly on her nose.

'What nonsense you talk, child! There . . .' she beat the omelette hard, '. . . this is ready to cook. Shall we eat it now before we bring baby in?'

They tried to behave as though everything was quite normal. Stella lay quietly while they ate, kicking and cooing endearingly.

They had just finished their meal when Alban opened the door and told Rose to come. Respy grasped her wrist but Rose just patted her shoulder and followed him instantly into the salon.

'Bring me some food and another bottle of wine.'

She picked up the empty bottle from his last meal, the dregs had spilled on the beautiful Aubusson carpet, but before she could go, he said unexpectedly, 'I did not mean to hurt you like that, Rose.'

For a moment she was too surprised to speak.

'I know that,' she said. 'I don't think you ever meant to hurt me. Forget it. It has passed.'

He began to speak quickly, the words tumbling out so incoherently that she could scarcely understand him.

'You are so different to any other woman! You tease and mock and tempt men, but you are never really afraid. I wanted to make you afraid. Perhaps . . .' He paused, then said slowly, 'Perhaps if I had time, I could. But I could never make you love me.'

'If it makes you happy to see me afraid, I can tell you I *am* very afraid. Since our return, I have been afraid all the time.'

'That is not what I mean. You are frightened now, but you are not frightened of everything. All the time. Of the war and those damned guns . . . or because of your Eastern blood . . . or of people sneering at you.' His voice was almost a whisper, his eyes haunted. Then he suddenly jerked, as though pulling himself together. 'Hurry now, and get the food. I shall go as soon as it is dark.'

287

She took him some food and wine and set it on the desk for him, and then returned to the kitchen.

She made coffee, hot and strong, and took him a cup, but he neither spoke nor glanced up at her.

She went back into the kitchen, and she and Respy finished their meal undisturbed. Rose bathed the baby, made her comfortable, then fed her and put her down. As she bent over to kiss Stella, she said, 'How pink and white she is.' She laid her hand upon the baby's soft forehead. 'Look – no one would think she was mine.'

In the bedroom they opened the windows wide and stood looking out. The sky was almost dark. There were thick shadows in the courtyard beneath the big plane tree. There was no sound in the apartment. She glanced at Respy and then went to the salon door and gently tried the handle. It was not locked – she opened the door wide. Alban was not there. The keys were on the desk.

She pushed them into the pocket of her skirt and ran to the courtyard windows. It was getting darker by the minute. But the courtyard was empty. From open windows came the clattering sounds of meals being prepared behind the blackout. It was windless, not a breath of air stirring the plane tree's leaves.

'Has he gone?'

'I don't know. There's very little light . . .'

And then, below their feet, they heard the lock being turned, and the grating sound of a door being opened, and then dimly they saw him, standing just below them. They shrank back behind the curtains. He was wearing the formal dark suit that Rose had brought him, a dark scarf pulled up about his face, and a wide-brimmed black hat. His hands were thrust into the pockets of his jacket. Rose thought, How absurd he is. He makes himself as noticeable as a theatre spy. And with this a terrible anxiety seized her, as though she was watching a child stepping into certain danger.

He seemed to stand there for a long time as though waiting for a signal. And then suddenly, as though he had found his courage, he went towards the archway that led into the street.

He sidled round the courtyard, skirting the by now dark

288

walls, turned into the archway which led into the street to the rear of the house, and vanished from sight.

'Let's go!' said Respy. 'Let us go now, while we can.'

'He won't come back,' Rose said. 'We'll wait a little . . .'

All at once there was the sound of rapid gunfire, a fusillade of pistol shots, and Alban came stumbling back, his hands gripped to his chest. He threw back his head and fell to the cobblestones. He did not move again.

Rose screamed then ran across the room, ignoring Respy's cry of protest. Her fingers fumbled for a second but the concealed catch gave to her touch. She plunged down the rickety spiral stairs, clinging to the rusty hand rail in the darkness of the wine cellar. With her hands stretched before her like a blind woman, she found the heavy courtyard door, scrabbled for the latch and lifted it.

The group of men standing round Alban's body looked up as they heard her, guns levelled. She did not see them. She ran straight across and dropped on her knees beside him, lifting his head upon her knee. His eyes were open. He looked up, smiled, and whispered, 'Rose,' wonderingly, as though at some inexplicable joy. 'You came back . . .' His head lolled against her arm.

There was a long moment of silence. Rose looked at the men around her and said, 'I could not help him. I really could not help him!'

Colonel Winterton took her arm and said gently, 'No one could.'

A terrible sadness engulfed her, remembering everything from their first meeting at Glockenschule when she had still been a schoolgirl – the gauche, clumsy, boastful young man trying to hide his terrible shyness behind a brash sophistication – to this moment when he lay dead on the cobbles at her feet.

She was barely conscious that Respy was standing beside her. She and Colonel Winterton took Rose back into the house.

'What would he have done?' she asked. 'Without money, or friends, or anywhere to go?'

'Maybe he was lucky to finish things this way. And there was no other course you could have followed. Alban was betraying his own country,' said Colonel Winterton. 'Intelligence had been watching him ever since they discovered that he knew Bridault. He was the man we really wanted, the Count was too slippery for us. He got across the Spanish frontier. Alban had to come back – we knew he was in Paris, but did not know where.'

'He was here,' Rose said. 'It's not surprising that you did not find him.' She crossed the room and pressed the hidden switch on the panelling. The door opened silently, and the foetid smell from below seeped into the room. 'That is where he was hiding. There is another hidden entrance in the old stables below.' She turned away, her young face drawn with unhappiness. 'I suppose he just hoped I would come, because I could get the things he wanted. Money, food, dope . . . and I had to because he held the baby here, and Respy. And then – I had to give him away . . . although I had hoped to help him. I thought I might persuade him to come to you, but he was beyond reason. What could he hope for? I still feel that I sent him to his death.'

'After what he did to you,' Respy burst out, 'what else could you do? Our lives depended on his getting away.'

'Rose,' said Colonel Winterton, 'you could do nothing else. He would never have got out of Paris.' He came across and took her hands. 'Look, my dear, you have gone through enough. I will telephone my wife, and you must come to us, you and Mrs Respigny and the baby, until you are fit to return to London.'

She looked round the beautiful room which she had made such a happy haven for so many people. Now it seemed a place of ill omen, haunted by ancient fears.

'Thank you,' she said, 'we'll be glad to leave this place. Tomorrow we will return to London. If I may, I will send a telegram to my brother-in-law and ask him to meet us.'

That night they both slept deeply from sheer exhaustion, and Mrs Winterton was happy to look after Stella. The following morning Colonel Winterton used his army influence to secure them places on the express to the coast, supplying his own driver to take them to the Gâre du Nord and manage their luggage for them. The driver, a rosy-faced boy, spoke with a strong West Riding accent and for the first time Rose felt she was going home.

Soon the train was running through Normandy, leaving the battle fields far behind. At Boulogne they stood on the deck of the cross-channel steamer, watching the town with its cathedral up on the steep hill behind, and its harbour full of naval shipping and service men, and both she and Respy thought of the time when Rose had made her first crossing nearly five years ago, a pert child of fifteen. Five years in which she had grown up to know both happiness and despair.

It was a fair crossing. Soon they were in the train passing through the fruit orchards of Kent, and then – at last – clanking into Victoria Station. When Rose stepped on to the platform with Stella in her arms, she saw Stephen and Marian waiting for her. His thick fair hair reminded her irresistibly of another boy who had once run down this platform to welcome her.

There were hugs of delighted reunion and it was minutes before anyone could speak coherently. Rose put her baby into Marian's arms.

Her eyes were filled with wonder. 'She's beautiful, Rose,' she said, and then burst out, 'I'm pregnant too! Isn't it wonderful?'

'She's so proud of it that she can't keep it to herself for a moment,' said Stephen. 'All the chaps at the Mill are telling each other that t'owld meister's lad's wife is expecting. I think half the town knew before I did!'

'You're as thrilled as I am,' said Marian. Rose saw the affection in his eyes, and her new confidence, and felt happy for them, and somehow desolate as well. She introduced Respy. 'My dear friend and foster mother, Madame Respigny. I would not have got through the past few days without her. But we'll talk about that later.'

Stephen looked older. He had filled out a little, was no longer a boy. Marian, in her pretty summer dress, was shining with happiness.

291

He had telephoned Mrs Dyson at the flat in Chelsea to say they would all stay there overnight, and travel on to Thornsby the following day.

'We've just moved into our own house,' said Stephen. 'We're only renting it because things are so unsettled.' He hesitated and Rose felt he was holding something back. 'Well, when Armistice is finally declared, we shall be able to decide what to do. But just now, I shall stay on at the firm.'

They took a taxi to Riverside Mansions and Rose felt as though she had been away for a very long while. Like all the buildings in wartime it looked a little shabby outside, but when Mrs Dyson opened the front door of the flat, before Stephen could get his keys out, Rose was back in Margaret's world again. The hall, immaculately polished, was full of the scent of fresh flowers and she seemed to smell the sharp, sweet, lemony perfume her aunt had always worn. And Sarah Dyson was as rosy as ever in her spotless apron, beaming a welcome.

'Ah, Miss Rose!' she exclaimed. 'It's grand to see you back again. And let's have a look at the little one.'

Rose put Stella into her arms. She cooed and dimpled, and Sarah exclaimed, 'Eh, she's a right Normanby, this one is! Just look at those eyes, blue as Mr Tom's ever were, and they were as blue as any eyes *I* ever saw!'

There was a little silence, and Sarah carried the baby off into the drawing room, saying, 'I've put you in your old room, Miss Rose, I thought you would like that.'

'Thank you, Sarah.'

'Everything's in order, though I've only just got back myself. Mr Stephen wouldn't let me stay here until after those Zepps had finished. I'll bring your tea in right away now.'

Stella, at last overcome by seeing so many strange grown-up faces around her, screwed up her little face and began to grizzle.

'Give her to me,' said Respy, 'She's used to me. I'll get her settled before her feed time.'

Rose took off her hat and turned to face Stephen and Marian.

'I'm afraid those eyes of hers will always give her away,' she said. 'I didn't tell you but I think you have already guessed. Stella is Tom's baby.'

'Oh, darling,' Marian said, hugging her. 'Of course we guessed! Don't worry about it. We thought we had better say nothing when we wrote, but you could have trusted us. What we couldn't understand was why on earth you should have married Alban!'

'I don't know myself now. It was some crazy longing for legitimacy for my baby. Alban asked me to marry him. When I told him I was pregnant, he still wanted it, and I saw it as an escape from Thornsby. People there will gossip just as much when they see Stella's eyes. I should have had the courage to tell you all at first. Now we'll just have to face it, Stella and I!'

Respy came back to join them and presently Sarah wheeled in the tea-trolley. Marian poured, and as Respy took hers she said suddenly, 'If you don't mind, I'll take this to my room. We have had a very strenuous journey and I would like to rest. I think, Rose, my dear, I would rather stay in London for a few days and not travel up to Thornsby with you. And then, if you don't mind, I will go back home.'

'Respy,' Rose took her hand, 'you must do exactly as you wish. You have been so wonderful and brave. I could never have got through it all alone. And perhaps next year the fighting will really have stopped, and the Armistice be signed, and then I will bring Stella to see you, as I promised.'

Respy looked a little self-conscious and said in her English school-marm manner, 'She has always been *such* an imaginative child!'

Stephen and Marian burst out laughing, but quite unperturbed Respy said: 'I shall look forward to that, my dear, but just now I really feel I have had enough emotion for a woman my age.'

Next day she said goodbye to Rose and Stella, and stood watching as the taxi drew away, waving until they were out of sight, then she went upstairs to the bedroom and all by herself had a good cry. Afterwards she rinsed her face in cold water, asked Sarah if she would kindly make a cup of tea, and settled down for an afternoon sleep. Only two days – yet it seemed so long since she had slept an hour without waking in fear.

Rose, in the taxi, suddenly felt an aching loneliness, and Marian said gently, 'You'll miss her.'

'I hadn't realised how much. She was so brave! For the hours we spent together, we were like comrades-in-arms. I wanted to give her some payment for what she had done for me, but all she would accept was my bed and board in Nice and her return fare to Menton. So I tempted her – when we slept at Colonel Winterton's apartment in Paris. I've always known how much she would like to have a dress from one of the great couture houses, so I telephoned Mr Brinkley at Margaret Normanby and told him to let her choose whatever she wanted, and to charge it to me.'

'Gosh!' exclaimed Marian. 'Fancy being let loose there with unlimited credit!'

'I wish she would take a whole new wardrobe but I know my Respy! She'll choose a very discreet suit and perhaps a white blouse to go with it, *if* the vendeuse does her work properly. Respy is incorruptible.'

Another journey, another train. A car was waiting for them at Leeds to drive them to the pleasant house Stephen had taken on the south side of Thornsby.

From the lawn Rose could see Cliffs Edge, square and white against its background of trees and orchards, the purple moorland rising behind it; the hazy murk of Thornsby town hanging beneath.

She could not see Danesfell Abbey, and was glad. It brought back all the stress and terror of the past few days. She did not want to be reminded of the fear-crazed boy who had held them hostage, or of that strange look in his eyes as he had died, as though for a few seconds he had really loved her.

She looked round the peaceful garden. At last the war seemed very far away.

'You have a lovely home here,' she said to Stephen.

'When the war is over,' he said, 'we might buy this house, or else build a new one in the district. At the moment Mother can't get over as she would like because of the petrol shortage. It's just far enough away from Cliffs Edge.'

Angela had already telephoned to ask them to dinner the following evening.

'Mother's invitations are like orders from H.Q.,' said Stephen. 'Marian has a very subtle way of evading them. However, I accepted provisionally – I said we'd go if you were not too tired. But if you don't want to, we'll put her off. How do you feel? Would you rather not go?'

'Well, I think I must. You know how hurt she can be by refusals.'

'I do indeed!' And they all laughed. It was the first time Stephen had heard Rose really laugh since her return. 'D'you know she telephones at least four times a day to ask how her future grandchild is getting on!'

'I wish I hadn't told her,' said Marian. 'I only have help in the morning, one of those wonderful Yorkshire women like your Sarah in Chelsea, so I'm free by the afternoon for Stephen's constituency work. Now sit down and rest while I get tea.'

Rose watched her run across the lawn to the house. She looked so happy and contented. Her baby brought no fears. There would be no shadows for Marian. She was as a woman should be in pregnancy, happy and secure.

Stephen saw the sadness in her face. She was still pale, and there were deep shadows round her beautiful eyes. He wanted to tell her that Tom was safe – but he had promised Tom to tell no one – yet. He was frightened of the reaction when Rose did find out. She was so tired, and so young to be so tired.

He drew her arm through his as they walked slowly along together. The garden, like Cliffs Edge, ended in a low stone wall dividing it from the rough moorland which sloped steeply down to the town. The mill stacks and rows of little stone houses could be seen below, and a tram winding its way along a high road.

'Marian does a great deal for me now,' he said. 'I'm glad you told us about the baby, even though we had guessed. And old Sarah is right – she's the image of Tom.'

'I'm glad she is, and I'm glad that people round here will know. I'll tell her as soon as she can understand. If we all love her enough, like your father and Margaret loved Tom, and do not care what people say, she will be all right. I was a fool to run away from it. I feel guilty, Stevie. I could have saved a lot of heartbreak if I had been brave enough to go my own way. And, maybe, Alban's life.'

'Do you want to talk about it?'

She gave a little shudder and said, 'I must. You have to understand why I married him. I thought I needed to be married for the baby's sake. I did not want my child to go through the petty humiliations that I suffered. I thought it was splendid of Alban to stand by his offer, and that I had misjudged him all those years. I never saw his obsessive jealousy of Tom, but it was growing in him like a malignancy. I had no one else to turn to.'

'You should have come to me.'

'No!' she exclaimed. 'No, no! You were engaged to Marian and were falling in love with her. She was so very much in love with you. I couldn't risk spoiling that. I was a coward. I should have told everyone or just gone away. I married him, thinking I could help him too, but it made everything worse. He could never forget that Tom had loved me first. That, and the fear of the war, the drugs – they were all destroying him. I couldn't help him. No one could. He had slipped over the edge into despair.'

'You must not blame yourself.'

'But I do! It was so awful, Stevie. When they shot him down like a dog, and he lay dying on the cobbles, I went to him and lifted his head upon my knee, and he looked up and spoke my name, and I thought for one minute he loved me and was forgiving me, but in that second he died. I sent him to his death, Stevie. I told Colonel Winterton that he was there.'

His hands gripped her shoulders. 'Don't say any more, *Chérie*, not if it hurts you so.'

'I feel so guilty. I grew old that day. In that moment, I grew old.'

'You cannot blame yourself any more. You must learn to be young again.'

He touched her cheek where the purple bruise and the mark of the lash still showed. 'Did he do that to you?'

'He did not know what he was doing. He had already slipped into madness. We won't talk about it any more. I *must*

296

face up to things. I should never have married him. I am not a poor girl. I had friends. There was an excuse for Alban, he was in mortal fear. But I can see no excuse for me.'

Rose and Stephen turned back towards the terrace where Marian was busily laying the tea things and arranging the chairs. She looked so happy and contented. It was strange how they had each fallen in love as schoolgirls and their lives had followed such different paths. Rose paused, her hand on Stephen's arm.

'So,' she said, 'we must not speak of Alban's desertion and treachery. Let us try to save his family from knowing the whole truth. It would be a deadly blow to them. Please, Stevie dear, let us try.'

Stephen stopped and turned to her with troubled eyes. 'Rose, I . . .' He shook his head, taking her arm again. 'Come, let's go to tea or Marian will be cross.'

'Not with you,' she said, smiling.

The terrace ran the length of the house and the teak garden table had been spread with white linen cloth inserted with fine white drawn thread work that Rose recognised as Angela's. She was continually making these elaborate cloths, and had actually given Rose two to take to Paris with her.

'Your mother's,' she said to Stephen.

'They always remind me of her at her most forbidding,' said Marian. 'Always when she has "had words" with someone she will take up her needlework. I'm sure they will all be museum pieces one day. Nobody will ever have the time to wash and starch and iron them! Now come along and eat something. You look so thin, Rose.'

The table was laid with all sorts of goodies – Yorkshire tea cakes, pastries, and jam scones. Rose took her tea and accepted a slice of the tea cake, and Stephen helped himself to cream and jam buns.

'Stevie's hardly ever here for tea,' said Marian, 'and it's just as well!'

'It's a plot between her and Mrs Heaton to make me fat,' he grumbled. 'She thinks no other political lady will notice my blinding attraction then.'

'Take no notice of him,' said Marian, laughing.

'This is a beautiful place,' said Rose. 'It's so free and open.'

'Yes. I hope we can buy it. It's so convenient . . . and it will be wonderful to have the flat in Chelsea, too, when Stephen's in the House.'

'Hey, hold your horses, love,' he protested mildly. 'I'm not elected yet. She's so like her mother! I could never understand how Mrs Palmer managed to bring up a family and nurse a constituency for her husband at the same time, until I learned that *her* father was also an M.P.' He took a scone and added, 'Or how my father-in-law manages to keep his figure.'

Rose sat smiling at their affectionate banter, watching the shadows lengthen across the lawn as the sun moved westward, painting the moors with colour and touching the factory murk with gold. She felt at peace here. How would she feel at Cliffs Edge?

The telephone rang and Stephen rose, saying, 'That will be Mother. I'll tell her we will be over tomorrow.'

They drove across at eight o'clock the next evening. Rose wore her dark blue velvet dress, and no jewellery except her wedding ring. She could not wear mourning for Alban.

Angela greeted her graciously enough and presented a cool cheek for her to kiss. Cliffs Edge was as immaculate as ever, not a hint of wartime shabbiness, and the food was so plentiful no one could have believed it was rationed. Angela confided that she saved all her meat and sugar rations for whenever Stephen and Marian visited.

She served sherry in the drawing-room before dinner as she always had, although Bates the butler had been called up months ago. She was dressed in black as though she was a relative of the Stoneberrys.

'You are not in mourning, I see. I suppose it is the modern fashion to show no respect,' she said to Rose.

'A good thing too,' said Stephen edgily, 'or everyone in this town would be in black.'

'I think Lady Stoneberry will expect it. Alban's death has come as a great shock to them. They had no idea there was any danger in Paris.'

'Everyone in Paris was in some danger,' said Rose. 'We were so near the battle front . . . it is only in the last few weeks that the sound of the big guns has receded. But I shall not be visiting Lady Stoneberry.'

'But you must!' Angela was truly appalled. 'And you should be in mourning for at least a year.'

'Oh, for heaven's sake, Mother, leave Rose alone! She has just travelled all the way from the South of France and has had a very difficult time. I don't see why she should go to Danesfell if she doesn't want to.'

'Stevie,' Rose protested gently, 'I would go if they wished to see me, but somehow I don't think they will.'

'Of course they will want to see you! They will want to know exactly how it happened.'

'I can't tell them that, because I know nothing about it,' Rose said firmly.'And I would rather not talk about it. I don't know what Alban's Commanding Officer told them but that would be how it happened.'

She could only repeat the lie. She could not tell them that the boy they had adopted and reared, but had never loved, was a traitor and a deserter, a seeker of strange pleasures in the night life of Paris. Had sold his country for money to gamble with and to buy cocaine to make his worthless, frightened life bearable. She prayed that they would accept Colonel Winterton's fabricated story, and not delve until they discovered the truth.

It was just after dinner, when Angela was pouring the coffee in the drawing room, that she said unexpectedly, 'I wish you had brought your baby girl tonight, Rose. I would like to see her. There was a lot of talk about you after you married so quickly and rushed off to Paris with Alban. Is she like him or like you?'

It was Marian who said thoughtlessly, 'She's a lovely baby with the most beautiful blue eyes just like . . .' She stopped, realising what she was saying, and flushed guiltily under Angela's surprised and suspicious gaze.

Rose gave her a reassuring smile and looked gravely at Angela.

'You will have to know sooner or later, and it is better that you hear the truth from me. My little girl is Tom's daughter. That is why Alban and I married so quickly, and why we decided to go away at once. I told Alban, of course, and it was

299

brave of him to stand by his proposal when he knew. But it is better that people should know the truth. I am sorry that you are shocked. You have every right to be so. I was wrong to marry Alban, it was a bitter mistake for both of us. But I am not ashamed of having Tom's baby.'

She rose suddenly, slim and graceful as ever, but her beauty was now clouded with grief. 'I should be grateful if you would tell Alban's aunt and uncle. I do not think they will want to see me under the circumstances. If you will excuse me, Madame? I need some air.'

She lifted back one of the heavily lined curtains and slipped out into the garden. There was a gleam of white moonlight before the curtain fell back into place.

Stephen sprang to his feet in distress. 'I must go after her,' he said. 'Tom's alive! He is at the cottage on High Moor.' They stared at him, and he stumbled into an explanation. 'He telephoned a few days ago and asked me to meet him in Leeds. He has been very badly wounded. He has lost his left forearm, amputated below the elbow. He asked me not to tell Rose or anyone yet. He wanted to be back in Yorkshire, on his own, to think things out. I could not even tell you, Marian. But I must tell Rose now. She has been through so much. I must tell her.' He lifted Marian's hand to his lips, 'Wait for me, darling.'

He caught up with Rose on the high ridge where the three of them had once stood looking across the valley to High Moor years ago. The little village stood out. Rose stood on the same ridge, leaning against the same tall flat stone, her dress blowing in the breeze like a carved figurehead at a ship's prow.

She was gazing intently across the valley. At his approach, she turned to face him with wide, excited eyes.

'Stevie, have you let Tom's cottage?' She pointed across the valley to the tiny white square of a building. 'Look . . . it's showing again! Someone *is* there!'

A gleam of yellow light shone briefly as the cottage door was opened and closed. 'Who is it? Did you see? Do you know?'

He said, 'Tom is there!' Bluntly, almost brutally, not knowing how else to tell her.

She turned her head and her eyes frightened him. He tried, haltingly, to explain. 'He came back several days ago. He telephoned me at the office asking me to meet him at Leeds. He would not go to Cliffs Edge or come to us. He wouldn't let me tell anyone . . . not even you. I had received a letter from him some time before. I didn't know how to break it to you. Or whether I should.'

'You are telling me that Tom is *alive* – and is there across the valley?'

'Yes.'

She gave a great cry. It seemed to be torn from her heart, and she would have fallen if he had not caught her. Slowly she recovered her strength, like someone waking from a nightmare. 'It has to be true,' she said. 'This time it *has* to be true. I don't deserve that it should be, but God forgive me and make it true!'

'It is.'

'Look – there it is again!'

The light flickered again and Rose stretched out hungry arms as though she would fly across the valley.

'He asked me to tell you first about how he was badly wounded and left for dead.'

'Tell me quickly.'

'There is so much to tell. So many horrors. His left arm was severed below the elbow.' She bit the back of her hand as though she felt the blade cutting into her own flesh. 'He had watched the Turks cut out his mens' tongues, and was sure they would do the same to him. For a long while after he recovered, he actually thought he was dumb. He did not want to return a maimed man. Then, when he fully regained his speech, he knew he had to come home. I had to tell him about Alban, that you had been married to him, and about his death. And the reason why you married him.'

'What did he say? Does he still love me?'

Stephen smiled, a little wryly. 'I don't suppose any man stops loving you completely. He just said, "Poor child . . . poor *chérie*." He looks much older. I think Tom feels you will find him greatly changed, maimed as he is. I think he feels you might go to him out of pity.'

Her eyes flashed and she said, 'I must go to him at once! I must go to him now, Stephen!'

'Come then – I will drive you across to High Moor.'

He put his arms round her. All tension between them melted, and the old sweet sibling affection returned. 'It was awful, not being able to tell you. No one else here knew he was alive except me and Arthur Sykes – he was with me when that first wonderful letter came. And having to tell Tom that you had married that stupid, sadistic young brute!'

'No,' she said, putting her hand over his mouth. 'A poor, doomed boy. We must let him rest in peace. Can we ask Marian to come with us? I think we both need her.'

Angela had gone upstairs to her room, saying she never wished to see or speak to Rose again. Marian smiled as she told them, and said, 'She'll forget when it suits her – she always does.'

'I'm driving Rose over to High Moor. Come with us, darling.'

It was a brilliant, windless night as they drove down into Thornsby, through the narrow streets, past the Grimshaw mills, looms thumping, working the night through to supply the armies still fighting a war that was staggering to its exhausted end. Over the old stone bridge where the Moor Beck flashed as it purled over the stones, up the moorland road, past the tall iron gates of Danesfell Abbey Manor, and up the far side of the vale, where the road wound round high stone outcrops until it ran down into the small village of High Moor. They went through the narrow High Street, past shops and pubs and houses, turned into moorland again until they came to the remote cottage, facing out over the valley, sheltered by woodland behind. It was surrounded by a neglected garden and perched high above the vale, looking across at Cliffs Edge five miles away.

Stephen stopped the car and the world was suddenly silent. The whitewashed cottage stood about twenty yards away, the windows shuttered and dark, showing no chink of light.

No one had spoken. Rose sat motionless, her heart racing. She felt it would burst in her breast. Her mind felt paralysed. She was unable to think or move.

Stephen said, 'Do you want us to come with you?'

She drew in a long, shuddering breath. 'Just hold my hands for a moment.' She thrust her shaking hands into theirs.

Stephen said again, 'Shall we come with you?'

She shook her head. Her hands were cold with fear. Marian began to rub the one she held, and Rose smiled, and sat up straight, and said, 'Do you really think he will still love me?'

Marian said crossly, 'Don't be so daft!' Rose kissed her, opened the car door and got out.

She stood there uncertainly, as though gathering her courage, then ran up the path towards the cottage. As she stepped into the porch, the door was opened.

Tom had heard the car drive up and stop. Yellow light from the lamp he held shone down upon her. She looked up at him, tremulous as a child, unsure of its welcome. He put down the lamp, and his good right arm came out and lifted her effortlessly over the threshold, and the door closed behind them.

It was so quiet. An owl cried somewhere in the woods behind them, and they saw it come sweeping down across the moor by the light of the rising moon.

Stephen put his arm closely round Marian and kissed her.

'How long do you think we should wait?' she said.

'No need to wait any longer. She won't come back tonight. Do you think you can manage young Stella until morning?'

'Just watch me!'

They stood face to face in stunned silence, as though they could not believe this was really happening. Then Rose touched the thick hair that had become silvery white. Tom's skin was so deeply tanned, darker than her own. The beard made her smile. Then she lifted his mutilated arm and rolled back his loose sleeve to the elbow, exposing the ugly red stump. With a cry of pain she lifted it to her lips, and then held it against her breast.

But she felt the vitality in him she had always known, as strong and sure as she had always remembered him.

303

He lifted her, and carried her across to the settee before the hearth. They had come through. They were alive and young and had found each other again, after all the pain and bitter sorrow had passed like a terrifying dream. They found their eyes were full of tears even when they smiled.

There was so much to tell each other, much that was ugly and that was still painful, and much of the joy of the baby Stella whom he had yet to see. But they could not talk. Slowly, almost shyly, they began to make love with a wonder that transcended anything they had ever known before.